A Spot of
Murder

Bill Siracusa

A Spot of Murder

Production copyright FurPlanet Productions © 2022

Text Copyright © Bill Siracusa 2022

Cover Artwork and illustrations © Jay Fitzmaurice 2022

Published by FurPlanet Productions
Dallas, Texas
www.FurPlanet.com

ISBN 978-1-61450-570-9
First Edition Trade Paperback

Table of Contents

Chapter 1: Final Week

Friday, May 11, 2018

"This is it!" called Professor Ino Reamer into the mostly-empty lecture hall. "It's all over for you! *This is the end!*" he cried.

He stared up at the huge room's only other occupants. The two remaining students stared back at him, wide-eyed.

The hyena started up the stairs and gave them a goofy smile. "Your final is over and so is this class." He tapped his watch. "It's 10:40! Summer has officially started. You're free! It's the end!" he said, smiling way too large. "Get out of my classroom!" he added.

The girl — Alanna, a caracal — rolled her eyes. The boy — Robbie, a large bull terrier — just stared back at him, horrified.

"That was not particularly funny, Dr. Reamer," Alanna said.

"Sweet Jesus," said Robbie, wide-eyed.

Ino frowned. "That wasn't fun? I thought it would be fun."

"It was not fun," Alanna told him. "It was the opposite of fun."

Ino sighed.

Robbie cleared his throat. "Besides." He pointed at the wall clock. "You're early."

Ino looked up at the clock and stared at it. It said 10:35. He frowned. The clock must be slow. Of course it was. "Oh. Well, five more minutes, then, and *then* it's the end." He trudged back down the stairs to the teacher's station at the base of the hall.

Ino sat down behind the large desk. After a few impatient seconds he leaned way back in the chair, putting his elbows up over his head, his arms tugging at the cotton of his button-down. He was probably a little over-eager to end the semester. This was the very last full final he was proctoring, and he was beyond ready for the week to be over.

At this point in the semester, the hyena was going on 4 hours of sleep for the 3rd day in a row, and he was so exhausted he had looped around from miserable all the way back to giddy. This was an entry-level Chemistry course and he probably should have made the final much easier. Like "make the whole thing 10 questions" easier. *QUESTION 1: ARE ATOMS REAL? Y/N.*

He looked wistfully out the window. It was probably close to 80 degrees out, unseasonably warm for early May, and yet not unwelcome. After a typical chaotic Indiana April of alternating sleet and sunshine, the warm weather had finally settled in to stay. The wild weather swings were a lot to deal with, but Ino welcomed it; his last school had been in Florida, where the summers rolled in early and stayed long, humid and miserable for most of the year. Now, nestled here in the temperate bosom of the Midwest, a stone's throw from Lake Michigan's cooling breeze, Ino loved the summer months most of all. Then again, the winters routinely hit 30 below, so there wasn't a lot of competition.

Leaning so far back in his chair he was in danger of tipping over, Ino thought about his summer plans. He had two solid weeks of freedom where his only objective was to chemically bond with his couch. Then the summer semester started, and Ino's schedule was amazing. He was teaching two repeat courses, both fully online, and only one in-person course. He only had to be on-campus three days a week. It was the perfect schedule to veg out all summer but still make enough money to comfortably pay his rent.

Watching a gentle breeze ruffle the trees, Ino thought about the next few glorious months. He could train for a 10K, or catch up on his reading, or just sit inside on his overstuffed leather sofa soaking up the air conditioning. It was going to be a great summer in his tiny adopted town.

Santiago, Indiana — pronounced in peak Midwestern dialect as "Sandy Aggo" — was wedged into the upper left corner of the Indiana. The town was close enough to the Illinois border to pick up Chicago radio stations, but far enough into Indiana that a good percentage of the county was made up of corn fields. Santiago's main street was only a few miles long, an island of local restaurants and storefront cafes surrounded by a few blocks of commercial and residential zoning, in a massive ocean of farm fields. It wasn't a tiny one-stoplight town, but by Ino's standards it felt miniscule, and he felt a little thrill living in a town that only had three Starbucks in the entire city limits.

The city had a population of 30,000, making it small enough to comfortably share the name Santiago with the University where Ino worked. Santiago University — Santi to the locals — was an equally-miniscule school of only about 3,000. Ino had come here from a huge state school in the south with a student body twice the size of the *town* of Santiago, so the move had been a culture shock and then a love affair. Indiana was slow and friendly (most of the time) and very relaxed.

It was a great fit for Ino at this stage of his life. He was 35 and comfortably single. He looked good — his metabolism had finally slowed down so he wasn't rail-thin, and he was finally putting on some decent muscle after twenty years of trying (and he was maybe developing a little tummy too, but he carried it well). He had a nice rental house with real furniture, a cool Jeep that ran a large percentage of the time, and a great job that he was good at. He finally felt like he was getting the hang of what millennials on social media referred to as "adulting."

Impatiently, he checked the wall clock again. It had only ticked 3 minutes closer to 10:40. He stole another glance out the window. Two months ago he had been slogging through half a foot of snow, and now all he could hear was the siren song of the hardware store's garden center. It was almost *too* gorgeous — especially for Finals Week. It usually wasn't in the 80s this early but it was now, and Ino had already dug out his shorts and flip flops.

He looked up and checked on his two remaining students.

Alanna, the caracal, was small and thin with round glasses and short natural hair. She was surrounded by a perpetual cloud of seriousness and was hunched intently over her exam. Ino guessed that she had actually finished her exam over an hour ago, probably before anyone else, and was now on her second *recheck*. Possibly her third! She was rounding the last page now, coolly reviewing her answers to ensure that her solid A++ for the semester was not in jeopardy. She was already well above 100% for the semester; if she landed any higher, Ino would have to come up with a letter grade above A.

Robbie, on the other hand, a large white bull terrier from the football team, looked like he was on the verge of cardiac arrest. He was also on the last page, but the dog had a solid frown and his ears were folded back. He had sweated out both armpits of his Santiago-yellow t-shirt and he let out a shaky sigh.

Ino glanced at the clock and raised himself out of his seat again. He walked up the stairs. "Sorry, guys, but it's really that time now."

Robbie looked up, eyes wide. "No!" he boomed. "I still have one question left!" He flipped frantically back to the middle of his exam, his ears pinned flat to his head.

Alanna brushed some eraser shavings off her Scantron exam form. "It's B," she said. She didn't even look up, though one of her tufted ears did swivel in Robbie's direction.

Robbie and Ino both stared at her.

The dog spoke first. "Uhhh, how do you know that? I didn't even say which question it was." He looked down at his exam and then up at her. He was visibly surprised.

She shrugged. "It's probably question 26, and you're probably stuck on choices B and D because the question is worded poorly." She finally turned to them. Ino thought he saw a hint of a smile.

Ino felt defensive for three-tenths of a second, but that was immediately overcome by his curiosity. "Worded poorly?" he asked. "How so?"

Raising an eyebrow, Alanna flipped her exam back open. "Here. *Which of the following is an example of a covalent bond?*" She pointed at the test and then at Ino. "*You* meant choice B, water — H_2O. A classic covalent bond."

He nodded. "Classic," he agreed. "Go on."

Alanna continued. "But choice D was Hydrogen. A hydrogen *atom* is not bonded at all, obviously. But a hydrogen *molecule*, even in its most basic form, is made up of *two* hydrogen atoms. They are bonded, and they do share electrons. That's a covalent bond. So D is possibly also correct, depending on the context." She looked up. "Which is not given. Thus making the question impossible to answer."

Ino stared at her, and then looked down at the test. He processed that for a moment. *Crap, I DID just mean the atom*, he thought. He had needed a random atom and literally just picked #1 on the Periodic Table of Elements, which was Hydrogen. But Hydrogen atoms never hung out alone — the molecule was always H_2. "Huh!" he said after a moment. "You're right! I guess I owe you guys an extra point!"

Robbie gasped. There was a series of thuds as his tail began wagging. "Really? What if I get it right anyway?"

Ino shrugged with a smile. "I guess you get an extra *extra* point then."

Robbie stared at him, eyes wide. Silently, he raised his hand. Alanna put hers up too, and they high-fived. The small cat had to lean way into the gesture to avoid being knocked out of her chair by the big dog.

Ino laughed. "Okay. Get the hell out of my class now, please!" he said. He reached for their desks and made grabby-paws motions at the Scantrons.

Robbie frantically filled in the last box and they both held up their papers. Ino checked them for names and course title, and tucked them under his arm. The hyena turned back toward his desk and tried not to prance happily all the way down the aisle. There were rustling noises as the two students gathered their things.

Behind him, Robbie took a deep breath and let it out as a heaving sigh. "I'm glad that's over. I think I bombed that. I'm doomed."

Without looking back, Ino rolled his eyes. "You're not doomed, Robbie!" he called over his shoulder. "You've gotten a B on every exam in this class. Also, as we discussed, you'll get at least *two* points." He turned, smiling.

Robbie did not see the humor. "I'm telling you!" the large dog proclaimed, his ears drooping. "I failed this and I'm going to flunk this class. I'm dead."

Alanna sighed. "If you've only gotten B's on every test before now, it is mathematically impossible for you to fail at this point."

Back at his desk, Ino stuck both their Scantrons into a file folder. He smiled. "See, Robbie?" he called back. "Mathematically impossible." Behind his desk, he finally looked up. "And if you really *did* bomb it, email me, and I'll send you the extra credit to do. I don't have to post grades until next Friday."

Swallowing, Robbie nodded. He was frowning, but he looked somewhat convinced. "Okay. Thanks, Doc," he rumbled.

Alanna opened her mouth to speak, so Ino put up a hand. "And YES, Alanna, I will send you the extra credit anyway. I, too, am interested in learning what the theoretical maximum number of points is for this class. I already have an email draft with your name on it."

Beaming smugly, she swung her large purse over her shoulder. "Thank you, Dr. Reamer."

He grinned at both of them. "You're welcome, both of you! Now get the heck out of here and go have an amazing summer!"

They said goodbye and headed out the back of the lecture hall.

Ino turned to pick up his bag, intending to power walk out of the lecture hall all the way to his office, when he froze.

The side door at the rear of the hall was open. A shadowy figure stood in the doorway.

The lights in the hallway behind the figure were turned off, so it took Ino a moment of startled alarm to realize it was Ethan Reed.

Dr. Reed was a rhino, another professor in the Chemistry and Biology departments, thirty years Ino's senior and tenured for what had probably been several decades. Dr. Reed was wearing a long-sleeved dark-gray button-down under a wool suit jacket, despite the heat. He was a big man, with a slow gait and a large clunky manner, and he was staring at Ino with barely-disguised contempt.

Before Ino could say a single word, the rhino grunted, and then disappeared silently down the hall. He left the door open behind him.

Wide-eyed, Ino stared. *Huh*, he thought.

Ino went right from the lecture hall to Dr. Reed's office. It wasn't a long detour — Reed's office was across the hall from his own. Originally Reed had been his faculty advisor, four years ago, and he was technically Ino's "faculty buddy," but Ino didn't really lean on him for anything at this point. Reed was... not easy to work with.

The door was slightly ajar. Ino rapped lightly on the thick oak with his knuckles. The door was open and Ino stepped a few feet into the office so Reed wouldn't have to yell across his office.

Reed's office was a standard 10-by-20 rectangle, lined, as most of the offices were, with tall, mismatched bookshelves, overflowing with textbooks, reference materials, and notebooks. There was a big window on the back wall, which Reed sat facing away from. Reed had a thick oak desk, which was probably older than Ino himself, and on one wall a tall steel file cabinet next to a short chest of drawers. Over the dresser hung three framed blown-up diagrams of stylized molecules. Ino recognized one of them — Hydrogen Chloride — because it was literally just two molecules stuck together (Hydrogen and Chlorine, unsurprisingly), but the other two were more complex and he'd never bothered to look them up. The bookshelves were littered with little models of molecules, marble statues and ceramic busts from Reed's many travels, and enough books to fill a small reference library.

The rhino was bent over his keyboard, peering at his computer monitor through thick reading glasses. He looked up, staring over his glasses. "Dr. Reamer!" he said. "I was just writing you an email." He was still wearing his suit jacket, even while sitting in his chair, and despite the fact that the room felt about 79 degrees.

The hyena stared at him. He smiled tensely. "Ethan, I *do* have a first name. Ino? Rhymes with Reno? Maybe I've mentioned that one or fifty times?"

The rhino stared at him for a moment, and then grumbled. "Back in *my* day, we used *titles*. It conveyed respect."

Ino chuckled. "This is still your day, Ethan. As far as I know you currently teach at this University, right?"

Reed snorted, reaching up to slip off his reading glasses with one thick, ponderous hand. He raised a bushy eyebrow. "That is correct, Dr. Reamer. You won't be getting rid of *me* any time soon. I'll be teaching at this school until I'm dead." He gestured at one of the chairs across from his desk.

Ino chuckled. "I have no doubt of that." He slipped into one of the chairs and crossed one leg up over his knee. "How's your summer looking?"

Reed thought for a moment too long, and then nodded. "Going up to Minnesota. Get out to the lake house. Don't know how many more summers I'll go up there, want to enjoy it." He looked up. "You? Something much more exciting, I imagine."

Ino leaned back in his chair and cracked a smile. "No sir! Staying put. Got a couple summer classes to run. Those real fun consolidated ones."

Reed frowned. "Oh, that's a shame."

Ino chuckled. "Not if I want to keep buying food! I think I've finally hit the sweet spot this year — I'm only teaching three. Two of them are online and the third one I've taught a couple times before." He shrugged.

"It should be a nice mix. I'll have some free time but I won't have to live on ramen for the summer."

Reed forced a smile across his thick pachyderm lips. "How… nice to hear!"

Ino suppressed a sigh. The rhino had never been a terrific conversationalist — this was about par for the course. "Did you need something earlier?"

Reed stared at him for a long time, and then nodded curtly. "Actually, I did. I have a few… questions… about your curriculum." He leaned forward. "Concerns, possibly."

Ino immediately felt defensive, even though Reed was really not in a position to have any input on Ino's teaching style. Reed was not above Ino in any org chart. Ino's actual boss was the head of the department; she was about 20 years younger than Reed and had nothing but good things to say about Ino. *Here we go*, Ino thought. He put a big fake smile on his face and took a deep breath. "Certainly! I always welcome feedback from my faculty advisor."

Reed blinked at him and then matched his fake smile. "Well, this would be colleague to colleague. I believe my tenure as your advisor ended… some years ago."

Ino beamed. "Oh, you're right! Sometimes I forget," he said cheerfully. He leaned forward. "What questions can I answer for you, Ethan?"

The rhino stared at him, *very* subtly narrowed his eyes, and let out a long, irritated sigh. "Extra credit, Ino?" he said, the derision plain in his voice.

Ino let out a long sigh and fought the urge to roll his eyes. "Ethan, I will not have this conversation with you again. *Yes*, extra credit. The class is for non-majors. It's supposed to be *passable*. Given that you expressly refuse to teach any of the 100-level courses, I would think you would leave the management of those classes to me."

Reed frowned. "What about that caracal girl? She's a science major." He pointed. "Genetics, in fact. She'll be in your 300-level classes next semester."

Ino frowned. "Alanna? She's also taking twenty-six credit hours this semester. She ran out of biology classes to take so the *department head* approved her to take an entry-level chem class, on the assumption that she'll probably teach it as a TA someday." He started to cross his arms but decided to deny Reed the satisfaction. "She's also getting 120% in the class, which is what I would expect for a major, in a non-major class."

Reed snorted again, his large nostrils flaring. The big rhino sat back in his chair, making the wood creak. "Honestly, I don't know how you can offer them extra credit *at all*. It's an easy class to begin with. Basic molecular structure. Simple chemical bonds. Half the experiments are computer simulations." He narrowed his eyes, leaning back in his chair. "A child could pass it."

Ino pursed his lips in irritation and then swallowed. "That is the *point* of a 101 for non-majors. Their job is to learn a little bit of science. If they like it, they'll take more. And some do! We pick up a couple every semester. If not, they've learned the scientific method and their critical thinking skills get a little more well-rounded. They've fulfilled their goal." He shrugged. "I'm not going to tank some business student's GPA because they don't know the difference between mitochondria and chloroplasts."

Reed rumbled with irritation. His large nostrils flared. "Did you know you're the most popular professor in the Chemistry department? You have a wait list. No one else does."

That didn't particularly surprise Ino. The hyena raised an eyebrow. "I'm sorry — it sounds like you're saying that's a bad thing."

Reed leaned forward. "It means you're *too easy*, Ino!" He sneered down his horn. "I wonder if you have enough respect for the subject material."

Ino stared at him, fighting an intense urge to roll his eyes.

Reed went on. "The science is *sacred*, Ino. It should be *respected*."

This time Ino did roll his eyes. "Okay. Sure. Sacred, why not. Respected, absolutely. Relevant to everyone? No, Ethan, it's not." He frowned. "Most of those kids will go on to Journalism and Political Science and Athletics. And I'm not going to make them believe science is any more important by failing them in a *gen-ed class*. A lot of these kids are here on scholarships, as you know, and a lot of scholarships depend on academic standing. This school is not cheap."

The rhino frowned at him. "Ah yes. *Speaking* of scholarships, I see more than a few members of the football team in your classes. Quite a... strapping lad I saw leaving your lab today."

Ino raised an eyebrow. "Yes? And?"

Reed watched him, eyes boring holes through him over the rhino's thick horn. "I just can't imagine what kind of class you're teaching if it's the preferred course of the football team.

Ino snorted. "You should read my final before you decide my class is *too* jock-friendly," he grunted.

Reed stared at him. "I don't believe the *course* is too jock-friendly."

Ino felt himself bristle. This was becoming a different kind of conversation altogether. "I don't know what you mean by *that*, Ethan," he all but growled.

Reed smiled inauthentically. "No, I'm sure you don't. Put another way, I see you're proctoring a make-up final for Sean Murphy in a lab later this afternoon. I don't believe there are any other students at that make-up. Isn't Mr. Murphy a member of the LGBT group you advise?" He cocked his head innocently. "Alone in a lab with you?"

Ino felt the fur on the back of his neck bristle up, and he suddenly knew with perfect clarity and absolute certainty that he would be mad about this conversation for the rest of his natural life.

"Ethan," he said, low and dangerous. "That is an offensive and absurd thing to even *imply*, and I will give you *one chance* to drop that topic before I make A Thing out of it." He kept the angry tremor out of his voice — mostly.

The rhino frowned at his obvious contempt. "Now, now, Dr. Reamer, I'm not saying anything inappropriate is going on..."

Ino smiled chillingly. "Of *course* not!"

"But," Reed continued with seeming obliviousness, "I just worry about *appearances*." He frowned with fake-looking concern. "I would think *you* would want to be on your best behavior at all times. Especially given the... *integrity concerns* at your last school."

Ino felt his stomach drop out.

The hyena narrowed his eyes, and now he didn't even bother to keep the anger out of his voice. "Well, Ethan. My *complete innocence* notwithstanding, there's a room full of lawyers at my last school who went to a lot of trouble to ensure that any alleged integrity concerns weren't concerns at all." He showed his teeth. "So I think we both know the only integrity concern here is the fact that you think you're somehow privy to whatever you *think* you know," he snapped.

Reed smiled frigidly back at him, showing a great number of flat pachyderm teeth. "I'm privy to a *great* deal more than you might imagine, Dr. Reamer."

Seething, Ino lifted himself out of his chair. "Well, if you find out about anything else, you can go straight to the Ethics Board and let them sort it out. Don't waste *my* fucking time with it."

He stood up and left Reed's office without looking behind him.

In the hallway, Ino had to take a deep breath to keep his hand from shaking long enough to put the key in his office door.

He shook his head. *All he had to do* was get through the rest of the day and he was going to have an amazing summer.

That was all he had to do.

Ino spent the rest of his afternoon angrily grading finals and working in his office. He debated working in the library to avoid bumping into Reed but decided not to give the rhino the satisfaction of avoiding him. Instead, he elected to work in his own office with his door open, while blasting Nine Inch Nails. The doors of the two offices didn't line up, and it wasn't a direct line of sight from one desk to the other, therefore Ino didn't have to make awkward eye contact with the rhino across the hall as he came and went. Ino enjoyed the idea of torturing the rhino by staying — he didn't even leave to eat his lunch, instead devouring it at his desk.

Once he finished grading all the written answers, Ino took his mon-ster stack of completed test papers and lugged them down to the Scantron room around 2:30. The machine kept jamming, so Ino stayed there trying to feed finals into it for some time, until 4:00 or so when he finally finished up the last class' worth. The Scantron machine was deep in a room down the hall from his own office, and at one point Ino thought he heard a yell from down the hall, just for a second. There was a lot of yelling on cam-pus during Finals week, though, and he couldn't hear anything else over the loud clacking of the grading machine, so he decided it was probably nothing.

At long last, the machine spit out the last test. It was Robbie Brandt's. Curious, Ino picked it up. The score was 94. Ino chuckled. "Guess you won't need that extra credit."

Returning to his office, Ino noticed Reed's door was closed.

He stared at it for a moment. *Bastard left without even saying goodbye.* Left for the summer no less. What a coward — start shit and then sneak out.

The hyena shook his head. And was that really a surprise?

Rolling his eyes, Ino disappeared into his office and slid back in behind his computer.

Poong! went Ino's Outlook calendar, interrupting his thoughts mid-sentence. He was nearly done with the syllabus for one of his upcoming online courses, *Single Celled Organisms 204*, and he had completely lost track of time. He checked the system clock. It was 5:40 pm, far later than he had thought. His stomach would have been screaming for dinner except there were two vending machines in the room with the Scantron reader and Ino had been scavenging continuously for the last three hours.

He looked at the reminder. MAKEUP FINAL-MURPHY. Ino stared at the screen. Whoops! That had come up fast.

Ino stood up, walked around his small desk, and propped open the door to his office.

Santiago University allowed students to reschedule finals if they had more than three exams in one day. This semester, only three of his students had been unlucky enough to meet that grim requirement, and two of them had finished out their finals earlier that week.

Only poor hapless Sean Murphy, the huskiest of huskies, had ended up with *four* back-to-back finals in one day, which required him to push Ino's Chemistry 101 Lab final all the way out to the last slot of the semester: Friday, at 6 pm. It was kind of a pain in the ass for Ino, since the lab final contained several measurement exercises and Ino would have to set up the equipment just for him, but Sean was a good kid, so Ino didn't mind.

Ino had finished his Scantrons and posted most of his grades to Blackboard, and moved on to updating the syllabi for his summer courses.

He figured he only had so much time before his motivation completely evaporated for his two-week break, and he wouldn't be able to budge again until the last-minute panic set in just before the summer session began. The only thing pushing him along so far was his righteous indignation at the asshole across the hall.

The hyena sat back down behind his desk, leaning back up in his chair. He put his arms up over his head, feeling the sleeves of his dress shirt tighten around his shoulders and arms. Ino had worn a nice outfit for finals week, proctoring today in tan dress slacks and a crisp white shirt, with a yellow fractal-pattern tie that offset his mustard-colored fur.

Ino always tended to dress up, which put him at odds with the university setting, since the entire rest of the university tended to dress down. He'd seen one of the Genetics professors in athletic shorts earlier. And the Humanities profs generally looked like they had just come from a three-week camping trip.

The hyena had always had a wiry build, but now that his metabolism was slowing down, he had packed on enough muscle to go up a shirt size in the last year. Ino wore mostly slim-fit tailored clothes, and he was really happy with his body for the first time in a long while. Ino wasn't Miami-hot but he was *definitely* Indiana-hot, and he was in good enough shape that he got second glances when he was jogging.

Zzzt-zzzt, buzzed his phone, on the desk.

Ino cracked a smile. "Oh! I bet that's a late husky." Ino's cellphone number was in all of his syllabi and the students were not shy about using it. If Sean was running late enough Ino could probably get to the vending machines one more time. Licking his teeth, he picked up the phone.

`1 message: Ethan Reed. (No subject.)`

Ino stared at it and narrowed his eyes. Ethan Reed? That was unexpected. He pondered. An apology, perhaps? Why would he disappear and *then* text him?

It was strange. In all the time he had known Professor Reed, the man had never once sent him a text message. Curious, Ino tapped on the message notification.

It was Ethan's name and a rectangle. Ino tapped the rectangle and the screen turned white. Puzzled, Ino closed the message and reopened it several times. There was only a little white rectangle with a thin black border around it, and when he opened it fully, the screen just turned white. It looked like a picture, but there was nothing there.

Dr. Reed had sent him a blank message.

Ino stared at the message, baffled. He started to tap out a reply.

"DOCTOR REAMER!" screamed a voice in the doorway.

Ino just about leapt out of his fur. "GAH!" he cried, flinching. He dropped the phone. It clattered down on the blotter.

Sean Murphy stood panting at the doorway. The Siberian husky was dressed for running, in high-cut black running shorts and a bright red tank top with a big UnderArmour logo on it. The young dog was wiry and fit, under all of his fur, which covered him thickly and was fluffed out at all conceivable angles, including his messy black hair. If Ino had to guess, the teenager was 2 parts muscle per 1 part fluff. He was a hair taller than Ino's 5'7" and smart and funny and in shape, and the girls were constantly after him. Ino found this particularly amusing, since Sean was the Student-Co-Leader of the campus LGBT group for which Ino was the faculty advisor.

The husky had a royal blue Adidas backpack over his shoulders and he was gripping the straps like it was a parachute. He was breathing hard, his muzzle wide open, and he had obviously just sprinted from the other end of campus, or possibly another University entirely.

"SORRY!" — *gasp* — "I'M!" — *gasp* — "LATE!" Sean panted, leaning against the door frame. He doubled over, putting his hands on his knees, and breathed hard for a moment. His long tongue lolled out several inches, tiny little drops of drool flicking off the end and onto the floor of Ino's office.

Wide-eyed, the hyena stared at him. He checked his watch.

It said 5:46 pm. Sean's final was at 6.

"Uhhh," he said.

Still doubled over, still panting, Sean held up one finger in the universal *hold on* gesture. "Whoof! Whoooooof!" he gasped.

Ino cleared his throat loudly. "You're *early,*" he said. He frowned. "Please don't throw up."

Sean raised his head and stared at Ino with disbelieving blue eyes. "HWHAT?!" he demanded.

Ino chuckled. 'It's like… quarter to six, Sean. You're fifteen minutes early. I don't think you ever even made it to *class* this early."

Sean stared at him, his ears splaying out sideways. "Are you kidding me? I thought the final was at 5:30!" He frowned. "Oh my God. I just beat my last 5K pace to get here this fast."

Ino shrugged. "Well, I can adjust it if you want. Let's make it 5:30! That's… one letter grade drop for every ten minutes late. You're starting at a C now. Is that better?" he asked, lowering his voice mischievously.

Sean stared at him, horrified. His jaw unhinged and dropped open. His curly tail even drooped.

Ino grinned. "Aww, I'm kidding. I would never do that to you. Are you ready to take this test?"

Swallowing, Sean straightened up. "I'm ready to be done with finals. Does that count?" He grumbled.

Ino chuckled. "I'll take it!" he announced. "Got your lab coat?"

Sean turned to show him his backpack, which presumably had his lab coat stuffed into it in a wrinkled mess, per the norm for most of Ino's male students.

"Okey-dokey. Aaand…" He leaned over the desk to look at Sean's enormous husky paws. "Closed-toed shoes — check! All right, we're in business. They've got us scheduled in…" He trailed off to turn to his laptop. He pulled up the email from the Registrar, who coordinated all of the makeup exams, so none of the rooms were double-booked.

Seeing the words in the email, Ino felt his jaw drop open.

BBSC 202.

Baker Brown Science Center.

That was all the way across campus, at least half a mile away, in a half-decommissioned science building so old that it was probably haunted. Ino had just assumed the test would be where he normally taught classes — right there in the Malerich building, where his office was. Down the hall, not across the campus. He hadn't even thought of Baker Brown in so long that he had basically forgotten it existed.

The husky watched him, cocking his head. "Uhhh," he said. "Somethin' wrong, Dr. Reamer? Where they got us, Notre Dame?"

Ino grimaced. He looked up and scrunched his muzzle into a sneer. "Oh my God," he moaned. "They put us in *Baker.*"

Sean blinked at him. "Baker? *Baker?*" He thought for a moment. "The *old* science building? Like by the Rec center?" He stared. "Across campus?" His left eye started twitching. "Where I just… *came from?*"

"That's the one." He winced. "I'm so sorry! I would have met you there." Ino grimaced. "That's my fault. I didn't check the room assignment. I haven't even *been* in Baker this entire semester. The labs here in the building must already be deep-cleaned and shut down."

The young husky shrugged. "Ugh. Don't worry about it. I'm already at like 35,000 steps today. What's another two miles?" He rolled his eyes.

Ino picked up his briefcase and the keys to his Jeep. "Not a problem. We can just drive."

Sean's eyes widened. "In… your car?" His ears tilted slowly backwards.

Ino smiled. "Uh… well, I mean, they might let me borrow a shuttle van, if I ask nicely. But the *plan* was my car, yes." He stared. "Is something wrong?"

Sean stared at the keys and then up to Ino. "Welllll… it's 79 degrees out… I just ran two miles across campus… and the whole rest of the day I've been sitting in finals sweating." He swallowed. "I'm surprised you can't smell me from there." He clenched his teeth. "Sure you want to be in a car with me?"

Ino laughed. "I'm sure it's not *that* bad." He smiled. "I mean, you did shower today, right?"

Sean stared at him for a moment, and then looked away, thinking. "Today's… Friday?"

Ino stared at him, and wordlessly put his car keys back down on the desk blotter. "Lovely night for a walk!" he announced.

Vacantly, Sean smiled.

Baker Brown Science Center was across campus, and as they started off on the 20-minute walk, Ino felt that the weather was starting to cool off — but not by much. After the long and frigid winter, and with the unseasonably early warmth, it still reminded Ino more than a little of Florida. The weather was still probably in the high 70s even this late in the day, and Ino was perfectly comfortable in just his shirtsleeves. Sunset was still a few hours off but the sun was low and there were a lot of clouds, so the heat was warming, and not oppressive. A warm breeze made the hyena's tie flap and gently ruffled Sean's thick fur. For the first time that year, Ino felt comfortable not running back upstairs for a hoodie.

They crossed in front of Wong Hall, the administration building. It was almost six, but there were still a dozen or more cars in the parking lot. A large thick badger, stuffed into a shirt and tie, was standing against the building, smoking. He glared at them.

"What's going on over there?" Sean asked. "The rest of campus is deserted."

Ino shrugged. "I think that's the administrative Accounting department. Like, the school's finances. Next month is the end of our fiscal year so they're all going a little nuts getting ready for it."

He waved at the badger. The large man scowled at him, threw his cigarette into the grass, and disappeared into the building.

Sean chuckled. "Wow, friendly guy."

Ino shrugged. "Don't worry about it. Finals Week sucks for everybody." His thoughts turned back to Reed. The hyena thought about the final he was about to give Sean and whether it was too easy or not. Annoyed, he went over Reed's words in his head again.

After a moment, he realized Sean was staring at him. Startled, he realized they had walked for three minutes in perfect silence.

He shook his head. "I'm sorry! Long week!" He offered a weak smile.

Sean stared at him, blue eyes a little wide. "Something wrong? I was quietly angsting and then I realized YOU were angsting too."

Ino smiled. "No, nothing. Just… teacher stuff." He shrugged.

There was a short pause, and then the husky grinned. "Is it Dr. Reed?"

Ino felt his pulse quicken and then stared. "What? *How* did you know that?"

Sean chuckled. "It's not hard to figure out. You're the only two left in that building and he is *absolutely* a weapons-grade asshole."

Ino stared at him in surprise, and then had to fight to keep the smile off his face. "Wow, that is remarkably apt! However, for administrative reasons, I am required to disagree with that statement." He felt his short hyena tail lash mischievously behind him.

Sean laughed. "You don't *have* to agree with me. I know the truth. That guy is the *worst*. I can't believe you have to like, share the department with him. Somebody should run that dude over with a Ford Econoline."

Ino blinked. "Wow, *that's* vivid." He thought for a moment. "And very specific!"

The husky narrowed his eyes dangerously. The expression looked out of place on him. "I had to drop his class last semester. I was two *tenths of a point* away from a C and he wouldn't give me any extra credit. *"A D is a D, Mr. Murphy,"* he said, in an exaggerated deep voice.

Ino frowned. The extra credit thing again. "Ugh, were you able to drop the class? Take an incomplete?" He grimaced. "Or did you end up with it lowering your entire GPA?"

Sean shrugged. "No, I dropped it, but only 3 days before the drop-dead. Which is way too late to sign up for another class. So I totally wasted three credit hours off my scholarship because Professor Reed is a dick." He rolled his eyes again. "Sorry. Excuse my language."

Ino let out a low whistle. "Wow. That's terrible." He frowned. "I guess I know why I always have a waitlist and he doesn't."

Sean grinned at him, wagging.

They walked for another short while in a comfortable silence.

They moved onto one of the asphalt paths criss-crossing the campus. The air was heavy with humidity and the smell of greenery, the sun just starting to make its final descent toward the horizon.

After a few moments, Ino realized that Sean had been silent for a hitherto unprecedented length of time. He glanced at the husky, who seemed to be deep in thought.

"Something on *your* mind?" the hyena prompted.

Sean blinked, startled, and then looked up at him, blushing. "Can I ask you something personal?" He glanced around, looking over his shoulder. "Like… gay stuff," he said, dropping his voice to a whisper. "Is that inappropriate?"

Ino watched him. He hated that Sean felt the need to lower his voice. "I mean, I *am* the advisor to the student LGBT group. And you're on the leadership panel for that group." He smiled, lopsidedly.

Sean watched him, and then let out a shaky sigh. "So… I have a boyfriend now."

Ino nodded. Sean was smart and funny and adorable; it would be a shock if he *didn't* have a boyfriend. "Uh huhhh," he said.

Sean swallowed. "And he's… in the closet kind of."

Ino nodded again. He took "kind of" to mean "completely."

Sean looked away, embarrassed. "And he wants to come out. He wants to start telling people that we're dating."

Ino blinked. "Oh! That's great!" He stared.

Sean frowned sourly back at him, with an annoyed little sneer that only huskies and cats could truly manage. "*Is it?*" he snapped.

Ino stared, surprised. "That's… not great?" He considered and then cocked his head.

Sean scowled. "No, it's not great! It's *horrible!*"

Ino blinked in surprise, but he didn't want to minimize Sean's feelings so he eased into his response. "Ahhhhh, what's horrible about it?" he asked, gently. They were passing the English building now. It was a short five-story cream-colored brick building and it was slated to come down in the next couple years.

Sean tightened his backpack straps, fidgeting. "It sucks! It's horrible. People are horrible." He frowned.

Ino nodded. Ah. He had a guess what was contributing to these feelings. "Did you have a bad experience coming out, Sean?"

Sean let out a long harsh sigh, his ears drooping. "I knew you were going to ask that." He sighed. "YES, I was in high school, and I told *one person*, and three days later the entire school knew. My senior year was a nightmare. I almost dropped out of school."

Ino grimaced and nodded. "Wow, that's *awful*. I'm so sorry. Where was this?"

"Home. Ohio," Sean answered. "In my tiny high school of four hundred kids. People were *merciless*. Someone made a Facebook page for it. *Sean Is Gay* on Facebook dot com."

Ino winced. "Oh my *God*." He frowned. "Okay, so — hope I'm not overreaching here, but I'm guessing you're worried about the same thing happening to your boyfriend?" He let out a breath. "I can't say I blame you."

Sean swallowed, hard. "He acts tough but he's really a sweet guy. People are going to eat him alive." He watched the ground, sadly.

Ino nodded. "Well... I don't want to... minimize your concerns, but... college is pretty different for the coming out experience." He watched Sean carefully. "You know? I've seen lots of students make the journey and come out here at Santiago. It's a... more mature set than high school, and people at the college level generally have their own lives. It's rarely a big deal." He shrugged. "I was out of the closet when I came on board here and I don't think it's even ever come up." He thought about Reed's horrible insinuation. *Well... almost never.*

Sean made a very husky-specific grunt-grumble-growl. "I know but what if it's NOT easy?" He looked at Ino, wide-eyed. "What if it's *miserable?*"

Ino frowned. "Have you talked about this with your boyfriend?"

Sean nodded.

"And does he still want to do it?"

Rolling his eyes, Sean nodded. "Yesss," he groaned.

Ino nodded thoughtfully. "Well... if you want to be on his side, really the best thing you can do would be to support him, in whatever choice *he* makes. You can voice your concerns, of course, but ultimately the decision has to be his." He thought for a moment. "On *this* topic," he added hastily. "Not if he like, tries to get you into poppers or something." He tried to keep a grimace off his face. *I am not good at this.*

Sean blinked at him. "What's a popper?"

Ino grimaced. "Nothing! Don't do drugs!"

The husky stared at him blankly, and then rolled his eyes. "Okay." He sighed. "I knew you were going to say that." He furrowed his brow. "The supportive part, I mean." He wrinkled his muzzle. "Not the drugs part. That was pretty random."

Ino nodded. "Right!" He aggressively steered back on-topic. "Coming out is a very personal decision. Everyone is ready at a different time, and if he's ready, he's going to *need* your support."

Sean grumbled, annoyed. "Fiiiine," he groaned. "Ugh, I knew you were going to say all of this."

Ino cracked a smile. "If you knew what I was going to say, why did you ask?"

Sean kicked a little stone. "*Because* I knew what you were going to say." He looked up. "But thank you. I feel better now."

Ino smiled broadly.

Sean sighed. "I'll support him in whatever he does, but I'm like… so nervous about it."

Ino blinked. "Is *he* nervous?"

Sean snort-laughed. "Not at ALL. Dude is fuckin' fearless."

Ino smiled.

Sean let out a sigh. "I guess we can tell the other guys in the frat while most of them are home for the summer…"

Ino blinked. *Other* guys in the frat? Sean was dating a frat boy?

"And then the rest of the football team after that … "

Ino's eyes widened. *FOOTBALL team?* Wow, times were changing!

"…and then anybody else we missed, and then…" He shrugged. "I guess that's it?"

Ino considered. "Parents?"

Turning to look at him, horrified, Sean's left eye twitched.

Ino grimaced again. "Oh God, I'm sorry, forget I said that. Take it one step at a time."

Sean blinked, and then shook his head. "No, it's fine. I was just thinking about how my parents are going to freak when I tell them I'm dating a dude. I've met his parents, and they already love me." He pranced forward, wagging.

Ino laughed. "Ha, really? Well, that's all you really need then." He beamed. "Who cares about the football team? You're in with the parents."

Sean snorted. "Yeah, I guess so."

Ino nodded. "Really! Those might be your in-laws someday!"

Sean stopped dead and stared at him, horrified. "Oh my GOD, Dr. REAMER!" he exclaimed. "I am *nineteen!* Stop it!"

Ino thought about Sean's parents. He'd never met them, but he knew from the group that Sean was having some trouble. "So… are you going home for the summer?" he asked, delicately.

Sean shook his head. "Naw, I have a part time job at Starbucks. I want to make some money. Get that sweet barista bread."

Ino nodded slowly. "Bread" was money, he was pretty sure. "So are things… good at home?" They picked their way onto a concrete path under a series of sweeping pines. They were almost to Baker.

The husky blinked at him, and then thought about it. "They're okay, I guess." He shrugged. "I mean, I'm an only child, so they're still trying to deal with no grandbabies." He shrugged. "I don't know. My dad is kind of a blue collar guy, so he's never going to be *thrilled*."

Ino cracked a smile. "He might surprise you."

Sean smiled lopsidedly. "I mean… that would be nice, but I'm not holding my breath. My Uncle Travis is pretty cool about everything, though." He looked up. "He works here at the school."

Ino blinked at him. "Really?"

Sean nodded. "Yup. University Security."

Ino thought for a moment. "Oh yeah. I think I've seen him around. Big husky, right?"

Sean chuckled. "You think?

Ino cracked a smile. "I suppose that wasn't a huge logical leap. Sorry, I'm done thinking for the semester. Unlike *you* since you still have to take your CHEMISTRY EXAM!" He spread his arms wide. "Which is right now!"

They stopped at the steps leading up to Baker Brown Science Center. The building loomed above them.

They both stared up at it.

Santiago University boasted a variety of hundred-year-old stone castles, and brand-new state-of-the-art glass-and-steel modern block buildings. Baker… was neither of these.

Constructed in the early 1970s, Baker had a wide, flat patio with eight or ten brick steps and painted brown metal railings which gave it a dated appearance even upon first glance. A huge planetarium made up something like a turret on the left side, with a series of unimpressive amber glass doors up front. The building was one story, floor-to-ceiling brick, with a faded metal cap at the roofline. The hall was boring and reliable — solid, uncomplicated, imposing, simple; all brick and browns and the occasional window. There was a brass plaque on the short brick wall in front of the building, which read simply, BAKER BROWN SCIENCE CENTER 1971, and even that had weathered to a dull dark tobacco color.

Baker was already living on borrowed time, eventually slated to be bulldozed as part of the University's master rehabilitation plan. Malerich Hall, where Ino worked, was already a much bigger and better science building, with huge towering glass walls, in view of the school entrance and Route 30. But Baker was still functional — the labs had fume hoods and thick slate countertops, and the building was perfectly serviceable for the lower-level science tiers and several extremely unlucky Humanities courses. Even the Nursing department had some classes in Baker. The building wouldn't be on any tours for prospective students, but the roof didn't leak and the lights still worked, and so it stayed. For how long was anyone's guess. Basically, until they got the budget to tear it down.

The building was nestled in an open lawn, nearest to the Athletic Center and the football stadium. Baker backed up to the side wall of the Center where it met the football stadium, a towering 40-foot wall that ran the length of the field.

The only other building in sight was the old bookstore — already closed for the summer, never to reopen. There was a much newer bookstore in the new Student Union, and this small standalone store would be demolished in the coming year.

Across campus, the bell tower in the chapel started bonging out the tones for 6:00 pm.

"Oh hey!" Ino said, grinning. "Right on time!"

The two of them started up the brick steps and onto the wide patio. Sean went first, and yanked on the door. It rattled loudly in its frame and didn't open. He turned to look at Ino. "Oops, it's locked!" he announced, gleefully. "Final is canceled!"

The hyena chuckled. "You should *be* so lucky. Guess we're not going to have any company. Yours might be the only final in this building the whole day." He walked past Sean to the far-left door, which had an RF-card reader sticking out of the wall next to it, one of the building's few modernizations in the last fifty years. There was a little LED light in the flat black reader, glowing red. Ino's ID badge was clipped to his belt. He held it up to the RF reader and after a moment the red LED turned green. The door's latch retracted with a loud *whunk!*

Ino pulled the door open and they slipped inside. All the lights were on, but the building was empty and silent, their footsteps echoing down the brick and vinyl halls. This late in the evening during Finals week, even the cleaning staff had come and gone.

Ino looked around. "Oh wow. I have not been in here in *forever*. Let's hope there's actually some usable equipment in the lab. It was always a crapshoot with this place." Ino would already have to set up all the equipment while Sean was taking the written portion of the test. If he had to hunt for pH paper or test tubes it was going to take a lot longer.

Sean pranced in ahead and looked around. "That's fine! You can just give me freebies for the questions we don't have the equipment for." His tail wagged excitedly behind him.

The hyena chuckled. "You're looking a lot more chipper. You weren't nervous about my test at all, were you?!" He smiled.

Sean looked at him, and then outright grinned, looking much more in-character. "*Your* test? No way. You're a pushover, Dr. Reamer."

Ino gasped in mock horror. "Oh really? What class are you in, again? *Advanced Inorganic Chemistry?* I think I'll give you *that* final instead."

Sean chuckled and bounded down the empty hallway. "Oof! You don't gotta do me like that, doc!" He turned back with a grin again, except then something happened.

The young dog froze in his tracks, his smile evaporating off his face. His shoes actually made sharp squeaks on the vinyl tile.

Ino stopped dead, staring at him. "Uhhh, is something the m —"

"Do… do you smell *gas?*" the husky asked, wide-eyed.

Ino stared at him, his jaw dropping open. *Gas?*

They were in a science building. Most of the labs had some kind of gas hookup for Bunsen burners. And the building was old — it wasn't totally out of the question.

Holding perfectly still, Ino sniffed the air delicately. He smelled a lot of things — floor wax, humidity, unwashed Finals week students, the mildewy smell of an old building — but he didn't smell gas.

The hyena frowned. "Gas? Like *gas* gas? Natural gas? Are you sure?"

Sean cocked his head, turning around in a half-circle. "Uhhhm… it was just a whiff." He walked a few more feet, his black nose twitching delicately. He turned back toward Ino, and suddenly his eyes widened again. "Oh shit, there it is!" He took off down a side hallway at a fast walk.

Ino still didn't smell anything. He re-adjusted his briefcase and took off after the young husky.

Sean was walking fast down the west hallway, which ran between a series of classrooms on the outer wall, and large labs, on the inner wall. These were the oldest labs in the building, many of them still full of glassware from the fifties and sixties.

The husky loped down the hallway, sticking his nose into doorways, and continuing down the line, frowning.

Ino trailed after him, rushing to keep up. "Sean, I still don't smell anything. Are you sure you didn't catch a whiff of one of your classm —"

And then the smell hit him. Rotten eggs. It made his nose wrinkle and his forearm fur stand on end.

The hyena stopped dead in his tracks. His fur bristled. "What the *hell?*"

Sean turned to him and frowned. "I *told* you," he grunted. He dash-hopped down the hallway to the next classroom.

Ino ran after him. "Sean, if there's a gas leak, we need to leave this building and tell Maintenance right now!" he said, sharply.

Sean was already two classrooms ahead of him, at Lab 103. The husky was at a closed door, and when he looked through the glass, he gasped sharply.

The look on his face was pure horror, and from twenty feet away Ino felt his stomach drop.

Oh God, he thought.

Sean turned. "*Dr. Reamer!*" the husky cried.

Ino sprinted the rest of the distance. The smell of gas was like a weight in the air now, filling his nostrils and making his stomach turn over.

By the time Ino reached the doorway, Sean was already aggressively rattling the handle, to no avail. The door was a thick wooden door with a 24" x 36" glass window in it, the old kind with the metal latticework throughout. Ino appeared at Sean's side and peered through the glass.

The lights were on. This was one of the light-duty labs, meant for twenty or thirty students doing concurrent experiments, with two long counters running the length of the classroom and a wide aisle between them. They were covered in thick black slate countertops, interrupted every few feet by an electrical outlet and a stainless steel gas connection.

There was a sprawled body on the floor in the aisle, half-hidden behind the first cabinet.

Ino stared for half a moment, his brain refusing to process what he was seeing. Dr. Ethan Reed was flat on the floor, laid out on his back, his arms stretched up above his head. His legs and waist were hidden behind the base of the first countertop. His eyes were closed and he wasn't moving. He looked like he might be sleeping, except he was still fully dressed in his suit jacket.

The rhino did not look good. He wasn't moving.

The smell of gas was overpowering.

Snapping out of his shock, Ino dropped his briefcase on the floor and felt frantically at his side for his keycard ID. "Move," he ordered Sean. The husky sidestepped instantly and Ino thrust his keycard at the room's ID reader.

Nothing happened.

"Dr. Reamer, I don't think he's breathing," Sean whimpered, still peering through the door.

Ino glanced up worriedly, and then hit his ID against the card reader several more times, with similar lack of effect. The green light never activated. The red light wasn't lit, either.

Ino grabbed the doorknob and yanked hard, shaking the door violently in the frame. The door rattled explosively but did not budge. The tiny movement of the wooden slab stirred the air, and for a moment the scent of gas washed over them like a soaking rain. It hung in the air like humidity.

He looked through the glass at the fallen rhino, and then up at the counter. There was an assortment of beakers and test tubes out on the counter, as well as the base of an unlit Bunsen burner. The tube was not connected to the countertop gas hookup. In fact, *nothing* was connected to the gas hookup. The valve was all the way open. In a moment of silence, he could hear it hissing.

"Oh, God. He's going to asphyxiate." He straightened up. "Sean, run and get help. Get out of the building and hit an emergency button. I'm going to stay here and —"

Sean's eyes left Ino's face to look over his shoulder, back into the lab. His ears flattened against his head and his pupils actually dilated as the husky focused on something at the back of the lab, and with rising terror Ino snapped his head around.

It only took him a moment to see it.

At the rear wall, one of the fume hoods was open. It was a small oven-sized cavity with a glass door for performing experiments that produced harmful gases. The hood door, a heavy affair that slid up and down, was open a few inches. The light inside was on.

As Ino watched, the light blinked out. A moment later it clicked back on, then off again. It seemed erratic. Like the bulb wasn't fully screwed into its housing.

Sean swallowed loudly. "I-i-is that going to spark, Dr. Re —"

Ino reached over and physically turned the husky around, facing away from the room. "Run," he said. "Now!" he barked. He shoved the husky.

Sean raced away in a full sprint. Ino lunged forward and flew after him.

They thundered down the hallway, flying all the way down the first floor hall and barreling around the corner into the main hallway, charging forward for the last fifteen feet to the front doors.

Sean hit it first and hit it hard, slamming into the crash bar at a full run. The vestibule door flew open and slammed into its neighbor, shattering the glass down the center with a loud, wet crack. It slowed him down a hair, and by the time he hit the outer door, the husky's momentum had decreased; Ino caught up to him just as they reached the steps.

He looked out into the quad. There was no cover for yards.

They weren't going to make it.

Behind them, there was a *whoosh*.

At the front of the building, next to the ten steps down to street level, there was a drop-off that descended the entire eight-foot height of the patio, leaving a short brick wall. Ino changed course for the wall and grabbed Sean around the waist as he went, lifting the smaller dog off his feet — God, he was *so light*, much lighter than Ino expected — and yanking him to the side. They barreled sideways over the edge and dropped a gut-wrenching eight feet, straight down into the grass.

By the time they hit the ground below, Baker Science Center was in the process of vaporizing.

Sean hit the ground first and let out half a yelp before Ino couldn't hear anything else. Ino pinned him and held on. It was all he could do. It was all he had time to do. He got one hand around Sean and one over the back of his own head and that was it.

There was a deep explosion, like thunder except it kept building nano-second by nanosecond until it was so loud Ino couldn't hear it anymore, couldn't hear *anything* anymore. He flinched violently as the ground rumbled and then actually shook underneath them. The sound awakened absolute horror in him and he felt his adrenaline surge.

A huge cloud of smoke and fire and dust blasted out of the front of Baker Brown like a sideways volcano, moving fast, moving *astonishingly* fast. It roared out over their wall in half a second and then 20 or 30 feet into the quad and then Ino couldn't see anything anymore. The billowing cloud overtook them, and Ino could see a dull, deep glowing red, and he realized with absolute existential horror that this wasn't a dust cloud passing over them, but a *fireball.*

Ino couldn't see or hear anything moving, but he could *feel* objects rocketing out into the night. He could just tell from the disruption to the atmosphere, by the violently rushing wind that was moving his fur and clothes. Years ago, a bad baseball pitch had once missed Ino's head by a fraction of an inch, and this was the same skin-prickling sensation. He knew there were objects with incredible mass — glass, metal, bricks — rocketing past a few feet over their vulnerable bodies. He was absolutely certain they were going to die.

Some of the things flying out toward the quad didn't quite make it, and tennis ball-sized chunks of debris rained down over them. Something hard and jagged — it felt like an entire brick — grazed off the back of Ino's knuckles and scraped his hand raw, even through his fur. It would have hit him in the head if he hadn't been covering it. More debris hurtled and bounced over them, like a hailstorm made of construction debris, and Ino had never felt more vulnerable or exposed.

The hyena pushed Sean hard up against the base of the brick wall, over countless unidentifiable objects already in the grass. Dust was shaking *out of* the wall itself, clinging to the bricks like steam. After 4 or 5 seconds, objects started raining down around them. Ino felt hard, violent impacts close by, way *too* close, reverberating through the dirt underneath them. *That's the roof,* he thought, in some distant dissociated part of his brain, *it went straight up and now it's coming down in pieces.* He pinned Sean up against the wall and covered him as best he could, squeezing the husky and hunching his head. Sean's entire body was tensed and so was Ino's.

Something massive and heavy slammed down on the top of the wall hard enough to shake the ground underneath them. There was a pause where Ino waited to be hit with shattered stonework from the wall above, and then suddenly the brass dedication plaque dropped out of the wall and hit Ino square in the back. "*Guh!*" he grunted as all the air left his body, and he heard Sean let out a squeak as the hyena flattened on top of him. It hurt *immediately* but Ino also felt a hard thud and heard a loud *whang!* As a heavy piece of dropping stone or metal bounced off the plaque about level with Ino's mid-back, and Ino noted with some interest that the stupid Baker Brown dedication plaque had probably just saved his life.

Pieces of rock and brick rained continuously down on them, rocketing out of the sky like gravel hailstones, pinging off Ino with a stinging little bite every time something made contact. As he cowered, the stone hail finally started to taper off. The trickle of bricks and chunks of wood died off, and then stopped finally.

The last huge thing to come down was a huge piece of shredded pink insulation, the size of a twin mattress. It wafted gently to the ground directly next to them, and then the worst of it seemed to be over.

It was a long time before Ino felt safe moving again.

Reeling, his heart thundering in his chest, he just held perfectly still for a minute, trying to breathe, as if hiding from a predator. Sean was on his side underneath him, breathing hard. Ino held his breath.

Silence.

Cautiously, he wiggled in place. He moved his arms and rolled his shoulders. His whole upper back felt numb, but he didn't think anything was broken. There was at least ten or fifteen pounds of tiny chunks of debris on his back, not counting the brass plaque, but nothing had come down hard enough to break any bones.

Cautiously, he raised his head and opened his eyes.

The air was dusty. Red and dusty. Great clouds of dust and smoke coursed over them. In Ino's immediate vicinity were a lot of broken bricks and glass and jagged pieces of wood and great snowy tufts of insulation. But the air was hazy and he couldn't see very far — it was like being underneath a waterfall or next to a dumpster fire. He smelled wood smoke and brick dust. Pieces of paper, some whole, some in bits, drifted down all around him, like snowfall. It looked like December again, except now there was ash mixed in. Everything felt silent and slow.

Sean was still underneath him, shivering violently.

Ino lifted himself onto all fours, letting the huge bronze commencement plaque slide off of him, causing a cascade of brick chunks to slide off. His ears were ringing. "ARE YOU OKAY?" he asked, too loudly. He couldn't tell how loud his own voice was — even to Ino he sounded like he was underwater.

Sean looked up at him and nodded yes, but he didn't *look* okay, he looked like he was having a heart attack. He was covered in dust, like he had fallen into a pile of unmixed concrete, and tears were running down his face, leaving long dark gray streaks in the dust dulling his fur.

"It's okay," Ino told him. "I think it's over. Okay?"

Clenching his teeth, Sean nodded. He was shaking, his blue eyes wide and terrified.

"Don't move!" Ino told him. He lifted the rest of the way up, and a couple jagged chunks of bricks that had been sitting in the small of his back rolled off of him. There were bricks everywhere, Ino realized. Hundreds, maybe thousands. Ino's head abruptly started pounding and he realized that both his arms and his entire back felt tender and bruised. His knees and elbows hurt the most, and the back of his hands were so raw they didn't even hurt yet, but his whole body already ached. Both of his shirt-sleeves were ripped open at the wrist, open up to the elbows, and his neck felt like he had fallen asleep stuffed in a closet. Even his tail hurt.

The hyena looked and felt the husky over, gently touching his limbs to feel through the fluff, looking for blood or limbs bent the wrong way. Nothing, except skinned knees and palms of his hands. Other than that and a thick coat of dust, Sean looked unscathed. He was even still wearing his backpack, though Ino noticed that both of his shoes were missing. *Jesus.* Was that from the explosion or their tumble over the ledge?

The backs of both of Ino's hands were bleeding, the blood bright red in the washed-out gray dust covering him. He felt the back of his head and came away with blood smeared over his palm. It wasn't a lot of blood at all, but as soon as he saw it the back of his head started throbbing. Ino reasoned that he couldn't be hurt too badly or he would be bleeding a lot more.

Ino smelled the blood and suddenly felt like he was floating, and he realized with some interest that he was disassociating. Well, that was to be expected. Everything felt funny and nothing felt real. He wasn't entirely sure what to do.

What were they always yammering on about for active shooter training? ABC, was it?

A was AREA: VERIFY THE AREA IS SAFE. He couldn't remember what B or C stood for, but that seemed like a good start. He should probably see if Baker was on fire. Ino staggered to his feet, feeling lightheaded.

Sean's eyes widened and he grabbed at Ino's arm. He looked terrified. "D-Dr. Reamer!" he whispered, urgently. Or maybe he shouted it. Ino's ears still weren't working quite right.

The hyena turned back. "I need to see if we're safe." He squeezed the husky's shoulders. "I'm not gonna leave you. Stay here!"

Swallowing, Sean nodded and released Ino's shirtsleeve.

He lifted himself to his feet. There was still a haze of smoke and dust in the air but it had started to dissipate. He could see the outline of the front of Baker now. Ino could make out the low, wide rectangle where the doors had been, except now the rectangle was missing its top, and the entire shape was backlit by bright red and orange light. The top of the building was definitely missing. And they had been on the *other side* of the building from the explosion.

That was… concerning.

Ino stepped to the stairs and gingerly picked his way up the steps. He had to pick his way up carefully, planting each ruined dress shoe with careful deliberation. Many of the brick stairs had big, fresh jagged chunks missing from their fronts, and Ino didn't want to take a nasty tumble down the stairs.

He got to the top of the steps and stared.

Baker was *gone*. The only thing left was the lower portion of the front wall and part of the sides. The planetarium had dropped into a pile of bricks no more than a quarter of its original size, the dented brass roof heaped in the center. The interior, as far as he could tell, was completely destroyed. The air was still smoky but Ino could clearly tell there was nothing between him and the rec center. Half of Baker had been swept clean off its foundation as if by a tsunami, and the other half had collapsed into a pile. Wreckage was everywhere, covering every square foot of ground for yards in each direction. Ino couldn't tell where the grass, paths, or parking lot were, or even where the building's walls had been. It was all just scattered bricks and wood and insulation. He could see pieces of furniture — a lab stool, part of a vending machine, an entire intact file cabinet — but the whole structure of the building was like a popped balloon. Ino could barely tell where he was.

The only clear part was at the base of the overhang. The blasted debris had shot out and over them — as he had hoped. Swallowing, he wondered what would have happened if they'd been even a touch slower. Well — that wasn't *that* difficult to theorize. They both would have been blasted into ground beef.

In the far corner, a few hundred feet away, was a thirty-foot tower of flames, burning like an oil rig fire. That was probably the main gas line. Nearby was a burst water main, gushing straight up like a casino fountain, but the gas main was the obvious point of focus. It shot a pillar of flame straight up into the sky, coloring the entire quad glowing fiery yellow. It looked like a funeral pyre.

Ino thought of Dr. Reed.

A funeral pyre was not inappropriate.

Abruptly the ringing of Ino's ears started to fade, and suddenly he could hear all sorts of noises. There was a symphony of car alarms, sounding from every corner of the campus, and in the student parking garage over the ridge, Ino could see headlights and tail lights from a hundred different car alarms flaring like searchlights, blinking and lighting the building up erratically, like a gigantic Christmas tree. The fire alarm in the rec center was going off — Ino looked and saw shattered windows all over the side of the building. As Ino looked around, the campus emergency sirens kicked in. They were long, screaming air-raid style sirens, coming from several points on campus, and Ino could hear them overlapping and warbling across campus.

All of the sounds were distant and jumbled, distorting as they ran across campus, and the sirens overlapped one another and screamed into the night. There were other noises, including yelling, and Ino could hear what sounded like a car horn being held down. There were sirens in the distance, drawing ever closer. It was a jumbled mess of noise that Ino had never heard before, and now he felt like his brain truly was going to shut down.

He picked his way back down to Sean, looked down, and found one of Sean's gray sneakers. He fished it out of the pile of building pieces and miraculously, quickly found the other one. He handed both of them to Sean, who looked at him in confusion, and then looked down at his bare feet, startled. He still hadn't noticed.

"*LET'S GET OUT OF HERE*," Ino told him, over the noise.

Slipping his shoes back on, Sean nodded. He was still shaking faintly, looking dazed. Ino realized all his fur was poofed out. He rubbed the poor husky's back. Sean leaned into him, swallowing hard, choking back a scared little noise.

There was the sound of running. Ino looked up and saw a large tiger running toward them. The tiger was wearing dark-blue maintenance coveralls, and he was running at an absolute full-tilt, yelling. "HEY! HEY!! ARE YOU OKAY?!" the man screamed, racing toward them. His eyes were very, very wide.

Ino saw other people running, mostly campus employees, and then the first Santiago University Campus Security came screaming down Chapel Drive, red-blue lights painfully bright against the fading daylight, sirens deafeningly loud. Two more squad cars — city cops this time — and a massive fire truck came roaring in from three different directions, and after that the scene was quickly swarmed.

The next few hours passed in an absolute blur for Ino. He was separated from Sean immediately by a group of EMTs — Sean didn't like it but Ino assured him it would be fine — and Ino was briefly inside an ambulance, and then outside of it under a thick medical blanket, and then back inside a different ambulance. All the while he was talking to people — paramedics, and firefighters, and campus security, and city cops, and university physical plant employees, and workers from the gas company, and a bunch of people he didn't have the wherewithal to identify.

There were so many inquiries that the paramedics didn't even take Ino off-site — they checked him out and cleaned him up right in the back of an ambulance, all while Ino was being interviewed by everyone who approached. There was at least one FBI jacket and two people from the ATF. He answered their questions without much thought, feeling numb and foggy. One of the paramedics planted him on one of the metal pathway benches, still wrapped in a thick navy-blue blanket. Ino was all too happy to stay there until his butt went numb.

The paramedics had cleared him of life-threatening injuries. He had a small scrape on the back of his head that they shaved and bandaged, and they gave him an ice pack for the back of his neck. The backs of both of his hands were raw and bleeding, so they shaved and cleaned his wrists and fingers and wrapped both of his hands in light gauze. Ino looked like a boxer after a match and felt like one too — and not the winner, either. He had two skinned elbows and two skinned palms and his entire body felt stiff and injured.

While he was repeating his story twenty times, Ino asked questions too, as he thought of them. There was no rhyme or reason to who he asked — as he thought of questions, he asked whoever happened to be in front of him.

Nobody else had been scheduled inside the building, a big Facilities tiger told him.

There was only one known death so far, said a lapine EMT, as she quickly checked Ino's vitals and then hurried off to help someone else. She was in such a hurry she pulled off her vinyl gloves and left them next to Ino on the bench.

All students were accounted for, a big beaver with an *Indiana Gas* polo told him, but he wasn't certain, just repeating what he had heard around the site. The man looked guilty telling him, like he was spreading hurtful gossip. "I shouldn't really be telling you that," he said, and then made Ino retell the entire sequence of events.

There were a *lot* of injuries, Ino learned from direct observation.

As he sat on his bench, Ino watched a seemingly never-ending line of people stream out of the rec center, in bloody white t-shirts and ripped pink spandex. Apparently, every window on the near side of the building had blown in, with bricks and cement blasting through office windows, and the false ceiling of the fitness center had come down on top of a dozen people, foam and metal crashing onto them on their treadmills and yoga mats and weight benches.

Most of the injuries were minor, but a handful were very serious. A security officer who had been close enough to get caught in the blast was hurt pretty badly. He was covered in so much blood, smeared all over his face and neck, that Ino couldn't even tell his species — just that he was black and white and red all over. After a moment he saw Sean pacing worriedly by a few feet away and realized the officer must have been his uncle.

Horrified, Ino leapt to his feet to rush over, but as soon as he did, EMTs rushed the two dogs into an ambulance and carted them away. He could hear the bigger dog protesting loudly until the moment the ambulance doors were slammed. Stunned, Ino sat back down.

The sun started to descend and the site descended into darkness. It was getting dark, *too* dark, and Ino couldn't figure out why, until he turned in a slow circle and realized that an entire block of pathway lamps and streetlights had been annihilated by flying debris. He could see the column lamps, in steel gray posts every ten or fifteen feet, bent at bizarre angles, glass shades smashed out, tipped over, flattened into the grass. The light pole closest to Ino was bent over at a 45-degree angle, like a fishing pole stuck to a pier piling, except it was 15 feet tall.

He looked around at the devastated campus. He really was lucky to be alive.

Colossal work lamps on stands suddenly appeared; abruptly, the area was lit up like a night game at the stadium. More bright lights appeared at ground level in the distance, kept at the periphery of the scene, and after a few moments of confused staring, Ino realized they were news vans with reporters filming on-scene. Dozens of people picked over the wreckage. There was still a haze in the air, and with the bright work lights and the foggy air, the former site of Baker looked to Ino like an underwater research site. He still didn't feel like any of this was really happening.

Ino shook his head, pulling the blanket tighter around himself. How had Ethan Reed, a career scientist, made such an obvious and avoidable error that he had killed himself, and nearly killed Ino *and a student?* What had Reed even been *doing* in there, working in a closed lab at this time of night? The hyena frowned. None if it made any sense.

It finally occurred to Ino to check his watch. He pulled up his ripped sleeve. His watch face was smashed, spider-webbed like a tiny car windshield. The hands were jammed into the faceplate, forever stopped at 6:04.

He fished his phone out of his back pocket, and found its screen miraculously un-shattered. The battery was dead, however.

Suddenly, the commotion grew quiet. Ino looked up.

Walking slowly over the chunks of brick and concrete, two burly EMTs were carrying a canvas stretcher with a large vinyl bag holding a substantial load in the vague shape of a humanoid figure. Silently, they walked down the steep front steps and slowly picked their way to a waiting windowless black van.

Something bothered Ino about the scene, and he was close enough to be in earshot, so he just said it. "Is that Dr. Reed?" he asked.

The two EMTs looked at each other.

Ino swallowed. "That doesn't look big enough."

The two EMTs exchanged a long glance, and then the older one cleared his throat. "It's, uh, it's not *all* of him," he said, softly.

Ino processed that for a long moment, and then before he even knew what was happening, he found himself fast-walking across campus, and he didn't stop until he got to his office.

Chapter 2: Operator Error

Saturday, May 12, 2018

Riiiiiiiiiiinnnngggggggggggggggg!

Groggily, Ino grunted awake. The phone was ringing. It was an old-style desk phone, with a real bell. A loud, jarring bell.

He sat up, confused. He didn't *have* a landline at his house.

Blinking, he looked around. He wasn't *in* his house. He was in his office at school, on the couch, still in his clothes. After spending three hours on the phone with concerned relatives who had seen him on the news, he'd gotten as far as taking off his clunky dress shoes and his tie and then laid down on the loveseat "just for a second" and then immediately fallen asleep. Now it was daylight out. Early morning light strained in through half-closed blinds.

Riiiiiiiiiiinnnngggggggggggggggg! His desk phone rang one more time, and then cut out mid-ring. Who the hell was calling on the landline? Must have been a wrong number.

Grunting, Ino squirmed around in a circle, sitting up on the couch. His whole body hurt, from his ear tips to the end of his tail, and he needed to pee. Squinting, he checked his watch, and again found it smashed. Clumsily, he worked it off of his wrist and dumped it on the table next to the tiny loveseat on which he had somehow slept the entire night. He checked his phone again, plugged in next to the sofa, now at 100% battery. 8:41 am. Jesus.

His eyes still half-open, Ino staggered to his feet. "Ungh, God, owwww," he rumbled. Every part of his body ached. Even his *fur* felt like it hurt, though it was probably just a thousand little cuts and abrasions all over his body. Grimacing, the hyena attempted a stretch, and only succeeded in raising his bruised arms halfway over his head before his shoulder twinged and he stopped. His bandaged hands and head felt clunky and awful. His mouth tasted like the bottom of a trash can.

Ino had a small dorm-style mirror mounted to the wall between two bookshelves, and he briefly checked his appearance.

Shirt hopelessly wrinkled and so caked with dust it was now a deep gray, tie missing, sweat stains under both of his arms. He had washed his face in the restroom but his hair was still full of brick dust. Bloody patches at the elbows of his nice dress shirt, permanent rips in the cuffs of both sleeves, rips in both his knees, and both hands bandaged to the wrists. With his destroyed shirt clinging to his chest and little spots of blood around the collar, Ino would not look out of place in the last ten minutes of a horror movie.

"Perfect," he mumbled, trying and failing to at least smooth out his hair. Like all hyenas, Ino had dark brown hair that, no matter how he cut it, ended up looking like a short spiky mohawk. He had the big radar-dish ears typical to his species and fur that was normally mustard-yellow with rich coffee-brown spots. At the moment his fur was both greasy and dusty and he could not wait to get into a shower.

He inspected the back of his hands. They were bandaged in thin white strips of gauze, wound up like a mummy. He had bled through in several places, but not by much, just in spots here and there. His shaved fur felt weird even under the bandages, and he could only imagine how bizarre it looked. The rest of his wounds had been superficial, and Ino felt lucky that he hadn't been one of the many people carted off to Beirne Memorial Hospital for stitches.

Turning away from the mirror, Ino briefly staggered around looking around for his briefcase. After a few moments he remembered that he had left it on the floor outside the lab where they had found Dr. Reed, and he would need construction equipment and a search team to locate it. With that thought came a torrent of memories that he stuffed back into his brain.

"I am not dealing with *that* right now," Ino grunted, reaching for his car keys, which he had fortunately left in his desk the previous day. He had a tobacco-brown backpack in a storage closet which he used on campus sometimes, and he stuffed his laptop inside it along with a few other essentials. "Keep it together, Ino. You just need to get home to the shower."

He opened the door to his office and stepped outside.

A figure in a sharp suit was standing at the doorway of the office across the hall. She jumped when Ino pulled his door open, which in turn made Ino jerk violently in surprise.

"*Oh!*" she cried.

Ino's eyes snapped open, and he immediately felt fully awake. "Dr. Greeley!" he cried at the cheetah standing across the hall from him.

She lowered her head, letting out an affectionate sigh. "Ino," she chided, her long tail lashing back and forth behind her. "For the hundredth time, Ino — please, call me Susan. How are you?"

Ino took in the sight of her — she was shorter than him, a slight cheetah of perhaps 5'4", or maybe 5'6" in heels. She had a sympathetic smile and she was the picture of professionalism in a light sage-colored skirt and jacket with unassuming pumps. Dr. Greeley was in her late 50s or early 60s but looked 40, and most importantly, she was the esteemed 8th president of Santiago University.

Ino managed a weak smile and decided to avoid the question. "I can't *not* call you Doctor. It's bad enough you won't let me call you *President.*"

Susan gave him a warm smile — a canned "oh you" response — but her smile quickly faded when she looked him up and down. Her expression quickly changed to horrified. "Ino… did you… did you *sleep* here?"

Ino looked away, feeling his cheeks heat up. "Uhh, yeah. Not on purpose. My mom and brother saw me on the news. Like… me personally. It took me a while to talk them down and by then I was too tired to go home." He felt his cheeks starting to heat up.

The cheetah nodded sympathetically. "I am so sorry to hear. I understand you were quite close to the explosion."

Ino swallowed. "I also found Dr. Reed."

Susan winced. "Ino, I want you to know that you have the full support of the University behind you." She paused for a moment, looking pained. "Have you already been to the hospital?"

Ino shook his head. "No, I was just cut up and bruised. They took care of me in an ambulance."

Susan took a deep breath. She was the picture of sympathy. "Is there anything we can do? Anything *I* can do? Do you need a ride home?"

Ino was about to brush off the question, but something did occur to him. "Do you… do you *know* anything?" He frowned. "Can you tell me what the hell *happened?*"

Susan processed the question, and then nodded thoughtfully. "Of course." She took a deep breath. "Well… of course we're in the opening hours of what will be a full investigation, but… it looks like Dr. Reed accidentally caused a terrible tragedy."

Ino felt his jaw drop open and didn't bother to hide it. "An *accident?*"

Susan stared at him, her blue eyes surprised. "Well… of course. You didn't think there was something else going on, did you?"

Ino stammered for a moment. "I just, uh, I didn't… I just didn't think it was possible for a whole building to explode by accident."

The cheetah swallowed. "Well, of course, not without *some* cause. The fire chief suspects Dr. Reed was working on an experiment, turned on the gas system for a Bunsen burner, and accidentally bumped one of the nozzles. They think he was overcome by the gas, and then of course the loose bulb you mentioned ignited the gas." She shook her head. "Such a tragedy. I'm so glad no one else was in the building."

Ino stared at her. "I don't understand. Why didn't he smell the gas?"

Susan stared at him. "Dr. Reed had no sense of smell."

Ino felt his jaw drop open again. "*What?* Are you serious?"

She nodded. There was a pause. "I thought you knew. You worked so closely together."

Ino frowned at her.

Susan stared sympathetically back at him. "Ino… I'd like you to think about counseling services."

Ino felt his eyebrows shoot up and at this point he didn't even bother to hide his astonishment. "Wh…" He trailed off. "I'm sorry, what?"

She nodded, and Ino could see her characteristic look of determination. "We've put a lot of money into keeping our students and faculty safe in the event of a catastrophe. All the experts agree that counseling should take place as soon after an incident as possible."

He processed that for a moment, his jaw hanging open. "I, uhhhh… I'm sorry, Dr. G… Susan. I really don't feel like I need a therapist. I'm still kind of processing what happened." He gestured to himself. "I haven't even showered yet."

The cheetah looked him over again, frowning, and Ino had the sudden thought that evoking his new zombie-movie look probably wasn't the best method to prove his stability. He swallowed.

Susan set her jaw. "Dr. Reamer, I insist. In this day and age it's all the more important to value the guidance of experts in the field." She nodded. "And if you need any other support, such as lightening your summer class-load, you have the full support of the University."

Ino felt his chest tighten as visions of reduced paychecks popped into his brain. He tried to keep his eyes from bugging out of his head. "Uhh, no need for *that*," he said, too hurriedly. He swallowed. "Maybe I will look into counseling. Do you know where I can get the information?"

Susan smiled at him. "I'll email it to you myself," she said.

Ino nodded weakly. "Thanks," he squeaked.

Susan nodded. "Thank you, Ino." She looked around. "Why don't you go home and get some rest."

He smiled. "And a shower."

They both chuckled.

Ino found himself looking over her head, at the door across the hall. *Huh.*

He cleared his throat. "Did you, uh… did you need something?" He gestured across the hall with his muzzle. "From in there?"

The plate on the door said ETHAN REED, PHD.

Susan Greeley took a deep breath, and let out a long sigh. Her ears gently drooped. "I'm afraid not," she said. "Just being sentimental." She smiled a sad little smile. "Dr. Reed and I worked together for a long time."

Ino nodded back at her, managing a weak smile. "I'm sorry for your loss."

She smiled, letting out a sigh. "You, too," she said, softly. She reached up and patted him firmly on the shoulder. "Go home, Ino."

"Yes ma'am," he said.

Ino went home and took a long shower after peeling off the scabby bandages off of his hands. The fur was indeed shaved stubble-short and it did, in fact, look ridiculous. The hyena was covered in a thousand little cuts and scratches, even on his big ears and short tail, that burned like fire as he worked hot water and soap into his fur. The pain was worth it to get rid of the crawling, itchy sensation of being covered in greasy, gritty dirt. He had to shampoo himself, head to toe, four times before the water ran clear instead of milky grey.

Ino had a nice fur dryer built right into the ceiling of the shower stall, and he stood under the hot air for a long time with his eyes closed, just aching. The heat was nice but even the ruffling of his fur stung a little. Once he was done, he put on athletic shorts and a loose-fitting t-shirt that an old boyfriend had left at his house.

Ino thought of poor terrified Sean Murphy while he was in the shower, and as soon as he was dry, he sent him an email since he didn't have his phone number. He kept it short. *Hope you're holding up, hope your uncle is OK. Let me know if you need anything. Take care of yourself.*

After that, his phone started ringing, and then his Saturday passed in a loud rush of people coming and going. News of the hyena's close call got out quickly, and the people of Santiago did what everyone in a small Midwestern town does in times of tragedy: they showed up, by the van-load, with food. With so, *so much food.*

At one point on Saturday Ino's small house had nine people in it: Mrs. Gaard from down the street who Ino occasionally did yardwork for, three professors from Santiago University (Meteorology, Genetics, and French), his boss, and the entire family that lived next door, complete with bored teenagers on cellphones. Each of them (minus the bored teenagers) brought food, ranging from a grocery-store cut fruit platter, to a baked mostaccioli that Mrs. Gaard had somehow produced that morning.

Everyone talked about the explosion, and how shocked they were, and exactly what they were doing when they found out what happened, and if they could hear the explosion from where they were standing Friday night — if it rattled the dishes or shook the windows or set off their car alarm — and how everyone thought it was thunder until they saw it in the news the next morning.

It was noisy and overwhelming, but Ino also found it comforting. At the end of the day, it was really nice to have other people around. He also had enough family-sized dishes to last him the entire summer. Mrs. Gaard's baked mostaccioli alone would take him a solid week to scavenge his way through. He licked his chops just thinking of it.

Still feeling disconnected from the world, Ino went to bed preposterously early, at 7 pm.

The next day, Sunday, Ino staggered out to his lawn in a robe and slippers and his big square glasses, his tail hanging limply behind him. Now his whole body *really* hurt. He was covered in little abrasions which he could now feel as a forest of scabs through his fur, and both his knees were throbbing. The fur shaved off his hands was starting to grow back and it itched like crazy. His shoulder and upper back still felt like he had taken a cannonball to the shoulder blade. It was going to be a long week.

It was 75 degrees at 8 in the morning — shockingly warm for yet another day.

Wrapped in a black and brown plaid fleece robe, Ino limped down the driveway. He was still getting a physical copy of the *Post-Tribune* newspaper for some reason, despite never having ordered one. The local newspaper had signed him up *yet again* for something they described as a "trial period," which Ino described as "throwing trash in his driveway every day." Most of the time the unwanted paper went straight into the recycling bin, but today he actually wanted to see it.

On his front porch Ino had a rustic hand-made bench he had purchased at the Popcorn Fair. He parked his spotted rear on it, poking his tender tail through the slot in the back, and slid the paper out of its tube-shaped plastic bag. He wondered how much of the front page the explosion warranted two days later. Considering how slow Santiago usually was for news cycles, it would probably be a front-page story for six months.

He unfolded the paper and felt his jaw drop open.

POLICE: FATAL BLAST LIKELY CAUSED BY VICTIM

Ino gaped, setting his coffee down on the bench next to him. *"What?!"* He adjusted his glasses and carefully read the article.

SANTIAGO, IN: A Santiago University professor killed in a major explosion on campus Friday night most likely caused the blast, police say.

In a joint statement released by the City of Santiago Police and Santiago University Campus Security, police say that their investigation is ongoing, but the gas was most likely released accidentally by Dr. Ethan Reed, who died in the explosion. Reed, 67, lived in Portage and died in the May 11 explosion which also completely leveled a campus building and seriously damaged three others.

"While a full investigation is still in process, detailed maintenance records for Baker Brown Science Center find the building in very good repair as recently as March, and no other leaks were found in the building's records or during regular inspections. The gas regulator has been found and determined to be in good repair. At this time our most likely eventuality is the inadvertent release of gas, most likely the result of operator error," reads the statement.

Indiana Gas did not immediately respond to questions but did release a statement indicating they are cooperating with authorities and do not believe any of their equipment was to blame for the incident.

The gas explosion, which was reported from as far away as Schererville and detected via instrumentation as far as Chicago,

completely destroyed the 32,000-square
foot Baker Brown Science Center and seriously injured 34 faculty and staff. Reed
was the only fatality.

Reed joined Santiago University in 1987,
teaching in the areas of Chemistry,
Biology, and advanced Genetics.

Porter County has not had a deadly residential gas explosion since 2014, when a
Chesterton home exploded due to a faulty
stove, killing two.

Ino frowned. An *accident?* That didn't seem possible. Was Reed really that careless? What had he even been doing in there? He thought back to the objects on the lab counter. It had been a series of beakers and lab equipment. It didn't look like any experiment that Ino knew — all the pieces looked like they were pulled at random from the glassware cabinet, and not by anyone who knew a damn thing about science. It looked *staged.* Ino wasn't even really sure that a single gas output *could* fill a room to explosion saturation.

There had to be something else going on.

Shaking his head, the hyena turned and loped slowly back into his house.

Chapter 3: The Tent

Monday, May 14, 2018

On Monday, Ino was right back on campus.

Even though it had only been three days since the semester had ended, the school had basically emptied out in its entirety. As it did every summer, the campus felt like a dying shopping mall. Only two cafeterias were open (out of six), most of the dorms had only two or three students per floor (if they were open at all), and the only fully-occupied building was Wong Hall, the administration building. Ino walked all the way from the parking lot to his office without encountering another person.

Ino was dressed casually, which for him was golf shorts and a navy-blue athletic polo shirt, tucked in with a white leather belt. Normally in the spring he would have opted for pastels, but he wanted something darker in case one of his scabs cracked and he ended up bleeding through it.

Unlocking his office door was no louder than usual, yet to Ino it sounded like dropping a stack of acrylic Petri dishes in a silent and empty lab. Ears back, he slipped into his office as silently as he could.

He stared. This was his first time back after the explosion. He looked around.

His ruined necktie from Friday was still sprawled out on the floor. And now in full daylight he could see his small office sofa was smeared with what looked like dust and ash. He leaned forward and there were definitely a few soaked-in spots of dried blood.

Picking up the tie and dropping it into the trash, Ino reflected that the sofa was probably due for a replacement anyway. He could throw a blanket over it in the meantime and start looking for a new one over the summer.

Sitting down at his desk, Ino docked his laptop and pushed the power button on the docking station. He was glad he still had the computer at all — he had almost brought it to Sean's final. There had been an iPad in his briefcase (University-issued) that had not been so lucky. He logged in with his network credentials, played some streaming pop music through the laptop's tinny little speakers, and worked for a couple hours until he was distracted by what sounded like heavy machinery.

Blinking, Ino stopped what he was doing and turned. It sounded like there was a backhoe outside.

Curious, he stood up, turned around, and peeked through the blinds, ears straining forward. His office was on the second floor, and he looked down into the parking lot.

Whirrrrrrrrrrrrrrrrrrrrrrrrrrrrrrr! Sounded a loud truck in the lot.

There was a huge flatbed tow truck outside, its diesel engine idling loudly enough for Ino to clearly hear it rumbling even through the glass. There was a small fluffy snow leopard in a blue mechanic's jumpsuit working industriously to attach cables to the back of a silver Toyota Camry.

Ino blinked at the car. Who the hell was getting towed out of a *faculty* lot? The car looked too new for a breakdown. It was only a few years old. It looked familiar, but every third car in the state was a silver Camry so he couldn't place it.

Frowning, Ino noticed a thin layer of dust on the car's back window. Everything on campus had been covered with a thin layer of brick dust after the explosion, but most people had hosed their cars down. This one had obviously been parked unattended since the night of the expl…

A chill ran up his spine. Ino winced and the fur on the back of his neck stood up. "Oh God," he said out loud, his voice low and flat. "That's *Reed's* car." He stared, horrified.

Frowning, Ino watched the snow leopard walk back to his truck. Using controls on the side of the vehicle, the driver tilted the flatbed of the truck upward. Whirring loudly, the flatbed tilted inexorably toward the orphaned Toyota.

Shivering, Ino sat back down and stared into space, trying not to listen to the sound of the truck.

After a moment he stood back up. Reed's car had been *here?* It was a twenty-minute walk to Baker Brown. Reed wasn't exactly the athletic type. Had the rhino really walked all the way across campus? *Why* would he do that? It looked like his office had been closed up for the summer. Nothing had given Ino the impression that Reed would be coming back to their offices in Malerich Hall. And yet, here was his only mode of transportation.

Ino frowned. This was not helping his feeling that the circumstances had been strange.

Reluctantly, he went back to his schoolwork.

An hour later, Ino decided he'd had enough, and shut down his computer to pack it up. All of his surviving personal effects were already conveniently in the spare backpack, so he decided to keep using that until he could go briefcase shopping.

Spotting his smashed wristwatch on the floor, Ino threw that in there, too. There was probably nothing that could be done to save it, but he didn't want to just throw it in the trash.

Leaving his office, Ino noticed something he hadn't noticed before.

Dr. Reed's door was slightly open.

Ino stared at it, wide-eyed, frozen. *What the hell.*

The plain wooden door offered no hint.

Ino stepped slowly toward the door, unconsciously taking light steps, and gently pushed on the wooden door.

It swung wide open, slowly, creaking loudly, and the light from the hallway shone upon a vacant floor and four empty walls.

The office was completely empty. There wasn't a stick of furniture in it. No desk, no chairs, no loveseat, no huge framed prints of chemical bonds up on the wall, no vivid rug from Dr. Reed's once-in-a-lifetime trip to Burma. Just vinyl tiles and white-painted walls.

Startled, Ino looked at the door. He hadn't noticed earlier, but even the door plate was gone. It was just another featureless wooden door in an academic building.

It was like Dr. Reed had never been there at all.

Feeling seriously creeped out, Ino decided to take a walk. He left his car in the parking lot, three spaces down from where Reed's car had left a perfectly normal-looking empty space, and started to walk briskly across campus.

It was colder now, a lot colder than it had been the previous week, in the low 60s. The cooler weather wasn't the only reason Ino felt a chill.

He loped briskly across campus, along the path that he and Sean had taken, and tried to picture Reed undertaking the same walk, late on the Friday of Finals Week. The rhino had been plenty able-bodied, but why leave the car? It would have been a long, pointless walk between two parking lots, and then another long, pointless walk back to his car to go home. Maybe Reed had just wanted a long walk (which Ino found unlikely at best at the end of an exhausting exam week), but otherwise it just didn't make sense. Especially in a suit jacket.

On the way, Ino thought about all the other things that didn't add up. Reed was a trained scientist, and Ino couldn't picture him opening a gas burner by accident, or forgetting he had one open when he turned on the main supply. Even if he did, he should have heard the hissing of escaping gas. It was a sound they had both heard thousands of times — Ino would hear that sound over the noise of a construction site.

Shaking his head, he frowned as he crossed the straightaway onto Old Campus. The huge athletic field and Rec center loomed in the distance, yellow caution tape strung across its doors. The building was temporarily closed to replace several dozen windows that had been blown out, which were already boarded up with huge pieces of plywood. Ino saw a small army of pickup trucks and windowless white work vans filling the parking lot like a car dealership, as engineers and contractors worked on the building.

Ahead of him, where once Baker Brown had stood, loomed The Tent.

Ino had heard about it but not seen it yet — it was a massive white picnic tent that Santiago used for alumni events and Homecoming. It was colossal, forty feet tall at its apex and half the size of the football field, humongous pieces of white vinyl in the shape of a huge oval, falling away down to ground level. The last place Ino had seen it was in the huge grassy space between the Arts Center and the Chapel for Homecoming, but now it had been erected over the wreckage of Baker. Instead of a blasted foundation and twenty tons of brick debris, there was now a big white tent the size of a small apartment building concealing the site. It had struck Ino as completely insane, but the officials at Santiago did a lot of completely insane things in the name of preserving the University's squeaky-clean image. The tent looked absurd, but it had also kept daytime pictures of the blasted building out of the local papers and national news.

As Ino approached the site, he was amazed at how much work had already been done. The bent-and-destroyed light posts were already mostly removed and some had even been repaired or replaced. Walking down the sidewalk, Ino noticed several chips out of the pavement where a flying chunk of brick or metal had gouged a wound in the cement. They were already circled with bright orange marking paint to signal a point of repair.

He blinked. Wow. That was a fast mobilization. He frowned. Reed's car wasn't even out of the parking lot and they already had his office emptied and started patching the sidewalk?

Shaking his head, he rounded the corner. He had been unconsciously gravitating toward the bench where he had sat and been swarmed by paramedics, but as he got closer he saw it was already occupied. He stopped, startled.

The hyena took another ten steps forward and stared cautiously at the occupant, who was staring into space in the general direction of the tent. It was Sean Murphy, in athletic shorts and a tank top, leaning forward tensely, headphones in his ears. The husky's tail drooped limply behind him.

Ino slowly edged into view until the husky noticed him. The young dog started in surprise, and reached up to pull out his earbuds, blushing immediately. "Dr. Reamer!" he said. He frowned. "Ugh, sorry I never replied to your email. This probably looks bad."

Ino blinked at him. "Don't worry about it." He frowned. "Bad? Why would it look bad?"

Sean grunted, playing with his headphones. "I don't know. Coming back and just sitting here. Staring at where we almost died." He played with his hands.

Ino frowned. "I mean... I don't think anyone can blame you for being a little... preoccupied."

Sean let out a sigh. "Thanks, Dr. Reamer."

Ino edged toward the bench. "Mind if I join you?"

The husky nodded. "Of course not." He scooted to one side. His ears perked up a little.

Ino sat down on the bench next to him. "How's your uncle?"

Sean turned to him, confused. "How did you —"

"I saw him the night of the explosion."

The husky blinked. "Oh." He let out a sigh. "Oh, *God*. He had a bad head wound. They stitched him up, he's okay now. They had to shave half his head. Head wounds bleed... a lot." He swallowed. He looked shaken.

Ino grimaced. "It looked pretty scary."

Sean nodded. "It was. He'll be okay, though. Huskies have pretty hard heads." He managed a weak smile.

Ino smiled at him. "Glad to hear it." He watched the young dog. "How are *you* doing?"

Sean looked away, and swallowed. "Oh, you know, uh, fine. Th-thanks for saving my life," he said, quietly.

Ino blinked at him, and then stared. "You're thanking *me*? *You* smelled the gas."

Sean frowned, tight-lipped. "I know we survived because you knocked us over the ledge. And I know you laid on top of me on purpose. I didn't have a scratch on me." He looked at Ino's shaved and scabby hands.

Ino nodded. "Think nothing of it." He looked over the young husky. Sean looked overtired and frazzled. His fur was unkempt and his eyes looked bloodshot. He actually looked worse now than he had looked during Finals week. "Are you... okay right now?" he asked, gently.

The husky glanced at him sideways, frowning, his ears folding back. "Yes. I'm fine. Why does everybody keep asking me that?!" he snapped, narrowing his eyes.

Ino stared at him, his eyes wide.

Sean frowned, looking away. "I'm sorry. That was rude."

Ino suppressed a grimace. "It's fine. It's also..." He pondered how to proceed. "It's also okay to not be okay. You know? We did just almost d — " He swallowed. "... We did have a pretty close call just the other day." He frowned. "I'm pretty stressed out myself." He thought about it. "*Really* stressed out. That was a really serious thing, you know?"

Sean frowned. "Yes. I'm fine."

Ino looked the husky over, dubiously. He didn't look fine. "What are you still doing on campus? It's pretty deserted."

The dog watched him. He shrugged noncommittally. "I'm staying for the summer. I have a job. I wanted to have a summer to myself for once."

Ino stared. "Are things still bad with your parents?" He blinked. "Is that… why they're not here?"

Sean stared at him and then shook his head. "Oh. Over the gay thing?" He snorted. "No, it hasn't even come up once. Now they want me to come home." He chuckled humorlessly. "They're stuck on a cruise right now — they were on it when they heard and they can't get off the boat." He looked up. "When they heard about the explosion, my mom tried to charter a helicopter to get here. She was going to fly from Bermuda to Indiana in a literal helicopter."

Ino smiled. "I mean… they love you, Sean. I'm surprised she didn't swim here."

Sean chuckled. "She's way too out of shape to swim." He let out a sigh. "Anyway, I don't think they care about the gay thing anymore. I think they're just happy I'm not dead."

Ino processed that for a moment and then leaned back on the bench. "Wow," he said. "That's… pretty heavy."

Sean nodded, swallowing. "Yup. About as heavy as that commencement plaque that almost squished you."

Ino cracked a little smile.

They sat in silence for a moment.

"So are you… *alone* here?" Ino finally asked.

Sean shook his head. "Naw. Uncle Travis is here." He played with his hands. "Though he's been pretty weird since the explosion." He frowned. "I dunno. There's a couple of guys from the frat here. I live in the frat house so I don't have to move out." He shrugged.

Ino watched him. "Is your boyfriend still here?"

Sean smiled tightly. "Nope!" he said. "He's taking summer courses but he had to go back for the break. And he couldn't tell his parents why he needed to stay without telling them *everything*."

Ino frowned. Finally he just decided to say it. "Sean, I'm worried about you," he said. "Are you sure staying on campus is the right call?"

Sean stared at him, surprised, and after a moment he scowled. "Dr. Reamer, I can't just leave. I have a job. We don't have enough baristas already." He stammered for a moment. "A-and I have… like… *plans*."

Ino watched him for a moment, and then nodded slowly. He thought for a moment. "All right, look. Only you can know if home will be a better support network for you. Buuuuut…" He pondered. "I just want to make sure you're not… over-prioritizing certain things." He watched him. "You know? Like, I know it seems like a big deal to quit your job and move back home out of state, but Starbucks will be just fine without you, right?" He searched for the right words. "Sometimes in life you have to upend everything and reprioritize. And that's okay!" He shrugged. "But you should decide on what's right for *you*."

Sean stared at him, a little shocked, and then amazingly, seemed to consider. After a moment he frowned. "I had this big plan for the summer, though. I had it all planned out." He looked up at Ino sadly, his ears drooping.

Ino ignored his shattering heart and nodded. "You can change your plans, Sean. You're allowed. You have to take care of yourself."

Frowning, the husky nodded. "I just hate to leave them short-staffed at work."

Ino chuckled. "Sean, you're going to have a hundred shitty jobs in your life. Trust me, in ten years you'll look back at this and be amazed you even considered the coffee shop in the equation."

Sean stared at him, and then let out a long sigh. "Okay." He played with his phone and his earbuds. "They made me see a counselor right after the explosion and I have to see her again this week. I'll ask her about it."

Ino let out a sigh. "That's good to hear. Thank you for tolerating my unsolicited advice."

Sean chuckled. "No problem." He let out a long shaky breath. "You should have heard my mom when I said I was going to stay on campus. She offered to pay me fifty bucks a week to quit my job and come home."

Ino laughed. "Wow. If you were a Finance major you could have gotten her up to a hundred."

Sean smiled.

Ino put his arm around the dog's shoulders. He squeezed him gently.

Sean grunted sullenly.

"And I'm glad you're talking to the therapist," Ino said. "You're way too young to be grappling with your own mortality. That was going to be my next unsolicited suggestion."

Sean rolled his eyes. "Yeah, well, President Greeley beat you to it. Came to the frat house herself and went right to my room. I answered the door in my briefs and the freaking president is standing there."

Ino stared at him, and couldn't keep the laugh from escaping his muzzle.

"Shut up! It's not funny!" Sean snapped, but he was smiling too. His smile slowly faded. "Anyway. Greeley insisted. She acted like she was personally responsible for the explosion or something. I'll see what the shrink thinks about the home situation when I go later. If she tells me I should leave, I'll consider it." He played with his hands, his tail flopping back and forth behind him.

Ino nodded. "Good." He gave Sean another little squeeze and released him.

Still frowning, Sean let out a long, shaky sigh. "It's just… all of this is so fucked up."

Ino nodded. "It sure is."

"Do you believe this tent?" The husky gestured with his muzzle. He looked annoyed.

Ino glanced at it, and for the first time he noticed there was a uniformed campus security guard standing in front of the entrance flap. He chuckled humorlessly. "I mean… yes. Santiago is pretty image-conscious so it's not really a surprise. But it *is* pretty ridiculous, even by our standards. It looks like we're having a big barbeque."

Sean snorted humorlessly. "Right?!"

They were silent for a few long moments.

They sat for a moment, watching the near wall of the tent push slowly outward, fueled by a strong breeze on the other side. It looked like the tent was breathing. Or like it was going to pop. Ino stared at it, wondering if the bricks and glass of Baker had bulged out like this, for a fraction of a second, before the entire building had shattered and blasted out over them into the quad.

Finally, Sean broke the silence.

"Did you see the papers?" he asked, quietly.

Ino nodded.

"They say Reed did it. That this was all an accident." His voice was barely a whisper.

Ino nodded, slowly. He watched Sean intently. The husky was actually *cowering* now, his shoulders hunched and his ears flat against his head. Ino frowned.

"Do you, uh," Sean asked, staring at his hands. "Do you believe that? Like a-as an explanation?" His voice was shaking.

Ino stared for a moment, and he couldn't quite figure out why, but he knew his answer was extremely important. He cleared his throat to stall for time. "Why… do you ask?"

Sean swallowed. He was still fidgeting and he refused to make eye contact. "Uh, because *I* don't believe that," he said softly. "I think something was really wrong, and I keep like, *telling* people, but nobody believes me. Like, my parents, and the city cops, and even Uncle Travis, everybody tells me it was all an accident, but I was *there* and it was" — he took a deep shaky breath — "it was *so not* an accident. So, um…" He swallowed again, hard. "I guess I feel like I'm going insane a little, so I guess, ah, I just wanted to see what you thought about it, and decide if I'm really losing my fucking mind or not." He said it all in one big rush, and still wouldn't look up. To Ino's surprise, the young dog reached up to rub at his eyes.

Ino stared at him. He was shocked to see the husky this upset. For a second, he debated lying to keep Sean out of whatever was going on, out of a weird impulse to protect him, but the husky was clearly at his limit and lying to him wasn't going to do him any favors.

Ino took a deep breath. "I… I don't think I believe that," he said, softly. "The whole thing… felt… like…" He searched for the word. "Staged," he said, finally.

Sean took a deep, jagged breath. He nodded, grimacing, and kept nodding, and finally let out a long, shaky breath. "Okay," he said, softly. "Thank you."

Ino frowned. He reached over and squeezed Sean's shoulder. "You're *not* crazy," he said, gently. "No part of that made any sense at all. The door lock, the gas. Why would Reed be in a lab across campus after classes were over? What kind of experiment was he even doing?"

Sean nodded, swallowing. "Thank you," he croaked. He leaned down and put his face in his hands, rubbing at his fluff. "Jesus Christ, I thought I was losing it."

Ino frowned. "If you are, we *both* are. Do you know Reed's car wasn't even at this building? It was back at *my* office."

Sean turned to stare at him, blue eyes wide and horrified. "Really?"

Ino frowned. "Yeah." He leaned back on the bench. "They just towed it out this morning. So, no — I still have a lot of questions." He frowned. "I should *not* be talking about this with you, but if it makes you feel better, I was really surprised to see that article too."

Sean nodded. He reached up to wipe his eyes again. "Thank you."

Ino frowned. "Is that what was bothering you so much?"

Sean let out another sigh. "Yeah." He sighed. "Like, you don't understand, *every single person* has told me he did it by accident." He swallowed. "Did you tell anybody you think that's a bullshit theory?"

Ino shook his head. "Not yet. I've just kind of been thinking about it. I didn't have anything really conclusive. Just a gut feeling."

"*Will* you talk to the cops?" The husky swallowed. "Nobody is listening to me." He frowned. "I could use some backup."

Ino frowned. "I was definitely going to. I don't even know who to talk to. The FBI? Homeland Security?" He considered.

Sean glanced at him with a humorless snort. "Naw, they're long gone. DHS, FBI, ATF — they run their residue tests in a couple hours and as soon as they determine it's not domestic terrorism, they're out of here." He shrugged. "It's with the local people now."

Ino blinked at him. If the feds were gone, that left the local cops. That was… non-optimal. Ino had only had a few run-ins with the local cops, and none of the situations had particularly impressed him. As far as he could tell, their core competency was issuing speeding tickets, and then their efficacy went downhill steeply from there. He frowned. "So who has jurisdiction?"

The husky stared at him. "I told you: local. Campus Security."

Ino laughed. "Haha. Good one."

Sean stared up at him, deadly serious. His ears were forward and his jaw was set. He wasn't joking.

Ino felt his eyebrows raise. "Wait, that isn't a joke? Campus *Security?*" He stared in disbelief. "Santiago University Campus Security has jurisdiction. Of a suspicious death investigation." He blinked. "They gave a *murder case* to SUCS?"

Sean glared at him. "You know, they *do* know what they're doing. My uncle and the chief are both damn good at their jobs. They're trained investigators and they both used to be State Troopers when we lived in Ohio." He narrowed his eyes. "That isn't helping *me*, since they both still think I'm a five-year-old, but it does help the *investigation*," he grumbled.

Ino blinked at him. "Wait, did you say *the chief*? You personally know the... what's he called. Chief Security Something?"

Sean glanced up at him. "Chief Security Officer. They just call him *Chief*: Chief Archer. Yes, I know him. Older guy. He's worked with Uncle Travis for... like, forever." He played with the wire of his headphones. "I used to call him *Uncle Jack*." He looked a little embarrassed. Ino had the tiniest flash that Sean was nursing a crush, and then he was overwhelmed with confusion by the geography.

Ino blinked at him. "Wait, *Ohio*? They're from your hometown? What the hell are you all doing here in Indiana?"

Sean glanced up at him. "The outpost closed. There were big budget cuts and the station got shut down and everybody lost their jobs. Uncle Travis got some severance money and he helped me with my tuition a little. He was a city cop for a while and he hated it, and there were still a lot of security positions open here at Santiago. After the, uh... you know." His ears tilted back.

Ino stared at him. "Oh God. Right. After the shooting. Yeah, that would have been the year before." He grimaced. What a terrifying day that had been. The lockdown, the barricades, the hundreds of cops and EMTs and reporters. "I'm glad you weren't here for that. I'm not at all surprised that half of Security quit. The school had to contract private security for almost a year."

Sean nodded. "I know, I'm a sophomore. They were still here when I started."

Ino blinked. "Oh right. Heh."

Sean shrugged. "Anyway, Uncle Travis knew a couple of the guards here from my Freshman year when I had an, um, incident." He swallowed.

Ino blinked at him and waited for Sean to elaborate. The husky didn't, and he looked like he was dealing with enough, so Ino didn't push it. He did, however, file it away for mental reference.

Sean coughed. "So Uncle Travis moved here, to be a guard. And then Uncle J — uh, *Sergeant Archer* came in as head of Security, and I think one of the admin people came over too, but I can't remember who."

Ino nodded. "Wow. Lucky for you all."

Sean chuckled. "Yeah, except I came here to get *away* from my family. I'm surprised my parents didn't move to town, too."

Ino smiled. "They still might. You're only a sophomore."

Sean rolled his eyes, but he was smiling, too.

Ino cracked a smile. He thought for a moment. Well — former cops was better than nothing. Probably.

"I will go talk to campus security tomorrow," Ino said. "I promise."

Sean watched him for a moment, evaluating his seriousness, and then nodded. "Thank you. It means a lot." He thought for a moment. "And, ah… do an internet search on the station before you march in there. Some of them are really sensitive about the whole '*security guard*' thing. Nobody is going to listen to you if you piss them off." He looked up.

Ino nodded gratefully. "Thank *you* for mentioning. Probably saved me from a bit of awkwardness."

Sean stared at him for another moment. "There's probably a *couple* things you'll want to know before you head in there and talk to the Chief. You're single, right?"

Eyes widening, Ino stared at him. "What's *that* have to do with anything?"

Sean thought for a moment and was about to answer when he was interrupted by the loud bang of a car door. They both jumped.

It was the back door of an unmarked white van, parked in amongst the work vans outside the Rec center. A short shrew and a tall bison, both in gray canvas zip-up coveralls and black boots, each hefted a large toolbox and walked toward the tent.

The security guard nodded at both of them and held open a gap in the tent.

Ino frowned. "Those don't look like crime scene investigators."

Sean shook his head, disgusted. "They weren't even wearing non-contamination suits. Did you see that? One of them was *chewing gum*."

Ino frowned.

The young husky turned to him. "They're not taking this seriously."

Ino grimaced. "I'll talk to them."

Sean let out a long, relieved breath. "Thank you."

Ino nodded. "Of course."

They sat for another few moments, both staring at the tent.

"It's gonna be a long time before this place feels normal again," Sean said, quietly.

Ino nodded. "I think you're right," he said. He let out a long breath. "I think you're right."

Silently, they watched the tent.

Later that night, now safely back at his rental house south of town, Ino peered over his laptop on his breakfast table. He stared at the tiny laptop screen, his glasses perched on his face. He had a cup of decaf Earl Grey tea in a big mug next to him, the TV on in the next room, and only a few lights on in the house.

Ino's main living space was one huge rectangle — a big square kitchen at one end, a tiny breakfast table in the middle in front of the sliding patio door, and then an entire open wall to the square living room. It made furniture placement awkward but for a rental unit on his salary he was lucky to have it. He had a desk in the 2nd bedroom upstairs but most of the time he just worked at the breakfast table.

He scrolled through his syllabus for the 17th time.

ATTENDANCE

```
Class attendance is mandatory with 1 miss
permitted. 5% of your grade is attendance
(pass/fail).
```

- ```
  Extensions of due-dates because of
  other class conflicts are permitted,
  but only if cleared with me within 2
  weeks of class start. (Check your other
  syllabi!)
  ```
- ```
  Since lowest quiz score gets dropped,
  no make-up quizzes will be given for
  missed attendance. Missing a quiz day
  ```

CHAPTER 3: THE TENT

will double-impact your score if you are past the one allowable absence.

- Make-up exams (unit tests, midterm, final) can be given, but only for university-approved absences (cleared in first 2 weeks of class) or for medical emergencies, sickness, bereavement, and at professor's discretion.

Ino frowned. He typed one more line.

```
Or unless the building explodes! But what
are the odds of THAT happening again? :3
```

Putting his head down on the table, Ino groaned softly. He was updating his GEN-200 syllabus for his summer class, and as usual, he was over-thinking it. The hyena *hated* writing syllabi because it required supernatural long-range planning skills — and the hyena's preference would be to write his lesson plans the night before he gave them.

Theoretically he should just be updating the dates, but in his experience, his students would pore over the document like amateur detectives looking for loopholes. One year he had to throw out an entire class's lowest-graded exam because in one key sentence he had typed "and" instead of "or." It was like working with a classroom of 35 teenage lawyers.

He glanced down at the computer clock. It was past 11:00 pm. There was really no urgency since the class didn't start for another two weeks. His back hurt from sitting for so long — the plaque injury was, for some reason, a lot worse when he stayed in the same position for a while — and his head was throbbing.

"Okay. We're done!" he declared. He slapped CTRL-S on his keyboard. The word processing program he was working on labored to save his file, even though it was only a text document. Ino was accessing his faculty drive via the VPN, and it was like being on a dial-up modem circa 2003. Every professor had a drive that could be accessed from any place with an internet connection, and it had unlimited storage. Since it was a convenient place to put things and access them anywhere, Ino saved all of his important files to that drive. It was nice centralization but the load times were really a pain in the ass sometimes.

Irritated, Ino watched the saved percentage climb up one percent at a time, finally hitting 100% so he could close it. He slipped off his glasses and rubbed his eyes.

He glanced at the clock again. It was probably time to sleep if he was going to crawl out of bed at a reasonable hour. He wanted to go visit campus security.

What had Sean said? Google them? He'd said something else weird too but they had been interrupted and Ino had forgotten to follow up. He frowned.

Ino cracked open a web browser, and typed in SANTIAGO UNIVERSITY CAMPUS SECURITY.

The first article came up. SANTIAGO UNIVERSITY NAMES NEW HEAD OF SECURITY. It was from the Post-Tribune and dated March 2017, a little over a year ago.

He opened it.

SANTIAGO, INDIANA. Santiago University has named former Ohio State Troopers Sergeant Jack Archer as Vice President of Public Safety and Chief Security Officer after a 9 month vacancy following 2016's deadly campus shooting.

University President Dr. Susan Greeley made the announcement Wednesday that the Board of Directors had approved the hiring of Jonathan "Jack" Archer of Columbus, Ohio. Archer has been an Ohio State Trooper for 19 years, most recently Staff Sergeant in the I-80/90 corridor and takes the role of Santiago University Security Chief after a brief gap in employment.

"I am pleased to announce the filling of a
vital role with an individual who espouses
Santiago's relentless commitment to excellence and shares our values," said Greeley
in a press release. "Sergeant Archer has
the credentials and experience to protect
our most important assets — our students,
faculty and staff."

Ino chuckled. That sounded like something Susan had said, all right. Super positive, relentlessly polished, and not really conveying any useful information. He read on.

Archer is a four-time nominee of the
Midwest Union of Law Enforcement's Profiles
in Excellence award for his work in community outreach.

Santiago University is a private Lutheran
college with an attendance of 3,000. In
May 2016 former student David Andrew Milne
opened fire in the student union, injuring 6
before fatally shooting himself. Security
Chief James Mason of Merrillville left his
position the following June.

Ino stared at the article, swallowing. He thought of the afternoon of the shooting, and as usual, his mouth went dry.

He arrowed back to the main search page. Almost the entire front page of search results consisted of links that were just re-wordings of that article, most of them clearly sourcing heavily from the same press release.

He was about to close the search results when the last article on the page caught his attention.

SUCS DOESN'T SUCK: SANTIAGO UNIVERSITY HIRES LGBT SECURITY CHIEF, it read. Ino stared, his eyes widening.

LGBT Chief??

Oh God, THAT'S what Sean meant, Ino thought. He was shocked — he'd had no idea about the Chief. As the professor running the campus LGBTQ+ outreach group, Ino was fairly certain he knew every non-straight person on campus, and he couldn't believe he hadn't heard this information. Though Ino hadn't so much as laid eyes on the Chief — the hyena mostly kept to the science circles. And who would have brought it up — *"Hey Ino, I heard there's another queer on campus!"*

"Actually, that sounds *exactly* like something someone would say at this school," he muttered, clicking the link.

The article was on a site called RAINBOW NEWZ, and a quick scan of the headlines in the sidebar showed mostly stories about social policy and entertainment in addition to some softer news articles. The main article was about a girl in a K-POP group being bisexual, though to Ino it looked like there were thirty teenagers in that group so that was probably just a matter of statistical sampling. Ino frowned. An article about Santiago's head of security was on *this* site?

A gigantic pop-up ad opened in front of the entire article. It was an ad for a gay cruise featuring a scantily-clad lion and a hulking brown bear, both with perfect abs and naked except for tiny, *very* revealing, package-hugging speedos. GET SOME IN THE SUN, the ad copy read. Frantically, Ino rushed to click the X to close it. "I hope IT doesn't see me cruising on this site," he hissed, wishing he had Googled this from his personal computer instead of his work laptop. How would he explain *that?* *"Oh, a student said I should visit that!"*

Finally, he looked at the article. He was already flustered.

THE SCOOP: LGBT CSO???

What can you find at Santiago University in northwest Indiana? The world's biggest University Chapel, a killer meteorology department, a Popcorn Fair every September, and now — a gay head of Campus Security!

Supercop Jack Archer — four-time nominee of the Central US Union of Law Enforcement's Profiles in Excellence award — is leaving behind his tiny trooper outpost in northern Ohio to lead a swarm of Santiago Security. Chief Archer is out and proud.

Why should you care? Santiago University is a Very Serious Religious Institution, purchased by the Association of Lutheran Universities (did you know that was a thing?) in 1918 and enjoying a storied history of super-fun religion ever since. Whee!

We all know how Indiana went in the last election — and, yanno, EVERY election — so hiring an out-and-proud LGBT chief like Mr. Archer on his merits is a big show of support from University President Susan Greeley. Greeley is the school's FIRST female President (!) since it originally opened (!!) in 1859 (!!!!?!?!?). Probably for this reason, she clearly Does Not Have Time for systemic oppression and chronic under-representation of minorities. Girl, big mood.

While the LGBT community has obviously had a contentious past with law enforcement (Stonewall Inn, anyone??), our boy Jacky has been a very good dog — his efforts include improving de-escalation training for all of northern Ohio and chartering after-school community programs in his district's high-poverty areas. Archer has

spoken to advocate for early non-incarcer-
ation intervention for minors and reform-
ing the state's juvenile detention program. In Ohio, the independent Foundation
for Ethical Law Enforcement rated his outpost 3.7 out of 4 stars for social justice
initiatives — the 2nd-highest score in the
entire state. WHO'S a good boy?

WE rate him 5 stars out of 4 for smolder-
ing handsomeness. Nothing gets us going
here at Rainbow Newz more than a combo
of an all-American German shepherd hottie
in uniform, and a healthy respect for the
social and systemic factors that drive the
school-to-prison pipeline and exacerbate
the incarceration crisis in this country.
Woof on all counts! Maybe it's time to
take some night classes…

Frowning, Ino felt himself blushing. Sean was trying to set him up! *That
husky…* What a little schemer! Rubbing his suddenly-hot ears, Ino resisted
the urge to Google-Image search the security chief and instead hurriedly
closed his browser window. With his luck he would land on LinkedIn or
some other site with viewer tracking, and the Chief would see that Ino had
been creeping on him. He could see the email now: *"DR. INO REAMER
viewed your profile and is already kind of into you!"*

Ino was comfortably single right now, after a messy breakup a few years
earlier with a very long-term boyfriend. No one believed the "comfortable"
part, so Sean would hardly be the first person who had tried to set him up.
He would *definitely* be the first *student* to do so, however.

If he hadn't been done working before his internet misadventure, he
sure was done now! Leaning back in his chair, Ino disconnected the VPN
and then turned off his computer.

He frowned. It was too early for bed. Probably a good night to fall
asleep in front of the TV.

Glancing back at the computer, he thought of the article again. *Just don't let that influence your behavior, Ino,* he told himself. *There's a serious matter here. The only thing that matters is getting to the bottom of this case.*

Closing his laptop, he stood up.

"I better go lay out something nice to wear," he mumbled, wandering off.

Chapter 4: Swiss Cheese Theory

Tuesday, May 15, 2018

The next day was pretty average weather for May — in the mid-70s and windy. Ino wore heather-gray dress slacks and a crisp white button-down shirt. He was on vacation, so it would have been nice to dress a little more summery, but he didn't think that showing up in shorts and flipflops would encourage Security to take him seriously.

The Santiago University Campus Security building was a short one-story brick building, not unlike Baker had been, having also been erected in Santiago's 20-year-long "boring brick buildings" phase. The building was tucked into a shaded pocket on the northeast corner of campus, down a sweeping hill and nestled in a grassy knoll in the shadow of one of the larger dorms. The structure was surrounded by 60-foot-tall silver maples and flowering hostas that had been there for 30 or 40 years, and looked more like a cozy library or a charming used book store than an active security station. Minus, of course, the side lot overflowing with black and white SUVs.

Ino steeled himself. He was surprisingly jittery — given his connection to the case he had plenty of legitimate reasons to inquire on the status, but he still felt a little like a meddling kid.

Setting his jaw, he stepped confidently through the front doors. It was the exact same framework that he and Sean had sprinted through on their way out of Baker. The two buildings could have been built from the same set of raw materials. It was creepy.

There was a young woman in a uniform at the counter, a ferret that looked at least six inches shorter than Ino. Her long hair was up in a severe-looking ponytail but she gave Ino a warm smile when he walked in.

Her nametag said REESE. "Hi there, help you?"

Ino smiled. "Hi, yes, uhhhhh I was wondering if I could talk to you... or the Chief... or... someone? I was at Baker the other night."

The ferret nodded animatedly. "Dr. Reamer! I remember you."

Ino blinked. "Oh. I'm sorry. Did we meet the other night?" He grimaced. "My apologies."

Reese laughed. "Yes, it's *very* rude of you not to remember me on the night you face-planted off a landing and almost got incinerated. How are you feeling?"

Ino blinked at her, and then smiled. "Like I face-planted off a landing and almost got incinerated."

Reese chuckled. "Sounds about right. I did a tour overseas — I know that feel. Did you get anything good for the pain?"

Ino blinked at her. "No, actually. They didn't give me anything."

The ferret smiled. "Good. That shit is a lot harder to stop taking than it is to start. Did you remember something about the other night?"

Ino debated how to answer, and then shrugged. "Something like that."

She nodded knowingly. "I figured. Give me a second." She picked up the desk phone.

Ino stood aside and pretended to study the pictures on the wall in the reception area. There were a bunch of posters about reporting sexual assault on campus and the importance of consent, and even more about being vigilant for shootings and planned shootings. Ino frowned. Grim stuff.

"Dr. Reamer would like to see you. Yes, from Baker," Reese was saying behind him. "Mm-hm. Yes. Mm-hm. Uh-huh. Yes."

Ino tried not to listen to the never-ending parade of filler words. His heart raced. He was nervous for no apparent reason.

On the other wall of the reception area was a line of 8"x10" framed photographs, each of them in front of an American flag, mostly in black and white — SU's chiefs of security, past and present. Ino studied the pictures. There were eleven of them, ten men and one woman, going back to 1952. Most of them were advanced in age, long in the tooth, probably comfortably retired for years before coming to run SU's sleepy security team. He skimmed them before coming to Jack Archer, the last in the line.

He stared at the picture in a panic.

Oh no! He's HOT!

Jack Archer was a handsome German shepherd, standard black and tan, staring impassively at the camera. He looked like he was in his late 40s or early 50s, little specks of gray and white fur just starting to creep into his inky black muzzle fur and short black hair. He had bright amber eyes, a square jaw, a muscled neck and broad shoulders under his black collared uniform shirt. He looked like he was in very good shape and he was undeniably handsome even from his employment photograph.

Ino felt his heart start pounding even harder and he let out a shaky breath. It wasn't that Ino couldn't talk to attractive men, but he was already feeling like a child on a field trip, interrupting important official business, and the hot daddy shepherd was not going to help. He frowned. Why couldn't Chief Archer have been 75 and just clinging to employment before finding a nice comfortable nursing home to occupy?!

"Dr. Reamer!" called a voice behind him. Ino almost jumped out of his shoes.

He turned. "Yessss?" he asked.

Officer Reese smiled at him. "The Chief is ready for you. Head all the way down that hallway" — here she pointed — "and he's the last door on the left."

Ino nodded. "Thank you!" He nodded and stepped onto Reese's side of the desk. "Appreciate it." He zipped down the hallway, glancing back over his shoulder, hoping he hadn't made a total moron of himself.

He looked back to where he was going just in time to see a figure step out of a side hallway, immediately before slamming into that person.

"*Whoomph!*" Ino grunted, as he came to a sudden stop. Whoever he had crashed into was so solid he felt like a brick wall wearing a thin coat of fur. Ino twitched with his entire body.

"OW!" the man grunted, taking a staggering step back, and Ino was shocked to see it was Jack Archer himself. After a moment Ino felt something hot and wet, and he realized that Jack had been holding a little foam cup of coffee. It had squashed between them and run down both of their chests.

He stepped back, gasping in horror. "Oh my God! I'm so sorry!" he squealed. He had a big splash of coffee — with cream and sugar, judging by the smell — splattered all over his chest, but the shepherd had taken the brunt of it. The dog was dressed in a crisp black Santiago security uniform, complete with tie and utility belt, and even with the dark fabric Ino could tell that most of the coffee had ended up on his chest and run down his stomach. Jack was taller than Ino, 6'2" or 6'3", even more handsome in person than in his photograph, and looked like he had been hit in the dead center of the chest with a water balloon full of Starbucks.

"Dr. Reamer!" the dog said, through his teeth. Coffee dripped off the underside of his muzzle. "Jack Archer. Nice to see you this fine morning."

Ino felt all the blood drain out of his face. It actually felt like all of the blood had drained out of his body, but that would mean he was dead, which would have been welcome at that point. "I'm so sorry!" he said again. "Oh my God. Can I get you a towel or something?" He gazed upon the caffeine-soaked shepherd with undisguised horror.

Jack took a long, deep breath, and let it out as a weary sigh. He visibly composed himself and then offered Ino a tired smile. "No, it's fine," he said. He looked down the hall. "Seems like I took most of it. Would you mind waiting in my office? I think I should rinse this out before it stains." He gestured down the hall. "I'm down to my last uniform. Do you... need a rinse?"

Ino shook his head exaggeratedly. "No, no, I'm fine! I'll just bleach it." He shuffled awkwardly down the hall. After a moment, he turned over his shoulder. "Take your time! No rush! I'm so sorry!"

Jack stared at him, and smiled grimly. "It's fine. I'll be with you in a moment," he said, and turned back down the hall, wiping his big black paws on his uniform shirt. He was positively drenched whereas Ino had barely gotten sprinkled. "Thank you for waiting," he grunted.

"No problem!" Ino squeaked, and slinked down the hall.

He slipped through a wooden door that said CHIEF, wishing he could just sink into the floor and disappear.

Stepping into the office, he looked around.

It was a small office, perhaps 10 by 12, with a nicely-built but battle-scarred wooden desk and two uncomfortable-looking dull gray metal-and-vinyl chairs in front of it. The desk had a single computer monitor — the huge old kind, Ino noted with some surprise — and at least four different piles of papers on it, all of them covered in yellow sticky notes, paperclips, and spiky handwritten notes. Jack had a suit jacket hanging on the back of his chair, a tiny wardrobe in the corner of the room, and a series of framed commendations on the walls around the room, stuffed into every inch of available space between windows and file cabinets and bookshelves. Many of them were from Santiago or the states of Indiana or Ohio, which Ino found comforting. At least the dog was qualified.

He paced nervously for several minutes, still unable to comprehend what he had just done. On top of everything, Ino's crisp white shirt was splashed with cream-colored coffee in the shape of an impact splatter, as if he had slapped a Venti Soy Caramel No-Whip Mocha Latte out of an insolent barista's hand.

The hyena let out a long, tired sigh. This was going swimmingly already.

After about five minutes, Jack reappeared. He was wearing a white undershirt — also blasted with coffee — and his uniform pants, carrying his soaking wet uniform shirt in a grocery bag in his hands. He had a gracious smile and he stepped up to Ino with a friendly, outstretched hand.

"Dr. Reamer!" he said, brightly. "Nice to finally meet you. I've seen your name in a lot of reports."

Ino shook his hand. The shepherd had a damp paw — no surprise — and a firm, friendly handshake. He had the big hands and quiet dignity of his breed, even after being splattered with breakfast beverage. "Chief Archer. I really cannot apologize enough for that."

The dog chuckled. "It's fine. I was a state trooper for twenty years — I've been covered in a lot worse."

Ino was caught off-guard by that, and he actually laughed.

Jack set his soaking wet shirt on his desk and stepped into the room. "Ummm." He pondered for a moment and looked longingly at a wardrobe in the corner. "I have a change of clothes."

Ino nodded. "Right! Do you need me to step out?"

Jack heaved a sigh. "As I said, I was a state trooper for twenty years. I have literally changed in the breakdown lane. If you don't care, I don't."

Ino cracked a smile. He felt a little awkward but he was frankly desperate to be accommodating at this point. "Locker room rules are fine!" he peeped.

"Thanks." Jack smiled warmly and closed his office door. "So what brings you by, Dr. Reamer?" Crossing to the wardrobe, he pulled his undershirt over his head, flexing his thick back and huge arms. Jack's fur was inky black in a huge diamond pattern on his wide back, and then golden brown on his arms, bleeding into cream in the middle of his forearms but continuing through to his hands and fingers. He was not as muscular as his photo suggested. He was *way way more muscular*, Ino discovered — far more so than he had guessed, slim and toned from ears to tail. Ino knew that the dog would have a six-pack just based on his rippled back. Jack didn't look like a security chief in his forties. He looked like a stripper *pretending to be a security chief in his forties.*

Ino felt his jaw unhinge. He didn't answer. He *couldn't* answer. The dog looked like he could lift Ino over his head without really straining himself.

Jack opened the doors of the wardrobe and mopped at his chest with the clean parts of his undershirt. He unbuckled his belt and glanced over his shoulder, and finally noticed Ino staring with open-mouthed astonishment. The shepherd stopped and frowned. "Sorry," he said. "I didn't want to smell like a Starbucks for the rest of the day."

Ino swallowed. "Understandable!" he squeaked. He half-turned away, both out of respect and to reduce his chances of fainting.

The dog finished mopping his chest — he definitely did have a six-pack, Ino saw out of the corner of his eye, a beautiful white chest and belly and probably crotch too — dropped the shirt over a chair, and took a white button-down out of the wardrobe, on a metal dry-cleaning hanger. He put the shirt on with no undershirt, and finished taking off his pants. "So how are you holding up, Dr. Reamer?" he asked. He was wearing little gray briefs and they did not leave much to the imagination. White fur poked out down each of his inner thighs.

Now Ino fully averted his eyes, blushing hotly. "Fine, I guess! A little beat up but otherwise okay." He felt his face heat up and glanced back at the shepherd.

Jack nodded. "I hope I'm not overstepping, but if you're *not* fine there are a number of resources available to you," the dog said. He pulled a crisp pair of gray slacks out of the wardrobe, also on a dry-cleaning hangar inside a clear plastic bag. "The University has a variety of counseling services. You *did* narrowly survive a massive explosion, as well as find a colleague dead on the floor." He opened his pants and put one big bare foot through. "I can give you all their information if you like."

Ino blinked at him, jolted out of his awkwardness. He frowned. "What? No, I found Dr. Reed *before* the explosion." He stared, confused. "I saw him when he was still alive."

Jack was in the middle of pulling his pants up, the waist of the slacks around his thighs, when he froze. He stared straight ahead, frozen, his pants half up, and then after a moment, lifted his head and turned to look at Ino. His golden eyes were a little wide, ears fully forward and listening intently.

With the dog's startled expression, Ino figured it out.

He felt the blood drain out of his face.

"Oh God," he said. "Was he dead? Was he *already dead when I saw him?!*" His head started to swim.

Jack grimaced. He yanked his pants all the way up and quickly buttoned them. "Dr. Reamer," he said, gritting his teeth. "I'm so sorry."

Ino swayed on his feet. He felt dizzy. Dr. Reed had already been dead. He and Sean had seen a corpse. The image flashed back into his mind. Not overcome with gas. Not incapacitated. Already dead on the floor. Ino felt the world get further away.

"No, no, no, no, no," Jack said, moving swiftly toward him. "Dr. Reamer. Sit down. Here." He put a hand on Ino's shoulders and guided him toward one of the chairs in front of the desk. Ino sank into the chair without feeling it, and reflected that he probably would have toppled over if he had tried to remain standing another second.

"Oh my GOD," he said, feeling lightheaded.

Jack scrunched his muzzle up. "I apologize, Dr. Reamer. That was inappropriate. I shouldn't have assumed you knew." He grimaced again. "Can I get you anything? Glass of water?"

Ino blinked for a few moments, shaking his head. "No. No, I'm fine." He couldn't believe it. "He was *dead?*" he said again, softly.

Jack frowned. "Yes. I'm so sorry. The coroner's findings were released days ago." He looked genuinely sorry. "I thought you knew."

Ino processed for another few moments, and then took a deep breath. He let it out as a shaky sigh. "No, it's fine," he said. He swallowed, hard.

They sat for a few moments in silence.

You did find a colleague dead on the floor.

Ino thought about the reason he was there. Already, his mental wheels were spinning again.

"Was... uh..." He took a shallow breath.

Jack blinked at him, and cocked his head ever so slightly.

Ino swallowed. "It *was* the *gas* that killed him... right?"

Jack blinked at him, genuinely surprised, and then Ino watched confusion come over his face, and then suspicion. "Yes, of course," he said. The dog furrowed his brow. "He died in a room full of gas. What else would have killed him?" Jack set about tucking his shirt into his pants, finally reaching behind him to fasten his pants' tail clasp.

Ino ignored the question. "And like... you would *know* if the cause of death was something different, right?" He swallowed again. "Like... something... suspicious?" he finally squeaked out.

Finishing with his shirt, Jack stared at him for another moment, and then his face went completely blank. It was eerie, the extent to which any trace of emotion disappeared from his face. He looked just like his employment photo from the lobby. "I take it this isn't a social call, then," he said, flatly.

Ino took a deep breath. "I only mean like... hypothetically."

The dog leaned forward, raising just one eyebrow now. "*Hypothetically*, I wouldn't discuss the details of an ongoing investigation. Unless someone had something important to tell me." He narrowed his golden eyes. "Do you have something important to tell me, Dr. Reamer?"

Ino watched him. So much for his subtle approach.

Play it cool, he told himself. *Reveal nothing.*

Ino stared at him. "I think Dr. Reed was murdered."

The Chief stared at him for a few long moments.

Ino sweated. *Perfect! Nailed it.* Internally, he rolled his eyes.

Jack nodded thoughtfully. There was no startled gasp, no horrified stammer. The dog stared at Ino as if he had commented on the unusually warm weather. He sat slowly down in the other guest chair, facing Ino. "All right," he said. "What makes you say that?"

Ino stared at him, shocked at the lack of reaction. "Did you hear what I just said?"

Jack nodded. "I did. What makes you think Dr. Reed was murdered? Did someone want to harm him?"

Ino frowned. "No." He paused for a moment. "I mean, I don't know. That's the frustrating part. But nothing about the lab makes sense."

The dog nodded thoughtfully again. "Go on," he said, simply.

The hyena let out an annoyed snort. He felt like he was being interviewed about his favorite oatmeal flavors. "Look... it doesn't make any sense for him to have been in that lab. It's... suspicious."

Jack nodded. "How so?" He reached across his desk and picked up a little notepad.

Ino stared at him. Every part of his conversation was surreal. "Well..." he said. "First of all, what the hell was he doing in *Baker?*" He frowned. "It was an old lab, probably the worst of the science buildings. I'm amazed it wasn't torn down years ago. Like, we make it work for entry level students, but if he had anything important to do, I don't know why he would pick Baker. Or why he would have walked across campus to do it, when there are labs right in the building with our offices." He thought for a moment. "You did find his car at Malerich, right?" he asked.

Jack nodded slowly. "We did," he said, noncommittally.

Ino resisted the urge to scowl. "Well, that's a little weird, too. I don't know why he would have left the car there, locked his office, walked all the way across campus, done... *whatever*... and then walked *back* across campus just to drive home. You know?"

Jack nodded. "I see. Go on." He wrote a few things down on his little notepad.

Ino narrowed his eyes. "Second, what on earth *was* he doing? I've taught most of his classes, and there is no experiment you can do with what he had laid out. And no lab you would be running after the students were gone for the semester."

Jack cocked his head, finally appearing mildly interested. "Tell me about that. What do you remember seeing?"

Ino frowned. He felt like he was talking to a therapist. And not a good one. "Mostly glassware." He thought about it. "A couple beakers. Some big Erlenmeyer flasks — those are the ones shaped like upside-down cones with the column at the top. A beaker stand. The burner itself. Some hoses." He thought harder. "A pipet. A scale. A Bunsen starter."

Jack nodded. "What kind of lab work could you do with that?"

Ino stared at him. "Nothing."

The shepherd looked up, surprised, and then nodded again. "Let me rephrase. What was missing?"

Ino let out an annoyed breath. It was an intelligent question, at least. "So… it's pretty rare to set up an experiment from memory. I would expect a textbook or at least an iPad. We don't just like… make shit up. Also, I didn't see any chemicals." He swallowed. "All the reactants, except for like, distilled water, are in very distinct containers, and they're all locked up in cabinets most of the time. I didn't see a single one of them out. It's like…" He struggled for an analogy. "It's like standing in a kitchen with five saucepans, and no cookbook and no ingredients." He frowned. "It looked like a movie set, actually. The stereotypical nonsense you see on TV." He paused. "The sort of thing someone would put out if they didn't know anything real about science."

The dog nodded thoughtfully. "I see."

Ino stared at him. "Do you?" he snapped, sarcastically.

Jack raised his head, blinking. He raised his eyebrows slightly, and the surprise was plain on his face.

Ino stared at him. "It just makes absolutely no sense any way I think about it. It shouldn't have happened." *And you're really not listening to me AT ALL*, he thought.

The dog stared at him for a long moment, and then nodded. "I understand, Dr. Reamer."

Ino leaned back in his chair, sighing. He did not get the impression that Jack Archer did, in fact, understand. At the very least he was being cagey, and it was starting to make Ino mad.

They stared at each other for a moment.

Hell with it, Ino thought. "So… is this a murder investigation, or what?"

Jack leaned back in his chair too. "Not exactly. At this stage we are investigating *all* possibilities, including both accidental causes and the possibility of foul play. I can't comment on an ongoing investigation, but —"

Ino grunted. "Forgive the interruption, but this sounds like a press release. Are you *really* investigating this as a possible murder?"

The dog stopped, and frowned at him, finally displaying visible irritation. "*Yes*," he snapped. "Of *course* we are, Dr. Reamer. A man died. *A building exploded.*" He looked pissed off, and Ino was actually a little relieved at the first indication that Jack was hearing him at all. "That's not exactly a commonplace occurrence. *Yes*, we are really investigating this, and we *will* figure out what happened."

Ino leaned back in his chair, sulking.

The big dog frowned. "Most people are satisfied with that. We are a fully-functional law enforcement division, you know, and we do in fact know what we're doing." He narrowed his eyes. "Perhaps we should each stick to our particular area of expertise, unless you'd like some tips on scheduling your lectures," he said, icily.

Ino stared, straining to keep his jaw from dropping open. *So it's like THAT*, he thought.

Jack frowned sourly. "And not that *you* particularly need this information, but I do have crime scene investigators from Indianapolis coming in. Experts in explosions. So I'm certain we'll get to the bottom of this." He leaned back in his chair, raising an eyebrow. "Why don't you tell me about your relationship with Dr. Reed?" He flipped the page in his little notepad.

Ino stared at him for a long moment, and then shrugged. "Fine. There's not much to tell. I started five years ago. Reed started way before me — like decades before. He used to be my advisor — now it's the department head — but I did have an office across the hall. We were in the same department, so I saw him at a lot of meetings." He shrugged. "Nothing really much beyond that."

Jack nodded. "Did you ever visit him at home?"

Ino thought for a moment. That was an interesting question. "No... he was really private. I saw him outside of work a few times but it was always at like, a restaurant or something. Always a department event." He shrugged. "Science professors aren't really the social butterfly type."

Jack nodded, still taking notes. "I'm getting that impression," he said, not looking up.

Ino stared at him for a long moment, and had to strain to keep from baring his teeth.

Jack looked up after a moment, and if he was fazed by Ino's obvious rage, he didn't show it. "Anything else?"

Ino nodded. "Sure, there was the South American drug cartel he stole all that money from." He nodded. "Like, a *lot* of money."

The shepherd blinked at him in shock, and then frowned sourly when he realized it was sarcasm. "See, now *that* would be useful information,

Dr. Reamer." He closed his notebook. "Someone with a grudge, someone who hated him. Someone who got…" He searched for words. "Run out of the University. Forced out of a business. Foreclosed on. Cheated on. Sued. Robbed." The dog shrugged, leaning back in his chair. "Some evidence of foul play that —"

Ino narrowed his eyes. "I just *gave* you evidence of foul play," he snapped.

Jack screwed up his black muzzle into a scowl. "No, you gave me evidence of strange behavior. Strange behavior, Dr. Reamer, is caused by a lot of reasons, very few of them having to do with murder. What you *didn't* give me was a motive." He ticked it off on one fat black finger. "Or a suspect. Or a single piece of physical evidence that anyone else was involved, or even set foot inside that lab."

Ino scowled at him. "Isn't that *your* job?"

Jack frowned. "Yes, of *course* it is. And we're working on it. But most of that building is in pieces the size of a phone book, scattered over an area the size of a football field. It's going to take us some time."

Ino fought the urge to bare his teeth. "You seem pretty convinced already," he snapped.

Jack frowned, leaning forward and taking a breath like he was going to yell. Then suddenly he sighed and relaxed. "Look, I get it. You're right." He shrugged, spreading his arms. "I hear you. I *do* think this was a terrible accident. But this investigation is still open, and if we find a *shred* of evidence that foul play was involved, *literally* a shred, I will convert this into a full-blown murder investigation. I don't know what we're going to find yet, so we're using the strictest treatment of the evidence already. IF we find something, we can still use it in court. But for all intents and purposes…" He trailed off and lifted his arms.

Ino narrowed his eyes.

"Let's review." The big dog leaned forward, counting off on his fingers again. "Dr. Reed had no enemies. He wasn't in debt. He didn't own a business. He wasn't in a relationship. There's no will, there's no wife, there's no jealous mistress. There wasn't even an insurance policy." He stared at Ino. "I shouldn't even be telling you this. But usually by this point, if there is *anything* to find, we have found *something*."

Ino leaned back, processing that.

Jack let him think, frowning sympathetically.

"So, what the fuck happened here?" Ino demanded.

Jack thought for a moment, took a deep breath, and let it out as a sigh. "Probably the most likely explanation — Dr. Reed pressurized the system. He turned on a gas valve by accident and never smelled the gas, since he lacked a sense of smell. He was overcome by the gas and died, and some time later the gas reached ignition density." He shrugged. "It happens."

Ino nodded. "Right. I get it. Just this morning I bumped my bathroom faucet and turned it on for an hour."

Jack blinked at him. "How did you manage that?"

Ino narrowed his eyes. "I didn't, because it's *impossible.*"

The dog stared at him, realized Ino was talking about the gas valves, and rolled his eyes. "Are you always this sarcastic?" he asked, wearily.

"No," Ino snapped. "I'm usually quiet and demure." He frowned. "What about the key card? *That's* a little suspicious, don't you think?"

Jack tightened his lips. "Those card readers were thirty years old, Dr. Reamer. They were cutting edge in 1995 and at this point they are trash. They go in and out, as I'm sure you've seen." He cast an arm up. "We used to have them in this building too, and last year we went back to using keys because we kept getting locked out of our own building." He frowned. "Actual metal keys, Dr. Reamer. I'm stuck with those until I can get new RF readers in the budget."

Ino leaned forward. "So what about the security cameras?" He pointed a finger triumphantly. "I'm sure Baker had cameras. *All* the buildings have cameras, after the shooting."

Jack stared at him for a moment, and then let out a sigh. "We haven't found the tapes yet."

Ino stared blankly at him. "The tapes?" He stared. "You haven't found..." He gaped in disbelief. "The recordings were *in the building?* It was *local storage?* Are you kidding? How does that make ANY sense?"

Jack nodded slowly. "Look, I'm not proud of this but... the cameras were the fastest solution the University could come up with in the event of another shooting. In-building tape storage was the quickest and easiest way to implement that. I've been trying to get a centralized database for the last two years, but it hasn't been in the budget."

Ino felt his jaw drop open. "So the tapes were destroyed when the building blew up?" He gaped. "Are you *kidding?*"

Jack shrugged. "We don't know. We haven't found them yet, destroyed or otherwise."

Ino frowned. "And you don't find THAT the least suspicious?"

Jack cracked a humorless smile. "Given our budget? Not really."

Ino threw his hands up. "Well, it's all just a little convenient — don't you think?" He clenched his teeth. "The weird gas release, the sense of smell, the missing tapes, the broken door lock?"

Jack thought for a moment. He leaned back in his chair. "Dr. Reamer, you're the... scientific type. Are you familiar with the Swiss cheese model?"

Ino stared at him, and for the second time, he felt his jaw drop open. "The..." He stared for a long time. "Did you really just say the words *Swiss cheese model* to me?"

Jack cracked a smile, which Ino found *infuriating*, and nodded. "Right. The Swiss cheese model. It's a model of *accident causation*. Kind of... an analogy to describe what happens when a very complex system breaks down."

Ino just stared.

Jack either didn't notice or didn't care. "In the model, each piece of cheese is a layer of protection." He leaned forward. "They're the barriers we put in place to keep accidents from happening. Something is going wrong, it hits a piece of cheese, and it mitigates the issue, or stops a problem from happening entirely. You don't want planes to fly into each other? You give them radar. That's a piece of cheese. You don't want people to die in car accidents? Give 'em seat belts and airbags. Two more pieces of cheese."

Ino stared at him. "I hate every part of this conversation," he said. He meant it.

Jack continued as if he hadn't said anything. "So in this instance, the key card system is a piece of cheese."

Ino stared at him.

"It's a barrier," Jack said. "A cheese barrier."

Ino frowned. "But it has *holes*. Swiss cheese has *holes* in it." He was getting mad. "Have you *seen* cheese? Are you aware of the properties of cheese, Chief Archer?"

Jack grinned, and Ino realized that he had played into the shepherd's stupid hands. "Right! *Every* layer of security, whether it guards against people or accidents, has *some* holes in it. You can't plan for everything. Every safety barrier in existence has some little quirk that, if exploited in just the right way, intentionally or otherwise, will cause that level of protection to fail. Plane radars work great, but if the pilot and copilot each think the *other* is looking at it, it doesn't make a difference. Seatbelts and airbags are great, but they're not so great if you don't use the seatbelt or have your feet up on the dashboard."

Ino stared at him. The conversation defied logic. And yet...

"So those are our cheese barriers." Jack started ticking off on his fingers again. "The countertop pipes are switched off until you turn on the main valve. That's a piece of cheese. The lab is kept free of ignition sources. That's a piece of cheese. Natural gas has extremely smelly particles added to it so you'll smell if there's a leak. That's another piece of cheese."

"Dr. Reed had no sense of smell," Ino said, slowly. He was starting to get it.

Jack actually looked excited. "Right! Perfect example. That is a hole in that piece." He frowned. "It's not a big hole, but it's a hole. If you can't smell *anything*, you're not going to smell the gas."

Ino frowned.

"So, in most cases, if you're trying to get through a bunch of slices of Swiss, you get through one piece of cheese, maybe two, but you're stopped dead by the next one. Look at commercial plane crashes — if you really dig down, most jetliner crashes are caused by ten or fifteen different, unrelated factors, and if you changed any one of them, the whole accident would have been avoided. That's why plane crashes are extremely rare. But sometimes in life, when you get a big pile of sliced Swiss, take all different pieces from all different blocks, and randomly order them, *one* time out of a hundred thousand, the —"

"The holes line up," Ino said, quietly.

Jack nodded grimly. "Yes," he said, finally. "The holes line up."

Ino stared at him.

The dog continued, slower and more quietly, choosing his words carefully. "And something shocking and wildly unlikely, and usually horrible..."

He gestured. "Happens. A plane crashes. Or a power grid goes down. Or —"

The hyena frowned. "Or a building blows up."

Jack nodded. "A building blows up."

Ino processed that for a moment. He couldn't keep the frown off his face.

Jack leaned back, cracking a little smile. "You don't appear to be convinced by my explanation, Dr. Reamer."

Ino frowned at him skeptically, and then took a deep breath. "I mean... it makes sense as a *theory*..."

Jack nodded. "Right. Scientist. You'll need a practical example." He thought for a moment, looking up and away. "Here, I have a good one. It's quite relevant, in fact. Last year in Massachusetts, 30,000 people had to be evacuated because of one huge series of gas leaks. The gas company put in a new trunk line." He leaned forward. "But they left the *pressure sensor* in the old line. Which they were emptying."

Ino frowned.

Jack went on. "As the old line emptied, the sensors detected the pressure drop, and the system poured more gas into the lines to compensate. However, it put gas into the *new* line, which rose to *ten times* the pressure it should have had, all while the sensors said the pressure was falling. It filled a thousand houses with gas and a few dozen of them burned down." He leaned forward. "Do you know how many layers of protection had to fail before a commercial gas company *accidentally* pressurized residential gas lines to 100 psi? But it happened! It was real!"

Ino sat back in his chair, sulking. It *was* real. He had seen it on the news.

Jack looked up, smiled a sympathetic little smile, and continued. "Anyway. This is just a long way of saying, sometimes this shit happens, you know?" Sighing, he leaned back in his chair. "And it's impossible to get your brain around if someone you care about dies. It never makes sense and it defies logic every time. But that doesn't make it any different. It just makes it... harder to process."

Ino raised an eyebrow. "Is that what you think I'm doing? Processing?"

The shepherd took a deep breath and let out a long sigh. "Dr. Reamer... everyone handles trauma differently. You're an intellectual — I can't say I'm surprised that you're trying to figure out an explanation for something that doesn't have an explanation to figure out."

Ino thought about it. Was the dog right? He frowned. He didn't like the thought of himself thinking irrationally. But he *was* having a hard time buying this as an accident.

The hyena snorted. "No, it still doesn't make sense. Why would he be alone in a deserted lab?"

Jack shrugged. "Dr. Reamer, do you *watch* television? I can think of plenty of reasons that someone would want to be alone in an empty chemistry lab, after the rest of campus was gone for the summer. Sure you want to keep digging on that topic?"

Ino raised both eyebrows, astonished. "Dr. *Reed?* What do you think he was doing, making meth? I was kidding about the drug cartel, you know."

The dog frowned. "It's certainly possible. How well did you really know Dr. Reed, anyway?"

Ino wanted to snap back, but he didn't really have a rebuttal for that.

Jack shrugged. "Sometimes people go places they shouldn't, Dr. Reamer." He paused for a long time. "Sometimes they don't make it back out."

Ino processed that.

Finally he spoke again. "I think your theory is bullshit, Chief Archer."

Jack stared at him for a moment, and then a smile slowly crept across his muzzle. He nodded. "You're more than entitled to do so, Dr. Reamer."

Ino stared at him.

"We're going to keep looking," the dog said.

Ino stared at him some more. He sighed. "You better," he said, standing up. "Because I'm not going away."

The dog grinned at him, *genuinely* grinned, and nodded. "So I have deduced, Dr. Reamer," he said. He smiled at him. "I guess we'll just have to get used to each other."

After staring at the dog for several long moments, trying to decide what *that* meant, Ino scuttled out of the office, annoyed.

Ino was halfway across the parking lot on the way back to his Jeep when he saw someone he recognized. It was Sean's uncle, turning to lock a huge blue Silverado pickup truck, in uniform and apparently just showing up for a shift.

Ino really looked him over for the first time. The husky was huge, bigger than Sean, and dwarfing Ino. Like a lot of older huskies, "Uncle Travis" was packed with muscle but had lost his lean-ness. He looked like an off-season bodybuilder, with big arms, a square jaw and a modest little beer belly, with a thick fluffy tail curled up behind him. Ino wondered if Sean, with his perfect six-pack, would look like his uncle in another fifteen years.

Well, he wouldn't look *exactly* like him — Travis had different markings. His face was mostly white except for the back of his jaw, and he had dark circles around his shockingly-blue eyes, the black running down his forehead and up to his nose. His face looked a little like a skull, actually. Ino put that thought out of his head.

The last time Ino had seen him, the cop had been sporting a blood-soaked white crew cut. Now the husky was wearing a black SU Security baseball cap, which almost covered the shaved skin of his scalp and a long, bandaged injury. The wound started over his left eyebrow and disappeared up under his baseball cap. Both of his ears were still securely attached to his head, but the base of the left one was shaved and raw and scabbed. Around the edges of the bandage, Ino saw raw and exposed pink skin. It looked like it hurt. A lot.

The dog caught sight of Ino and his eyebrows shot up, his clear blue eyes widening.

Ino cracked a smile. "You must be Uncle Travis."

The husky frowned at him. Ino thought he saw a tiny little flash of teeth. "Officer MacGregor," the dog corrected, curtly.

Ino stuck his hand out. "I'm Ino Reamer. I was with Sean during the, ahhhh, excitement the other day."

The dog reached out, and shook his hand. He squeezed hard — *way* too hard. Ino fought the urge to wince as the husky's huge mitt enveloped his hand.

Travis narrowed his eyes as he crushed Ino's hand. "You're the reason my nephew almost died in that building," he said, low and dangerous.

Ino stared at him a moment in disbelief, and then forcibly yanked his hand back. "Excuse me?" He stammered for a moment. "Did those words really just come out of your mouth?" he snapped.

The officer glowered at him. "That building was closed. What the hell were you doing in there?"

Ino stared defiantly back. He was already pissed off. "Gosh, I guess it *wasn't* closed, Uncle Travis, because that's where *his* makeup final was scheduled."

Travis MacGregor stared angrily back at him. "Shouldn't'a been there," he growled, barely audible. "You're the professor. It's your responsibility."

On some level, Ino realized that the husky was just scared and traumatized over nearly losing his nephew and having his own face fricasseed, and at any other time he probably would have been sympathetic, but after the garbage conversation with Travis' boss, he just rolled his eyes. "Actually, I knocked him over the ledge right before the building exploded." He cocked his head. "And I laid on top of him. Did you know that?" He lifted up his hands, which were still raw and scabbed. "I stopped a flying brick from hitting that kid right in the spine. I'm the only reason your nephew is still alive."

Travis stared back at him, his eyes widening in disbelief. His jaw slowly opened and stayed open.

"So I guess I'll take responsibility for *that*," Ino snapped. Without a word, he turned and left the big husky stammering in the parking lot.

Having gotten nowhere with Security, Ino went straight to the next level of escalation, after a quick detour to his office for a clean shirt.

Now sporting a white polo and hoping he wouldn't bleed through it, the hyena walked slowly up the stairs to Wong building. Wong Hall had been put up in the mid-'70s and reeked of brutalism. It had big featureless white concrete walls, tiny windows that receded into its frame, and a structure composed of a series of interconnected block shapes that managed to be boring and distractingly nonsensical at the same time. It was horrendously ugly and it was absolutely Ino's favorite building.

Ino moved slowly down the hallway, just fast enough that he wouldn't get asked if he was lost. He didn't have much cause to be in the admin building on a regular basis, but he had a pretty good idea where he was going. After a short walk he ended up in front of a large frosted glass office door.

OFFICE OF THE PRESIDENT, it read.

Ino put on his best smile and was about to step inside when a huge skunk came thundering out of the office.

Ino recognized him. His name was Sebastian. He was Susan Greeley's husband. He was massive, and gorgeous. Sebastian Greeley was 6'5' and his tail was almost as tall. He was mostly inky-black with select white features, and he moved like a dancer, his huge tail suspended effortlessly behind him. Ino had seen him around and was always dazzled at the skunk's incredible aesthetics. Sebastian looked like a professional hockey player who was also a male model. Today he was poured into an expensive light-gray suit, with a white shirt and no tie, and he looked perfect.

"Oh!" Ino said. "Mr. Greeley!"

The hulking skunk stared at him for a moment and then smiled. "Ino Reamer! How are you?" He reached forward to shake Ino's hand. His hand was strong and enormous and he shook hard. Not rudely hard, just "huge buff guy" hard.

"Wow!" Ino said. "I can't believe you remember me!" He smiled. Finally, someone who was friendly!

The skunk nodded warmly. "Of course. We met at the 99th Anniversary Gala last year." His smile faded. "Susan told me about your close call. How are you feeling?"

Ino shrugged. "Better." He reflexively shifted in discomfort. "I got a pretty good whack but I'm starting to feel like my ribs are moving back into place now." He smiled.

Sebastian winced. "Oh, Jesus." He shook his head. "I'm glad you're all right. I heard you saved a kid. I'm trying to talk my wife into some kind of commendation for you."

Ino blinked at him and felt himself blushing. "I didn't *save* anybody; Sean smelled the gas before I did. I just had a good idea of where we should cower."

Sebastian grinned. "So modest." He winked. "Truly, though, I'm so glad you're okay. It was sad enough to hear about Dr. Reed."

Ino nodded. "Yeah," he said. He thought of Jack Archer's words. *Found your colleague dead on the floor.* He suppressed a shiver.

Sebastian let out a quiet sigh. "Well… if there's anything we can do for you, let us know." He reached out for a handshake again. "I'm sorry to say I'm running late. I'll see you at the anniversary Gala this weekend, though!"

Ino nodded. From what he knew, the skunk managed all sorts of art galleries and philanthropic grants. "Oh, sure!" He shook Sebastian's hand again. "Nice to see you again, Mr. Greeley!"

"Please, call me Sebastian!" The skunk grinned at him, and left.

Ino let out a little sigh as he went into the office. That had been… nice.

"Good morning," said the young lemur behind the desk. She was wearing a light pink blouse and her hair up in a severe-looking bun; Ino couldn't actually tell if she was a student employee or just looked very young. "How can I help you?"

Ino cleared his throat. "Hi, I was wondering if I could speak to the president?

She turned to her computer. "Do you have an appointment?"

Ino cleared his throat again. "No, it's really just an informal visit. If she can't see me, it's fine."

"Mmm, I'm afraid her schedule is pretty tight today," the receptionist said. "Are you on campus for the rest of the d—"

Susan Greeley appeared in the doorway of her office. "Ino!" she said, loudly.

Ino and the receptionist both looked up, eyes wide.

Susan smiled warmly at both of them. "It's fine, Lucy. Thank you so much." The cheetah turned to Ino and hit him with a 1000-watt smile. "Ino! Come right in!" she announced. She walked up to him, took his arm, and guided him aggressively into her office.

The Office of the President was very strategically laid out. It was a huge room for a single office, twenty feet on a side, with President Greeley's monstrous mahogany desk in one corner, tall walnut bookshelves lined with old books and framed photos and diplomas, and a large solid-wood conference table with six chairs in the other corner. It was lavishly appointed but only because this room had been the office of the Santiago University President for six decades — the desk was original and the conference table and bookshelves had become antiques during the tenure of their use. President

Greeley wasn't one to show off, but Ino knew she would be horrified at the thought of altering the beautiful and historical office.

She led him into the room, patting his arm, her tail trailing casually behind her. "Ino, how are you?" she asked. She gestured to one of the two large leather guest chairs in front of the desk — also antiques. They each sank into one. The cool leather felt nice after being out in the summer heat. "What brings you back on campus?"

Ino tried to relax, or at least look relaxed. "Oh, just cleaning some things out of my office before the summer term starts." He smiled. "I'm going to have to find a new couch. I bled all over my old one!"

Susan winced.

Ino frowned inwardly. *Great! Let's make this as awkward as possible.* "Also, it's nice to get out of the house for a bit. I wanted to get back to campus and see if things were any more normal." He frowned. "It's weird seeing Dr. Reed's office empty."

Susan blinked at him, and then let out a sigh. "Right. I imagine it is." She frowned.

Ino grimaced. "Do we really need the space that badly?"

The president blinked, and leaned back in her chair. "Truthfully, no. But we thought it best to…" She paused, searching for the words. "Pursue a goal of moving forward."

Ino nodded thoughtfully. "Wow. I see." He frowned. "And where is all his… stuff?" He frowned. "It didn't get like… thrown out, did it?"

Susan shook her head. "Oh, no no no. It's all right here in this building. There's some extra storage downstairs. We're going to hold it until we locate next of kin — I think Ethan had some distant cousin on the west coast."

Ino nodded. "Ah," he said. "That's… good to know."

She leaned back in her chair. "So, Ino. What's on your mind?"

For a moment, Ino debated dropping the entire thing. He could make small talk, and then just skate out. It would certainly be a lot easier. But then he thought of Sean and decided he needed to go for it. He let out a long sigh, considering his words. "I just… don't feel right about the explosion. I don't feel like it was an accident. I don't see how it could have been."

Susan nodded thoughtfully. "That's… troubling, Ino."

He nodded, taking a deep breath and letting out a shaky sigh. "You're telling me."

She leaned forward. "Did you bring these concerns to Security? We aren't handling the investigation *completely* internally, but Security is spearheading."

Ino nodded slowly. "I did. Chief Archer seems convinced that this was a terrible accident."

She nodded again.

Ino could tell she was deep in thought about her next words.

He grinned. "Let me guess. I should accept whatever conclusion that Security reaches?"

Susan took a breath. "Ino... both of us are used to being specialists of the highest esteem." She paused. "But that's restricted to our specific fields." She spread her hands. "We can't take the lead on this. We do have to acknowledge that the Security teams are the experts in this situation."

Ino cocked his head. "Are they?" he asked pointedly. It wasn't sarcastic. He was genuinely, but respectfully — he hoped — challenging that assumption.

Susan seemed to hear that, and spent a moment choosing her words. If she took the challenge personally, she did a good job of hiding it. "While I... *appreciate* that this is unique and outside the norm for a campus security force... Chief Archer and his team have plenty of experience in addressing various crimes and public safety concerns. We researched a number of candidates before we hired him, Ino. I thought Jack was by far the most qualified lead we had." She crossed her legs. "I still do. He has a long law enforcement career. We're lucky to have him."

He nodded. "I hear you. But I have to wonder — do State Troopers experience a lot of..." He searched for the correct term. "Structural explosions?"

The president smiled. "Always reviewing credentials. You know, I read your last publication."

Blinking, Ino looked back at her. "Seriously?"

She nodded. "Yes indeed. *Molecular Phylogeny of the Endemic Philippine Rodent*... uhhhhh... the..."

"*Apomys Muridae.*" Ino finished. He let his jaw drop open.

The cheetah laughed gently. "A lot of the hard genetics was over my head, but your research was so... *rigorous*, I couldn't help but appreciate it." He shook his head in disbelief. "Amazing. I can't even remember what your degrees are in."

Susan laughed again, genuinely. "Oh, Ino. I find your honesty so refreshing. The world of academics is usually so... staged." She beamed. "German Linguistics, Physics, and Economics. And my undergraduate was in Accounting, in case you were wondering. But feel free to forget before I see you again next."

He smiled.

She nodded. "Anyway. I understand your concerns and I absolutely share them. The security team has brought in a number of experts in fire dynamics, explosions scientists, and forensics. I've reviewed all of their credentials personally. I'm confident we have the right people on this."

He nodded. They were quiet for a moment.

Ino let out a sigh. "They already told you it was an accident, didn't they."

The cheetah gave him a little smile. "I don't think they've reached any definitive conclusions just yet."

He frowned and shook his head. "It just doesn't feel right."

Susan nodded slowly and thoughtfully. "Our friend and coworker died, Ino," she said softly. "It's *never* going to feel right."

Ino looked away, and to his surprise found tears forming and blurring his vision. He blinked them back for a moment, swallowing the lump in his throat.

The president frowned sympathetically at him, giving the hyena a moment to compose himself, and then rose fluidly up from her seat. "Here. I'd like you to see something."

Taking a deep breath, Ino lifted himself up from his chair.

The president went to the huge conference table, her tail lashing behind her, and Ino followed her. He hadn't seen it before, surrounded as the table was with massive leather chairs, but there was a sheer white sheet over something rectangular on the conference table.

Confused, he frowned.

Susan took a deep breath. "Before... all of this happened, the Board and I were working with one of our corporate donors. They've been considering a gift to the University for quite some time. We were thinking maybe next year, maybe the year after. But in light of this recent tragedy, they've decided to move up their timetable." Beaming, she lifted the sheet off the conference table. "I give you... the Reed Center."

Ino felt his jaw drop open. The sheet slowly retracted over an architectural model — a model of a building. It was big and square and all glass, at least two stories, maybe three. The model itself was twenty inches tall. The little fiberboard paths leading up the building and circling around it made it clear this was on the site of the former Baker Brown Science Center. He could even see the little bench where he had sat watching the flames. Freakishly, there was a little plastic figurine of a hyena on it.

"A-are you kidding me?" he choked out.

Susan stared at him, surprised. "What? What do you mean?"

Ino swallowed. "It's been... it's been *four days*." He shook his head, horrified. "How did you even get this made?!"

Susan stared at him, and then shook her head. "Oh no, of course. No, Ino, this plan has been in the works for years. These buildings take 24 months just to engineer. We've had this model since..." She thought about it. "February."

Ino stared, and then let out a relieved sigh. "Jesus."

Susan let out an awkward chuckle. "My goodness. No, Ino, this is part of the University's master plan. We're just working with an... abbreviated timetable, that's all," she said, cheerfully.

Ino nodded. He stared at the little mock building, taking it in.

Sensing Susan had expected more fanfare, he cleared his throat. "It's... very impressive!" he said, doing his best to sound enthusiastic.

The president beamed, and Ino smiled awkwardly back at her.

He looked back down at the building. "This looks expensive. How much is the donation?"

Susan stared at him, leaned in conspiratorially, slid a piece of paper out from under the model. She slid it toward him.

It was a copy of a legal document, written as a signed letter with two big signatures at the bottom. He skipped over the return address and moved directly to the text.

```
The    below-signed    Dublahm    Chemical
Corporation  LLC,  does  hereby  with  this
```

```
correspondence make expressly and explic-
itly clear its intentions to donate to the
above-named University of Santiago insti-
tution, a sum of not less than…
```

He stopped reading as soon as he got to the number. When he saw it, his eyes bugged out of his head. "Oh," he said. "Oh my GOD."

President Greeley smiled. Her tail swished back and forth behind her a few times.

Ino blinked at the figure. "Is that in MILLIONS?" He gaped at her.

Beaming, the cheetah nodded.

Ino let out a long breath. "Wooooooooooooow." He took a step back and stared at the model. "So Dr. Reed gets a memorial building."

She nodded. "Yes. And we're creating a program for low-income local high school students, where they can take advanced courses and get college credit. And there will be an endowment scholarship fund for current students in Ethan's name."

Ino stared, feeling breathless. The little building didn't look at all like it could really be built. He couldn't picture it. It looked way too modern for Santiago.

His sense of decorum abruptly kicked in and he looked up to give the president a big smile.

"He would be so happy to know," he said, hollowly.

President Greeley beamed back at him, and nodded.

Ino let out a breath. "Wow. It's… a lot to take in," he said. He smiled, because he didn't know what else to do.

"Isn't it nice? Dr. Reed's memory will live on in a brand-new science and research building."

Ino nodded, feeling lightheaded.

"And just in time for the 100th anniversary," Susan added.

Ino lifted his head. "Hmm?"

She stared at him. "Don't tell me you forgot! Wait, I have something for you!" She turned to a side table with a large cardboard box on it. She reached into the box and retrieved a baseball-sized glass dome, inscribed in white with the Santiago University logo.

Ino stared at her.

She reached out a hand. "Here, take it! It's a big time for the University! The Gala is this weekend!"

Smiling awkwardly, Ino took the glass half-sphere. "Thank you, Susan," he said, slipping his backpack off his shoulder and sliding the paperweight into it. He slipped the bag back onto his shoulders and it felt like it weighed about five pounds more. He swallowed. "And thank you for the... uh, the comforting news."

Susan nodded, beaming again. "Just make sure you don't tell anyone. The press release hasn't gone out yet." She took one end of the sheet. "Would you mind helping me cover this back up?"

He blinked, and then hurried to take the other end. "No no, of course."

Together, they lifted the white sheet, up and over, completely covering the Reed Center. The sheet draped over it, hugging its form and barely concealing what lay beneath.

Ino swallowed a lump in his throat.

They stood back, staring at the sheet with the shape under it.

Something occurred to Ino. "Wait. Did that say *Dublahm Chemical?*"

Susan's eyes widened, and then she looked guiltily away. "I... shouldn't discuss that."

Ino grimaced. "From the news?"

Susan frowned, and then let out a sigh. "Unfortunately, yes."

Ino let out a low whistle. "Wow. I guess they're in damage control mode." He thought of the number on the signed legal document. "*Aggressive* damage control."

The cheetah frowned at him. "We can't always pick our benefactors, Ino. We can only ensure we do good works with the results of their partnership."

Ino nodded slowly. "I... see. And they just decided to donate all this money because of Dr. Reed's m... accident?"

Susan nodded. "They were... eager for the opportunity to build good will. Locally."

Ino nodded. "Wow."

They stared awkwardly at one another, and then Ino cleared his throat. "Well, I should probably be going," he said. "I don't want to take up any more of your time. Thank you for seeing me."

Susan smiled, returning to her desk. "Very good. Thank you for stopping by. And remember, Ino!" she said.

He turned back, his eyes wide.

"Don't say a word!" Susan told him with a large warm smile. She was showing a lot of teeth. "Or you'll regret it!"

Smiling awkwardly, Ino waved and slipped out the door.

Feeling lightheaded, Ino staggered around to the back of the building.

He couldn't believe it. The site of the exploded Baker Center hadn't even been cleared yet and President Greeley was ready to break ground on its replacement building. He shook his head.

Sliding his backpack off his shoulder, Ino stuck his hand in and fished around for a little paperboard box he knew was hiding somewhere at the bottom. It was probably stale and he was going to regret it, but there was a reason he had saved it for so long.

Finally, his fingers closed around a square object — it had fallen deep into the bottom, attracted by the gravitational pull of the huge paperweight — and pulled out his very last pack of cigarettes. It had been eighteen months since Ino's last smoke but he was more than ready for one now. He took the green box in his hands and slapped it against his other palm several times. The action felt familiar and totally foreign at the same time, like getting on a bicycle after a break of many years.

Ino had a bright yellow lighter on which he had drawn little brown hyena spots with permanent marker. It was in the pack with the cigs. Ino hung a cigarette into his muzzle, held the flame to it, and sucked in deeply.

The smoke hit his lungs like he was huffing bleach.

"*Blearrrgh!*" he hacked, dissolving into a coughing fit, his body seemingly trying to eject his lungs via his esophagus. "*Whuh huhhhgh hurrrgh,*" he gagged, letting the cigarette drop out onto the sidewalk, and spitting repeatedly into the bushes.

He had a buzz and his heart was racing, but he couldn't tell if it was from the nicotine or from the dry heaving. The hyena staggered down along the back patio of the admin building, clearing his throat and coughing. There was a tall line of hedges and shade trees ringing the back patio, and Ino was on the other side of the hedge, obscured from both the building and from the parking lot. At least nobody could see him.

Shaking, Ino shook his head, letting his doglike tongue hang out of his mouth. "*Jesus*," he said, to the pack of cigs in his hand. "*Et tu*, Newport Menthol?" Swallowing one final time, Ino squished the pack and threw it like a baseball. The smushed-up pack arced perfectly through the air over the hedges, and landed directly in the center hole of a public trash can. "Even *you* have betrayed me."

Grimacing in disgust, Ino looked around to make sure nobody was watching him talk to an inanimate object. He took a couple minutes just to catch his breath, since he still had tiny spots at the corners of his vision, and sat on a little bench in a shady area ringed by hedges.

The hyena was just standing up to leave when there was a bang as the back door opened.

Wide-eyed, Ino froze.

A big figure clomped out the back door, walking swiftly towards the parking lot. Ino could just barely make him out through the bushes.

Ino watched him, holding perfectly still, his eyes wide. He hadn't meant to be sneaky — he'd just been embarrassed and startled. But now if he moved he would seem like even more of a creeper.

Ino caught a glimpse of black and tan as the figure strode past. He blinked in surprise.

It was clearly a big German shepherd, wearing a baseball cap and aviator sunglasses and a plain white t-shirt. Ino could tell he was handsome, even with the hat and glasses.

Suspiciously handsome.

Holding his breath, Ino peered through the foliage. Was that Jack Archer?

The dog thumped down the stairs and stepped into the parking lot. Ino heard a door open and he leaned forward a little closer, peeking. Jack had gotten into a massive Ford Bronco, one that was a dusty red and couldn't have been newer than 1989. He climbed in, fired the engine — it sounded like a piece of construction equipment — and slowly pulled out. He took the long way around the parking lot, away from the building, rumbling off onto Church Street.

Ino stared. What the hell had Chief Archer been doing here? And why not walk out the front door? Why park in the back behind the trees? And had he *changed his clothes?*

Ino furrowed his brow. There weren't many people in the building now. Half of the admin building was empty, except for the accounting people, and they barely left their desks this time of year. Who else could the dog have been here to see but President Greeley? The timing, right after Ino had left, was definitely a bit strange.

Frowning, Ino watched the old SUV recede down the middle of campus.

"Hup!"

Ino clapped his paws over his muzzle, wide-eyed. After a few seconds, he determined that he really had just *hiccupped*, and with that decided that he had embarrassed himself in public enough for one day. He scampered back to his car.

Next, Ino decided to do what he always did when he didn't like how a plan was going: research the everloving hell out of it.

The hyena was buried in his favorite research nook: a giant conference table in the middle of the ground floor. The library was built into a gently rising hillside, and the beautiful granite front entrance was on the higher side, facing Church Street, so the "ground floor" was effectively the basement. It was poorly-lit and stuffy and Ino's favorite place to hide. The hyena had about fifteen books spread out on a huge table intended for six people, in such a way as to advertise he would be needing the entire surface and no one else should attempt to join him. Hyenas were highly territorial, after all.

He was halfway through a book called "So You've Decided To Solve A Murder" when a shadow appeared over him.

"Hey nerd — don't you know it's summer?" said a smooth female voice.

Ino looked up, startled, and it took his brain a moment to recognize who he was staring at.

Vivian Chen was a slim pine marten in her late 30s, in a narrow black skirt and, despite the heat, a billowy eggplant-colored sweater. She was chestnut-colored with long straight black hair and thick-framed black plastic glasses, small and slight, with a miniature-scaled purse and an absolutely gigantic black leather backpack.

"Vivian!" he gasped, scrambling out of his chair, sweeping the marten up into an embrace. He laughed. "I didn't know you were back!" He squeezed her and they released, both sinking down into chairs.

"Are you okay?!" Vivian demanded. "The rumor mill is saying you were in the building when the explosion happened. Is that true?"

Ino forced a smile. "Don't worry about it! When did you get back? Why didn't you call me? I would have brought you dinner! How was your trip?" He screwed up his face. "I mean… you know what I mean." He felt himself blushing fiercely. "I know you were at a refugee camp. Oh my God, I can't believe I said that."

She chuckled. "I know what you mean. I got back yesterday but this is my first time back on campus. I took a night to decompress. And Turkey was… rewarding. I'm happy I got to stay an extra three weeks thanks to the GoFundMe. Thank you again for donating." She beamed.

Ino nodded. "Of course, it was my pleasure. I'm happy to help." He leaned in. "Is it weird being back? Santiago is so… *Santiago*."

She nodded. "It's… an adjustment. I feel like I'm equipped to handle the transition, however."' She beamed.

They both laughed. Vivian Chen had advanced degrees in clinical psychology and taught several courses at the University. Most recently, the marten had spent eight weeks in refugee camps in the Middle East consulting on a program to administer crisis therapy. She certainly was equipped to handle re-adjusting to culture shock. In fact, Vivian was qualified to teach a course on the topic.

Ino nodded. "Well, I'm glad to see you back. I'll donate again if you decide to go next year."

She smiled warmly and reached out to touch his forearm. "That means a lot to me. Thank you, Ino."

He leaned back in his chair and checked the time on his phone. "Do you want to get dinner? I've just been doing some, uhhhh… light reading."

They both looked down at his books. The top one said *METHODS AND TECHNIQUES OF FATAL ACCIDENT RECONSTRUCTION AND ANALYSIS, 1945-1971.*

Vivian raised an eyebrow. "Ah, some beach reading," she said, flatly.

Ino chuckled weakly.

Vivian adjusted her glasses and dug through the pile. "Why don't I join you? I think I'll head up to the Dunes and spend a leisurely afternoon flipping through" — she slid a book out from the bottom of the pile — "*Practical Arson and Fire Investigation, Second Edition.*" She held it up. "Wow. With *full-color* autopsy photos." She turned the book like she was looking at the pinup in a dirty magazine, beaming. "Fun! This is so much better than the *first* edition."

Ino looked away, feeling himself blush.

Vivian smiled and leaned forward. "Something on your mind?" she asked, innocently.

Ino sighed. "Have you been talking to people since you got back? I feel like I'm going crazy. Everyone is acting like nothing happened and it's all I can think about."

Vivian frowned. "Well... I've only been back for a day or so, but... this isn't really that uncommon. People are capable of some fairly impressive mental gymnastics when they want to move on from a trauma. Some people just want to put it behind them and get on with their lives as soon as possible. Don't you remember that after the shooting?"

Ino blinked at her. "Oh. Yeah, I guess I do."

Vivian nodded. "Right. Having said *that*, people who are more *directly* affected sometimes have... trouble moving away from it."

Ino felt his face heat up. "I think I'm fine."

She raised her eyebrows. "Are you, Ino?"

He frowned. "I really do think so. Anyway, that's not what's bothering me. It's just how *weird* everyone is acting."

Vivian frowned. "How do you mean?"

He told her about President Greeley's full-speed-ahead plans to renovate the University and Jack Archer's seeming impatience to close the case as an unfortunate accident.

She nodded, reaching up to push her glasses up her nose. "That doesn't surprise me about Greeley. Susan is one of the smartest people I've ever met but she's not... overflowing with emotional intelligence." She shrugged. "The architectural plan is a very..." She pondered her word choice for a moment. "*Calculated* response. It's the best next step for the University and it doesn't surprise me that she's not getting caught up in the details."

Ino nodded. "The security chief is the one that's killing me."

Vivian shrugged. "He's probably just lying to you."

Ino stared at her. "You think so?" he asked, astonished.

Vivian considered. "Sure! Especially if he's a former cop. Law enforcement lies all the time. Usually to get confessions, but they're constantly withholding or changing information if they think it will help them get new evidence. Or even just to save time in an investigation. For all sorts of reasons." She stared at him. "People assume they're honest because they're law enforcement, but like, they're in no way legally *required* to be."

Ino blinked. "But why would he lie to *me?*"

She shrugged again. "Does he have any reason to tell you the truth?"

Ino frowned. "Wow, I don't remember you being this cynical."

Vivian chuckled. "No, I mean, think about his motivations — what are his priorities?"

Ino thought about it. "Uhh. Close the case." He raised an eyebrow. "As quickly as possible, if I'm being realistic." He rolled his eyes.

Vivian nodded. "You're right about that. It's bad PR for the University to have an unsolved death open. A school the size of ours lives or dies on its reputation. So, is closing the case definitively progressed, in *any* way, by telling *you* everything he knows about the incident?"

Ino considered that, frowning. "Huh. I never thought of that. I guess not. I'm sort of… irrelevant to that goal?" He pondered. "In fact, telling everything might *hinder* him because I would be all up in his business." He sat back in his chair. "Hhhhhuh. I guess that makes sense." He frowned. "By the way, how come nobody told me the Security Chief was gay?"

She raised her eyebrows. "You didn't *know?* That was all anybody was talking about for like two months."

He frowned. "Nobody said anything to *me.*"

Vivian stared. "What did you expect, someone would run up to you and say *Hey! We found another gay person in Indiana!*"

He raised an eyebrow.

She considered a moment. "You know what, now that I've said it, I am actually *genuinely* surprised that no one did that."

He smiled. "Right?! That's what *I* thought!"

She nodded. "I could picture it as soon as it came out of my mouth." She shrugged. "Anyway, I was *sure* you knew. Don't you get some kind of gay newsletter or something?"

He scowled.

Vivian stared and then grinned. "Why, are you into him? Is he single?"

Ino snorted. "No and I don't care! He's an asshole! Especially if he's not even being honest."

Vivian chuckled. "I figured you would say that. Though, to be fair, that's just a guess. He could easily just be incompetent. We do work with some fairly stupid people."

Ino snort-laughed, covering his mouth in the silent library. "God, I missed you."

Vivian smiled broadly. "It's good to be back." She adjusted her hair and crossed her legs. "So… what's this all about?" She gestured broadly at the table.

Ino blinked at her. "Pardon?"

She narrowed her eyes. "You've never been one to police people in a professional capacity before." She considered. "Generally, you're quite happy to let people make fools of themselves. So why *now*?"

Ino felt himself blushing. "I don't want to tell you. Everyone else thinks I'm insane."

She smiled. "They don't know the meaning of the word."

Ino sighed. "I suppose."

Vivian widened her eyes crazily. "I mean they *literally* don't know the meaning of the word."

Ino shook his head. "Okay, fine! MY GOD, woman!"

They both started snickering.

"SHHHH," came a voice from deep in the stacks.

They hunched down.

"So what's going on?" Vivian demanded.

Ino frowned. "I think Reed was murdered."

"*Murdered?!*" Vivian gasped.

"SHHH," Ino hissed.

Vivian clapped her small hands over her muzzle.

After a moment Vivian removed her hands and put them back in her lap. "I believe I've recovered. What makes you say that?"

Ino stared at her, narrowing his eyes. "Were you *acting* shocked just now?"

Absolutely deadpan, Vivian nodded. She stared directly at him with the perfectly-still stare that only small mustelids could truly master.

Ino sighed. "You *knew* I was going to say that." He threw his arms up over his head.

She shrugged innocently. "I mean... there is kind of a theme going on at this table." She gestured at the books.

Ino sighed. "My God. Could I be more of a cliche right now?"

Vivian grinned. "I think you could. I read a *lot* of mysteries. Do you have any desire to adopt a cat? Or open a bookstore?" She leaned forward excitedly. "Or a bakery?"

Ino glared at her.

Vivian widened her eyes. "Or a combination bookstore slash bakery?"

Ino narrowed his eyes. "I mean, *obviously*, it would be a combination. What kind of hyena business do you think I'm running?!"

Vivian laughed and then quickly hushed herself. After a moment, she leaned forward again. "So... who do you think did it?"

Ino blinked at her. "Pardon?"

Vivian leaned one elbow on the table, propping up her chin. "Who killed Dr. Reed?"

He stared. "I... I have no idea!" He was startled at the question.

The pine marten looked disappointed, pursing her small snout. "Oh." She recovered quickly. "Well, who would *want* to kill Dr. Reed?"

Ino shrugged. "I don't have a clue! Chief Archer says he didn't have any significant others, or heirs, or enemies."

Vivian smiled. "I don't want to know what Chief Archer thinks. I want to know what *you* think. You worked across the hall from that man for five years. I think you know him a little better than campus security."

Ino thought for a moment. "Well... I mean... he definitely wasn't regularly seeing anyone. So it wasn't a jealous wife or girlfriend." He thought, looking up and away. "Only child, parents are dead. He was married, but they divorced..." He thought. "Probably in the '90s? And I don't think he had much money. I mean, not like... *get murdered* money." He felt his face heating up. This was a weird conversation.

Vivian nodded, cocking her head. "So who would have a motive? Who benefits from his death?" She considered. "Who had he pissed off?"

Ino shrugged. "Well… a lot of people, I guess."

Vivian blinked at him, her dark eyes intrigued. "Seriously?"

Ino shrugged again. "Sure. He wasn't shy about confrontation."

Vivian leaned forward at full attention. "Give me an example." She propped her chin up on her hand again.

Ino smiled humorlessly. "Well, the day he died, he implied that I'm a shitty professor and I was kowtowing to the football team. That's both insulting as a professor *and* as a gay man, depending on how you interpret it." He elected to leave out Reed's allusion to the incident at his previous school.

Vivian chuckled, leaning back in her seat. "Oh, great! We've established a motive for *you*."

Ino couldn't help but smile. "Awesome! Thanks for your help!"

Vivian grinned, and then pondered for a moment, lost in thought. "Who else?"

Ino shrugged. "Well… in a weird way, the University."

Vivian stared at him, raising an eyebrow. "What? How?"

He explained about Dublahm Chemical's massive corporation donation and their last-minute decision to offer it up all at once so the school could start work on the replacement science center.

Vivian wrinkled her small muzzle. "Hm. That's definitely an amount of money that someone might kill for. But I don't buy it as a motive for murder. It's not like a will. You couldn't know for sure that a huge company would decide to donate millions of dollars."

Ino shrugged. "I mean… you *could*. You would just need to work it out with them ahead of time."

Vivian raised a skeptical eyebrow. "Like, secretly get them to agree to make the donation to improve their own horrible public image?" She pondered. "I *guess* I could see it. That would make them complicit in a murder, though."

Ino nodded. "I mean… they're being investigated for gross safety violations right now. It wouldn't *really* surprise me. If you struck a horrible deal with them you would just need to decide who to… uh, who to kill."

Vivian leaned back in her chair. "Well! Dr. Reed would certainly be an excellent candidate."

Ino stared at her, his eyes widening.

The pine marten frowned. "I mean, *academically*. No family, no spouse."

Ino wrinkled his muzzle.

Vivian rolled her eyes. "I mean, if you had to do it to *someone*." She sighed. "What did Dublahm do, anyway?"

Ino grimaced. "Uhh, they had a big fire at their processing plant outside of town. Two people died and there were a lot of injuries." He shook his head. "They had to evacuate half the west side of town. It was while you were away. It was insane. They're getting dragged in the news for it. Every day it seems like something else comes out that they should have done, but didn't. Or shouldn't have done, but did!" *Oh God*, he suddenly thought. *More Swiss cheese.*

Vivian nodded. "That would certainly establish motive. Every day they're in the news for this they lose hundreds of thousands in shareholder value." She shrugged. "But they'll make it back the next time they release a new product. Who else we got?"

Ino pondered. "Can't really think of anyone."

Vivian thought about it, resting her chin on her palm, drumming the base of her muzzle with her fingers. "I hate to bring it up but… what about… that thing last summer?"

Ino stared at her. "Uhh, could you be more specific."

Vivian watched him. "Where he brought up the data thing. With the student. At your old school."

Ino stared. So much for not bringing it up. Reed had played that card once before, the previous summer. It had been just before they departed for the year and Ino had been too shocked to react. He'd gone straight to Vivian's place and fumed about it for hours. He swallowed, hard. "Ah," he said, softly.

Vivian watched him. "All the blood just left your face." She pointed.

Ino let out a long shaky sigh. "I really hate talking about this," he said. "It wasn't a great time for me. I really didn't picture a full ethics investigation a few years into my career."

Vivian nodded. "Understandable. Which is kind of my point."

He raised an eyebrow over his glasses. "What do you mean?"

Vivian cocked her head. "My point is, what if he pulled something like *that* on the wrong person?"

Ino thought for a moment. The first time Reed had dropped that bombshell, Ino had just stammered in surprise. The second time, the morning of Reed's death, he had yelled. But he'd *wanted* to do a whole lot more. "Hhhhhhhhhhuh. You may be on to something there."

Vivian nodded. "It's as plausible as anything else."

Ino swallowed. "Jesus."

The marten shrugged. "Okay. Well then, figure it out."

The hyena blinked at her. "Excuse me?"

Vivian lifted her arms. "Find out what *he* found out. You know where to look. You know what circles science professors run in. Would Jack Archer ever think to look at journal publications? Fighting for grant money? How a chemistry professor thinks?"

Ino stared at her. "Why are you encouraging me?" He cocked his head, genuinely curious.

Vivian grinned. "You mean, you don't accept my sudden burning desire for justice?"

Ino stared her down.

Vivian chuckled. "Do you want my professional opinion?"

Ino scowled. "I don't *want* it but I probably need to hear it."

Vivian nodded. "Ha! You'd be surprised how often that is the case. Okay, I think one of two things is happening. First — you think this was a murder because it *was* a murder. You're smart, you notice things. Maybe something you subconsciously noticed is eating at your brain and that's why you have these nagging doubts."

He frowned. "Okaaay. I'm scared to ask what the second choice is."

She smiled humorlessly and her tone softened considerably. "Ino... you could have been killed. In a freak accident completely out of your control. And you're having a hard time accepting that."

He grimaced. "Is that common in this sort of scenario?"

Vivian processed that for a moment. "Not... particularly." She shrugged. "But everyone processes trauma differently. Denial is definitely in the range of possibilities."

He frowned. "Do *you* think I'm in denial?"

She shrugged. "I haven't fully completed my analysis."

Ino stared at her, and then felt a grin spread across his face. "Okay. Fair enough. Next question — what's the clinical benefit of having me investigate?"

Vivian smiled. "Well, if there really was a murder committed, you could uncover valuable evidence. You knew the man fairly well. You know the people he talked to, and his habits. A little internet sleuthing could easily make up the difference." She shrugged. "Don't break any laws, obviously, but you might look somewhere the investigators didn't think to look."

Ino narrowed his eyes. "And if not? What if there wasn't even a crime?"

Vivian shrugged. "Even better. You'll prove to yourself that nothing happened." She gestured at him. "You're a firm lover of the scientific method. Don't you think you'll feel differently about the incident if you chase down a dozen leads and all of them lead back to the same innocuous conclusion?"

He thought for a moment, and then slowly cocked his head. "So I have two working hypotheses. I just need to determine which is the correct one."

Vivian smiled warmly. "There you go."

There was a short silence.

Ino nodded. "I think I actually feel better about this," he said.

Vivian chuckled. "That was easy."

He smiled. "I try to be a cheap date," he said, softly.

Vivian reached over and squeezed his forearm.

"Thank you," Ino said, quietly.

Vivian nodded. "Of course." She tugged up her sweater sleeve and checked her watch. "Unfortunately, I can't stay. I'm speaking to a women's group tonight."

Ino chuckled. "Of course you are."

Vivian beamed. "Of course I am. And since I didn't say so… I'm really, really, really glad you're okay, Ino." She reached forward and squeezed both of his forearms, and when Ino looked up he was surprised to see tears in her eyes.

"Aw, no, don't do that!" he begged, lifting to his feet and sweeping the pine marten into a firm hug.

Vivian laughed and squeezed him back. "Now be careful, and don't do anything illegal. I'll call you when I get settled and we can have coffee and talk for nine hours."

He laughed. "Coffee, nothing. How about breakfast? Eggs Benedict?"

She nodded. "Bloody Marys."

He smiled. "Of course. What do you take me for?"

She chuckled. "Never one to disappoint." She hugged him again. "Talk to you soon! *Try* to stay out of trouble, please," she stage-whispered as she headed for the stairs.

"No promises!" he called, as she walked away. He watched her sweep up the stairs and disappear.

Sitting in his house that night, Ino frowned.

He had a blank legal pad in front of him. Most of his students used iPads or Chromebooks these days for note-taking, but Ino still preferred his old standby: taking notes on a stolen legal pad from the supply closet at work.

He was parked at the breakfast table. The TV was on in the other room. The A/C was cranked so high that Ino was wearing his robe but he dared not turn down the A/C since it was his only defense against the humidity. He had a gin and tonic in a glass tumbler next to him, the glass coated in condensation on the outside and carbonation on the inside. It was the perfect time for sleuthing.

Except I have no idea what I'm doing.

He wrote down HYPOTHESIS on one side of the yellow paper. Under it, DR. REED WAS MURDERED.

Under that he wrote WHY?

Under that he didn't write anything else.

He frowned. This would have to get filled in later.

He wrote down ALTERNATE HYPOTHESIS on the other side of the page.

Under that he wrote I AM JUST LOSING MY SHIT.

Frowning, he leaned back in his chair. Maybe he wouldn't fill that one in yet either.

Ino signed. "Okay, I'm getting nowhere. What do I do when I'm stuck on a research project?" He frowned. "Consider the known variables."

He flipped to a new page and wrote down INFORMATION.

When had it started? He pictured Sean Murphy standing ten feet away from him in the Baker hallway, all the blood draining from the husky's face as he caught sight of something through the glass window of a metal lab door.

Ino shook his head, shaking off that image.

No, it hadn't been then. It had been half an hour earlier.

"Jesus, I completely forgot," Ino rumbled. Slipping his bare paws back into his slippers, Ino padded away from the table and retrieved his cellphone.

He opened the message icon and sat back down.

Rufus Reamer	bro u idiot call me lol	4:55 pm
21525	Automated Message: INO, your RX i…	11:21 am
Mom	thx u 2 sweetie	7:07 am
Novi	Let me know if u want to talk. Miss u…	May 14
Formalwear Outlets	TODAY ONLY: extra 30% off clearance, $29…	May 13
Alan S	OK, let us know if you need anyth…	May 12
Wolf From Gym	glad your ok !! see u soon	May 12
Cain Seward	CALL ME PLS I JUST SAW YOU ON THE NE…	May 12
+1-219-555-5000	Santiago ALERT: All clear issued fo…	May 11
ETHAN REED	No Subject)	May 11
+1-847-550-2145	dr. Reamer its Maddie i lost my syllab…	May 10
Unknown Number	You w0n a FREE! 1phone X! click here…	May 10

Ino opened up the message from Dr. Reed. As previously, there was nothing in it. The screen opened up white and nothing further appeared.

On the legal pad he wrote:

DR. REED ATTEMPTED TO SEND ME SOMETHING. SENT EMPTY MESSAGE INSTEAD.

He checked the timestamp. 5:41 pm.

He stared at the phone. Jack had said Reed had been dead at the time the explosion happened. Assuming he was telling the truth.

Ino frowned. That… didn't seem right.

He picked up his pen again and started writing down times.

5:41 PM. REED MESSAGES ME.
5:45-ISH. SEAN SHOWS UP FOR HIS FINAL (EARLY) (THINKS HE'S LATE) (HUSKY BRAIN)

He knew that one off the top of his head. He'd commented on the specific time after reading it off his watch. 5:46 pm.

When had the explosion been? They had walked to Sean's final but at a pretty good pace.

He knew that one, too. The campus bell tower had started ringing at 6:00 pm, right as they were walking up the steps.

6:00 PM. ARRIVE AT BAKER.

And how long had they been inside the building? Not long. And yet what a time it had been. It felt like it had taken an eternity, but it also had felt like ten seconds.

He thought about it. Sean had smelled the gas almost immediately — fortunately, thank God for sensitive husky noses — and they had run straight to the lab with Reed in it. Realistically, the whole thing had probably taken only two or three minutes.

So that left the last event of the timeline.

6:03 PM. REED DEAD.

Ino stared at the pad.

5:41 to 6:03. That was 22 minutes.

22 minutes.

Reed had gone from sufficiently alive to send a text message, to "already dead," in Jack's words. In 22 minutes.

Ino frowned. That didn't seem right. It didn't seem *possible*. How long did it take to asphyxiate? It didn't seem possible that a person could go from awake and alert enough to type on a touchscreen, to demonstrably dead from gas in an autopsy *even after* being blown up, in less than half an hour.

The gears started turning in Ino's mind. What *was* the accident timeframe? Reed sent the text after collapsing, just before passing out, dazed on the floor? Why had he texted Ino instead of calling or texting 911? Was he that disoriented? Was any of that consistent with gas asphyxiation anyway? And how could a room possibly fill with gas that fast from *just one* open jet?

Ino frowned. Or was Reed staring down the barrel of a gun and realized he wasn't getting out of there alive? What if the intended final message had been the identity of the killer?

He swallowed. How did he even know *Reed* sent the message? He could have been dead well before that point. In which case, there was really only one person who might have been on the rhino's phone at the time: the person who had killed him.

His tongue lolling out, Ino shivered. God, he had to tell Jack about this. He couldn't believe he'd forgotten the message, but everything that happened before the explosion felt like days or weeks ago. But it had actually been so close to the incident that it might establish the time of death.

In fact, if Reed truly was the one who sent the message, *it was probably the last thing he ever did.*

Ino's phone idled and went black. Jerking, startled, Ino picked it back up and hurried to close the message. He didn't think he could handle unlocking his phone later and being surprised by Reed's final message as the first thing that appeared.

He backed out of the message to the main screen of the text app.

Staring at it, Ino frowned. He looked at the message above it.

It was the Santiago University shelter-in-place warning. It still had a little orange dot next to it, indicating it was new and unread. Frowning, Ino tapped on it to clear the "new message" flag.

```
6:37 pm SANTIAGO ALERT: All clear issued
for Santiago University and surrounding
area. Do not approach Baker Brown Scnc
Ctr. Do not interfere with emergency work-
ers or law enforcement. Immediate threat
is cleared.
```

```
6:16 pm SANTIAGO ALERT: SHELTER IN PLACE.
Alert remains in place. An unspecified event
is threatening campus.Please shelter in
place NOW.Lock Doors.Turn Off Lights.Stay
Quiet.Wait for All Clear. THIS IS NOT A
DRILL.
```

```
6:09 pm SANTIAGO ALERT: SHELTER IN PLACE.
2nd notification. An unspecified event is
threatening campus.Please shelter in place
NOW.Lock Doors.Turn Off Lights.Stay Quiet.
Wait for All Clear. THIS IS NOT A DRILL.
```

```
6:03 pm SANTIAGO ALERT: SHELTER IN PLACE.
An unspecified event is threatening campus.
Please shelter in place NOW.Lock Doors.
Turn Off Lights.Stay Quiet.Wait for All
Clear. THIS IS NOT A DRILL.
```

Ino looked at the original warning and let out a long sigh. *An unspecified event*, indeed. "I guess they don't have a message template for a building being leveled," he muttered.

Shaking his head, he reached his thumb toward the DELETE button but something caught his eye.

Blinking, Ino stared at the timestamp for the first message.

6:03 pm.

It stuck out.

But why? What was weird about that? 6:03 pm. It was a perfectly normal time.

He frowned. That was fast. He looked back at his notepad. *6:03 pm. Reed dead.*

That seemed… confusing. How could an alert have gone out at the same time the explosion was happening? Maybe he had incorrectly estimated the time they spent in the building. But how could he tell how long that had been?

But wait. He *could* tell.

Excited, Ino padded off and searched until he found his work backpack in the corner. After a few minutes of digging inside, he found his smashed wristwatch.

It had been a cheap watch, a no-frills affair that he had gotten in a mail-order men's fashion box that he had canceled after two months. It had a black band and a black face, with a simple silver bezel holding the crushed glass in place. The watch face looked like a tiny smashed windshield, various shades of white with a jagged triangle dip in the center, where it had obliterated the center post and jammed both hands against the watch face. The watch looked like it had been bashed with a ball peen hammer. Ino's wrist still hurt.

He walked back to the table and held the watch next to his phone. The shelter order text message was timestamped at 6:03:15.

The watch was stopped at 6:04 and 10 seconds.

He stared at the two objects for a long time.

Surely… ?

"That is *impossible*," the hyena said, the sound of his voice sounding out-of-place in his own head.

And yet, the evidence was right in front of him.

Had he really received the lockdown text message almost a full minute *before* the building exploded? He certainly wouldn't have noticed it, busy running for his life. Or possibly still trying to jimmy the lock open to reach the dead rhino.

No, it wasn't possible. What if his watch was just five minutes fast? He vaguely remembered a mismatch with the classroom clock but *none* of the classroom clocks were accurate. Surely someone would have noticed if the explosion had come *after* the campus warning had been issued.

"… *Right?*" Ino asked, no one in particular.

After a moment, he was startled to realize that his house was completely silent.

Shaken, Ino padded silently into the living room. The TV was still on but the picture was pure white. He'd left it on a public access channel, which must have switched off for the night.

His heart pounding, Ino switched to a music channel and filled the house with '90s pop. He disappeared back into the other room. The phone screen had dimmed again, while he was out of the room. Now it was a blank rectangle on the table.

Ino regarded the dead watch and the dark phone.

Surely it was impossible. Someone would have put the pieces together if the explosion had happened *after* the alert had been issued. Right? After all, who could have issued the alert at all if the explosion hadn't happened yet?

Ino felt his blood run cold. "Because you knew there was going to *be* an explosion." What better way to get everyone inside and away from flying debris? Maybe this killer had a conscience.

Ino stared at the two objects for a long time. He picked up the watch and peered at it. Was there anyone nearer to the explosion than he and Sean had been? It was 6 pm on a Friday and most of campus had been closed. Housekeeping was gone for the night. Campus security was too far away to even hear the explosion.

And even if someone *had* noticed the timeline, they would probably have assumed that someone smelled gas and called it in. And why not? That was a perfectly reasonable explanation.

But Ino knew what no one else knew: the only ones around to smell gas were himself, Sean, and the killer. Dr. Reed had already been dead by then.

Shivering, he set the watch back down on the table.

"I think I need to ask Jack Archer who called in the security alert," he said, softly.

Getting ready for bed, Ino thought about the watch. He had suspected foul play for days but presented with the first real indication of something fishy, he felt a newfound sense of urgency. He also felt a newfound sense of being *majorly* creeped out. Shivering, he snuggled under his massive duvet.

This wasn't *really* enough to go on, though. Jack would take days to verify what he had said, verifying eyewitness testimony and looking for physical evidence... assuming he took Ino seriously at all. And what if Ino's watch had just been running fast? He needed something *real*.

Frowning, Ino thought about Dr. Reed. Despite what Vivian had suggested, Reed didn't really have enough of a digital footprint to give Ino any confidence about finding something. Ino might find a publication from 1979 that someone had scanned to an internet archive, but that would be about it. Reed didn't even have a professional portfolio page, let alone a Twitter or a Facebook where he spilled his heart out and broadcast his secrets.

So where did that leave Ino? He knew the man loved keeping dirt on other people. He also knew that Reed was a fastidious note-taker and quite forgetful. He could hear the rhino in his head, muttering in his deep voice. *Better write that down, I'll never remember it otherwise, bleahhhbblblb-blblblbll.* And where were all the things he had written down?

Ino frowned into the dark. They would have been in his office. The contents of which were now stored somewhere in Wong Hall.

Don't do anything illegal, he heard Vivian's voice saying in his head.

The hyena sighed.

He was going to break into the administration building.

Chapter 5: All That Was Left

Wednesday, May 16, 2018

His heart pounding, Ino turned his Jeep onto campus. The weather was gorgeous. After a few cooler days, it was starting to warm up again — the temperature was in the high 80s, hot and windy, not too humid, with huge gusts of dry wind blasting across the prairie.

It was a beautiful day for a felony.

This is dumb this is dumb this is dumb this is dumb he thought, as he rolled into a parking space in front of his office. Ino's only mode of transportation was a two-seater Jeep Wrangler Sport that he had bought from one of his youngest brother's little gay hipster friends, when he had moved from the humid hellscape of northern Florida to the snowy hellscape of northern Indiana. The car was eight years old, bright yellow, and small and uncomfortable, plus it ran like a 30-year-old dump truck. About half the dashboard warning lights were lit at any given time (which *specific* lights were on varied seasonally, and with use), and none of his colleagues understood why he even kept it. Ino loved it.

Unfortunately, it was also a shade of bright yellow that could only be described as "fluorescent," so if Ino was going to use it to do crime he would need to park it far, far away from the action.

Ergo, he parked at his office and hoofed it the quarter-mile or so to the administration building. It was still roastingly hot out so Ino was already lightly sweating by the time he got to Wong Hall. His various wounds had finally stopped actively bleeding, so he had been able to dress seasonally — khaki golf shorts and a lime-green polo. It wasn't exactly camouflage, but it was *one of* the greens in camouflage, so Ino was hoping it was somewhere at the index of sneaky and fashionable and he could skate by.

Coming up to the building, Ino stared at the front door. There was probably a security camera there. Maybe he should go around back.

Creeping along the side wall to the back entrance, he slipped along, looking for the big double doors Jack had used the previous day. At least he was behind a line of hedges and several tall trees, and behind the outcropping of foliage he wouldn't be seen. It had come in handy when he had been trying not to throw up after attempting to start smoking again.

His muzzle wrinkled up. Actually, it kind of smelled like smoke *now*. He got to the well-hidden back doors in the shade of several large trees.

He frowned. Next to the back door was an ancient trash can, so old that it had an ashtray built into the top of the can cover. Inside the ashtray was a single cigarette butt. It was still smoking.

"Jesus, that was close timing," Ino muttered.

"*What* was close?" demanded a loud voice behind him.

"*ARP!*" Ino yelped, leaping a foot off the ground. He crashed back to the ground and whirled around.

Leaning against a tree and staring at him was a 6'4" badger, in a white shirt with a narrow black tie. It was the unfriendly guy from the Accounting department. He was an American badger, tall and stocky, with jagged face stripes and a pissed-off expression. He had slicked-back hair, broad shoulders and a well-established paunch. He looked to be in his early fifties.

The badger watched him, unimpressed, flicking a lighter and lifting it up to another cigarette in his jagged badger muzzle.

"Jesus! Nothing!" Ino snapped, his heart pounding. "What are you doing back here in the bushes?"

The badger raised one eyebrow, holding up his cigarette.

Ino swallowed, snorting. "Right. Of course. You should quit. Those things'll kill ya."

The badger rolled his eyes. "Oh, really? I've never heard that before. Thanks for the hot tip."

Ino turned to slip through the back door, paused, and glanced back at the badger. He thought of the stale pack of cigs he'd crumpled out and thrown into this very trash can the other day.

What the hell. He'd been seen already.

He turned back. "Actually, could I bum one of those?"

The badger stared at him, raising an eyebrow. "Seriously? What are you, sixteen?"

Ino narrowed his eyes. "I don't have any. I quit a year and a half ago."

The badger stared at him, horrified. "Well, don't *start* again! I been tryin' to quit for twenty years!"

Ino wrinkled his muzzle. "It's been a rough couple of weeks."

The badger grunted, irritated. "Here. Take a drag off this." He stretched his hand out toward Ino with the lit cigarette he was smoking.

The hyena stared at him, irritated, before finally deciding that was better than nothing. He reached for the smoking cigarette, stuck it in his mouth, and took a long drag.

"*Whurrhurrhurrhurrrghhh!*" he coughed, doubling over. He spent a few long minutes coughing before raising himself up, his head spinning while he tried to maintain consciousness.

When his vision finally cleared, he found the badger grinning savagely down at him.

"*Hurk!*" Ino grunted, spitting into the bushes. He wiped his mouth with the back of his hand. "You knew that was going to happen."

The badger grinned, showing his teeth. "Just remember that. *Don't* start up again, you moron. This shit'll kill you."

Ino sighed. "I suppose that's the best advice I'm going to get today." He looked around. "God, I hope nobody saw that."

The badger chuckled darkly. "Just me."

Ino nodded, and let out a long sigh. He resisted the urge to glare at the badger. "Well, uh, thanks for the... help." He turned around and reached for the back door.

"Say... you're in the Biochem department, aren't you? Did you work with that Reed asshole?" came the badger's deep voice behind him.

Ino froze in mid-reach for the door handle. He turned to look over his shoulder, his eyes wide.

The badger stared darkly at him, lifting his cigarette to take a long drag, holding it for a moment and then blowing it out his nostrils like a steam locomotive. The man had dark eyes, and just for a second he angled his head so his eyes caught the light of the flame and reflected subtly green. He didn't wait for Ino to answer. "You know, he made our staff accountant quit."

Ino lowered his hand, turning to face the badger, still not quite sure if this conversation was really happening. "Wh… what?"

The badger lifted the cigarette for another drag. "Real nice girl. In her twenties, right out of college. Graduated from Santiago just last year." He exhaled as he talked, a puff of smoke accompanying every word. The badger took another long drag. "I guess her father wasn't quite all the way documented. You know? Reed found out, and while he was dropping off an expense report… *happened* to bring that up in conversation." He spat into the bushes on one side. "You know. As one does."

Ino stared at him in shock. He didn't know what to say.

The badger snorted. "Guess she took it as a threat. She put in her notice the next day." He exhaled two last gigantic puffs of smoke and dropped the smoking cigarette next to the trash can with the ashtray in it. "Been gone almost six months now."

"Jesus Christ," Ino said, slowly.

The badger chuckled darkly. "Yeah, I would call that an appropriate reaction." He put his arms over his head and stretched, and Ino saw the older man's shirt strain against a considerably thick and muscular hide. The badger wasn't a bodybuilder but Ino sure wouldn't want to fight him. "I was going to have a word with the good Dr. Reed but…" He smiled grimly. "Guess I didn't get the chance."

Ino nodded dumbly. "Uhhhh," he said. "Guess not."

The badger flashed a toothy smile and slipped past Ino. The hyena stepped aside to make room. Even though he was huge, the badger moved perfectly silently.

As the badger put one huge hand on the door handle and heaved it effortlessly open, he glanced back over his shoulder. "I know you're in the same department, so… I hope you won't make the same mistakes Dr. Reed did."

Ino felt his eyes widen. "Noooo, *sir*," he said, emphatically.

The badger grinned humorlessly. "Good to hear. That probably bodes a lot better for you than it did for him."

Dumbly, Ino nodded.

The badger nodded back. "Have a good rest of your day, Dr. Reamer!" he said, cheerfully, and then he disappeared into the building.

Ino shivered as he crept down the hallway of the admin building. He wasn't nervous anymore. Nothing that had been in Dr. Reed's office could possibly be more terrifying than what had just happened. Did he even need to look at the office contents anymore? The badger was definitely *Prime Suspect Number One*. Ino briefly considered just yapping his way straight into Jack Archer's office, but decided that due diligence demanded he at least have a passing look at Dr. Reed's displaced belongings.

He theorized about where, exactly, that might be. Susan had said inside Wong Hall, but hadn't specified where. Theoretically there were storage areas all over the building, but if Wong was anything like Hagerman or the SU Center for the Arts, there would be a series of large storage cages in the basement behind tall chain-link walls. Ino hoped they would be the kind of walls that stopped two feet from the ceiling, and he could just wriggle his way over and down into the cage where Reed's things were being kept.

Padding lightly through the building, past rows of single-occupant offices and big glass-walled student assistance areas, Ino located a stairwell and slipped through the heavy wooden door. He descended down the concrete steps, trying to be quiet but look normal at the same time.

The basement didn't look any different from the upstairs, more concrete walls with old '70s-style wooden doors lit by bright fluorescent lights, but it just *felt* like a basement. There was a lot less airflow down here and it smelled a little damp. Plus there were occasional random items just parked in the hall — an ancient metal fan on a tall post here, a pile of metal chairs there. The basement was definitely used for storage and not offices.

Ino passed two restrooms that probably hadn't been updated since 1978, slipped through a set of large metal doors, and found himself in a series of storage cages.

Frowning, he looked around. Everything smelled old and musty. He could see through the chain-link walls, and it looked like mostly classroom supplies. There were three entire cages full of elementary-school-style stacking metal-and-plastic chairs. Another cage was filled floor to ceiling with plastic storage tubs, but there were also a few signs for student organizations. Ino saw a storage unit for Alliance that he hadn't even realized belonged to them, even though he was faculty advisor for the group — there was a yellowing posterboard that said ALL ARE WELCOME AT

ALLIANCE! with a bunch of pictures that couldn't have been from later than 2002.

He frowned. He didn't see anything of Reed's.

After looking around for a frustrated moment, Ino saw another set of metal double doors. The last doors Ino had gone through had big glass windows in them, crisscrossed with metal reinforcement. These doors were solid, gray-painted steel.

Frowning, Ino reached for the handle. He expected it to either hold fast, or to activate an ear-splitting burglar or fire alarm.

Neither happened. The heavy door opened with a *clunk*. Surprised, Ino slipped through it.

He entered a short concrete hallway with crisp white cinderblock walls. This hallway was cool and dry. It felt considerably more climate-controlled. There were a series of gray metal doors in the wall, and then the hallway turned around a corner.

The first door had a window in it. Ino stuck his muzzle up to the glass.

It was a storage room, about 10 by 10. There were a half-dozen pieces of large framed artwork, and some kind of huge statue under a white sheet.

Ino furrowed his brow. It took him a moment to remember that there was an art museum on campus, in the Center for the Arts. This must be overflow storage.

He looked around. So this was high-value storage.

Walking down the hallway, Ino glanced at the doors. There were eight of them, only one of which had a window, and then another big gray door at the end of the hall. That door said MAINTENANCE, NO ADMITTANCE. Ino frowned. Up until this point, he could plausibly say that he was just wandering around, or exploring, or looking for a room. If he went past *that* door, his plausible deniability evaporated.

Ino turned and walked back down the hallway. Might as well check here then.

Each of the doors had a quarter-inch gap at the bottom. Listening intently for the door at the end of the hall to swing open, Ino got down on his hands and knees and peered under the metal. Frowning, he turned on his phone flashlight and pushed it close to the floor.

The first room had a ton of file boxes. Ino couldn't make out any of the words but they looked very old. The second room was empty. The third room had a bunch of old boxes and a dressmaking form, which scared the shit out of Ino until he realized it wasn't *actually* a person.

The fourth room was impossible to make out, except for the bottom two inches of a rolled rug. Ino recognized the pattern.

Ino gasped.

He tried the doorknob, shaking the handle up and down. Nothing. It was locked.

He stared at it. *Well, that was a short trip.*

He frowned. So close.

It was time for Plan B.

Ino had to go back up to the main floor to execute the second part of his plan.

He found the maintenance office off one of the side hallways. It was really more of an ambitious broom closet, crammed into a corner between the south restrooms and a loudly-chugging room which Ino assumed must contain the HVAC equipment.

The door was open. Ino stuck his head in and found the maintenance man.

He was a lion, probably in his late thirties, in thick gray work slacks and a blue short-sleeved button-down work shirt. The big cat had two enormous paws — *bare* paws — lifted up onto a huge old metal desk. He was leaning way back in an ancient wheeled desk chair, watching something on a cellphone. As Ino watched, the lion snickered loudly, his big shoulders shaking and his fat toes curling over.

The dude was pretty hot, but Ino couldn't get over the bare feet. The lion had tawny paws and baby-pink paw pads.

"Seriously?" Ino said, loudly.

"*Waaareowr!*" the lion yowled, jerking in shock and tipping precariously back on his chair. He dropped his feet to the floor and waved his arms frantically, crashing back onto the front wheels. Wide-eyed, he stared at Ino. He had a big bushy mane and long hair tied back into a short bun. His tail lashed agitatedly behind him.

Ino tried to keep the smile off his face. "Keeping busy?"

The lion scowled at him for a moment, and then softened and chuckled. "Sorry!" he said, loudly. "Didn't even know anybody else was here!" He reached under his desk and pulled out a pair of enormous tan work boots, which he industriously worked to stuff his huge feet into.

Ino raised an eyebrow and chuckled. "You have a whole Accounting department right down the hall!"

The lion grunted. "Yeah, but you keep them in coffee and toilet paper and they never even leave their corner." He looked up at Ino and grinned, roughly tying the laces of his boots. "Help you with something?"

Ino blinked at him, feeling his face heat up, and then let out a sigh. "I hope so. It's kind of a weird request."

The lion blinked at him, and then grinned broadly. He had blue eyes and an easy, endearing smile. "That's fine. Already sounds better than what I been doin.'"

Ino felt his face heat up a little more, for a slightly different reason. The lion was… super hot. The hyena cleared his throat. "Uhh, okay. So. I'm sure you heard about Dr. Reed."

The lion nodded. "The building exploding was kind of hard to miss."

Ino nodded. "Right. I know Dr. Reed's office got emptied out. I think all of his stuff is here, down in one of the storage rooms. I was wondering if I could… get access to his things."

The lion's eyes widened.

Ino grimaced. "I know. It's horrible. But he borrowed — he *was borrowing* — a book of mine when he died. We worked together, you see." He paused a moment. "I'm Ino Reamer. I work in the Chemistry department." He reached forward with one hand.

The lion reached up and shook his hand firmly, grinning his dazzling grin. "Doug Miller." He angled a thumb over his shoulder at a wall of tools and cleaning supplies. "Maintenance."

Ino laughed. "So I figured."

The lion winked at him. "I could tell you were a smart one."

Ino definitely felt himself blush. Was the lion flirting? Ino hadn't counted on this. "Anyway, uhhhh, this book, it was…" He coughed, trying to remember his cover story. "It's very old. A first edition. I had borrowed it from another professor. I'm worried if I have to request it from Security, it'll take months to get it back." He paused. "I was hoping you could let me in to just… take it."

The lion blinked at him, and then grinned at him conspiratorially. "How 'bout *that!* You aren't as innocent as you look." His big tail flicked back and forth behind him. His eyes twinkled.

Ino felt his ears heat up too.

"Well, ain't nobody supposed to go in *that* storage room," the lion rumbled. "But since you worked together and all…" The lion lifted himself to his feet, grabbing at his desk for an enormous pile of keys with a ring buried somewhere therein. He clipped it to his belt. "Let's go, Professor Reamer. I think I can make an exception."

The lion led him toward the storage area without further pomp or circumstance. Ino looked the lion over as they walked. He was a big man, taller than Ino by four or five inches, thick with muscle — triceps and lats that showed even through the thick fabric of his shapeless work shirt. Ino surreptitiously snuck a look at the lion's rump, too, and found that the big cat was definitely not skipping leg day. He even smelled good.

Ino swallowed. This had not been part of the plan.

The lion clumped his way down the stairs and down the hall, headed right for the storage unit that Ino had found.

The big cat glanced up at him. "How did you know this stuff was even down here?"

Ino smiled vacantly back. "I think one of the workers mentioned it when they were moving everything?" he lied. "My office is right across the hall."

Doug nodded somberly back at him. "Did you know him very well?"

Ino grimaced. "Yeah, I would say so. We worked together for many years."

The lion nodded. "Sorry for your loss."

Ino smiled back awkwardly. "Thanks," he said, not sure what else to say.

Finally, they turned the corner to the climate-controlled hallway.

"Here we are!" Doug announced, his big voice booming in the small space. "You want some help in there?"

Ino stared at him for a moment. "Uhhhhhhhh, no, actually!" he said, loudly. He thought furiously for a moment and lowered his voice. "I would, uh, actually prefer to be alone." He nodded with his best impression of somberness. "I'm feeling quite… emotional."

The lion blinked, and then nodded at him. "A'course. I'm sorry to hear that."

Ino stared back at him, not sure what else to say. Maybe nothing?

The lion stood awkwardly for a moment, his tail lashing behind him, and then cleared his throat. "Right, well then, let's get you in there." He took an enormous keyring off of his belt and began flipping keys.

Ino exhaled. *Whew.*

"Anyway, just don't tell anybody I let you in here," the lion rumbled, finally selecting a key and aiming it at the door. He pushed it forward into the keyhole. "I could get in serious —"

Before he turned the key, *or* the knob, the door made a loud *clunk* and creaked open a few inches. A wide band of darkness was visible inside the room.

"… trouble," the lion finished, slowly.

They both stared at it.

"Uhhhhhh," Ino said. "Was it unlocked?" *It wasn't when I tried it five minutes ago,* he thought.

The big lion frowned at it. "I don't *think* so." He reached down for the handle and tried to turn it just like Ino had. It refused to even budge. "I don't think it's unlocked *now,*" the lion said, baffled. "It looks like it was locked but the latch wasn't engaged all the way."

Ino stared at him.

Wide-eyed, Doug pushed the door the rest of the way open. Cautiously, he reached in and flicked on the light.

There was nothing in the room but a rolled-up rug, a few stacks of furniture, half a dozen bookshelves, and dozens and dozens of boxes.

The lion grinned winningly down at him. "Don't worry, Dr. Reamer — nobody in here!"

The hyena chuckled. "Good to hear. Thanks for checking." *Yeah, but who WAS in here, before me?* he thought. "And please, call me Ino."

The lion blinked at him, and then grinned. There was something predatory about it. Like, in a good way. "Awesome. And hey… come and see me on your way out, huh?" he said, smiling a big dopey grin. "I'll need to lock it up. And it *is* the summer… it's nice to have company."

Ino froze, a grin plastered on his face. *Oh God, he's definitely flirting.* What was he supposed to say to that?

"Will do, haha!" he said, awkwardly. "Maybe I can… show you my book." *OH GOD, I'm flirting BACK!*

The lion blinked at him a moment, and then grinned a devilish grin. "Sounds *amazing*, doc," he said, and winked. "See ya soon." Then he was gone.

Shaking his head, Ino let out a shaky breath. *What the hell was THAT?* he thought. Landing a huge blue-collar lion was not part of the plan. He was researching a murder here.

Well… a *possible* murder.

He thought of the big maintenance lion one more time. He hadn't been wearing an undershirt. He probably looked pretty good shirtless. Maybe he *should* be part of the plan.

Shaking his head clear of *that* thought, Ino turned to the door behind him. He checked the doorknob to make sure it was unlocked, and then checked to make sure the latch was fully engaged, so it wouldn't suddenly swing open and scare the shit out of him.

He had to push against the door hard from the inside before it would finally click. No wonder it hadn't latched properly. But that was only part of the mystery — the real question was, who had been in this storage unit before him?

He didn't think the movers or the administration would be so careless as to leave the door without checking it. So somebody else had possibly snuck down here. Somebody high-ranking or connected enough to get access to the room.

Ino turned to examine the large piles in the storage room.

There was a massive quantity of cardboard boxes — all file-size, all the same beige cardboard. They were carefully labeled in permanent marker, stacked in piles six boxes high against the back wall, in the left corner. In the right corner were several large wooden bookcases which Ino remembered seeing in Dr. Reed's office. The room smelled like old books and dust.

Ino stared for a moment. This was all that was left of Dr. Ethan Reed at Santiago University.

He shook his head. How sad.

Okay. Where to start.

First, in case he was interrupted, Ino needed to establish his cover story. He went to the pile of file boxes and read the labels. There were at least two dozen boxes in the front row and all the ones he could see were simply labeled "BOOKSHELF."

Ino took the box off the top one, and was hit with a wave of book dust and mildew smell. He poked through until he found a suitably-old-looking tome. It was called *Elements of Modern Chemistry*, by Charles Adolphe Wurtz, and it looked about a hundred years old. At the very least, the name "Adolphe" hadn't been popular in *any* form in at least a few decades, so the hyena decided the book was suitably aged. He fished it out of the box and tucked it under his arm.

He looked in the rest of the box. There were a few dozen books, a carved stone figure, and a decorative glass bowl. Ino frowned.

The last non-book item in the box was an ancient-looking clay vase. It had a fresh chip cracked out of the rim, which it had definitely not been sporting the last time he had seen it on Dr. Reed's bookshelves. *Ethan would be so upset*, he thought, and to his surprise he found himself overcome with sadness.

The hyena looked through four more boxes labeled "BOOKSHELF" before he decided he wasn't getting anywhere.

He thought for a moment. What was the plan? He'd been so preoccupied with getting in here that he hadn't really thought the rest through. So what was he expecting to find?

Reed liked secrets and he was *not* shy about confrontation. Since he had no close family or friends, and a random assailant probably wouldn't go to the trouble of blowing up an entire academic building, the most likely avenue to pursue was someone that he had pissed off.

Assuming the offending party had been stupid enough to send threatening emails, phone messages, or another electronic format, Jack and the rest of the security team would probably track them down pretty quickly. If not, the killer might have sent threatening letters — and the only way to do that anonymously would be a physical piece of paper.

He thought for a moment. It was a long shot but it was the only thing he could think of. He pictured a letter made out of letters from cut up magazines. "YoU'rE fINisHed, ReEd!" Did people still do that? He frowned.

Looking around, he tried to gauge where the contents of Reed's desk would be. That would have been the last thing Reed was working on. It would be the most recent, and therefore a decent place to start.

He poked around until he found a box that said DESK.

The first box was full of office supplies, most of which had been relegated to the outbox of history. Ino found a cast-iron three-hole punch and a pad of sticky notes that said "FAX CONFIRMATION." He found three bottles of correction fluid and an envelope adhesive moistener. Staring into space, he tried to remember the last time he had sent a physical letter, let alone a *fax*.

The next box had a bunch of top-of-desk items as well as a pile of papers. Inside it was a keyboard, a laptop docking station, a mousepad that was at least twenty years old yet still somehow smelled noticeably of rubber, and a few other items.

Bingo! Ino pulled the box out and set it on the top of Reed's desk.

The box was full to bursting. Something glinted in the dim lighting. Ino reached in to fish it out.

He hefted out a three-pound glass half-globe and held it in his hands. *SANTIAGO UNIVERSITY: CELEBRATING 100 YEARS.* It was a monster anniversary paperweight like the one that President Greeley had given him. But he'd only gotten it the previous day — and Susan Greeley had pulled it right out of the shipping box for him. When had she given this one to Reed? His things had been sitting here in storage since Sunday. And Ino hadn't yet seen another one in the entire school yet.

Shaking his head, he put the glass paperweight back. The light refracted through it, and cast a rainbow beam onto a red-leather bound book.

Ino's eyes widened. It was a date book.

Dr. Reed had not been computer-savvy — he swore his Outlook calendar was out to get him. Everything was liable to be in his paper calendar.

Ino pulled it out and flipped to the 11th, the day of the explosion.

At the bottom, the last entry was written in red pen. *LAST FINAL*, it said. Ino winced. "Ugh," he whispered. "That's a bit on the nose," he muttered.

The other appointments were:

9:10: BIO 415. The slot was blocked out for two hours. That would have been a final exam.

12-1 was blocked out, presumably for lunch.

1:30 CALL

There was only one more appointment: 4:00: S.G.

Ino scrunched up his nose. S.G? What was that?

He looked down at the paperweight. "Susan Greeley?" he whispered, out loud.

He kept digging, emptying things out onto the desk as he went.

There was no computer, and there was no cellphone. Ino wondered if Reed had brought them to the lab. He didn't remember seeing either of them, but of course, the last time he'd been in Baker he had been a little bit... otherwise occupied.

At the bottom of the box was a stack of papers.

Eyes widening, Ino swallowed. If there was a clue to be found, it was probably in this pile.

He hefted out the stack of papers. On the top was a heavily-marked exam. Underneath that was a syllabus, and under that was a pile of 10 or 15 pieces of mail, all the same kind of crap that Ino got.

Invitations to paid conferences, ads, etc., most of which went into the trash unopened. The pile was huge, but Ino flipped through, looking at every document.

On the bottom, he found something that looked very out of place. It was a printout of a computer program screenshot. Ino frowned. That was strange in and of itself. And it certainly didn't look like anything related to chemistry or genetics. He held it up and read the header.

JOURNAL ENTRY		1/8/18
ACCOUNT	DEBIT	CREDIT

There was a lot more under that but it didn't make a bit of sense to Ino.

"*Journal entry?*" he whispered. "Isn't this an accounting document?" He frowned. What the hell was Reed doing with something like this?

He looked over the document but it was all just account names and numbers. He frowned. It didn't mean anything to him but it still looked out of place.

Frowning, he swung his backpack around to his chest and slipped the document inside, between his laptop and his stolen legal pad.

Turning back to the cabinet, he flipped through the rest of Reed's paperwork. He didn't find anything else that appeared to be remotely significant.

Straightening up, he frowned. Not exactly the smoking gun he had been looking for. He puzzled for a moment.

Reed printed *everything*. There must be something else floating around in the office.

Ino raised himself up and looked around until he spotted Reed's file cabinet, towering over the sea of file boxes like a rocky outcropping on a sandy beach. It was a massive metal file cabinet, probably from the '60s or '70s, and it appeared to have been moved directly from Reed's office without having been emptied. That must have been a feat since the cabinet itself probably weighed 200 pounds.

Ino waded over to the cabinet and tugged open the top drawer. Peering inside, his eyes widened.

Dr. Reed had his files neatly organized by class and topic. Apparently *all* of his files were paper, because there were dozens upon dozens of them. Ino scanned the headers.

GEN 101, GEN 102, GEN 202, GEN 203, GEN 203-L, GEN 210, GEN 215. Genetics classes.

BIO 204, BIO 204-L, BIO 300, BIO 405, BIO 505, BIO 505-L, BIO 510, BIO 510-L. The higher-ranking Bio classes and labs. Reed had left the lower-level 100 classes almost exclusively to Ino. He hadn't taught any of the 200s in years and the 100s weren't even in the file cabinet anymore.

ANA 101-300, HCL 101, PHYS 101, 300 and 500. EVS 100-400. MCR, ORG CHEM, INORG CHEM. Ino could hardly believe how many classes Reed had taught in his tenure at Santiago. He opened the rest of the drawers to check. There were probably 40 files in each drawer and every drawer was full.

He stared. This… was going to take a while. If Reed had anything good and it was just hiding in a specific folder, Ino would never find it.

He went back to the top drawer and scanned the tabs: GEN, BIO, HCL, ANA, PHS...

HCL 101. Frowning, the hyena stopped at that one.

HCL? What the hell was HCL? Ino knew the abbreviation HCL, which was *very* familiar to him, but not as a class. To Ino, HCL was *hydrochloric acid*, a very common and — despite popular belief — fairly harmless solvent. It was used in a lot of experiments, included in most anything that required a fairly robust dissolving agent. But it wasn't a *class*.

He thought of the pictures on Reed's wall. One of them had been made up of two molecules — Hydrogen and Chlorine.

Hydrogen Chloride. Hydrochloric acid.

He stood there a moment and frowned. Were they related?

Swallowing, Ino pulled out the file folder. It had only one piece of paper in it.

He read it.

Frowning, Ino stared at it. It wasn't a class document, or even related to chemistry, but it still didn't make any sense:

It was a form, an internal Santiago form. It said VENDOR REGISTRATION FORM in all caps at the top, under the Santiago logo. Underneath that, the form read NEW VENDOR REGISTRATION: FILL OUT ALL FIELDS.

There was a business name written in. *Triton Landscaping, LLC.* It was a semi-local address, way out south of Route 30, out in the sticks. Ino didn't recognize the business. But then, he had never paid much attention to the landscaping trucks on campus. There was a signature at the bottom but it looked like just a scribble — Ino couldn't make it out.

He frowned. What did this mean? And why did Reed hide it? Ino recognized it as an accounting document — another one! Should he take it out and march upstairs and ask them to explain it? He thought of the badger upstairs and frowned. Maybe not. He slid the form into his bag, next to the other one.

Ino pondered. He'd found two unusual documents, and they might actually be clues. In any case, the vendor form was something Reed had intentionally hidden. And the key to find it had been hung on the wall — a literal sign, except only someone in the field would have noticed it.

Ino narrowed his eyes. There had been two more molecules up on the wall.

He looked around for the other pictures.

It took a little time, but he finally found all three huge 20" by 30" posters pushed behind Reed's desk. They had been shoved behind the filing cabinet with a few other large framed photos.

The top one was Hydrogen Chloride. Hydrochloric acid. He'd already found that one.

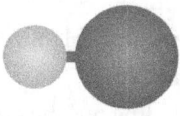

The next one was a little more complicated.

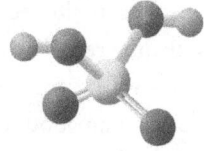

Ino stared at it. The two little guys were probably Hydrogen again. Hydrogen was a tiny element and was commonly drawn as such.

H_2, something, something 4.

He stared at it and a rhyme popped into his head. He groaned. It was an old chemistry joke — very old, like "19th century" old.

Our Willie passed away today
His face we'll see no more
For what he thought was H_2O
Proved H_2SO_4.

H_2SO_4. Two Hydrogen, 1 Sulfur, 4 Oxygen.

"Sulfuric acid," he said out loud. Another common lab solvent — and, even though it looked exactly like water, H_2O, would prove harmful or fatal to drink. Hence the joke. Ino shook his head.

Turning back to the cabinet, Ino started looking again.

He finally found something under HSO-24. Again, not a class.

He pulled out another file folder that contained only a single document, a small stack of stapled papers. Another clue! He slid it out of the folder.

THE FLORIDA STATE UNIVERSITY, said the letterhead. It looked instantly familiar to him.

Ino blinked at it, eyes widening. He had worked at FSU. He checked the date in the top right corner. 2012.

"You have GOT to be kidding me," he groaned. He scanned lower.

INVESTIGATION OF DATA FALSIFICATION CHARGES AGAINST DR. REAMER, AND THREATS AGAINST STUDENT, NAME WITHHELD.

"Reed, you insane bastard," he whispered, his voice shaking. He looked over the document. He hadn't ever actually seen a copy of it before. "Great," he mumbled, feeling his ears turning red. "I've now *proved* my *own* motive." He didn't even want to keep it — if he got caught, this document on his person would do a lot more harm than good. Ino decided it was better off where it had been. He stuck it back in the folder, stuffed the folder back in the cabinet, and comforted himself with the fact that Security probably wouldn't have an extensive knowledge base of chemistry jokes from the late 1800s.

Swallowing hard, Ino turned back to the third picture. He stared at it for a long time.

This one was just as tricky, and no helpful rhymes popped to mind.

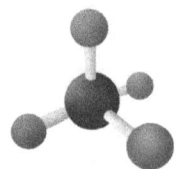

Frowning, Ino stared at it. "How do I decode THIS?" he thought. "Ugh, this is like one of my stupid test questions."

He frowned. The other two had been common lab solvents. This was probably another "chemistry professor" joke. But this was probably not a liquid. The tiny molecules were probably Hydrogen again, and with four of them it was probably *super* reactive.

He stared at it. "What has Hydrogen combined with a stable element, is extremely reactive, and is relevant to a chemistry lab?"

Eyes widening, he found a chemistry book to confirm his suspicions. METHANE GAS. Lab gas. CH_4. One Carbon, 4 Hydrogens.

Ino wrinkled his nose. That was… unsettling. For the final clue in this weird little creepshow repository, Reed had unwittingly selected the cause of his own death. Under his collar, his neck fur stood on end.

Ino had to check for METHANE, METH, GAS, and CH-4 before he finally found it under LAB/GAS. He had flipped right past it several times and would never have found it if he hadn't been looking specifically for it.

This time it was a photocopy of a newspaper clipping.

EMBATTLED TROOPER OUTPOST SCHEDULED TO
CLOSE DUE TO BUDGET CUTS.

CLEVELAND: Amid strong budget cuts for the 2016/2017 fiscal year, Trooper Outpost 212 is scheduled to close in April of next year, the Ohio State Comptroller announced via press release today.

Outpost 212 was known for a record-breaking drug seizure in April of 2015 worth over 1.4 million dollars, and then again in that year for the subsequent disappearance of a 1kg brick of heroin worth approximately $54,000. The theft from the police station's evidence room remains unsolved.

That last sentence was highlighted. Frowning, Ino read on.

```
The Comptroller Office did not immediately
respond to questions, but did specifically
call out in the press release, "The clo-
sure of Outpost 212 is strictly due to bud-
getary reasons and unrelated to any pend-
ing investigations or failures in outpost
security." This is widely considered to
be the latest jab between the office of the
Ohio Comptroller in their feud with the
Ohio State Troopers, said a source close
to the Comptroller's office.

Twelve employees will be impacted by the
station closure, including outpost com-
mander Sergeant Jonathan Archer.
```

Ino felt his eyebrows shoot up. Jonathan Archer? Jonathan *"Jack"* Archer?!

The document was a Xerox of one corner of a newspaper. Ino looked closer at it. It was from the Cleveland Register, and dated November 11, 2015. That timing was certainly right. It had to be — this was about his station closing… which meant it referred to when he and Travis MacGregor both lost their jobs.

What had Sean said? Budget cuts? Ino frowned down at the clipping. So much for that. An unsolved theft of 54,000 dollars' worth of heroin was a *slightly* different kind of problem.

Ino frowned. But what did it mean? And what the hell was Ethan Reed doing with a photocopy of this article? Did he know something that wasn't printed on this page? What if Travis or Jack weren't just doing a poor job of investigating Reed's murder — what if they were *involved* in the murder in the first place?

Shaking his head, Ino folded up the photocopy and stuck it into his backpack. This one seemed extra-serious so he put it in the little document sleeve behind the computer. He stuffed the now-empty folder back in the drawer.

This was really unsettling. Ino's theory had been that Reed had been killed by someone after revealing he had dirt on that person. Now Ino had a newspaper article about what had to be a felony, and the people most relevant would be the security team investigating the crime. Unless that was just Reed digging for dirt? What if the real clue was the Vendor Form? Or none of it, because the psychotic badger in the Accounting department had clearly just murdered the hell out of Reed and was now going around saying as much?

Frowning, Ino closed the drawers, and put the lids back on top of the boxes. He had come down looking for clues but now he had way too much to even process. How was he supposed to solve this now? It's not like he could just turn everything he had over to Security. *"Hi, I found this while I was breaking into a dead man's belongings. By the way, did one of you kill Reed over a heroin bust? Thanks in advance!"*

Leaving the storeroom, Ino pulled the door shut behind him. He shook it vigorously in its frame, making sure the door was actually closed. He decided to skip speaking to the lion and get back to his house as fast as he could. He had a lot of research to do.

Hopefully I can get out of here without anybody else seeing me, he thought, rushing down the hallway.

He turned the corner in the basement and crashed into a tower of black and tan. *"Awrk!"* he squealed, flinching with his entire body.

The impact felt… familiar.

Ino flinched, gasped, and staggered backward a foot or two.

Standing directly in his path, in full uniform, with an impressively sour expression on his face, was Chief Jack Archer.

Ino stared, wide-eyed, up at the imposing dog.

"Find your book?" the shepherd asked, grinning sadistically.

Ino swallowed loudly.

They sat in Jack's squad car for a long moment. Ino was relieved to find himself in the front seat, instead of the back. Or in handcuffs. Yet.

They were parked behind the administration building, on the other side of the hedges where Ino had encountered the badger. The German shepherd behind the wheel took his time starting the car, answering a radio call, and fussing with a notepad.

Ino decided the dog was waiting for him to talk, and also decided not to give him the satisfaction. He sat in silence, though his heart was pounding.

Finally, the handsome dog looked at him, with a decidedly un-handsome frown on his black muzzle. "Do I even have to *tell* you how much trouble you're in?"

Ino stared at him for a moment, weighing his responses. He should probably say something vaguely conciliatory, while being careful to avoid anything that might sound insulting.

"None, because you've already decided this was a terrible Swiss cheese accident?" he snapped. *Or, you know. I could say THAT.*

Jack stared at him, and then actually laughed. "You know, I've *heard* you don't take any shit, Dr. Reamer, but it's quite another thing to see it in person." His smile faded. "You want to guess again?" he growled.

Ino ignored the question. "Heard from *whom?*" he asked, indignantly.

Jack stared at him, his golden eyes widening. "Not really important right now! Are you *crazy?!* I found you raiding the deceased's belongings during an active investigation! What's the matter with you?!"

Ino felt his face heat up. "I was not satisfied with the impression I got from our meeting."

Jack snorted. "Oh, that's fine, then! Awesome! Have a great rest of your day!" He gestured sarcastically for the door. "Let me know if you need anything else."

Ino narrowed his eyes. "Look, I still think nothing adds up. I didn't find any magical experiment guidelines that use *only* a Bunsen burner and five pieces of empty glassware. And I had forgotten at the time, but Ethan Reed sent me a blank text message the day he died. From right around the time he was dying. Would you like to see it?"

The dog raised his upper lip. "No thanks, we already subpoenaed the phone records." He looked like he was biting back a growl. "Look, Dr. Reamer, you're entitled to think my investigation is bullshit. It happens a lot. I'm used to it. What you are *not* entitled to is felony breaking and entering! What about that idiot maintenance man you conned into letting you in there?" He gestured broadly back at the building. "He could get fired over this!"

Ino leaned forward. "Hey, it's not MY fault you put *the janitor* in charge of the evidence!" He pointed too, though his arm swing was a lot more frenetic. Hopefully nobody was looking at them, watching two yelling people, both wildly waving their arms at an administration building.

Jack scowled back at him. "It doesn't matter who was in charge of it!"

Something occurred to Ino. He sat back in his seat. "Wait a minute, why *would* you keep all this shit in the Admin building?" He frowned. His mental gears started turning again. "I'm sure there's plenty of room in the Security building. It's not like we have anything else going on at this school."

Jack stared at him, perfectly expressionless.

Ino stared back at him, his jaw dropping. "Oh my God, you did this on *purpose!* You left it here so you could see if some idiot would come digging around through his stuff! That's why you showed up so quickly." He flopped back in the seat, gritting his teeth. "Oh my God! It was a *trap!*" He swallowed. "Ugh, and *I* was the idiot that fell for it!"

The shepherd stared at him, his expression betraying nothing. "Dr. Reamer," he said, slowly. "I love the idea — in theory," he said, slowly. "But you know our little Security building is plenty old. We just don't have a gigantic evidence room like city stations." He smiled vacantly back at the hyena. "This was all here *only* because this is where the school had room for it."

Ino stared skeptically at him, frowning. Was he giving the dog way too much credit? Or did Jack Archer have a perfectly-polished "dumb hick cop" facade?

Jack didn't give him the opportunity to decide. "*Anyway,*" the shepherd grunted, "I'm going to let you off with a warning this time. But for God's sake, Dr. Reamer, this is an active investigation. If one of the other officers had found you, we would have to charge you with trespassing at the very least."

Ino sighed. "I know. I'm sorry. I just want to know why this happened."

Jack nodded. "Thank you. I understand." He stared at the hyena a moment longer. "So, did you find anything?"

Ino pondered. Should he tell Jack anything? What if someone on the security team really was behind the murder? Then again, Travis was the one acting weird. And what if it was completely unrelated? Then he would just be withholding evidence. If the Vendor Form was a real clue, Ino might be the reason the killer went free.

Ino frowned at the chief. "I don't know. I'm not sure I should tell you."

Jack grinned broadly. "Great! Whom should we notify that you've been arrested for obstruction of j —"

"Fine, fine," Ino grunted. "Hold on a second." He picked his backpack up off the floor. "Yes, I found something. There were secret files. They were coded to the chemical structure of the molecules in those pictures on the wall." He dug for a moment, ignoring the document pocket with the article about the police station. After a moment he felt Jack's eyes on him and looked up.

The shepherd was staring at him with open-mouthed astonishment. "He had *coded… files…* and the key was *the molecular structure* of the *pictures on the wall?*"

Ino cracked a smile. "Yeah. Kind of felt like a video game." He thought for a moment. "Not a good one, though."

Jack frowned. "How did you know what the molecules were?"

Ino stared at him. "You… *do* understand what I do here, don't you, Chief Archer?"

The dog furrowed his brow. "What did you find?"

Ino swallowed. "Ah, two of them were empty," he lied, "but I did find *this.*" He slid the Vendor Form out of his backpack and passed it over to the dog.

Jack blinked and then scowled. "I wish we'd had a chance to fingerprint that," he grunted. He took the paper and looked at it for a long time.

Ino watched him review the paper. The dog's expression completely changed as he intently studied the document. He looked more like a surgeon working on a patient than an investigator with a random piece of paperwork.

It was very intense and… kind of hot.

Ino looked away, feeling a blush start to creep in.

After a moment, the dog looked up, frowning in bafflement, and the dumb detective was back. "I don't get it. What the hell is this thing?"

Ino sighed. "I have no idea. I know it's a vendor form, but that's all I know. You fill one out when you want the school to hire someone to do some kind of work."

Jack nodded. "I know *that* much. I have to approve these when we get any work done. We had to use a locksmith when we went back to keys for the Security building."

Ino nodded. "Beyond that, I have no idea. I've never heard of Triton Landscaping."

Jack nodded. "I'll look into it." He raised an eyebrow. "Anything else?"

Ino nodded. "Yes. The calendar. Reed had a meeting a couple hours before the explosion. I think with President Greeley." He shrugged. "S.G. But I guess that could be any number of people."

Jack nodded. "Mmm-hmm." He didn't seem surprised.

Ino stared. "You knew that already."

Jack raised an eyebrow. "We DO investigate, Dr. Reamer. Yes, I saw the calendar. Greeley says they didn't have a meeting and her secretary confirmed she didn't leave her office. That could have been anyone, and the meeting could have been canceled, or a call, or an old entry. We'll probably never know."

Ino nodded slowly. "Right, of course." He was silent for a moment. "Anyway, that was it." He wasn't going to cough up the news article and the journal entry from the desk was probably garbage. He was already embarrassed enough.

Jack nodded. "All right. You're cooperating *now* and you did find a lead, but *please* leave the dirty work to us from now on. Okay? I'm not going to charge you with anything."

Ino nodded, still blushing. "Thank you."

Jack stared begrudgingly for a moment. "And nice detective work. Didn't figure you for the Perry Mason type."

Ino cracked a smile. "I'm more of a Jessica Fletcher."

The dog stared him down. "Didn't really care for that show. She always made the cops look like idiots."

Ino opened his mouth to say something, reflexively, and then exercised supremely good judgement and shut it.

Jack's eyes tightened around the edges. The man didn't have crow's feet yet, but Ino had a feeling he might be developing them soon.

After a few moments passed, the dog let out a long sigh. "Thank you, Dr. Reamer. You're free to go."

Ino paused for a moment, thinking of the desktop box. "Actually... there's one more thing."

"What's that, Dr. Reamer?" the dog asked, exasperatedly.

Ino took a deep breath. "Well... there's two things I'm hoping *you* have already. Because I didn't see either one. And if you don't have them, it's pretty suspicious that they didn't turn up in the office."

Jack stared at him blankly. "Nothing from the office has been entered into evidence. What do we not have?"

Besides a kilogram of heroin? Ino thought. "A computer. Or a cellphone."

Jack nodded slowly. "Ahhh. Mmm-hmm." He didn't seem surprised.

Ino leaned forward. "Did you find either one when you searched the explosion site? He never did get his full message off to me. His phone might tell you what he intended to send."

Jack stared at him for a long moment, and then took a deep breath. "All right. I shouldn't have told you anything about the investigation, and I *really* shouldn't show you what I'm about to show you, but... as a show of good faith, I think you need to see something."

Ino swallowed.

The gigantic tent over the explosion site still looked like an outdoor wedding from the outside, if the gift table had exploded and blown big furrows into half of the lawn. Ino felt his ears fold back as they approached it.

"Let me know if this is too much for you," Jack said as they walked down the same path that Ino had walked with Sean. The shepherd's voice had changed. It was softer now. "I'll drive you back to your office afterwards. I saw your car there."

Ino frowned. "How do you know which car is mine?"

The dog chuckled. "That fluorescent yellow thing? It's pretty hard to miss, Dr. Reamer." He cracked a smile, which slowly faded. "Seriously. I know this is probably hard for you."

Ino nodded, clenching his jaw. "It's fine. I have to face this sooner or later." He trailed a few steps behind the dog.

Jack nodded slowly, turning to walk up the path. "All right, here we go."

The entrance to the tent didn't line up with the path, so they had to walk around the side of the tent to get to it. As they stepped into the grass, Ino noticed that the turf was shredded pretty much everywhere, for yards around the building, with torn and yellowed grass billowing up at the edges of the tears like dead skin around a wound. Ino looked up and saw a Santiago University pickup truck parked with rolls of sod in its bed. Glancing back at the pathway, he noticed a lot of the sidewalk repairs were already completed — little irregular patches of new, bright-white concrete dotted the darker sidewalk like hyena spots. The sidewalk was done and they were already starting on the landscaping.

He shook his head as they rounded the corner.

"What's HE doing here?" snarled a loud voice.

Startled, Ino snapped his head up, to see Travis MacGregor blocking their path. The large husky was stuffed into a slightly different uniform, still barely concealing the ugly gash in his head underneath a baseball cap. His ears were tilted aggressively forward and Ino could see his front lip just starting to pull back into a small snarl.

Ino couldn't see the security chief's face, but he thought he saw the dog cock his head in confusion. "Uhhhh, Dr. Reamer has volunteered to assist us in our investigation?"

Travis narrowed his blue eyes at Ino and frowned sourly. "Oh yeah?" he growled. "Says who?"

Now Jack definitely did stiffen. "Says *me*," he snapped, curtly. "Any other questions?"

The shepherd's angry tone finally caught the husky's attention, and he seemed to jolt out of his ire. He glanced sideways at the chief, his ears tilting back, and nodded quickly, scooting out of their way. "'No sir," he grumbled, as they went past, through the white flaps of the tent.

Ino stepped past. Behind him, he heard Jack say "You good, Trav?" but after he saw the sight in front of him he didn't hear the response.

Eyes widening, ears folding back, Ino took in the scene.

The light in the tent was dim, filtering in through gaps in the tent and huge plastic skylights in the roof, made of milky opaque vinyl. There was a ton of visible dust in the air, and each sunbeam lit up a beam of dust as the light struggled to reach the bottom of the tent. The debris had covered a massive range, and someone had clearly bulldozed the piles of building material to fit into the tent, because the shattered building pieces were like giant snow banks made of brick and timbers and huge shredded swaths of insulation. The high sides and the filtered light made it look like a cave, deep below the earth.

Ino stared, his jaw hanging open.

Jack appeared at his side, holding two bright green respirators. "Here," he said. "This building was asbestos age."

Ino nodded, dazed, and slipped a respirator over his muzzle. It had a rubber strap that went behind his head. Jack did the same.

Ino looked around.

As dim as it was in the tent, it was still brighter than it had been the night of the explosion, when Ino had last seen the site. There were bricks, and pieces of bricks, scattered absolutely everywhere, like giant irregular hailstones. But there were also entire walls that had apparently fallen over more or less intact. The roof was in the highest number of pieces — Ino guessed it had been a timber construction, because there were long, thick beams criss-crossing the debris field. In fact, that seemed to make up most of the building material — large wooden planks, bricks, and gigantic ripped pieces of insulation. There was surprisingly little fire damage — restricted to a charred ten-foot circle around where the building's gas main had been, on the east exterior wall. Other than that, it seemed like the gas had ignited and then gone out without burning too much of the debris. Baker had popped like a balloon, blasting the roof straight up in a thousand pieces, and blowing out or knocking over all of the exterior walls.

Ino started walking forward.

"Whoa, whoa, whoa," Jack protested, his voice reverberating weirdly through the mask. "This isn't a sightseeing trip, Dr. Reamer!"

Ino edged away from him. He turned back, scowling. "Oh yeah?" he sneered. "What is it, then?" He waded deeper into the pile, carefully picking his way through the bricks. He still had sidewalk under his feet but after a few moments he came to the stairs.

Jack hustled after him. "I just wanted you to see what we're dealing with!" Jack called after him, as loudly as he could through the mask. "Why we didn't find a computer. Or a phone."

Ino mounted the steps at the front of the building. He had a much better view from up here.

Jack scrambled up the stairs and appeared at his side, glaring. "Look, you see?" he said. He pointed at a twisted and mangled metal frame at their feet. "This is the one of the front doors. That's *welded tube steel*, Dr. Reamer." He stared at him, his golden eyes piercing over the mask. "If this blast did that to pure steel, what do you think it would do to a laptop?"

Ino stared at him. He frowned. "Is *that* why we're here? That doesn't mean anything. The door was the path of least resistance."

Jack stared angrily at him for a moment, and then in confusion.

Ino rolled his eyes and turned. He stared for a moment.

He spied a large buried object on the other side of the building's foundation. It was on the east side, in the opposite direction of where Reed had been. "What's that?" he asked, already starting toward it.

"Dr. Reamer, *please*," Jack grunted, picking his way after the hyena. "This is not safe."

Ino chuckled, carefully balancing on top of the shattered building materials, nimbly climbing onto the side of a caved-in file cabinet. It was like walking on top of a garbage dump. Jack was clearly trying to catch up to him but Ino was a lot faster. "Don't worry, I'm sure the Security team is insured." He came to the object of his interest.

He was on the east side of what had been Baker Brown, the furthest corner from the explosion. This side seemed mostly to have collapsed, rather than being blown into pieces. The roof was still similarly shredded but Ino could see huge segments of brick wall. It looked like they had simply toppled outward.

Several sections were laying on top of what had previously been a late-model Ford Explorer. It was unquestionably a security vehicle, painted black and white with the shattered plastic remnants of a red-and-blue bar light on top. The bright plastic pieces had littered down the roof and the hood of the truck like jagged plastic confetti.

The Explorer was so destroyed it was hard to picture it ever having been functional. It was covered in huge, deep dents on every outer surface. The hood and roof were so smashed that Ino could clearly see the underlying framework, the metal bent around the frame like heat-shrink plastic. Half of the paint was gouged or scraped off, revealing bare gray metal, and the windshield was a great pitted mass of shredded glass, with huge tears in the top of the glass. The whole thing was covered in dust as thick as fallen snow.

The hyena peered inside. The seats were light-tan leather, and both the driver's seat and the passenger seat were covered in blood. In the driver's seat it had pooled in the crease between the seat and the seatback, and dried to a deep shoe-leather brown. There was a massive red-orange smear on the white sill of the driver's door, and long rivulets of dried blood running down the outside of the door, all the way down to the ground. It looked like a prop from a horror movie.

Ino shivered. *Jesus*, he thought.

He turned back to the shepherd. "Was this Travis MacGregor's car?" he asked, grimacing under his respirator.

Finally catching up to him, balancing on top of a dented air-conditioning unit, Jack nodded solemnly.

Ino nodded thoughtfully. "And this car was never moved?"

The dog frowned at him. Ino couldn't see his mouth, but he could still tell. "Does it look drivable to you, Dr. Reamer?"

"Wow. This is *close*." He looked around for some sense of position. The Explorer had obviously been outside the building but it was hard to tell what had been "inside" and "outside." He looked down.

Ino was standing on ten or eleven inches of drywall and insulation, but in the gaps underneath his feet he could make out the thick base of the wall. The base was mostly intact, terminating two or three feet above foundation-level, in a jagged, irregular cutoff, with peaks and valleys like a mountain range. The Explorer was just a few feet away. There was a mangled sign next to the SUV, bent over at a 30-degree angle, reading DO NOT BLOCK, FIRE LANE, one corner bent over and peeled back like the lid of a sardine can.

Ino shook his head. The older husky had been parked right up against the building and the wall had collapsed right on top of his cruiser. He really was lucky to be alive.

Ino turned back to the dog. "Most of your experience with explosions has been with explosive *devices*, right, Chief Archer?"

The shepherd stared at him with surprised yellow eyes. He blinked. "I suppose so," he rumbled loudly, his voice muffled and nasal through the mask. "Depends on your definition of *explosive device*."

Ino nodded. He started off again, picking his way over the top of the debris pile, past Jack in a moment. He was wearing black boots, which he had embarrassingly picked to sneak around in the basement of the admin building, but which were still coming in handy here. He still picked his way carefully through the debris. Large timbers from the roof still remained, but a lot of the roofing material had obviously been cleared away. Ino was mostly climbing over dusty broken bricks, plywood, and insulation. He took off with as much speed as he could muster.

Jack grunted and started after him. "Dr. Reamer!" he called. "Get back here!"

Ino ignored him. "Explosive devices. Like a pipe bomb. A stick of dynamite," he called, as loud as he could be through the respirator. "Something with a chemical trigger. Right?"

Jack scrambled after him. "Yeah, sure," he said. "So what?"

Ino picked his way up to the top of a pile. He figured he was where the main hallway had been. He was probably only five or eight feet up. It was amazing how much Baker had... compressed. "Well, that's a different *kind* of explosion. It's a chemical reaction and a chemical process. That kind of explosion *annihilates* things. It has a small radius with very high concussive forces and most of the things in it are absolutely destroyed." He stopped and turned.

Puffing and straining to keep up with him, the shepherd scrambled after. He glared. "Yep!" he snapped. "Sounds like an explosion, all right!"

Ino frowned. He turned and kept picking his way along where he thought the main hallway had been, and at this point he could occasionally catch glimpses of dirty white vinyl tile through the debris. "But a *gas* explosion is different. The expansive forces are much lesser. It's really a force of *pressure*." He looked over his shoulder.

Jack was closing in on him. The shepherd unclipped his tie, and Ino was startled to see it was a clip-on. Did they all wear fake ties? "What's the difference?!" the dog demanded.

Ino still had a wide lead so he stopped and let out a sigh. "A stick of TNT will pulverize a rock face because the energy it's releasing is exceeded by its ability to dissipate. But a gas explosion doesn't do that — it doesn't release enough energy. It's like inflating a balloon until you pop it — but the balloon was the building. The force is just... expansion."

Now Jack stopped too. He frowned. "That's still an explosion!" he called.

They were about twenty feet apart now, each standing on a peak of a pile of bricks. Ino estimated he was about thirty feet down the hall from Lab 103. This would have been about where Sean took off running.

Ino stared at the dog across the debris field. "Of course it is. But if you pop a balloon because you overinflate it, or you pop a balloon because you *blow it up with a stick of dynamite*, you end up with two very different balloons, you know?"

The dog narrowed his eyes.

Suddenly, Ino's brick pile shifted underneath him. The hyena yelped sharply as his pile of bricks settled underneath him, rattling with a sharp clay-on-clay staccato clacking noise. He flailed his arms and kept his balance, if only barely.

Jack gasped, ears flattening, reaching out, as if he could close the gap.

Ino's pile stopped crumbling, and he settled, holding his arms out. Eyes wide, he watched a number of bricks avalanche down the side of his pile. One of them landed in a pile of already-broken glass, disrupting it with a crash.

Jack's concern melted into anger. "Are you out of your *mind?!*" he demanded.

Ino frowned at him, and then turned. "Possibly." He started picking his way along. "Anyway," he called over his shoulder. "What I was saying earlier — the doors and even the walls were blown out because that's the path the expanding gas took out of the space it was confined in. The gas ignited and expanded to many times its original volume, and as it sought equilibrium of pressure, the structure was a barrier between the gas and the outside air." He straightened up and looked around again. Almost there. "But an object *in* the room wouldn't have been a barrier to exit. The entire lab was equally pressurized — and the ignition of exploding methane couldn't have pressurized the room to more than a few hundred PSI." He turned back to the shepherd.

Jack was further behind now. He was sweating and looked irritated.

"Also — methane is *lighter* than air — so the gas would have collected near the ceiling! It wouldn't have gathered near the floor like propane would, which would blast debris up and out. The methane gathered near the ceiling, and when it exploded, it blew everything —"

Suddenly, Ino reached the lab, or more accurately: the pit where the lab had been. Where the floor of the lab had collapsed into the basement.

"… straight down," he finished.

Baker Brown had been constructed of brick and masonry, its basement consisting of heavy, load-bearing cinderblock walls with a wooden ceiling, which also formed the ground floor. The basement and ground floor rooms had the same floorplan, carrying the load all the way up to the roof. Thus, as the gas blew the walls out of the building and blasted the roof straight up, it also blew the floor straight down into the basement.

Lab 103 was now a colossal pit.

Jack growled at him, twenty feet away, strangled through his mask. "How do you KNOW ALL THIS?" he demanded.

Ino turned to look up at him. "Has someone explained to you what a chemistry professor does, Chief Archer?"

Jack scowled.

Ino turned back to the gaping hole in the floor of Baker Brown Science Center.

The edges were ringed with splintered plywood subfloor, dangling down into the pit like a debris waterfall, in many cases still wearing the occasional stubbornly-stuck vinyl tile. A lot of the roof had gone straight up and come straight back down. Beyond the building material dangling down around the edges like vines, the edges were *shockingly* clean, showing Ino that the floor collapse had clearly followed the outline of the lab itself. There was a clear division between where the explosion had punched through into the floor and where it had swept like a great wind across the ground floor of the building.

There were lights down in the pit, and a bright-yellow construction ladder set up at the edge of this division.

Ino scampered to the ladder, and before the dog could reach him, he swung his leg over and hurried down the rungs.

Jack saw him and gasped. *"That's enough, Dr. Reamer!"* Jack roared. "We're done here!"

"I just need to check for one thing!" He quickly skittered down the ladder.

"No you don't!" the shepherd yelled, his voice muffled through the respirator but not reduced in volume. His ears were fully forward and he looked mad. "That is an accident scene! You are *done!*"

Ino zipped down the ladder as fast as he could and reached the bottom. He looked around. The base of the pit — which was really the basement floor, about fifteen feet down — was covered in what looked like shapeless piles of debris, but as Ino's eyes adjusted to the weird lighting, came out as recognizable shapes. A lot of items were crushed and destroyed but for all intents and purposes the floor of the lab had just blasted into the basement, followed by the roof. Ino could make out large sections of the lab floor, the slate countertops, chunks and pieces of the building's ceiling, hundreds of pieces of shredded insulation, and a wide variety of lab machinery. There had obviously been quite a lot of water in the pit — probably from the fire hoses — but it had apparently been pumped out some days ago. Ino picked his way along the top of the pile. A quick glance told him that Jack had reached the top of the pit.

Suddenly, he found something. The hyena gasped.

"Here. Look. You see?!" Ino said, reaching down. He bent down and picked a half-buried object out of the debris.

It was a digital scale, white and silver, made of aluminum and cracked, dusty plastic. It had a square metal plate with a huge dent in it, and the plastic was crushed at the base. The bottom of the scale had cracked open, exposing the circuitry, and letting a 9-volt battery dangle out of the bottom, hanging by its lead wires. The entire device was dusty and dirty and looked like Ino had dug it out of the sand at the Dunes.

"LOOK!" he cried, triumphantly, holding it up over his head.

Jack had reached the ladder but paused to peer down at him from the edge of the pit. The shepherd looked baffled, even with the mask on, and as Ino watched he even cocked his head like a confused puppy.

"What is th —" the shepherd started.

"It's a SCALE!" Ino snapped.

Jack raised an eyebrow. "Not a whole scale. It's *some* of a scale."

Ino rolled his eyes. "Don't you get it? This thing is made of cheap plastic and it's still mostly intact. These forces weren't nearly enough to completely pulverize a laptop computer *or* a cellphone."

Frowning, Jack looked back and forth from the scale, to Ino's face, back to the scale.

Ino huffed loudly into the mask. "Haven't you ever seen pictures of a gas explosion? You can have an entire wall and roof blown off and a stack of cheap plastic containers still stacked up, completely undamaged. If something is not *in the way of the gas* as it seeks equilibrium, it should be intact. As long as the fire didn't burn it, everything should still be here."

Jack narrowed his eyes, glancing toward the ladder into the pit. "Why do we care, Dr. Reamer?"

Ino snorted at him and turned back into the debris field. He headed toward what he thought had been the front of the room. "I think Dr. Reed was trying to tell me something or send me something. He wanted to send me a file but he never got the chance. If we can find his personal effects we can figure out what it was." He turned and glowered. "Aren't you at least curious where the man's *phone* is?! Who's the last adult you saw without a cellphone on them?"

Glaring, Jack swung one leg over the ladder into the pit.

"Ack!" Ino gasped, turning back to the pile. He picked his way along a thick roofing timber, which went to the top of a pile of what looked like crushed industrial shelving. There were huge pieces of plywood splintered in the debris with vinyl tiles stuck on to them, and bits and pieces of what Ino recognized as the long wooden cabinetry that had run the length of the room. There were big chunks of black slate everywhere — the countertops had basically shattered as the room blew into the basement. Like all solid stone, it was incredibly strong, but very brittle under extreme forces. Ino steered clear since broken slate could be incredibly sharp.

The slate countertop had been at least two inches thick. It had broken, but there was a good chance that in doing so, it had absorbed the force of the blast, and protected something else.

Feeling like he was scuttling over a bone pile, Ino scurried to the north side of the room.

Jack was halfway down the ladder. "Where are you *going?!*" he growled.

Ino glanced back over at him as he mounted a pile of splintered wood and insulation. "We work with a lot of corrosive chemicals in these labs," he said. "And college freshmen aren't exactly the most careful with materials. Do you know what hydrochloric acid will do to an iPhone?"

"*So what?*" Jack roared.

Ino picked his way forward. There was a huge section of the roof, ten by ten at least, with splintered wood on the edges and black plastic sheeting stuck to the top. The section of the roof was propped up by the crushed cabinetry on one side, like a crudely-constructed lean-to.

"So, I don't know a single professor who doesn't keep their phone in the same place."

Rounding the debris pile, Ino came to the back wall of the basement room. On top of industrial shelving, still somewhat connected to the displaced floor of Lab 103, was a crushed mess of cabinetry that the hyena recognized as the teacher's station.

He pictured it in his head — a four-foot wide section of cabinet at the head of the lab. There *had* been a slate top on this desk, but all that was left was construction adhesive and dust and, ominously, a lab gas jet sticking straight out of the cabinet. The base of the station had split and compacted, and it was only about twenty-four inches tall now.

The insides of the top two drawers were partially exposed, visible through big broken slabs of slate. Both drawers were full of what looked like ten pounds of unmixed concrete dust and pieces of wood and slate. The whole thing was partially covered by the huge section of roof. But they were clearly drawers — Ino recognized the stainless steel handles on the front.

He grabbed the one on the right and pulled.

The drawer was off its tracks, of course — in fact, they weren't really tracks to speak of anymore — but the wooden box shrieked reluctantly out of its housing.

"*Hey!*" Jack cried. He was at the base of the ladder now. "That's *evidence!*"

Ino snorted. "You've had a hundred techs through here! The best in the business, Dr. Greeley tells me!" He picked a pencil out of his pocket and started jabbing through the debris. A lot of it was heavy and didn't want to move, and it was all so dusty it looked like someone had dumped an entire five-pound bag of flour inside. "Besides, evidence of what, Swiss cheese?" He kept poking, faster now.

Jack growled at that — actually *growled*, Ino was startled to hear — and started picking his way angrily toward him. "Dr. Reamer, if I have to drag you out of here in handcuffs, don't think I won't!"

Ino finished poking through the box. He could recognize a couple items, but nothing of importance. Most of it was office supplies and had probably been in the desk for years.

Grabbing the handle on the left, he wrenched it out of its housing. The wood squealed in protest and the entire thing almost dumped onto his feet. The contents jostled, stirring up a cloud of dust that coursed over him.

He saw something.

"*Dr. Reamer, final warning!*" Jack roared. His voice filled the pit and echoed through the ruins of the building.

Ino barely heard him.

He stared into the drawer, wide-eyed. Had that been a… ?

The Chief finally appeared in front of him. He was starting to sweat through his uniform and he looked dusty and pissed off. "Did you hear me?!" he hissed, angrily.

Reaching into the drawer, Ino picked up a flat rectangle.

The phone was in a thick plastic case, one of the hard industrial ones that contractors and construction workers carried. It was impossible to tell the color, since it was completely covered in brick dust, and the screen was unquestionably shattered. Grit and dust were gathered into the deep cracks in the phone's slick black screen. But it was definitely a cellphone.

It looked like Reed's.

Balancing it between his thumb and forefinger, careful not to hold it too hard, Ino held it up in front of the dog. Wide-eyed, he said nothing.

Jack blinked at it a moment, and then Ino got to see a sight he thoroughly enjoyed — the shepherd's eyes grew perfectly round in astonishment.

"Wh-wh-*what?!*" the dog gasped.

"Oh my God," Ino told him. "I can't believe it."

"Shut up," Jack told him. He looked horrified. The dog fished in his pocket for a handkerchief. "Do not move!"

"I can't believe it!" Ino gasped. "Like, I kind of thought, but I never *expected* —"

"I said, *shut up!*" Jack snapped at him. He hurriedly produced a handkerchief and reached for the phone.

Suddenly, the phone buzzed in Ino's hand. *ZZZZT!*

They both jerked in surprise.

Ino almost dropped the phone but managed to hold it at the last moment. "*Ahh!*" he cried. "How is this battery not dead?!"

Jack's eyes widened angrily. "You're holding the power button!" he snapped. "You turned it on! *Give* me that!"

ZZZZZZZZZZZZZZzTTTT! the phone buzzed, and then the screen lit up.

It was at full brightness and it hurt Ino's eyes. It showed the Apple logo, clear even through the dust and the cracks. Ino resisted the urge to wipe the screen clean.

WELCOME, the screen said. **CHOOSE A LANGUAGE.**

They both stared at it.

"Uhhhhhhhhhhhh," Jack said.

Ino stared at the phone.

It was a list in cheerful font. *English. Deutsch. Español. Francais.* Japanese characters and then Korean. It kept scrolling.

"What… what is that," Ino asked.

Jack frowned at the screen. As they watched, the screen detected the low light and dimmed accordingly.

They both stared at it.

"That's the *setup screen*," Ino said, slowly. "Isn't it? This phone has been wiped." The implication slowly sank in. "Someone… someone *erased* it. They wiped the whole damn phone."

Jack looked up at him, darkly. "We don't know that."

Ino stared for a moment, and then rolled his eyes. "Oh really?" he snapped. "We don't?"

"No, we *don't*," Jack snapped. "There are plenty of explanations for this."

Ino narrowed his eyes. "Really, Chief Archer? Like what?" He stared. "Did the explosion blow it back to factory settings?"

Jack glared back at him. "I have to get this back to the station."

"Hey, I have an explanation," Ino offered. "How about, Dr. Reed was *obviously* murdered, and whoever killed him wiped his phone to remove the evidence of *why* they killed him? Before blowing up this building to cover up the crime."

The dog glowered at him, bristling with annoyance, but for once he didn't have a rebuttal.

Finally he spoke. "Are we done here?"

Ino stared at him. "Kind of looks like we're just getting started."

Jack let out an exasperated sigh. "Okay. OUT," he ordered. He pointed at the ladder.

For once, Ino didn't protest.

They took their time getting out of the debris pile. By the time they got to the top, Travis MacGregor was just inside the tent, wearing a respirator and shining a flashlight around the debris field. The big husky spotted them as they crested the debris pile.

"Sir?" MacGregor called. "Everything OK?" Ino couldn't interpret the husky's voice through the dog's respirator — Travis was either very concerned or pretty pissed off, but the hyena couldn't tell which one.

"Everything is FINE," the shepherd snapped, as the two of them came down off the debris pile onto the concrete pad in front of the building.

Ino trailed after him. Inwardly he felt triumphant but he understood that the Chief was probably embarrassed so he wasn't going to push it.

Travis furrowed his brow in confusion at his boss' tone, but then he saw the dusty cellphone in his handkerchief and his blue eyes widened in horror. "Oh my God. Is that — ?!"

"This tent is on lockdown until I say otherwise!" Jack snapped. "Nobody gets in. *Especially* the CSI techs and those *experts* Greeley brought in. *Nobody.* Is that understood?"

The husky stared at his boss, dumbfounded, his ears tilting back. "Yes sir!" he barked.

Silently, Ino frowned. The experts *Greeley* brought in?

The shepherd sailed past his officer without so much as a second glance. Ino passed by the dog too, and as he passed him, the husky's expression unquestionably clouded into anger.

Okay, that settled that. He was pretty pissed off.

Ino decided to push it after all. "Something wrong, Officer MacGregor?" he asked.

Travis' eyes narrowed to angry slits and he took a breath to yell something back when the other dog interrupted him.

"*You!*" Jack spat, pulling his respirator up off his face. All of his black muzzle fur was matted to his face with sweat, the straps of the respirator making it stick up in weird peaks. "Go home. Do not tell *anyone* about this or I will arrest you for interfering in an investigation. Do you understand me?!"

Ino pulled his mask off and narrowed his eyes. "Is this a murder investigation now?"

Jack's jaw actually dropped open, and Ino saw his eye twitch. He started forward.

Whoops, too far! The hyena held up one hand. "Okay, okay, okay! I retract the question." He stared the shepherd in the face. "I won't tell anybody."

Jack stared at him, searching him, and finally nodded, frowning. "Okay. Thank you. Go home, please."

Ino nodded. He put his respirator back in the box by the doorway and slowly started forward.

The Chief whirled and walked swiftly back toward the street, grumbling under his breath.

After a moment, Ino thought of something. "Chief Archer!" he called.

Stopping in his tracks, the dog turned his muzzle upward. "What?" he snapped, whirling.

Ino swallowed. "Can you please check something for me." He closed the gap.

The dog frowned at him. "What, exactly?"

Ino jogged after him and lowered his voice so Travis wouldn't hear. "Can you check the exact time that someone called in the lockdown alert?"

Jack stared angrily at him. "What? Why?"

Ino swallowed. "Probably nothing. But I was hoping you could settle something for me."

"Settle?!" Jack demanded. "Dr. Reamer, this is not a *game*. And my time is not to be spent checking into every little whim that you deem noteworthy."

Ino stared at him, feeling his adrenaline surge. The dog was *insufferable*. "A whim, huh?" he asked, casually. "Like that whim in your handkerchief?"

Jack's eyes widened, and he looked like he was about to start snarling. The dog stared at him, his eyes wide and angry, but after a moment he visibly calmed down. The dog took a deep breath, and let out an exasperated sigh.

"What do you need to know?" he asked, flatly.

Ino stared at him, and then nodded. "Just the time the alert was called in." He took a deep breath. "I think it might be important."

Jack nodded, his jaw set. "I'll find out."

Ino let out a relieved sigh. "Thank you," he said, softening. "Really. Thank you."

Jack nodded. "Okay. Please go home, Dr. Reamer."

The hyena nodded. "Won't stay here another minute." He glanced back at the husky. "I get the feeling it might be dangerous for me."

Travis stared at him, and then lowered his eyes into a murderous glare.

Muttering angrily to himself, Jack stomped back to his patrol car.

Ino stood in the path, and then slowly turned.

Travis MacGregor stared angrily back at him.

It was time to go.

Sitting in his bright yellow Jeep with the engine running and the A/C blasting, Ino let out a shaky sigh. That had been… intense. Jack had been pissed off. And Travis had been *really* pissed off. *I better not get mugged anytime soon,* Ino thought. *I've pissed off the entire security force.* Well — that nice Officer Reese probably still liked him. If he got jumped in the parking lot, he would make sure he talked to her.

He thought of the last couple hours. It had been… eventful to say the least. He needed a debrief. And a shower. And maybe a beer. Maybe several beers.

Fishing his phone out of his pocket, he slid to his contacts and dialed the third number.

Vivian picked up on the second ring. "*What* did you *do?*" the pine marten demanded by way of greeting.

Blinking, Ino stammered into the phone. "Uhhhhh," he said. "What do you mean?"

"I just saw the head of security go screaming down Church Street in a squad car and he looked *furious.* I've only known one person who can get people that mad without trying. Was that you? Didn't I tell you not to do anything illegal?!"

Ino laughed. "Haha! Wow, I really think *you* should be the one solving this mystery. Guilty as charged."

There was a pause. "You do mean that... *figuratively*, right?"

Ino chuckled. "Come over and I'll show you."

The pine marten sighed. "Wouldn't miss it! I'll be there in an hour."

By the time Vivian showed up, it was dark out. She was wearing black leggings and a thin crimson sweater, and holding two huge bags from the Golden Dragon restaurant and a six-pack of Stella Artois. The beer was ice-cold, right from the liquor store, judging by the condensation sparkling on the bottles. It was a warm night and as soon as he saw the frosty beer his mouth started to water.

Ino stared through his front door, open-mouthed, at the objects in her hands. He had totally forgotten to feed himself and Vivian had probably guessed that on the way. "Marry me," he insisted.

Standing on his doorstep, Vivian laughed. "No. Haven't we been over this?!"

Ino grinned, pushing open the storm door and holding it open, crowding against the doorframe so the slim pine marten could slip by. "But why not? I would be such an *amazing* gay husband."

Vivian laughed as she slipped into the house. "If you think *very* hard about what you just said, you'll find you have answered your own question."

The ground floor of Ino's rental house had a huge open floorplan with a dining area in between the kitchen and the living area. Ino had a table that could seat six (eight if he put the leaf in), *and* an eat-in kitchen with a sparkling quartz island with a bar sink and breakfast bar, and two expensive barstools that Ino had gotten as hand-me-downs from his oldest brother.

As per usual, Ino and Vivan ignored all of the designated Grown-Up Eating Areas, and went straight for the overstuffed living room sofas.

Ino pulled up two brown fake-leather ottomans, each of which had a cushion that flipped over to reveal a wooden tray, while Vivian disappeared into the kitchen only long enough to retrieve two white Corelle plates and cutlery.

They opened their bags and the scent of Kung Pao Chicken and fried rice filled the air. Ino felt himself start drooling. He licked his chops as Vivian doled out chicken and rice and crab Rangoon.

"So, whatcha got?" she demanded, as soon as they were half-settled. She sat back on the couch, balancing her tray on her lap, ears forward and demanding.

"I found Reed's cellphone inside Baker. Also, they have all his stuff in storage, and I broke in. I found a bunch of clues!"

The pine marten stared at him, her brown eyes wide. "Are… are you *serious?*"

Ino chuckled, blushing.

Vivian frowned. "Aren't you worried about being *arrested?*"

Ino shrugged. "Jack Archer found me. He yelled at me but I think I'm off the hook." He began stuffing his mouth with fried rice.

Vivian threw her hands up in exasperation, miraculously not disturbing the tray balanced on her thighs. "Did I not *specifically say* to not do anything illegal?"

Ino ate an entire Rangoon in two bites. "Yeth, twithe actually! But I found a *bunch* of thtuff," he said, his mouth full.

Vivian shook her head. "I *swear*, Ino —"

He shrugged, picking up a beer. "It's fine! I think the whole security team already hates me anyway." He pawed at the cap, twisting it repeatedly to no avail. It wouldn't come off.

Vivian stared at him, expressionless. "That cap is not a twist-off," she advised, raising an eyebrow.

Ino raised a finger and pointed at her. "*This cap*," he declared. "Is *not* a twist-off." He leapt out of his seat. Vivian handed him a bottle opener that she had brought from the kitchen.

Ino looked at it. "I should just leave this thing out here," he said.

Vivian rolled her eyes. "I think you should be less concerned about how the Chief feels about you, and more concerned with going to jail." She shook her head. "So you found Reed's *phone?* Was there anything good on it?" she demanded.

Ino shoveled another mouthful of fried rice and Kung Pao into his face. "No, thath the thimg, we couldn't atthteth anthy-."

The pine marten stared at him down her short muzzle. "SWALLOW YOUR FOOD, PLEASE."

Ino gulped hard, blushing. "Sorry! I'm just excited!" He wiped his mouth with a paper napkin. "*Yes*, I found the phone. Jack took me to the explosion site. I think he did it to prove that none of Reed's belongings could have survived the blast. But the concussive forces in a gas explosion aren't strong enough to *really* destroy a device like that."

Vivian nodded. "As a psychologist, I obviously knew that."

Ino grinned toothily. "Naturally! Anyway, we found the phone, which miraculously still turned on, but was totally blank. As new. Factory reset."

She stared at him. "It… it was wiped?"

Ino held both his arms up. "*Right!* That's what I said! So whoever killed Reed reset the phone, and then planted it, thinking it would be blown to bits. Except it wasn't blown to bits and I found it *immediately*." He popped an entire Rangoon into his mouth and chomped it to bits. He eyed the bright-orange sauce, and as he chewed, wondered if Vivian would object if he downed the entire thing at once like a shot.

"How is that possible?" she asked. "I thought that *several* teams went through there."

Ino shrugged. "Allegedly they did."

She narrowed her eyes. "So where was the phone?"

"In the teacher's station." Ino shoveled another forkful of rice into his muzzle.

Vivian frowned. "Wouldn't that be the *first* place you would look?"

He smiled. "It *was* the first place I looked!"

Vivian shook her head. "That doesn't make any sense. Are you sure somebody didn't come back and plant the phone later?"

Ino blinked at her. "I mean… I guess they could have." He thought about it. "I kind of doubt it, though. I think somebody from security is there all the time."

Vivian frowned. "It's a *tent*, Ino. It's not a bank vault."

He leaned back in his chair. "Huh. I suppose you're right!"

The pine marten's brow furrowed. "Well. Assuming it's not just broken, there's something on that phone that someone was trying to keep quiet." She puzzled for a moment. "Or something Reed didn't want anyone to see. He could have wiped it himself."

Ino pondered. "Hm. I didn't think of that. But you could be right. Anyway, in either case, whoever killed him didn't want to raise a red flag, so they left the phone, thinking the investigation team would only find chunks of it." He nodded emphatically, pausing before shoving a huge forkful of Kung Pao chicken into his muzzle. He reached for his beer and downed half of it.

Vivian watched him, eating slowly with chopsticks. "Did you forget to eat for the entire day again?"

He nodded.

Rolling her eyes, Vivian let out a sigh. "Self-care, Ino. You should at least be better at it than our students are. If I have to coach you any more in taking care of yourself I'm going to start charging your insurance." She shook her head. "Who brought in the crime scene teams, again?"

Ino frowned. "That's the thing, Greeley said they were Archer's teams and she just signed off on them." He raised an eyebrow, scraping his plate clean. "But Archer said, don't let *Greeley's* teams in here. They both told me the other one picked the investigation teams."

The pine marten blinked at him. "That… could be University politics at work."

Ino nodded. "Orrrr…" he prompted.

Vivian shrugged, letting out a resigned sign. "OR Susan Greeley *intentionally* forced terrible investigators on the security teams in order to purposely botch the investigation." She shook her head. "I see we're pivoting back to President Greeley again," she said. "Did you find anything about her in the office?"

Ino nodded. "Yeah. His calendar said 'MEET S.G.' on the day of the explosion." Ino looked at her plate and she was barely a quarter of the way through. He picked up another food container and started eating directly out of the box.

Vivian stared at him. "You're kidding."

The hyena nodded slowly. "Two hours before he died."

Vivian frowned. She thought about it, and then after a moment shook her head. "Eh. It's circumstantial at best. I still don't buy the corporate donation angle. And how do you know that was even her? That could have been anybody with those initials. Anything else?"

Ino nodded. "He had a paperweight."

Vivian put her arms up, in an exaggerated shrug. "Case closed!"

Ino burst out laughing. He came dangerously close to emitting a shrill hyena-laugh but managed to choke it down at the last second. "No, hear me out! A University paperweight. The anniversary one."

Vivian blinked at him. "The glass one? That thing that weighs like... five pounds?"

Stuffing his mouth with rice and chicken, Ino nodded.

The pine marten frowned. "That's... strange. I only saw one for the first time this afternoon. Susan is giving them out like party favors but I don't think I've seen one before today."

Ino nodded. "Right. Greeley gave me one yesterday morning, and she took it right out of the box. I think I was only the second or third person to get one."

Vivian stared at him, frowning.

Ino gestured with his fork. "But *Reed* had one *in his office.* Which means he had it on the day of the explosion, the 11th." He leaned back on the sofa. "So how the hell did *he* get it a week before anyone else on campus did?"

Vivian stared at him. "Hhhhhhuh. I don't know."

Ino nodded. "Greeley brought it to him. Right before she killed him to get a gigantic donation for the University."

The pine marten snorted. "Oh wow! There you go. I'll notify the press." She popped a piece of chicken into her mouth. "She probably..." She gestured with her chopsticks, her eyes widening. "She probably killed him... *with*... the paperweight!"

Ino cracked a humorless smile. "I mean... you *could.* It weighs as much as a fire extinguisher."

Vivian nodded. "It sure does. Speaking of fire, did the authorities ever figure out what happened at Dublahm Chemical?"

Ino nodded. "Yeah. It was a big explosion."

Vivian blinked at him. "At the chemical plant? I'm surprised the whole place didn't go up."

Ino nodded. "It was outside in the refinery part."

She frowned. "How do you have a fire outside?"

Ino considered. "Well, it was a flammable gas leak, so it was basically a huge methane fireball."

"Huhhh." Vivian thought for a moment. "And how did Baker blow up again?"

Ino blinked at her. "Uh, a natural gas explosion." He thought for a moment. "So basically a huge... methane... fireball." He trailed off.

Vivian raised an eyebrow. "Well! That's an interesting little detail, don't you think?"

Ino considered. "I suppose it is."

They stared at each other for a moment.

Ino leaned forward. "I have a wayyyy better suspect, though."

The pine marten narrowed her eyes. "Do tell."

Ino nodded gravely. "I had a suuuuper weird conversation outside the admin building." He told her about the angry badger with the grudge against the late professor Reed.

Vivian blinked in surprise. "Wow. That is... *blatant*."

Ino shrugged. "It sure is! I was going to tell Jack about that first thing in the morning."

Vivian stared at him in disbelief. "Kind of surprised you didn't bring it up earlier."

Ino sighed. "We didn't end on a great note. When I find out about who called in the lockdown I'll tell him about it."

The pine marten pondered. "So what's your theory on the badger? He murdered Reed to avenge his coworker? Seems like a bit of a stretch."

Ino shrugged. "I don't know, but he clearly *hated* the guy. And maybe the weird angle triggered something. An old guy cruelly victimizing a young girl is, like... I could definitely see at least a fight breaking out over that. And he's a *big, big guy*. Maybe a verbal argument went south, he punched him in the face, broke his neck... needed to cover it up." He thought about it. The badger had *towered* over him. Ino wouldn't want to fight him. He could easily see a heated exchange going into "accidental murder" territory.

Vivian considered and then shrugged. "Well, that's definitely a sort of murder that happens in real life."

Ino nodded. "Right. Except... I mean... it's a bit *too* on the nose, isn't it? Why would he tell me about it? He has to know that makes him the prime suspect." He frowned. "Unless he's covering up for the real killer or something ridiculous like that."

The pine marten stared at him, the corners of her lips turning up. "Well, make sure you're not falling for the trope of the *criminal mastermind*. I would not be at *all* surprised to learn of a murderer explaining, in detail, exactly what his motivations were for murdering the victim." She chuckled. "That definitely happens in real life too! People only act like criminal masterminds in the movies. In real life there's all sorts of tells. Some people even lay clues all around them, because subconsciously they *want* to be caught." She took another bite. "That's why *you're* probably the prime suspect right now."

Ino choked on his beer. He spurted half of it back into the bottle, making it foam. "*Me?!*" he demanded. "What?!"

Vivian stared at him. "I mean... obviously."

He stared, his jaw hanging open. "Not obvious!" he squeaked in protest.

The pine marten stared at him. "Ino. Come on. Do you know who the first suspects are in a murder investigation?"

Ino frowned. "No." He sighed. "This feels like more information I don't *want* but probably *need*."

Vivian ticked off three fingers. "The spouse, the person who found the body, and the last person to see the victim alive."

Ino pondered that. His jaw hanging open, he set down his fork. "Uh-oh."

Vivian nodded, raising her eyebrows. "Right. You're two of those three people, and the third one doesn't exist." She shrugged. "And it's less common, but I think that people being overly helpful in a police investigation automatically get on the list too."

Ino swallowed.

Vivian shrugged. "But I'm sure they know you're innocent." She smiled wickedly.

Ino felt himself blush, frowning. "That's not *really* funny," he mumbled.

Vivian tut-tutted. "I'm really not worried. You were with your student across campus during Reed's final moments." She shrugged. "And immediately going back to the building you had rigged to explode is not exactly the work of an evil genius."

Ino frowned. "I suppose you're right." Annoyed, he bunched up the paper bag from his Chinese into a tight ball. He stood up and pitched it into the other room.

The paper ball sailed thirty feet through three rooms and landed perfectly centered in the kitchen sink.

Vivian *ooo-ed* exaggeratedly. "Wow, perfect aim! That was amazing! Did you used to play baseball?"

Ino blinked at her. "Yes. In high school. I was the starting pitcher. Seriously?? You knew that!"

She stared at him in disbelief. "Of course I do, you've told me a hundred times!" She frowned. "That was the joke. Wow, I was about to compliment you on your detective skills but now I think it was beginner's luck." She laughed. "What else you got?"

The hyena thought for a moment, and then walked to the breakfast table, where his work bag was hanging out. "Yah. You're gonna flip your shit when you see *this*. Reed had a bunch of hidden clues in his file cabinet."

The pine marten stared at him. "You had time to go through that entire monster cabinet?"

Ino blinked at her. "No. The good stuff was in phony class files, and the key to finding them was in the molecular structure of the pictures on the wall."

Vivian finished off her beer, staring at him. "I retract my recommendation that you not do anything illegal," she said, somberly. "*Apparently...* you are like... *terrific* at it." She sounded a little tipsy, which made her gravitas all the more amusing.

She took a few moments to read it, sipping on her beer. "Wow, look at *that*. Look, he even highlighted it!" She read it out loud. "*The theft from the police station's evidence room remains unsolved.* Boy, that would do it!"

Ino nodded. "You aren't kidding. That's *definitely* a felony, right?" Ino sat back down so he wouldn't be tempted to scavenge Vivian's rice. "A former cop trying to stay out of prison? If Reed found out Travis was the one who stole the heroin, all he would have to do is mention it and there's your motive."

Vivian raised an eyebrow. "Travis? Why Travis?"

Ino shrugged. "He worked there. And he's constantly acting like he wants to beat me up." He frowned. "I think he feels guilty that he almost blew up his nephew by accident, along with the guy he actually *meant* to kill."

The pine marten frowned seriously. "Jesus, I hope not. Anyway, it could just as easily have been Jack Archer. Either of them could have taken the drugs."

Ino stared at her. He took several long moments to process that information. "Uhhh. I hadn't thought of that." He frowned.

Vivian nodded. "Or *anybody*. We don't know who else might work at the University now. That police station was only a couple hours away. Anybody from there could work here now, and anybody who worked there is a suspect. For all we know some admin or analyst came too. They could work right in Wong or Malerich and we would never even know the difference."

Ino nodded. "Well, I have an easy way to tell if it's Travis. I think the blast was called in *before* it happened."

She stared at him. "Do you."

He nodded.

Vivian narrowed her eyes. "Don't you think that would... stand out, just a touch?"

He rolled his eyes. "Yes, of course. But would anybody put *all* the pieces together?" He frowned. "Think about it. Only a few people would know the exact moment the call came in. The security office was too far away and too insulated for anyone to hear the explosion. They wouldn't even know if it happened after they put the alert out. Footage doesn't help — every security camera in this school probably has a different timestamp." He shrugged. "And any students who got the alert before they heard the explosion would assume that someone smelled gas and put out the alert." He frowned, feeling self-conscious. "It's not like the whole story has gotten out — the newspapers haven't even so much as mentioned me or Sean."

She stared at him, considering. "It's... possible." After a moment, she shrugged. "Eyewitness testimony is lousy. I concede it is within the realm of possibility." Setting down her plate, Vivian frowned. "Still kind of a stupid move," she said. "Really setting yourself up for failure, that would be — calling in your crime before you commit it."

Ino shrugged. "It might be worth it if you didn't want to kill anyone else." He shrugged. "Maybe he thought the explosion would be smaller —

like too small to see — and he wanted everyone else out of danger. I doubt whoever did this was a munitions expert, and that applies to any of the suspects — for all we know the killer was only going for a small fire, not to level the entire building."

Vivian nodded thoughtfully. "I could see it." She pondered. "Anything else?"

Ino let out a sigh. "Just some paperwork. But they're both accounting documents. One is a Vendor Supply Form, which was in the file cabinet. Have you ever heard of Triton Landscaping?"

Staring blankly, Vivian shook her head.

Ino sighed. "Didn't think so. I gave that one up to Archer — I didn't even know where to start with it. We'll see if he gets anywhere. The other was this weird accounting document and it looked a lot more interesting. Based on where it was packed, this one would have been right on top of Reed's desk."

He dug out the journal entry and set it out on the coffee table.

They both stared at it.

"What the hell is this?" Vivian asked.

Ino sighed. "I don't know. I was hoping you did. I recognize that it's a journal entry but I don't know anything else about it."

The pine marten nodded. "Makes sense. Reed was a CPA before he went back to academics."

Ino stared at her. "What?! Are you serious?"

Vivian nodded, her eyes wide. "Yes. I thought you knew that."

Ino grimaced. "Ugh, that's even more clues pointing toward the accounting department." He shook his head. "I wish I could get this explained by someone in University Finance, but I have a funny feeling that badger is involved." He let out a sigh. "I really don't want to, but I think I'm going to have to take this one to Jack, too. Let's hope he has better forensic accountants than he has crime scene investigators." He frowned. "There's nobody else to ask that isn't likely to be directly involved."

Vivian stared at him. "Are you serious right now?"

Ino blinked innocently at her.

Frowning, the pine marten sat back in her chair. "Ino, you do realize we work at a *University*… right?"

Chapter 6: Balance Check

Thursday, May 17, 2018

CLARA CALDER, PROFESSOR OF ACCOUNTING, read the door plate.

Ino stood outside the office, frowning. It was one thing to harass the chief of security with his theories. But he was surprisingly shy about interrupting another colleague with what could turn out to be a completely absurd supposition.

At least he'd called ahead.

Lifting his hand, Ino knocked very gently on the door.

"Come in!" proclaimed a voice from inside.

Ino took a deep breath and opened the door.

Dr. Calder was a calico shorthair with mostly white fur. She had a black patch of fur over her left eye and an orange patch over her right eye, with straight shoulder length hair, and thick cat's-eye glasses in bright red plastic. She was seated at her desk in an academic office a little larger than Ino's, behind a sleek metal desk. The woman looked older than Ino, probably 40 or 45, plump, looking very put-together in a crisp white silk blouse. She didn't look up from her computer as he walked in. "One moment, Dr. Reamer, be right with you," she announced, with authority.

"Thank you," Ino said quietly, looking around. Dr. Calder's walls were lined with bookshelves, covered in terms that Ino didn't recognize. There was a whole shelf titled COST ACCOUNTING. There was an entire *bookcase* about tax law, each book about four inches thick. Ino was not inspired to seek a career change.

Dr. Calder continued furiously typing at a rate that Ino had seldom observed, and then finally stopped. She hit the button on her computer mouse with a flourish, and then turned her full attention to Ino. She smiled warmly at him and folded her fingers in front of her. "Thank you for waiting, Dr. Reamer. How may I be of service?"

Ino suddenly felt his face heating up. "Please, call me Ino." He took a deep breath. "I apologize in advance if this is a waste of your time, but I found something, and I was hoping you could tell me what it is."

The cat blinked at him. "Me? What on earth would you need an accountant for? What did you find, an abacus?"

He laughed. "No! Nothing as interesting as that. I should... tell you the background." He reached into his bag as he spoke. "I worked very closely with Dr. Reed," he said. That was mostly true, right? The man was across the hall. That counted as close. "Dr. Ethan Reed. I found something in his papers. I think it's an accounting document."

He looked up. Clara Calder was staring at him with wide eyes. "Goodness, Dr. Reed who just passed away?"

Ino nodded solemnly.

Clara frowned. "I'm so sorry for your loss. What an absolute tragedy."

The hyena nodded. "Thank you." He thought of the thundering roar of Baker Brown Science Center blasting into pieces. "It was... quite a shock."

The cat nodded sympathetically. "I know we've just met but please do let me know if there's anything I can do."

Ino swallowed. "Thank you. Everyone has been really great." He slid the accounting document across the desk in front of him, inside a plastic zip-top bag. "And maybe you can help me... I was hoping you could tell me what *this* is."

Clara's brown eyes widened again. "You have that in a plastic bag? Is this *evidence*, Dr. Reamer?" She leaned forward, and Ino couldn't tell if the expression on her feline face was horror, interest, or both.

The hyena felt his face heating up, and he wished he'd thought this out a little better. "No! No, I'm... I'm probably being ridiculous about this whole thing," he said in a rush. He swallowed, feeling his ears tilt back. "I just don't want to damage it. I... I found this in Dr. Reed's desk, and it looks like an order form or something. I just wanted to make sure it wasn't something that needed following up on." That was also true. He swallowed. "There's some huge numbers in here and I just want to make sure I don't throw away anything important."

"Of course," Dr. Calder purred. "Understandable."

They both looked down at the document.

JOURNAL ENTRY		1/8/18
ACCOUNT	DEBIT	CREDIT
Investment dividends 4042300	$2,565,400.70	
Vacation accrual 303030	$27,750.08	
Raw materials purchased 206000	$6,560.10	
Interest Payable 3710000	$21,320.02	
Cash JP Morgan ***51015 3010101		$24,576,577.30
TOTAL	$2,621,030.90	$24,576,577.30
Variance check		$0.00

He stared. "Can you tell me what this is?"

Clara stared at it for a long moment. She put her glasses back on, gently tugged it toward her, and sat it on her desk as if she was afraid it was going to leap up at her.

"Well…" she said. "I'm sorry, Dr. Reamer… I'm afraid I can't!"

He stared at her. "Uhh… what?" he questioned, blinking at her.

Dr. Calder stammered for a moment. "It's not *anything*. I mean… it is an accounting document, sort of, but…" She struggled for the words. "It doesn't make any sense at all. It's basically gibberish. This document is essentially… meaningless."

Ino stared blankly at her, trying to understand. "Ahhhhhhhhh…" he trailed off.

Dr. Calder nodded gravely. "I know that look. You have *no* idea what I'm talking about."

Ino grinned. "Do you get that look a lot?"

The calico rolled her eyes. "You have *no* idea. Hold on one second. I have to teach you a little bit about accounting for this to make any sense."

She stepped up from her chair, walked around from her desk, and scanned the bookshelf. She pulled a book from the shelf. Ino read the title as she pulled it down — BASICS OF ACCOUNTING.

He let out a relieved sigh. "Oh, thank God. Basics. I like basics."

Clara moved to the other visitor's chair, across from Ino, and sat silently down. She flipped through the book as she sat down, and continued flipping as she spoke. "What you have found, Dr. Reamer, is… a journal entry." She glanced briefly upwards at him. "It's a document that is one of the most basic transactions of accounting. Here."

She set the book open on the desk in front of them, laid open. Ino noticed they were only 20 or 30 pages into the book — barely past the introduction. Wow — the lesson he was getting was *basic*, all right. They were barely past the Table of Contents.

There was a quick definition — Ino only read the first sentence — and then another "entry" on the page. It looked a lot like the document he had found in Dr. Reed's office.

A **JOURNAL ENTRY** IS USED TO RECORD A BUSINESS TRANSACTION IN THE ACCOUNTING RECORDS OF A BUSINESS.

JOURNAL - ENTRY - ABC
Company   March 4 2004

ACCOUNT	DEBIT	CREDIT
Employee payroll	$20,000.00	
Cash		$20,000.00
TOTALS	$20,000.00	$20,000.00
Balance check		$0.00

Ino nodded thoughtfully. "I see, I see."

Dr. Calder stared at him. "Do you?"

He shook his head. "Not at all."

The cat cracked a toothy smile, and continued. "What you're looking at is a record of a single *transaction*. Every time a business does something with money, that's an accounting transaction. Every time they buy something, or sell something, or pay the workers — they're all accounting transactions. A journal entry documents that."

Ino nodded.

Dr. Calder continued. "Each journal entry is entered into the *general ledger*. When you hear someone refer to a company's "books," that's what they mean. They used to be literally books. It's a record of everything they've done with their money, or their assets — which is something they own that is *worth* money — and their expenses."

The hyena nodded again. "Ahhh. So this is like… the amino acid of a business' financial protein structure."

The cat stared blankly at him.

Ino smiled vapidly back as his joke died on the floor. "Maybe just pretend I didn't say that." He shook his head. "So! Back to the journal entry. This one has something wrong with it?"

Dr. Calder nodded. "Well… I would go a step further and say it's basically nonsensical. But let me show you what I mean."

He nodded. "Please do."

She pointed at an example journal entry on the next page. "Look at this example."

JOURNAL ENTRY - XYZ
Company   May 2 2004

ACCOUNT	DEBIT	CREDIT
Raw Materials Purchased	$10,000.00	
Cash		$10,000.00
TOTALS	$10,000.00	$10,000.00
Balance check		$0.00

"This is to document a purchase. Specifically, the purchase of a bunch of raw materials. Say you make guitars. You run Dr. Reamer Guitar Company."

He smiled.

She kept talking. "You go out and spend $10,000 on guitar wood. *This* is how you would record that." She pointed at the top line. "This is your account for raw materials. That's just what it sounds like — material you turn into something else. A debit to that account increases its value — you bought stuff, so you have more stuff now!" She moved one line down. "Cash is your bank account. You *spent* money, so you have *less money* now. In accounting, that's recorded as a *credit* to cash."

Ino nodded. "I see." He frowned. "And why is this such a big deal? Who cares?"

She laughed. "An indelicate, yet thoughtful question! At some point you're going to finish and sell those guitars, Dr. Reamer. Now let's say you only make *eight* thousand dollars selling them."

He thought about that, and slowly frowned. "But that's less than they cost to make! I spent *ten* thousand on just the wood!"

She nodded enthusiastically. "Right. And wouldn't you want to know that you'd thrown two thousand dollars in the toilet?"

He thought about that for a moment. "I see." He processed that. "Huh. Accounting!" he said, cheerfully.

She nodded sagely. "Accounting," she agreed.

Ino looked down and mentally processed the document. "Ok, this makes sense to me." He cocked his head. "So what's wrong with the one I brought?"

Dr. Calder reached across the desk and plucked Dr. Reed's entry off the surface. She set it in front of them, resting on top of the accounting book.

"Well… first of all, none of these accounts have anything to do with one another. Factory Assets is a facilities account, and Interest Payable is a liability account. Completely unconnected — you would never see a transaction affecting both of them. But the *real* problem — is here." She slid out the claw on her index finger to point at the totals.

Ino looked down at the last two lines.

TOTAL	$2,621,030.90	$24,576,577.30
Variance check		$0.00

"*These* two numbers should match," Dr. Calder said. "They're supposed to cancel each other out." She frowned. "This document, Dr. Reamer, quite literally… does not add up." She shrugged. "When I said it was nonsensical, I meant it."

Ino frowned. "What do you mean match?"

She pointed to the two previous examples.

"See? Look. 20,000 here… 20,000 there. 10,000 here… 10,000 there. The amounts should be the same or it doesn't follow the transaction, which is the whole point of accounting. If that doesn't work, you're not really explaining what's happening to your money. It's just... disappearing." She frowned. "Sorry I couldn't be of more help."

Ino stared at her for a long moment, and then let out a long sigh.

"Unfortunately, I was afraid you were going to say something like that." He frowned. "I appreciate your help, Dr. Calder, but I think I need to take up a little more of your time." He swallowed. "There's someone else that needs to be here for this."

Jack Archer was there in ten minutes.

Ino heard him coming from the end of the hall, not *quite* stomping with irritation, but definitely not skipping down the hall with happiness, either.

"I hope you have something good, Dr. Reamer," the dog boomed, from halfway down the hall.

Ino stuck his head out the doorway. "I'm sure you won't be —" He cut himself off mid-sentence.

On the phone, Jack had said he was in the middle of something. That something had apparently been a workout, because the handsome shepherd was only wearing a pair of running shorts — tiny little running shorts — and a cutoff shirt. The t-shirt had apparently started out as a full garment — it said HARVEST DAYS, NOVEMBER 10-11, 2007 on it — but the sleeves had been cut off, halfway down the sides of the shirt. The sides were cut so low that Ino could even see some of the white fur over the dog's muscled stomach. He had huge arms and Ino felt the urge to stick his hands in his shirt and rub the dog's six-pack.

Jack stomped up to him, frowning, and stuck his salt-and-pepper muzzle right in Ino's face. He was accompanied by the strong scent of Right Guard, and a little haze of dog sweat.

Ino swallowed. "—won't be disappointed," he finally squeaked out.

Jack stared at him with half-lidded eyes. He let out a heavy sigh directly in Ino's face.

They stared at each other from inches away. *Oh God*, Ino thought. *Are we having a moment right now? It sure feels like a moment.*

After a couple seconds, Jack glanced away. His eyes settled *immediately* on the document in the zip-top bag on the desktop. The dog narrowed

his eyes angrily. "You have *ten seconds* to hand over any other evidence you stole, or I'm arresting you right now."

Welp! We are not having a moment.

Ino pointed meekly. "Over there." He pointed at the top of the desk.

Jack nodded. He stepped into the room and approached Dr. Calder. "Jack Archer," he said, extending his hand. "Chief of Security. Please ignore my outfit."

"Clara Calder," the cat said, raising her eyebrows. "Accounting." She turned to Ino. "The *chief* of security? I thought you said this wasn't evidence, Dr. Reamer."

Ino was in the process of working up a world-class blush when Jack answered for him. "Don't be alarmed, Dr. Calder," he said. "Dr. Reamer just has my number and he's not shy about using it." He glanced at the desk, and then turned his withering gaze upon the hyena. "Anything else?"

Ino thought for a moment, swallowed, and let out a shaky breath. "Well… one more thing." He reached into his bag and slipped out another document.

Silently, he handed over the article about Jack's station closing.

The shepherd took it and swiftly looked it over. Ino braced himself for the inevitable explosion.

Jack stared at it for a few silent seconds. Finally, he looked back at Ino, perfectly expressionless. "Is that it?"

Ino stared back at him in disbelief. The shepherd had *absolutely* no tells. He'd just seen a piece of evidence that incriminated everyone who had worked at his station in a horrible murder… and he didn't look so much as *perturbed*. His ears hadn't even moved. He had a total lack of expression. He looked like Ino had just handed him a takeout menu.

It was a perfect poker face. Ino stared in disbelief. *It's Cop Face,* he thought in wonder.

Jack raised an eyebrow, as if he was waiting for Ino to tell him the ambient air temperature. "Anything else, Dr. Reamer?" he asked, again.

Collecting himself, Ino shook his head. "N-no. Nothing else. Sorry about that." He put on the charm and grinned at both of them. "And I'm sorry. I didn't think I had anything of value OR interest. Until I ran it by Dr. Calder just for a sanity check."

The shepherd nodded. "Mmm-hmm." He slowly turned. "So what *do* we have?"

Ino cleared his throat. "Uhhhhh when I was… checking out Dr. Reed's things, I found this in a weird file." He laughed nervously. "It didn't make sense to me so I showed it to an expert." The hyena swallowed. "Ahhhh, maybe Dr. Calder could explain what this is again."

Jack looked back and forth between them. "I'm all ears," he said, dryly.

Ino swallowed. "Dr. Calder, would you be so kind?"

The calico nodded. "Certainly! What you're looking at is a journal entry. This is a record of a single *transaction*. Every time a business does something with money…"

Ino zoned out as the other professor explained about the purpose of a journal entry. It was basically the same speech verbatim. This time the example was Archer Guitar Company. Hiding a smile, Ino wondered how many dozens of students over the years had been subjected to this exact same speech.

Looking unimpressed, the shepherd looked back and forth between the textbook examples and the document from Dr. Reed's office.

"… so that's the purpose of a journal entry," Dr. Calder finished.

"I see," Jack said.

"The problem with *this* journal entry is —"

The shepherd looked up. "It's out of balance. So what?"

Ino felt his jaw drop open. Stunned, he stared at the dog. Clara looked similarly surprised.

Jack blinked back at them, frowning. "What?" he asked, flatly.

The calico finally smiled. Her tail swayed behind her. "How did you know that?"

The dog frowned defensively. "It's obvious. You have two examples with the same dollar amounts in both columns." He pointed at the textbook. "It doesn't take a genius to spot the pattern." He set his jaw. "Why do we care?"

Clara frowned. "Why do we *care*? It seems fairly obvious this is something that was done intentionally."

Jack raised an eyebrow. "*Intentionally?* It looks to me like Dr. Reed was just bad at math." He crossed his arms. "I don't see anything intentional here, except maybe intentionally staying out of the accounting field. For good reason, I would say."

Ino frowned. "Chief Archer... are you quite sure? This looks like a fairly obvious indication left behind on purpose."

The dog shrugged. "We found a lot of things in that office that look like Dr. Reed was just playing around. I'll have a forensic accountant check this over, but I don't think it's the smoking gun you're making it out to be."

Clara frowned. "You don't understand, Chief Archer. This isn't just a printout from Microsoft Excel or Google Sheets. This is a screenshot from an actual piece of accounting software."

Jack stared at her. "And... ?"

The calico narrowed her eyes, and despite just meeting her, Ino could tell she was getting pissed off. He resisted the urge to shake his head in disbelief. The dog was one stubborn son of a bitch.

Clara leaned forward. "Even the most rudimentary accounting software has a balance check *built into* it." She pointed at the *balance check* box. "This box here is *not* a suggestion. The software completes a running total and will throw a big flashing error if any part of your entry is out of balance. Accuracy is the foundation of good accounting. *Every* part of *every piece* of software is designed to *prevent you* from having math errors like this."

The shepherd frowned. "So what? He found a way around it."

The cat narrowed her eyes. "Excuse me?"

Jack shrugged. "Reed was a CPA for over ten years. He found a way to override it. Or he just didn't know what he was doing. So what?"

Clara crossed her arms.

"Fire your gun," she said.

The dog stared at her, his golden eyes widening slightly. "Wwhhhhhat?" he asked, dumbly.

She leaned back, her arms still crossed. "Fire your gun... *but*... don't switch off the safety."

The shepherd frowned. "The safety."

Clara nodded. "Yes please. If you wouldn't mind. You can shoot my tax books, if you like. Quite an opportunity!"

Ino saw Jack's left eye start twitching, and Ino had a feeling the dog was a moment away from literally snarling. "Even if I wanted to, which I do *not*," he said through his teeth, "that is literally impossible."

Clara raised an eyebrow. "Oh, now, tut tut. I'm sure you've carried a gun for many years. You're the *Chief of Security!* You're a subject matter expert! How hard can it be? So just leave the safety on and let 'er rip. I'm sure you can find a way."

Jack's eye twitched. "Of course I can't!" he snapped. "The entire point of the safety is to *prevent* the gun from firing. How the hell do you expect me to circumvent something that's *entire purpose* is to prevent me from —"

The dog fell silent, and Ino watched understanding hit him like a truck.

"Ohhhhhhhhhhh, I get it," the dog grumbled.

Ino and Clara made eye contact. They both tried — unsuccessfully — to hide a smile.

The dog nodded, thinking. "Okay, I get it." He frowned, looking up, irritated. "So how does *this* exist then?" He pointed at the very-incorrect "Balance Check" box on Dr. Reed's entry.

Clara shrugged. "That, I can't say. No accounting software on earth would let that out. So you would have to create it artificially." She shrugged. "Photoshop, some kind of imaging software. You might want to check with the Graphic Design department."

Ino raised his eyebrows. "Somebody *faked* this?" he asked, incredulously.

Clara nodded, frowning. "I would guess so. It just couldn't be natural the way it is."

Jack nodded slowly. "So Reed didn't just… screw this up," the dog said. He looked up again. "He went to a *great deal of trouble* to screw this up."

The calico nodded. "I would certainly say so."

Jack nodded. "Okay. Sorry to doubt you, Professor."

Clara smiled smugly back at him, but she did nod amiably. "Not a problem."

Jack sighed. "All right. I guess I'll get a forensic team on this." He frowned. "We'll see if anything on here is important to the case."

They all frowned at the document for a few moments.

Ino stared at it. What a strange way to screw something up. What was Reed trying to *say* with this? It was another riddle.

The man never came out and directly stated anything. But he *did* put it out in the open. The pictures had been the same way. The files were hidden, but the keys to finding them were literally hanging on the wall in thirty-inch frames. Ino had the information to solve the puzzle staring him in the face. He just had to connect the dots.

So what was hidden in plain sight on *this* document?

Ino pondered, cocking his head. "Hey… I have a question here."

They both looked at him.

Ino pointed to the balance check. "What *should* be here, but isn't?"

Clara stared blankly at him. "Pardon?"

Ino frowned, feeling his ears tilt back. This was a little embarrassing but he felt like it was important. "This balance check thing. How is this supposed to work?"

Clara stared at him. "Well… the premise is very simple. The left side and the right side are supposed to balance. The software totals up both columns, and then subtracts one from the other. If you're off by a dollar, it says, one dollar."

Ino nodded. "Okay. Got it. And if both numbers are the same, like they should be, you end up with zero. 10,000 minus 10,000 is zero."

Clara nodded. "It does the job."

Ino nodded. "So what *should* this number be?"

Clara cocked her head. "I'm sorry, I don't follow."

Ino thought for a moment about how to phrase it. "You said this box had to be overridden or faked. Right?"

The calico nodded.

"So if I put this in real accounting software, right now, what would I come up with? What would this say if someone *hadn't* doctored it?"

Jack's ears perked, *literally* perked. His facial expression didn't change but he was indisputably paying very close attention now.

Clara blinked. "That's… an excellent question, Dr. Reamer!" she said. "One moment please." She stepped back around her side of the desk and pulled out an enormous 10-key calculator. Her fingers flew over the keys, filling the screen with numbers. She frowned, slapped the delete key, and re-entered all of it. Then she did it again.

Nodding, Clara turned her calculator around. "Here," she said, simply.

The calculator said -**21,955,546.37.**

They both stared at it.

"Well, that's a hell of an error," Jack said. "This document is screwed up by *twenty million bucks*? I see why Reed decided to quit accounting."

Clara looked at him like he had started drooling. "You don't see it? Look again."

Jack grunted. "Just looks like a number to me."

Ino swallowed. "I have to admit, I don't see anything there besides, like... bad budgeting."

Clara rolled her eyes and pulled a pad of yellow sticky notes out of her top drawer. "And they say *women* don't have a head for numbers." She copied the number down without the commas. "Here. Let me give you both a big fat clue."

She drew two big slashes through it.

-219 / 555 / 46.37.

Ino felt all the blood drain out of his face.

Jack's eyes widened. "Oh my God. It's a phone number!" He stared at it, his jaw hanging open.

Clara frowned at him over her red glasses. "It sure is. And not just any phone number. That's a *local* phone number." She pointed. "Obviously 219 is a big section of Indiana. But if 555 looks familiar, that's because those are mostly University numbers. That prefix is connected to our internal system. The last four digits will be someone's room number or office extension." She extended a claw and tapped on the post-it repeatedly. "This is a *University* phone number."

Jack let out a long breath. "Son of a bitch. It *is* a deliberate clue. He's pointing us right *to* someone." He shook his head in disbelief. "Unbelievable." After a moment he asked the obvious question. "So... whose extension is 4-6-3-7?"

Ino finally took a breath. He let it out as a long, shaky sigh.

"It's *mine*," the hyena squeaked. "4-6-3-7 is *my* extension."

They both turned to look at him.

Jack's eyes narrowed. "*Is* it now," he asked, slowly.

Ino swallowed.

Once again, Ino found himself in an SUV with a silent Chief of Security. This time it was apparently Jack's personal vehicle. Ino recognized it as the ancient red Ford Bronco he had seen leaving the administration building a few days ago. He elected not to bring that up.

They sat in silence again for a moment.

Ino coughed. "This is a funny-looking squad car."

Jack narrowed his eyes. "I told you, I was off duty."

Ino frowned. He was feeling hot for some reason. And he could smell the dog, who was giving off a light aroma of sweat and aftershave. It wasn't a *bad* smell, just a smell of which Ino was growing acutely aware. "You know, if you had a car from this decade, you could enjoy such modern benefits as air conditioning. It's like 86 degrees out."

Jack frowned at him. "I'm perfectly comfortable."

The hyena snorted, looking at Jack's bare arms. "You're also wearing half a shirt." He stole another glance at the dog's exposed flanks.

Jack nodded. "I suppose that's true."

They sat for another moment.

"Am I under arrest?" Ino finally asked.

Jack frowned at him, and let out a shallow breath. "No. Not yet, anyway." He stared at Ino for a moment, and then asked the question the hyena had been dreading. The dog narrowed his eyes. "Where were you on the evening of the 11th?"

Ino swallowed, feeling his face heat up. He'd known this was coming, but hearing it out loud still made his stomach turn over in a slow, nauseated roll. He sighed. "I assume you mean *before* the explosion. I was walking across campus with Sean Murphy. He can vouch, and so can that psychotic badger in the accounting department. He saw us walking past at around ten to six."

The dog stared at him. "What about before that?"

"I was sitting in my office grading finals and emailing." He thought for a moment. "Nobody saw me, I don't think. But there will be computer network activity. Which is tied to my password." He considered. "And I have a unique login on the Scantron machine." He tightened his lips. "And I might have been on a security camera somewhere. I went to the vending machines at like… maybe 4:30? I walked past the front of the building, I assume there are cameras up there."

Jack stared at him.

Ino felt his face heat up. "What?!" he demanded.

The dog shrugged, and cracked a humorless smile. "Nothing. I just expected another sarcastic response out of you. This sure seems a lot more serious when it's *your* phone number as the clue, doesn't it, Dr. Reamer?" He smiled grimly.

Ino scowled at him. "This situation has *always* seemed serious. I almost died in that explosion, remember? Which, by the way, is pretty strong evidence that I *wasn't* the one who caused it."

Jack shrugged. "Not necessarily. Maybe you thought it would be half the size that it was. Bust a couple windows, maybe take the roof off. Maybe you don't know as much about gas explosions as you think you do." He raised his eyebrows. "Because I gotta say, Dr. Reamer, if you wanted to throw suspicion off of yourself, that makes for a hell of a good alibi!"

Ino resisted the urge to show his teeth. He felt his ears getting hot. "I. Would *never*," he growled through his teeth. "Have put *Sean* in that kind of danger."

Jack stared at him for a long time.

Finally, he looked away. "No, I don't believe that you would."

Ino let out a long sigh. "Thank you."

"That would make you more of a psychopath. I'm pretty sure this killer was just a garden-variety murderer."

Ino glared at him. "That's not funny."

Jack glanced back at him, no trace of a smile on his black muzzle. "It wasn't a joke, Dr. Reamer," he said, flatly.

Ino stared at him, and nodded slowly. After a moment he sat back in the Bronco's uncomfortable thirty-year-old seat. It felt like one big metal bar behind the thick vinyl of the seats. He frowned. "You don't *really* think I might be involved in his murder, do you?"

The shepherd considered for a moment, and then shallowly shrugged. "No. Your alibi is pretty good, and I don't even know if that stupid math clue was even connected to Reed's murder. For all I know he was just playing with paperwork. But you don't catch a murderer by asking polite questions."

Ino smiled humorlessly.

Jack stared off into the distance for a moment, and then turned back to the hyena. "You can go, if you like. Or I can drive you back to your hysterical yellow Jeep."

Ino narrowed his eyes. "Are you making fun of me?"

The dog shook his head seriously. "I would *never*." He stared at Ino, absolutely deadpan.

After a moment, the hyena rolled his eyes. He thought for a moment, and then heaved a deep sigh. "Actually... I was wondering if we could go back to your office. I think we need to discuss something. About me." He swallowed. "And Dr. Reed."

Jack stared at him, eyebrows slightly raised. After a moment he nodded wordlessly, and started the truck.

They rode in silence a short distance down Church Street, and when they arrived at the overly-scenic Security building, Ino trailed quietly after the German shepherd until they were safely inside Jack's office.

The dog turned to him. "Would you like some terrible coffee? I'm wearing street clothes if you'd like to throw it all over me again." His tail wagged behind him at the little joke.

Ino smiled. "Tempting! But I'll pass."

Jack took a seat behind the desk. Ino slipped into one of the chairs in front.

Something on the dog's desk caught the hyena's eye.

"I see you got your *anniversary paperweight*," he said, cracking a smile. He took the heavy glass globe off the desk and hefted it into his hands. It weighed as much as a hardcover book.

The dog frowned. "I sure did. You want it?" He scrunched up his muzzle. "Why do they even still *make* paperweights? I'm not sitting here with the damn windows open. I don't understand why they haven't melted down all the machines that make these things yet."

Ino grinned at the annoyed dog. "When did you get it?"

Jack raised an eyebrow. "Yesterday. Hand-delivered by the President herself."

Ino smiled to himself. "Huh," he said. "I got mine from her too. Tuesday." He looked up. "There's one in with Reed's things," he said, quietly.

Jack stared at him, and after a moment his expression went completely blank.

Good, Ino thought. *He's doing the math.*

"Really?" the dog said, nonchalantly. "You sure?" He looked down at the object on his desk. "One of these?" He tapped it with the thick black claw of his index finger.

Ino nodded. "Ayup. *Celebrating 100 years.* Just in time for the Gala this weekend. I wonder how Reed got one. When did you pack up the office again?"

Jack stared at him, and then a big smile spread across his face. "Not sure," he said. "I'd have to check."

He's turning on the charm, Ino thought. The dog was avoiding the answer. Interesting. At least that meant Jack understood how weird the timeline was — and that Reed had been with or around President Greeley shortly before his death. And that apparently his paperweight warranted a special delivery.

There was a short silence.

"I think there was something you wanted to tell me?" Jack prompted, gently.

Ino let out a long sigh. "I mean... yeah." He took a deep breath. "I think... I think I know why Dr. Reed was murdered."

Jack's eyebrows raised, and the shepherd blinked at him. After a moment of staring in surprise, he leaned forward. "Please," he said, encouragingly. "Go on."

Ino let out a sigh. "I was kicking this around already, but after seeing that he marked my phone number..." He trailed off. "I've been thinking a lot about conversations I've had with Dr. Reed." He looked up, over his glasses. "We weren't exactly the best of friends, so our conversations were almost exclusively about work."

Jack nodded. He was just letting Ino talk now.

The hyena looked down and swallowed. "There was... an incident at my last school." He looked up and away. "A student was failing my class and made a complaint to the school administration. He said I was falsifying data and sending him threatening messages." He took a deep breath and let out a sigh. "The data allegations were serious — I was running a pretty huge research program at the time, hundreds of thousands of dollars of

grant money involved — but the threats he said I was sending were…
intense. Really violent stuff."

Jack stared at him. "Were you?"

Ino rolled his eyes. "No, *Chief Archer*, I was not." He leaned back in his
chair. "What a perfectly obnoxious question."

Jack stared back at him. He cracked a smile. "Still worth asking."

Ino shook his head. "You are *insufferable*." He let out a huff. "Anyway,
no, I did not threaten one of my students, you black-and-tan cretin. He
said I was sending him texts and emails. *Obviously*, the administrators
checked those, and *obviously* they didn't find anything."

Jack nodded. "Obviously."

Ino glared at him but continued. "Anyway, that was case closed. The
student confessed almost immediately. He got a suspension and a chemistry tutor, the parents got called, and that was really the end of things." He
took a deep breath. "I was never charged with anything, not even infor-
mally. The student was 17, so he was a minor. It went into his record but
no charges were ever brought against him. He was just a stupid kid doing
stupid kid things."

Jack nodded, watching him patiently, waiting for him to go on.

Ino frowned. "So… move ahead a few years. I've now joined Santiago
University. I'm having a conversation with Dr. Reed about a student who's
failing my class." He paused, remembering. "I don't even remember what I
said, something like, I was going to encourage him to drop the class and
retake it next semester, and I said…" He paused for a moment, thinking.
He could still see the rhino sitting across from him, over paninis in the
Union cafeteria. "I said something stupid like," he raised the pitch of his
voice a little, "Oh, it's tough, but it's just part of the job! And he said…" He
cocked his head and dropped his voice to the deepest, most ponderous
bass he could manage. "Surely it's not *that* tough, Dr. Reamer. Not like that
business in Florida with young Mr. Kaminski." He leaned back, shaking
his head.

Jack frowned. "I… see." He leaned back in his chair. "I assume you had
never mentioned this to Dr. Reed."

Ino nodded shallowly. "Not a *word*. I never told anyone at Santiago."
He shrugged. "Nor was I obligated to. No charges were ever filed. In fact,
I'm obligated to *not* disclose it, since the student involved was a minor."

Jack nodded.

"So like…" The hyena leaned forward, narrowing his eyes. *"How did he know that?* I mean, that kid was underage. The record was sealed but Reed still knew *his name.* And why drop it like that? It was… very unsettling." He frowned. "I mean… it was *supposed* to be unsettling." He leaned back, sighing. "He was clearly relishing the moment. I didn't even care that he'd somehow found it out, I was more upset about the creepy way he chose to convey that. It was like a reveal in a bad suspense movie."

Jack nodded. "Interesting. And did you see this behavior any other time?"

Ino frowned. "Yes. Reed was not… well-liked in the department. I bet if you push people you'll hear a lot of stories like this one." He frowned distastefully. "A few years ago we had an Organic Chemistry professor who was having an affair with a research assistant. We had all guessed what was going on — they were *not* subtle — but nobody had said anything. At the Christmas party that year, Reed dragged the professor's spouse over to the research assistant and spent the evening pushing them into conversation. None of us could believe it."

The dog blinked several times. "Well, that's certainly a pattern all right."

"I think that's why he listed my phone number. He knew I would remember his little… games." He frowned. "He even went out of his way to mention it the day he died." He lowered his voice again to a mocking approximation of the rhino's voice. *"I'm privy to a great deal more than you might imagine, Dr. Reamer."*

Jack nodded, lost in thought. "So is that what you're suggesting? Reed found out someone's secret, and it was a lot more damaging than your sealed incident report?"

Ino nodded slowly. "It's kind of starting to feel that way."

Jack looked up at him, considering. He looked into the distance, and Ino could tell he was pondering the possibility. "And he sprung it on somebody, like he did to you. Another one of his *reveals.* And… they panicked." He mused. "A fight broke out. They killed or incapacitated him. They panic. They weigh their options, and decide to cover it up as an accident." He considered. "And all this time Reed has a clue that points to you as an insurance policy, in his desk where he knows someone will find it. Just in case his blackmail goes south."

Ino scrunched up his face. "I cannot *imagine* why else he would list my phone number, except to tell you *that* in case something happened to him."

Jack nodded slowly. "So the big question is… what did Dr. Reed find out?"

They sat in silence for a moment.

Ino swallowed. "Did you talk to anybody from the Accounting department?"

Jack blinked at him. "About the journal entry? You just gave it to me."

Ino stared at him. "I was thinking more like that large angry badger with the amazing motive for murder."

The dog cracked a smile. "You mean, the only guy who saw you *not* in a lab with the murder victim an hour before he died? Your alibi?"

Ino frowned.

Jack smiled a humorless smile. "That would be Mr. Giron, first name Samuel. Not currently a suspect. No priors and he was in or around the accounting building basically the entire night. They didn't even come out to see the explosion. I asked him about it and all he said — *screamed*, really — was *'June is fiscal year-end!'* Whatever that means."

Ino thought about how to continue delicately. "Did he say anything about a former employee? A young girl?"

Jack stared at him a moment. "Do you mean something along the lines of…" He retrieved a pair of black plastic reading glasses from a desk drawer and planted them on his muzzle. He looked shockingly adorable with glasses on.

Ino tried not to notice.

Jack shuffled through one of the stacks on his desk and lifted off the top papers. "… along the lines of: *'That bastard, he's the reason Sonia quit, I'm glad he's dead, my only regret is that I didn't get to fucking murder him myself'*?" He looked at Ino over his glasses.

Ino stared at the dog in shock. "He *said that*? To YOU?"

Jack grinned at him, looking genuinely amused. "I am extremely disarming, Dr. Reamer."

Ino blinked at him repeatedly. "Did, uhhh, anything come of that?"

Jack nodded. "His alibi still checks out. We checked her out too. She was out of state and so was her family."

Ino paused a moment. "Are you going to tell anyone that girl's father is undocumented?" he asked quietly.

The dog's face clouded over. "Nope!" he snapped, his face contorting into a resentful scowl. "I'm not doing Immigration's dirty work," he spat.

Ino stared at him. "Oh!" He stared for a long moment, blinking, and then nodded appreciatively.

Jack shrugged. "Not my department. What else you got?"

Ino thought for a moment. "Hold on." He dug in his bag. "Did you find out what time the first emergency call came in? The *exact* time?"

The dog stared. "Uh, yeah. Hold on." He turned to his computer, leaving his reading glasses on. Ino was still trying very hard not to find him adorable.

The shepherd peered at his monitor, hunching over the keyboard, and typed with the thick claws of his two index fingers. "Now where did I put it… what folder. Ope! Here it is. It waaaaas…" He frowned at the screen. "6:03 pm." He looked up over his glasses. "And five seconds." He turned the huge monitor, with some effort, so Ino could read: 6:03:05.

Ino nodded. He swallowed. Silently, he put the shattered watch on Jack's desk. The time read, and would always read, 6:04:10. Frozen at the time it read at the moment off the explosion — well *after* the call had come in.

Jack looked at it for a long time, and then frowned.

"Your watch was fast," he grumbled.

Ino narrowed his eyes. "But what if it *wasn't*. I was proctoring finals all week. None of our clocks are remotely standardized, but doesn't that seem a little unlikely to you? What if it's *not* fast?"

The dog narrowed his eyes. "You're saying the explosion was called in *before* it happened."

Ino crossed his arms. "I'm not committing to that. I'm saying it's a *possibility*."

Jack leaned back in his chair. "And you just think nobody noticed a call-in for an explosion that hadn't happened yet?" He raised his arms. "And a lockdown alert that *preceded* an emergency?"

Ino stared at him. "Have you talked to any of the students who got the alert *and* were close enough to hear the explosion?"

Jack stared at him, and his blank look told Ino his answer.

Ino shrugged. "Because if *I* got a warning, and then a building exploded, I would just think some nice person smelled the gas before it went up in flames, and notified the appropriate parties." He raised an eyebrow.

The dog stared at him, considered, scrunched his face. He opened his mouth, and then closed it again. "Hhhhhhuh," he said.

Ino nodded. "See what I mean?!"

The dog's brow and black muzzle scrunched up. "I mean… we *don't* have security footage with a timestamp on it… and it's possible that the timeline is…" He trailed off.

Ino was all set to grin smugly.

Suddenly, the dog furrowed his brow and shook his head. "No, that's still impossible," Jack said. "That would mean whoever called in the blast knew it was going to go off, so they were the one who set it. And Travis MacGregor is the one who called it in. Which would mean that Officer MacGregor is the murderer."

Ino stared at him, and raised a single eyebrow.

The chief stared uncomprehendingly at him for several seconds, and then his face clouded over with anger. "Okay. Thanks for coming by, Dr. Reamer." He rose out of his chair, making it squeak shrilly behind him. "Get the fuck out of my office, please."

"Wait wait wait!" Ino cried, raising his hands defensively. "You said it yourself. Nobody solves a murder by being polite!"

Jack's upper lip pulled back, and he slid stiffly back down into his chair. "You *cannot be serious*," he said, through his teeth.

Ino raised his eyebrows. His heart was racing. "Is this really such a surprise? You don't think that guy's a little *intense?*"

The dog sat back incredulously. "Intense? *Travis?* Travis is a big fluffy puppy! Are you kidding me, Reamer?"

Ino felt his jaw drop open. "Are we talking about the same Travis? 6'1", built like a brick chimney, huge angry husky? He's been borderline homicidal to me every time I've seen him. The last time I saw him he threatened me."

Jack shook his head in disbelief. "I think you've been inhaling a few too many chemical fumes, Dr. Reamer. I have worked with Travis MacGregor for fifteen years and he's one of the most gentle, soft-spoken officers I have ever worked with."

Ino wrinkled his muzzle. This didn't add up. "He's been nothing but snarls to me." He furrowed his brow. "Has he been through de-escalation training?"

Jack leaned forward, his yellow eyes piercing. "Been through it?! Travis *teaches* de-escalation training! And he's damn good at it." He sat back in his seat. "You must have really pissed him off." He raised an eyebrow. "Based on our previous interactions, I would say that is comfortably within the realm of possibility."

Ino gave him a tight-lipped frown.

Jack let out a long, irritated sigh. "Anyway, what the hell do you suspect Travis for, anyway? He almost got blown up, same as you did."

Ino nodded. "Right. He was close enough to keep an eye on things but technically out of harm's way."

The dog grimaced. "You should see how messed up his skull is before you decide that was *out* of harm's way. The man is lucky to still have *ears*."

Ino grimaced. "Fair point. But you see what I mean. He could have been watching the building without endangering himself while he waited for it to blow up, after setting Dr. Reed up to look like an accident."

Jack leaned forward. "But. *Why*."

Ino swallowed. "The article."

The dog sat back in his chair. "Ah. About my station closing." He frowned. "I can't believe you're still concealing evidence at this point. Maybe you *did* have something to do with this."

Ino let out a sigh. "Look, I know you probably don't want to talk about it, but what if Reed figured out who stole the heroin? That person committed a felony. I could see someone committing a murder to keep that information from getting out."

Jack stared dangerously at him. "Travis did not steal that heroin."

Ino frowned. "How can you be sure?" He narrowed his eyes. "Are you covering for him?"

Jack's jaw dropped, his eyes wide with anger. "Absolutely not! He didn't *take* it!" he snapped, his voice climbing in pitch.

Ino blinked at him. "Why not? How do you know?"

Jack frowned. "Because Travis MacGregor doesn't *use* heroin."

The hyena leaned back, shocked. "How can you possibly claim to know that? Do you drug test?"

Jack frowned. "No! Look, I spent over a decade working with MacGregor on a staff of *twelve*. The station was tiny, Dr. Reamer. We worked 12-hour shifts. We were around each other *way* too frequently to let something like that slip by." He scrunched up his muzzle. "You don't think I can tell if someone is *currently on heroin*, Dr. Reamer? I *was* a cop, after all."

Ino frowned. "Hm. Maybe he sold it?"

Jack darkened. "Absolutely *not*," he snapped.

Ino blinked at him, his eyes wide.

Jack shook his head, lowering his voice. "I'm sorry. I shouldn't expect you to know heroin like I do. That shit kills people, Dr. Reamer. Some of them fast, most of them slow. I cannot tell you how many bodies we recovered from overdoses over the years. Dozens. Maybe hundreds. You've read about the opioid crisis — Travis and I *lived it*. Heroin destroys lives, all the way up and down the social spectrum. If you sold a fucking *kilo* of heroin in rural Ohio, you would have your own personal death toll. I might have the conversation about a financial theft, but *nobody* at that station would be willing to commit mass murder."

Ino stared. "So that rules out Travis, and conveniently, everybody else from that station, including yourself." He frowned.

Jack shrugged.

Ino rolled his eyes. "Bullshit. Why have the article then?" He shook his head, his voice climbing in pitch. "I'm telling you, *he figured out who took those drugs!*"

Jack showed his teeth again. "And *I'm* telling you, none of those twelve people would use heroin *or* sell a block of drugs that dangerous. We would have seen about a hundred overdoses starting a couple days after that. It would have gone on for months!"

They sat in silence for a moment.

Ino frowned. "There must be some other reason then."

Jack blinked. "What?" he snapped.

Ino frowned. "There must be some other reason to steal it. Otherwise why risk a *felony*? If you weren't going to use it, and you weren't going to sell it, why the hell would you take it? *Somebody* had a very good reason."

The shepherd narrowed his eyes. "If you can figure it out, you'll be the first!" he complimented, sarcastically.

Ino thought for a moment. "How else do you benefit by stealing a brick of heroin but not using or selling it…" He trailed off.

The dog snorted. "I'm sure I have no idea. Unless you were trying to get *your own* station shut down, because that's exactly what happened."

Ino stared at him. He slowly widened his eyes.

Jack frowned. "What," he asked flatly.

Ino processed for a moment. "Get the outpost shut down." He leaned forward. "What if you *were*? What if you were *trying* to get the station shut down?"

Jack stared at him, and then snorted loudly. "What, like the local meth ring wanted more room to operate? I don't get it. It's not like there *weren't police* after we were gone."

Ino frowned. "No. Like someone had a grudge against you, personally. Or the station. Did you fire anybody before the theft?"

Jack stared at him. He thought for a moment, and then blinked slowly. "I… don't think so. I fired a dispatcher for drinking on the job but it was maybe… a year, a year and a half earlier. There *were* two officers I was bringing up on disciplinary charges but that's hardly worth a felony."

Ino nodded slowly. "Did anybody hate you enough to do it?"

Chief Archer frowned at him. "Me *personally*?"

Ino nodded. "It's a serious question."

Jack let out a long sigh. His ears drooped wearily. "I don't think so." He shrugged. "I was just a country cop. When I arrest someone, generally they deserve it. *And*, generally everybody knows it. If I picked somebody up, that person was well-known to the community, and not in a good way." He lifted his big black paws and rubbed at his eyes.

Ino thought for a moment. "Maybe a hate crime? People didn't like a gay sergeant?"

The dog's black eyebrows hopped up, the shock plain on his face. He put his hands down on the desk, eyes suddenly very wide, big ears flared up in surprise.

Ino blinked. He hadn't expected that reaction.

Swallowing, Jack nervously cleared his throat. "N-no," he grunted. "I mean… plenty of people weren't *thrilled* about…" "— he paused to swallow hard —"… me… but nobody would go to felony lengths over it. That's more of a… slash-your-tires situation." He looked away, and now the black fur of his muzzle was definitely tinted crimson.

Ino cracked a smile. "I didn't figure you for the shy type."

Jack looked away, still blushing.

Ino frowned. "I'm sorry. I didn't mean to put you on the spot."

Jack let out a shaky sigh. "No, it's fine. Don't worry about it. It just feels weird to talk about in this context." He smiled a tense little smile. "Or *any* context. I'm… still adjusting. I only, ah, came out a few years ago."

Ino blinked at him. "Wow. I'm so sorry! I got a totally different read."

Jack's eyes widened a little. "H… how so?" he stammered.

Ino shook his head. "I thought you had been out for a lot longer. I mean, I think I read a newspaper article about you."

Now Jack's eyes fully widened, and Ino swore he saw his pupils dilate. "Y-you *read that?*" he gasped. "The gay website article? The one where they called me *smolderingly handsome?!*"

Ino grimaced. "Oh God, I'm sorry. I was just looking for your name. I started Googling about who was in the position and that article just… came up."

"Oh my God," Jack groaned. He looked like he wanted to climb under his desk. He covered his face with his hands.

"Jack. Really. I'm sorry," Ino said, lowering his voice sympathetically. "I'll be more delicate on the topic in the future."

The dog frowned. "You really don't have to do that," he said, but he did look relieved.

Ino nodded. "I will. Assuming there's another instance where we have to discuss your sexual orientation and its relevance to a murder investigation, I'll be very chill about it."

Jack stared at him for a second, and though Ino could tell he was trying not to, the dog smiled.

Ino beamed inwardly. He decided to keep going. "And, to be fair, you *are* smolderingly handsome."

Jack frowned and glared sourly at him over his reading glasses. However, after a few moments, Ino heard the movement of air and thumping from behind the dog's desk.

Ino stared. "Are you… *wagging?*" he asked.

Jack's eyebrows jumped up in shock, and then he scowled. "Okay look, we're way off track here. Back to the actual crime — nobody outside my station could have gotten at those drugs. The evidence room was locked and the heroin was in a safe, and the whole room was under video surveillance." He frowned. "And also it was literally in a police station. That's why it was so confusing. Nobody on the outside would even have been able to physically get close to it."

Ino frowned. "So it had to be someone *currently* working there?"

Jack nodded slowly. "Right. In a station full of people with no motive. Now you see why no one ever solved this case."

The hyena shook his head, thinking of Dr. Reed. "Well," he said flatly. "I'm pretty sure *somebody* did."

Jack blinked at him, and sat back in his chair, crossing his arms. "Dr. Reamer. Unless you can identify which of my employees was actively seeking to put themself out of a job, you won't solve this."

Ino thought for a moment. "Did you get a severance?"

Jack stared back at him. He didn't move. He was processing. He opened his mouth, and after a moment he shut it.

Ino leaned forward. "When they fired you, did you get a lump-sum severance payment? Sean said Travis did. He said Travis helped him with his tuition. It must have been a lot, right? Did you get a decent payout? You both worked there forever. And I assume you guys were in the union."

Jack stared back at him, perfectly expressionless.

Ino raised his eyebrows.

Jack stared noncommittally back at him, and then gave the hyena a big grin. "Well, I mean sure," he said, turning on the charm. "But it wasn't really anything special. I would have to check what everyone else got."

Ino frowned back at him. Jack's expression didn't betray any background opinions. The dog's expression didn't convey *anything*. *He's hiding his reaction*, Ino suddenly realized. It was Cop Face again.

Interesting.

"Oh…" the hyena said, slowly. He narrowed his eyes. "Well, if you do think of anything, can you share?"

Jack nodded brightly. "Will do, Dr. Reamer! Thanks for sharing that tidbit about Dr. Reed. I'll put it to the team and see if that gets us anywhere."

Ino nodded slowly. "Chief Archer… I have to ask you something."

The dog stared at him expectantly.

Ino frowned. "If you knew Officer MacGregor was involved in this, *would* you turn him in?"

Jack frowned, and now Ino could tell the expression was genuine. "Yes. Of course. He's not above the law any more than I am. But I can tell you right now, he *isn't* involved."

Ino nodded. "Okay. Thank you." He took a deep breath and let it out as a long sigh. "And, like... in the meantime... please don't tell him that I said anything. I don't need to give him any more reasons to hate me if I'm wrong about this."

Jack stared at him, his eyebrows shooting up. "What was that?"

Ino blinked at him. "If I'm wrong about this, I don't want him to hate me any more than he does. What's so strange about that?"

The dog grinned savagely, full of teeth. "Oh, it's not strange, Dr. Reamer. I just wanted to hear you admit that you might be wrong about something."

Ino narrowed his eyes angrily, and then felt something inside him give way. He let out a long sigh. "I'm... I'm really not an asshole. You know?" He swallowed. "I don't go around accusing people of incompetence. Or murder." He swallowed. "I don't always think I'm right, either. I'm wrong. A lot, in fact." He let out a long, sad sigh. "I just... I just need to figure this one out."

The dog's face softened, and his lips tightened. He frowned, and then solemnly nodded. "I know. We will, Dr. Reamer."

The hyena rose from his chair. He took the watch off Jack's desk and stuck it back in his backpack. "Thank you for listening to me," he said, turning toward the door.

Jack cleared his throat. "Dr. Reamer... one more thing."

Ino turned slowly back.

"There's something I don't understand about all of this..."

"What's that?"

The dog frowned. "These clues... none of them point to *Travis*," he said, softly. "They all just point to *the station*." He looked up at Ino with his big golden eyes. "But there's another employee from that station right in front of you." He lifted his head. "Why don't you suspect *me* in all of this?"

Ino stared at him, and thought for a long series of moments. Vivian had even said as much. Why *didn't* he suspect Jack? Should he?

Finally, the hyena just shrugged. "I don't know," he said. "I just can't picture you doing it."

Jack got a funny, confused look on his face, and then he shrugged slowly with a grin. "I guess that's as good a reason as any."

Ino thought for another moment. "Besides," he said. "You're the Chief of Security. Surely *you* could think of a better way to destroy evidence than by blowing up a 30,000 square foot building."

The dog cracked an unsettling smile. He had his muzzle dipped, and it looked like he was narrowing his eyes.

Ino ignored the chill that raced up his back. "How *would* you do it?" he asked, slowly.

Jack stared at him, and then answered without a moment's hesitation. "Burn the body," he said. He picked up a stack of papers on his desk. "Fire isn't like the movies — it destroys basically all evidence. As long as you didn't use an accelerant, we would have a hard time even proving foul play, and if you covered up your motive effectively you would probably walk."

Ino stared at him for a moment. The hairs on the back of his neck stood up.

"But... but you *couldn't* burn the body," he stammered, slowly. "The lab had fire sprinklers. So does this building." He pointed to the stainless steel nozzle sticking three inches out of the ceiling directly above Jack's desk. "*All* of the buildings have sprinklers."

The dog grinned darkly up at him, his white teeth luminescent against his black muzzle. "Well, Dr. Reamer, you're right," he said softly.

Ino nodded, swallowing.

The dog cracked a humorless smile. "Guess I would just have to blow up the building, then."

Chapter 7: Upper Flammable Limit

Friday, May 18, 2018

The next day, one week after the explosion, Ino was back on campus to meet with a student. Alanna Johnson, one of the two late-finishers of his last final, was taking extra classes over the summer (of course she was) and wanted to present her extra credit presentation (of course she did).

This was *absolutely* not a required part of the extra credit. The assignment read: *Design a student lab for ongoing sessions of this class on a 1-page spec sheet. Include seating, size, equipment, and supplies needed (+10 pts). Bonus: Create a PowerPoint presentation pitching the addition of a new lab to the University board (+15 pts).* It was intended to make students reflect holistically on the course material as translated to practical lab work — nothing more. It was worth about the value of one bombed quiz, or two quizzes if a student did both parts.

Alanna, ever the overachiever, wanted to present hers to Ino personally, and Ino didn't have much else going on so he agreed. He figured Alanna was fishing for a few more points (*Get Prof. Reamer to put on pants and leave his house, +5 pts*), which he was willing to entertain, since she already had 116% in his class and he thought it would be funny to give her an A++++.

It was the last day before the final cutoff for grade submission. Ino had entered his second-to-last grade late the previous night, giving Sean Murphy an A+ for the make-up final he never ended up taking — Ino figured that correctly identifying methane gas was sufficient grounds to pass him with full credit. Now this was his very last box to check before wrapping up the Spring 2018 semester.

Since he was seeing a student, Ino wore a white button-down shirt, but he found one with short sleeves made out of super-light linen that he still had from his days teaching in humid Florida. He skipped an undershirt, and wore a pair of tan golf shorts with navy-blue canvas dock shoes on his big broad paws — no socks. He looked like he was going to spend the day shopping in Tampa, but it was almost 86 degrees even though it was only 10 am, and he wasn't wearing anything more than he needed to.

He got out of the Jeep, where he had been blasting the A/C, and the summer heat instantly penetrated his fur. He could feel his dark brown mohawk and mane heating up, and as soon as he had taken a few steps in the baking sun he felt the desire to pop the buttons on his shirt and maybe sprint all the way to the rec center pool. He slapped a set of aviators on his face and strode across the parking lot.

A hot, dry wind whipped across the open campus. It made his shirt flap in the breeze.

He found Alanna on the front steps of the library, looking serious and carrying a white leather bag with the side of a laptop peeking out. The caracal was standing in the sun wearing skinny jeans and a daffodil-colored smock-sleeved blouse. The shirt looked breathable, but Ino felt himself start sweating at just the sight of a pair of full jeans. *Jeans!* Her only concession to the heat was a pair of white strappy sandals. Ino could tell the moment she noticed him, even from thirty feet away, because her ears perked in his direction, and with her big ear tufts every movement was broadcast like semaphore.

"Hi Alanna! Aren't you WARM?" he called, incredulously.

Alanna laughed, and Ino was happy to get a grin out of her. The caracal was deadly serious most of the time. She waited for him to get a little close before responding. "I'm from Atlanta, Dr. Reamer. This is nothing."

Ino laughed. "Well. I know a school you would have loved in Florida. Shall we?"

Downstairs, Ino and Alanna parked at the same large table in the basement where Ino had set up shop the week after the explosion. There was nary a soul in sight.

The caracal looked around the empty library. "Wow. I thought we would need a conference room, but I guess there's nobody here to disturb!"

Ino grinned. "Yup, isn't it great? It's like a ghost town. I love working here, especially over the summer. We might be the only ones in the entire building besides the librarian." He waved at an older squirrel behind the downstairs reference desk. "Hi, Evelyn!" he called across the floor. She waved back and then put her finger over her lips.

Alanna nodded. "Good! I hate performing in front of crowds."

Ino cracked a smile. "Just me. Go ahead and start any time that you're ready."

"Thanks," Alanna said. "I've prepared a few notes ahead of time." Putting on a pair of huge plastic glasses, she opened her laptop. It was a PowerPoint presentation. The first slide read "NEW LAB PROPOSAL: MAY 18. PRESENTER: ALANNA JOHNSON."

Ino blinked at her. "Oh wow! You've got a whole... *thing* here! Well! Let's go ahead."

Alanna nodded. "Excellent. I'll start with the agenda." Her tail whipped back and forth behind her.

Ino swallowed. *Agenda??*

What followed was a fifteen-minute presentation that probably didn't surpass, but definitely *rivaled,* Ino's thesis defense. Alanna had schematics, equipment part numbers, supplies listed by type and value, and staffing requirements. She had even called a contractor for a renovation estimate. It was stunning, and for fifteen minutes Ino just watched in wonder.

"This concludes my presentation." Alanna hit the laptop's space bar and the next slide read DISCUSSION BLOCK. It had clip-art of several cartoon figures enthusiastically collaborating. She took out a brand-new legal pad and a ballpoint pen. "At this time I would like to discuss any shortcomings you feel require addressing in my proposed laboratory addition, as well as any potential updates or clarifications you would advise."

Ino blinked at her. "Nothing."

Alanna stared at him. She looked surprised. "Nothing?" She leaned forward. "*Nothing?* Was I not clear enough to make any assessments? Because I can cover some of the slides in greater detail."

"No — nothing, it was *perfect,*" Ino said. "I understood it completely. It's perfectly structured. If anything, it's *too* inclusive." He leaned forward.

"It was *amazing*. That's better than our actual labs. We should build it. I would be happy to teach in there."

Alanna beamed at him. "Really?"

Ino smiled back conspiratorially. "*Yes*, really. But you knew that, didn't you? You must have spent *hours* on this."

Alanna looked up and away, smiling innocently.

Ino leaned in, grinning. "C'mon, Alanna. You knew this was bullet-proof. Why are we even having this conversation? If anything, *my* input will make your presentation *worse*."

She sighed, blushing. "My mother insists I need more facetime to prove my worth with department professors, if I'm going to get picked over the boys in the program when it comes down to research assistants."

Ino stared at her. "Research assistants," he repeated.

She nodded, her ear tufts swaying.

Ino leaned forward. "Alanna, you're a *sophomore*. We won't be picking research assistants from your enrollment group for like… three years."

She nodded again. "Mm-hm. Never too early to start!"

Ino blinked a few times. "What's your mom do?" He thought for a moment. "Wait, let me guess. Ahhhhh… structural engineer."

Alanna frowned. "Civil. How did you know that?"

He laughed. "Lucky guess." He grinned. "I figured STEM. It's good advice. But you can cross *me* off the list of people to impress, because I already know you're smarter than any of the boys in your class." He frowned. "And I'm not currently doing any research." He thought for a moment. "Though I guess I could start, now that Dr. Reed left an opening." He sat back in his chair. "Huh."

Alanna nodded.

Ino cracked a smile. "It really was a kick-ass presentation, though."

The caracal beamed.

The hyena thought for a moment. "Actually, now that you mention it… do you think you'd have any bandwidth to help me run experiments for the Gen-Ed classes? I could really use another set of hands from someone who knows, like… what's corrosive and what isn't. Especially when I have thirty freshmen in the room." He considered. "I absolutely hate to offer something unpaid, but it would only be for two hours a week in the lab portion. It would probably put you *way* ahead of the pack if you still want to be a research assistant or a TA when you're actually in grad school, even if you don't want to do it with me."

Alanna lit up. "Yes!"

Ino frowned. "To work around *your* classes, of course. I don't want this to be a strain."

Alanna nodded. "Great! I appreciate the opportunity!"

He nodded. "Awesome! That would be a huge help for me. Robbie Brandt accidentally set his sleeve on fire last semester and I could just... really use another set of eyes."

Staring back at him, Alanna nodded slowly.

Ino swallowed. "I'll... show you where the fire extinguishers are." He decided to stop talking.

Alanna pondered, and then looked at her computer. "So... do I get the full extra credit?"

Ino laughed. "Yes. You currently have such a high grade in my class I have cycled back around to the Greek alphabet. You're currently marked at Alpha Omicron."

She smiled. "Great! I'm glad you liked it!"

Ino pondered for a moment. "Actually... would you mind emailing me a copy of that? I think I'd like to show it to the University execs."

Alanna stared at him. "*Really?*" she asked, incredulously, her golden eyes wide.

He nodded. "Sure, why not? It was a terrific presentation. And you hit on some pieces of equipment that we don't have in any of the labs in the Malerich building. And I like your desk layout better." He thought for a moment. "I can't share details, but I'm privy to information about... some new labs going in. I would actually like to send this presentation up the pipeline. I think you have good ideas here and I'm sure the school would love to use a student's design, even as a jumping-off point."

The caracal stared at him, wide-eyed, ears forward. "Dr. Reamer, are you being serious right now?" she asked, flatly.

Ino nodded, concerned. It was always a little alarming to get a wild cat's full attention. "Yes. Uh... if that's okay? No promises that they'll use it. But I'm sure President Greeley would love to see it."

"*Yes*, that's okay!" Alanna cried. She leaned forward and abruptly hugged him. Quickly she regained her composure and leaned back. "That's great. Thank you."

He beamed back at her. "Oh! Good."

Something occurred to Ino. He thought about the presentation.

"Actually… I do have a question."

Alanna stared at him. "Oh? About the presentation?"

Ino nodded. "Yes. But not about your choices. About… the counter-top gas jets."

The caracal watched him. "The lab gas hookups?"

Ino nodded and narrowed his eyes. "Yeah," he said, trying not to appear too interested. "What do you think the output is on those? Gas volume, I mean."

Alanna thought about it. "Hum. For a standard hookup? I don't know. A couple cubic feet a minute, maybe? It would depend on the system pressure. They're rated up to 125 pounds per square inch, but I imagine the pressure in the building system is probably way less than that. Maybe even in the single digits. 10 or 15 psi tops, if we're on city gas with a standard regulator."

Ino stared at her. "Huh," he said.

Alanna watched him. Ino felt her eyes boring into him.

"So, ahh, speaking of city gas. You wouldn't happen to know the ignition saturation point of natural gas, would you?"

Alanna considered. "Not off the top of my head, but it would be easy enough to look up. For methane, it's pretty low. I think it starts at four or five percent. For actual numbers I would need the volume of the la… space being filled."

They sat in silence for a long moment.

Alanna let out a long sigh and rolled her eyes. "Dr. Reamer, you can just *say* it's for Lab 103. I already figured it out."

Ino winced. "Oh God. Really? Am I that transparent?"

Alanna shrugged. "I mean, you *did* almost get exploded. I can imagine why it would be on your mind." She frowned. "I'm glad you're okay, by the way. I didn't know how to bring it up." Her ears tilted slightly backward.

Ino frowned. "Thank you," he said. "Sorry for my incredibly obvious questions."

Alanna leaned forward and lowered her voice. "It's fine. I'm sure you had the same thought I did. Could a single countertop valve *really* fill a full-size lab to *explosion density* before somebody noticed?"

Ino leaned forward. "*Right?* The output isn't like… ridiculous. Like, it doesn't knock you over! We don't get *ten-foot jets of flame* out of those things if you crank a Bunsen burner all the way up." He caught himself and gave her a tight-lipped frown. "I shouldn't be talking about this with a student," he said.

"You don't have to," Alanna said. "*I* can talk about it. No discussion needed." She rose abruptly from her chair. "On it!"

Ino's eyes widened. "Where are you going?" he asked.

Alanna marched with purpose directly across the floor to the librarian. "Hello!" she greeted, a little too intensely.

Evelyn the librarian smiled warmly back at her. "Hello, dear," she said.

The caracal smiled and nodded. "I have a reference question. Are the plans for the campus buildings stored in the library collection?"

Ino fast-walked up to the counter, horrified but also incredibly interested. It was a great question. Why theorize about the gas volume when they could look it up with certainty? He never would have thought to ask the librarians, but of course they were the perfect resource. He narrowed his eyes. Maybe he *should* snap up Alanna as a research assistant before anyone else had a chance to.

Evelyn thought for a moment. "No, dear," she said. "That would be a security risk. The University does maintain an *extensive* archive in the library, but the actual schematics aren't part of the accessible collection." She pronounced it with a little old lady accent, *Skee-matics*. "To see the blueprints you would have to check with Facilities."

Alanna beamed gratefully. "Thank you so much," — she looked down at the squirrel's nametag —"Evelyn. I knew you were just the person to ask."

The squirrel chuckled. "I'm just glad you didn't text me your question!" She giggled extensively at her own joke.

Alanna smiled. "Of course. Say, would you happen to know how to get in touch with someone from Facilities?"

The librarian nodded. "Certainly! Hold on one moment." She picked up the clunky plastic receiver of the phone in front of her.

Ino's eyes widened. This was moving a little fast. "Whoa, maybe we don't need to go this far *just* yet —"

"YES, HELLO!" Evelyn said, far too loudly, into her desk phone. "DOUG, HOW ARE YOU?"

Ino stopped in mid-sentence. *Doug.* Wait a minute. Was that the—

"YES, FINE. CAN YOU COME DOWN TO THE DOWNSTAIRS REFERENCE DESK? THANK YOU!"

Ino grit his teeth. He felt his left eye start to twitch.

Alanna looked back at him. *Sorry!* she mouthed.

Ino shook his head. *It's fine,* he mouthed back. He swallowed.

In a moment the stairs were darkened by an approaching figure, and to Ino's chagrin, it was the hot lion from the administration building. This time he had his boots on, and he was wearing similar dark-blue work pants and a light-blue Dickies button-down. As had previously been the case, he wasn't wearing an undershirt, and his thick arms strained at his shirtsleeves. Ino reflected that the shirt would be a lot less tight if the lion unbuttoned it and just walked around bare-chested.

The hyena felt himself start to blush immediately.

The big cat looked confused, until he saw Ino, and then his face lit up with a 1000-watt grin. "Well, hey there! What can I do for you?"

Ino cleared his throat. "Hello again. I thought you worked in the Wong building."

Doug grinned. "I go where I'm needed." He winked. "Looks like *you* need me now!"

Ino felt himself turn pink.

Alanna stepped directly between them. "Hello!" she said. "Can I have access to the building plans for the University science buildings? I'm designing a lab and I need a real-life reference point."

The lion stared at her. After a moment he looked up at Ino, wide-eyed.

Ino gave him an awkward little smile.

It took Doug a few seconds to regain his composure. "Uhhhhh that's not normally something we would let a student access?" He looked genuinely shocked. "But I guess if a professor signs off on it…"

Ino swallowed. "It's fine," he said. "She's designing a lab. It's a pretty big project and I'd like to get it in front of the President." Technically that was true. "As long as it's fine with you. I'll take full responsibility."

The lion stared at both of them for a moment, and then nodded. "Okeydokey!" he announced. "Follow me."

Surprisingly, he started down the hallway.

Ino and Alanna glanced at each other. Smiling, Alanna shrugged.

"So the building plans are stored in the library?" Ino asked. "That's weird. I figured you would have them… somewhere else."

The lion turned and grinned back at him. "Yup. We had a little moisture problem in the basement of the Wong building. It was pretty damp for a good long while down there. After all the plans got flooded out in the '90s they moved them here for good. The climate control is a lot better." He looked over his shoulder. "They got a Special Collection room in here too that I'm not even allowed in. Some books from the 1600s or something." He looked Ino in the eye, grinning savagely. "You like old books, don't you, Dr. Reamer?"

Ino felt himself wither.

The lion led them deep into a staff area past a bunch of offices and then into a 15'-by-15' office with a metal door and no windows. A nameplate on the exterior said FACILITIES. The room was cave-like in appearance and even sounded different from the outside hallway — inside, it was cold and muted. It was ringed by old metal filing cabinets, and in the center was a white melamine table that was probably from 1979. There was a stainless steel file cart — definitely older than Alanna, probably older than Ino — and a bunch of twitchy, painfully-white fluorescent lights in the ceiling.

One of the file cabinets was an absolute monstrosity, with two dozen short drawers, each only about an inch tall. It came out at least three feet from the wall, sitting squat on beige metal legs. It looked like a combination of a file cabinet and a pizza oven.

The lion gestured. "Here you go! Science buildings are Malerich, Kemper, and Baker." He frowned. "Though I suppose we should take that last one out."

Alanna narrowed her eyes. "I know which ones are the science buildings."

The lion blinked at her. "Oh? Is your boyfriend a science major?"

Ino felt his eyes widen in horror.

Alanna developed an expression somewhere between shock and homicidal rage.

The lion grinned. "I'm kidding, I'm kidding!" He put his arms up. "I'm sorry, I shouldn't even joke about that. It's inappropriate." He smiled charmingly. "I apologize. Please don't fire me when you're a department head."

Alanna stared at him for several long moments, and then rolled her eyes. "I won't," she snapped. "I'll be too busy."

Doug chuckled. "Good enough for me!" he said. He gestured at the cabinet. "Have a look at whatever you like. I can't let you take anything out of here, but feel free to take notes."

Ino nodded. "Do you want us to come get you when we're done?"

The lion cocked his head, raising a bushy eyebrow. He shook his head, which made his ponytail move. "Ah, I think I'll just hang out here," he said. "I'm sure you understand, after last time." He grinned at Ino conspiratorially.

Ino felt his ears turn hot. "Ah, heh," he stammered. "Sorry about that."

The lion chuckled deeply. "Not a problem."

Alanna looked suspiciously at both of them, but proceeded with her work.

"Let's pick… this one," she said, reaching for the drawer marked BAKER. "Do I need to do anything to pull this out?"

Doug shook his head. "Nothing besides be careful. It's pretty sturdy." He cocked his head. "I would probably pull the entire drawer out and put it on the table, if you want to support the bottom."

Alanna nodded and gently slid the metal drawer out to its full extension. She frowned, and gestured to the other side with her muzzle.

Wordlessly, Ino slid in and grabbed the other side of the drawer. It was big, at least three feet by four feet. They set it on the table and squinted down at it.

The caracal nodded thoughtfully. "I see what I need." She looked up. "Let me grab a notebook. I'll be right back."

She disappeared out of the room, leaving the two of them alone.

Ino felt the lion turn to him in his peripheral vision. He felt himself start to blush again immediately.

"Hmmmm," the big cat rumbled. "Alone together. This seems like another situation where I could get in trouble."

Ino winced. "I am so sorry about the other day." He grit his teeth. "I hope you didn't get written up or anything."

Doug chuckled. "Naw, man, it was fine. I just got a stern talking-to. That security dog had a few choice words to say about *you*, however," he said, grinning.

Ino snorted. "I have *no* doubt!" he said.

Doug cocked his head. He had a big blocky tawny muzzle. His fur looked soft and his mane was beautiful. The lion smiled again and this time it was definitely flirty. "I was more upset that you didn't come and see me afterwards." He crossed his big arms, his tail lashing back and forth behind him.

Ino stared at his arms. *Say something flirty!* he thought.

"I'm sorry!" he blurted. "I was busy committing a serious crime!"

The lion stared at him, eyes wide, and had just started to open his mouth when Alanna reappeared in the room.

There was a moment of awkward silence, and then Alanna turned to the desk.

Hovering over the blueprints, the caracal started at the exterior dimensions. She wrote down the total exterior length and width and kept going, copying down the measurements of the large lecture halls and then the smaller labs, until she had two neat columns of lengths and widths. Finally, she got to lab 103 and copied down the dimensions: *25' x 40'.* She carefully placed a little dash next to the last one.

She's obfuscating the true intent, Ino noted. She didn't want anyone to catch on to the fact that they were investigating the lab that had exploded. Smart.

I am DEFINITELY snagging her as a research assistant, he thought.

Alanna wrote down one final number, *144"*, the interior height, and drew a line next to all of the widths. She looked around the paper. "What year was this building put up?" she asked.

Doug blinked several times at her. "Uhhhhh. 1970-something, I think." He frowned. "There used to be a big metal plate with the year on it."

Ino winced. "Yes. 1971." He probably had a bruise that spelled it backwards on his back.

She nodded. "Very good." She looked up. "You don't have any of the lab equipment purchase records, do you?"

The lion blinked at her. "Hmmm… I definitely don't," he said, eyes wide. He thought about it and grimaced. "They were probably stored in the building."

Alanna nodded. "That's fine." She smiled. "It was a long shot. Most of these lab supply companies have been producing the exact same parts for decades so I can probably still find it." She turned to Ino. "I have what I need. I was within 3% on my guesses in my mock presentation. I expect to be graded accordingly."

Ino burst out laughing. "So noted!"

The caracal looked at the two of them. "I'm going to get started on my summary," she said. "I'll be outside if you have any other suggestions." Without a further word, she turned and was gone.

The maintenance lion looked over at Ino. "Watch out, doc — she's going to have your job someday."

Ino grinned. "That's fine. I can always go back to being a lab tech." He pointed at the drawer. "Help you with that?"

The lion beamed. "Sure — thanks!"

They grabbed both sides of the drawer and carefully slid it into place.

Ino watched the lion's thick forearms as the cat leaned over. He felt his face start to heat up again. "Thanks for your help. What are you doing here anyway? You keep the Wong building running, but you work here too, huh?" the hyena asked. "Is there anything you *don't* do at this school?" He beamed. *That was not embarrassing!* he congratulated himself.

The lion grinned coyly at him. "Nope. I do it all — maintenance, engineering, work on the University fleet vehicles. Sometimes I even pitch in with the landscaping." He leaned forward, smiling a big smile. "Would you like to come lay some sod, Dr. Reamer?"

Ino laughed. "Gosh, as tempting as that sounds… I don't have much of a green thumb. I think I'll leave it to the experts."

The lion stared at him for a moment, smiling a funny smile, and after a moment Ino realized why.

"How about coffee, then?" he asked.

Ino stared at him. So this was it! This was the culmination of all the big cat's flirting. After a brief consideration of his options, Ino decided to chicken out.

He swallowed. "Sure! Great! Absolutely! Ah… later. Right now is… just… a really really bad time." He grimaced. "I mean… can I get back to you? I have a lot going on."

The lion blinked. "Oh!" It took him a moment to recover. "A lot going on?"

I'm trying to solve a murder that maybe isn't a murder but is just instead me going insane; so far the only person truly implicated is me, and also summer semester is about to start. "Yep. I have a lot going on." He winced. "I'm sorry. I know that's a terrible answer."

The lion leaned in, grinning evilly. "I mean… are you sure it has nothing to do with that cop you left with?"

Ino felt his jaw drop open.

Doug laughed loudly. "I *knew* you guys were a thing. I figured he must have the hots for you or you'd definitely be in jail by now." The lion chuckled, his deep bass voice resonating in his thick chest. "It's cool! You like older men, he's a hot daddy." He shrugged. "I get it."

Ino felt his face heating up. "We are absolutely not a thing! He is *insufferable!*"

The lion nodded. "Well, no argument here."

Ino took a deep breath. "No, there's nothing there, and like, you, you're hot, like *super* hot — like those *arms*, and like, that *chest*, and I'm pretty sure you could bench press me, so like, uh…" He trailed off. "I forgot where I was going with that."

Doug smiled. "You were rejecting me."

Ino blinked at him. "Oh right!" He frowned. "I mean… not *right*…" He let out a shaky breath. "It's just… not a good time," he muttered.

The lion smiled. "It's fine. I believe you." He leaned in. "I am not gonna stop flirting, though."

Ino felt himself blush immediately. "I mean… that's fine," he squeaked.

Doug grinned. "Thought it might be."

He found Alanna back at the big downstairs table, in front of a notepad with twenty lines of notes on it. There were half a dozen books open around her. One of them had pictures of the desktop valves and Ino recognized it as a supplier catalog. Ino didn't know that vendor so his guess was that Alanna had ordered a copy specifically for her extra credit presentation.

"So, what do you th —" he started.

"Four hours," she said. "Minimum."

He slid into a chair, stunned, and stared at the caracal for a moment.

Four hours?? That meant the timeline was all wrong. The way Jack had been talking, they thought the nozzle would have been open twenty minutes. Maybe half an hour, *tops*. *Nobody* had made any mention whatsoever that Dr. Reed could have been lying there for even an hour, let alone *four* hours. That would have been... all the way back when Ino had started grading finals.

"That's impossible," he said, flatly.

She grinned. "See for yourself! Let's review my methodology."

Ino stared at her. "Nothing personal," he said, frowning.

"Oh no," she replied, leaning intensely forward, eyes a little too wide. "I *insist!*"

She slid the legal pad over to him so she could walk him through her calculations.

"Okay. That lab was 25 by 40, with 12-foot ceilings. That's 12,000 cubic feet of volume, even."

He nodded.

"Here's the flammable range for methane." She pointed to a chemistry reference book. *Wow, she found that fast,* he thought.

FUEL GAS	LOWER FLAMMABLE LIMIT (LFL) % by volume of air	UPPER FLAMMABLE LIMIT (UFL) % by volume of air

They went way down the page.

Methane	4.4%	16.4%

He nodded. "Got it. At 4.4% of the overall atmosphere, there's enough Methane to ignite. And at 16.4% it's too rich — it composes so much of the atmosphere that a flame couldn't sustain."

She nodded. "Right. So for 12,000 cubic feet, 4.4% is 528 cubic feet of methane, absolute bare-bones minimum. Round up to 600 to account for methane leaking out while the room is filling."

Ino thought about that. He *knew* methane had leaked out. They had smelled it all the way down the hall. He felt doubt gnawing at his stomach. That was… *a lot* of methane to come out of a desktop nozzle. It already felt sketchy.

"So," Alanna continued. "Here's a purchase catalog for the countertop gas nozzles. They're rated for 125 pounds per square inch, but the actual gas pressure was probably much lower." She gestured to her laptop. "Even for a commercial building using a lot of gas, 10 psi is probably the *highest* it could be. Most homes are 7 and you can deliver to a residence with as little as 0.25."

Ino frowned. He didn't like how this was shaping up. But it made sense. When he opened a desktop nozzle, he got a steady stream of gas, not a blast. It wasn't like firing up an air compressor. Otherwise it would blow the burner hose right off.

She continued. "So, based on the manufacturer spec form, a 3/8-inch nozzle at 10 psi will release 2.5 scfm. That's 2.5 standard cubic feet per minute."

Ino blinked at her. "*Two point five* cubic feet? *Per minute?* That little? I think my shower moves more volume than that."

Alanna raised her eyebrows and nodded. "Mmm-hm. From there, we just need to calculate how much time we need for that volume to spill out."

She slid a small ten-key calculator toward him and Ino tapped out as she spoke.

"600 cubic feet, the minimum explosive threshold for a room that size, at 2.5 cubic feet a minute, would take —"

Ino looked down at his calculator. *240.*

"Two hundred and forty minutes." Alanna tapped her legal pad.

Ino stared at her. "Or four hours."

Alanna nodded. "You bet. And that's assuming *very little* methane escapes. That lab wasn't airtight, obviously. This calculation doesn't account for HVAC or any other leakage. Or gas that seeped into the drop ceiling since methane is lighter than air. *And* it assumes that the gas found an ignition source as soon as it hit the minimum explosive threshold." She leaned back in her chair. "And I somehow doubt that the *minimum ignition threshold* would be enough to level the entire building. For closer to 10% you're talking... 8 hours or more."

Ino stared at her. "What if *all* the jets were open?"

Alanna blinked at him. "That would be... quite an *accident* to accidentally open all of the jets at once." She raised an eyebrow. "Wouldn't you say?"

Ino frowned but said nothing.

Alanna uncapped her pen again. "Do you remember how many gas jets were in the room?"

Ino thought about it. "Uhhh. Four per countertop, two countertops. Eight?"

Alanna keyed it out. "Eight times 2.5 cubic feet per minute is ... twenty cubic feet a minute, assuming they're all open full." She tapped it out. "For minimum explosive threshold... thirty minutes?"

He frowned. "Hm."

Alanna ticked off her fingers again. "Assuming *minimum* explosive saturation. I think it was probably closer to *maximum* saturation, which even with all eight jets open, would be —"

Ino stared at her. "Two hours."

Alanna nodded. "And *that* assumes 10 psi. If it's half that... more like four hours."

Ino stared at her. "Hhhhhhuh." He thought of the last time he had seen Ethan Reed. He had walked past his open office door around 2 pm. But had he *seen* him then? Or was that all the way earlier in the morning? Could Ethan Reed *already* have been lying on the floor of Lab 103 by the time Ino even left for the Scantron machine?

The caracal leaned forward, whispering. "They're looking at the wrong time, aren't they? Security checked everyone's alibi for Friday evening, I'm sure. The average person thinks you turn the gas on and five minutes later everything blows up. That's how it is in the movies. *Nobody* has done these calculations." She stared at him intently. "They were looking at the wrong time. They should have been checking Friday *afternoon*, or even late Friday *morning."* She leaned back in her chair and adjusted her glasses. "And at the very least, this was clearly not an accident."

WHUH-BURRrRRMMMMMMMMMMM! rumbled an incredibly loud bass noise from outside.

Alanna jumped, and so did Ino. It rattled the windows in their frames and for a moment the lights dimmed and flickered erratically. It went on for several seconds.

Ino and Alanna stared at each other.

"Jesus *Christ,*" Ino said, shaken. "Is that thunder?!"

Alanna nodded, startled. "I guess. Damn. They've been talking about it on the radio all week — high daytime temps and then these crazy random thunderstorms. The whole week is supposed to be like this."

Thunder boomed again. The entire library shook.

Ino frowned. "Wow! It's probably pouring, too. Do you want a ride back to your dorm so you won't get wet?"

She scowled. "I don't mind getting my fur wet. That's just a myth, Dr. Reamer."

He paled. "That wasn't... I didn't mean — !"

The caracal smiled. "You're fine. I'm just playing with you, Dr. Reamer. No — thank you, but I'm going to go work out so I'll probably get soaked anyway."

Relieved, he nodded. "Great!"

Alanna laughed. "The Fitness Center is still closed but they put a couple treadmills in one of the big conference rooms at the Union. And look!" She pulled a mini umbrella out of her big leather bag.

Ino stared. "And you were worried I would *underestimate* how smart you are?"

Alanna beamed at him.

Ino cracked a smile. "Okay, good deal." He thought for a moment and then sighed heavily. "Thanks for your help today. *Please* don't share anyth —"

"Don't discuss anything we talked about." She nodded. "*Obviously.* I don't want to endanger an ongoing investigation."

Ino nodded. "Right." He felt a little sick. "Do you mind if I make copies of your reference materials here?"

Alanna nodded. "Of course, but most of it is online. Do you want me to just send you the links?"

Ino thought about the creepy answer Jack Archer had given him. He needed to present this, but there was always the arms-length chance that someone on the Security team was somehow involved. And if there was even a tiny chance that Jack or Travis was involved, Ino wanted to keep Alanna far, far away from it.

He put on a fake smile. "Actually... I would prefer to keep this out of email. Can you just print them?"

Alanna stared at him a moment, surprised. "Of... course." She furrowed her brow, clearly seeing right through the implications, and frowned. "Just... be careful, ok, Dr. Reamer?"

He smiled weakly back at her. "Always!" he said, brightly.

Ino didn't have anything scheduled for the middle of the day, so he headed back home. He flung his clothes off as soon as he walked in the door and spent the next several hours in spots and little boxer briefs, working on lesson plans and then scrubbing and cleaning his townhouse with the air conditioner blasting. He lifted weights in the guest room for an hour, and then still had a ton of nervous energy so he ran a few miles on the treadmill.

He showered and headed back to campus for a dinner date with Vivian, opting for another linen shirt and little golf shorts, this time with sandals. The storms had been over by noon, and now it was hot *and* humid. Indiana was feeling more like Florida every passing year. Ino was already rotating through his hot-weather work shirts and it was still May.

He parked in the admin spaces and hiked to one of the few operating cafeterias — Chaney Hall.

The main eating space in Chaney was a long semicircle of windows, looking out over the quad. The outer wall was ringed with booths, flanked by four-person tables filling the open space, and a handful of bar-height tables with stools. Vivian was perched at one of these with a huge hamburger and a 30-oz soda. The rest of the cafeteria was almost empty — it was dinnertime, but between semesters the school facilities were always very lightly attended. Plus, students ate at weird hours during the best of times.

"Hey, nerd!" she greeted him. The pine marten raised her eyebrows when she saw him. "Wow, you're actually wearing shorts!"

Ino padded up to her, panting. He hated wearing sandals in public, and the air felt weird on his toes. "Oh my God, it's so gross! Do you believe it's not even June?" He looked at the pine marten and her jeans and thin white sweater. "Are you crazy, Vivian? A *sweater?!*"

Vivian chuckled. "What? It's a *white* sweater, at least! And look, I'm at least wearing a skirt." She swung her legs and showed him her navy-blue pencil skirt and white sandals.

He frowned. "I suppose so!" He shook his head. "Cute shoes. Hold on, I need food."

She smiled toothily. "Can't promise I won't finish before you get back!" He chuckled.

Two minutes later, he was back at the table with a hamburger and a mountain of french fries. He eyed Vivian's empty tray. "Wow. I guess you missed American food while you were away."

She stared at him and then at his food. "*Yes,* and you would too. It's so fatty and horrible and delicious." She grabbed a couple of his fries.

Ino laughed. "Hands off, woman!" he ordered.

She grabbed at his plate again. He pretended to swat at her hand.

The pine marten stuffed the stolen fries into her mouth. "I'm done, I promise. You're one to get upset, you filthy scavenger."

"You'd better be done!" Ino announced. "You know, hyenas aren't even scavengers." He gestured with a french fry. "We are *apex predators.*"

Vivian chuckled. "I know, I know. If I see any lions I'll set them straight."

Ino straightened in his chair, grinning. "You know, *speaking* of lions not being straight…"

She raised her eyebrows. "Wow, that's a hell of a segue."

Ino grinned. "You know that big hot lion in maintenance? Works in the admin building and the library sometimes?"

She nodded. "And the Union and the Chapel. I've seen him working on the lawn occasionally. He's like… gorgeous. He looks like the maintenance guy in a romance novel where the heroine falls for the maintenance guy."

Ino grinned. "He asked me out."

Vivian's jaw dropped. "Really?!"

He beamed. "Yah, like a couple hours ago!"

Vivian nodded. "That's great! When's the date?"

He stared at her. "Ehhhhh…"

Vivian's face darkened. "Ino. No."

Ino shrugged slowly. "Ehhhh. It's not really a great time for me."

The pine marten leaned forward, horrified. "When is it a bad time for hot lions?!"

Ino stifled a laugh and leaned forward. "Shhh, he works all over campus. He could be working here today. Or crouching in the salad bar."

Vivian nodded. "Hiding in a supply closet."

Ino nodded. "Crawling around in the vents."

The pine marten frowned. "You really turned him down? What the hell?"

Ino frowned, and then shrugged. "I don't know. I just don't feel like dating right now, I guess."

Vivian stared at him. "Ino. It has been *years* since your last relationship spectacularly self-destructed." She narrowed her eyes. "Are you developing intimacy issues?"

Ino blinked at her, his eyes widening. "I don't think so. Ummm, that's *your* department."

Vivian raised an eyebrow.

Ino shrugged, letting out a sigh. "I don't know. I don't know anything about that guy. It came up quick and I didn't know how to respond."

Vivian sighed. "You panicked."

Ino laughed. "I DID panic. But I can always go back and ask him out."

Vivian nodded. "You'd better. I worry about you. Cooped up in that little house all alone. What did you do all day anyway — work out and then deep clean your house?"

Ino's eyes widened.

Vivian grinned at him. "Nerd."

Ino swallowed a snicker. "Don't call me that so loud! The students will hear you."

Vivian grinned savagely at him. "I'm pretty sure they know already."

Ino snorted and set in on his hamburger.

Vivian stared at it, narrowing her eyes.

He blinked at her.

Finally, the pine marten let out a sigh. "I give up. I'm going to get another burger." She slid out of her chair. "I'm giving myself two more weeks of eating like crap and then I'm going back to real food."

Ino chuckled. "You gonna get fat," he said around his burger. He finished his bite and licked his chops. "You might finally break 110. And *then* what, Vivian?" He grinned sardonically at her.

Vivian rolled her eyes. "Why do I hang out with you?!" she lamented, and disappeared back into the cafeteria.

Five minutes later she was back with another burger, a small paper boat of fries, and a little tub of molten fake cheese.

Ino's eyes widened. "Cheese fries?!"

Vivian shrugged. "Thought I would really own it. You're helping me eat them, you mangy cretin."

Ino pondered for a moment, and then nodded. "Deal." He licked his fingers. "I missed you."

She smiled. "Same." The pine marten climbed nimbly back up onto her stool and in a moment had already unwrapped and started in on her burger. "So hey, listen, there might be something to your insane Susan Greeley theory."

He blinked. "Really?"

Vivian nodded. "Yeah. I found something out. My housemate's brother works in finance at Dublahm Chemical. That company is in a freefall right now. They just laid off a ton of sales and marketing people and he says general and administrative is probably next. He thinks he's going to get laid off. They are *hemorrhaging* money right now."

Ino leaned forward, his jaw hanging open. "Seriously?"

Vivian nodded. "Yeah. Which means they are *absolutely* not in a position to be making a thirty million dollar donation."

Ino frowned and leaned forward. "Should we even be talking about this? Isn't this, like, insider trading?"

The pine marten stared at him. "I don't know, are you going to sell 90,000 shares of stock when you get home?"

Ino scoffed. "I think in all my retirement accounts I probably have about... *five* shares? Maybe?" He frowned. "It's possible I have as many as six."

The pine marten smiled. "Good. Try to avoid mentioning this to any investment bankers. Anyway, there is absolutely no reason for that company to be throwing out a huge donation right now."

Ino shook his head. "God. I wonder if she has something on them?"

Vivian frowned. "Like what?"

Ino shrugged. "I don't know. They just had that big accident, didn't they? All the papers are saying negligence and cost-cutting. Maybe Greeley has proof that they cut corners. I *did* find an accounting document."

Vivian stared at him. She reached for more fries. "What's the Reed angle? How is he involved?"

The hyena thought for a moment. "He figured it out first," he guessed.

The pine marten frowned. "*How?*"

Ino blinked at her. "He's an accountant *and* a tenured professor of chemistry. If anyone could figure out how a chemical company cut accounting corners, it's him."

She thought about it. "Oh. Damn. Okay, that actually makes a shocking amount of sense."

Ino nodded. This felt kind of plausible. He continued musing aloud. "So, let's say he figures something out, and he decides to finally put a secret to good use and make a little money on the side. He decides to blackmail Dublahm Chemical."

Vivian nodded. She picked up the metaphorical baton. "He needs to get a *lot* to make it worth his while. But he can't explain a huge cash influx because he's just a private citizen."

Ino swallowed a huge bite of his hamburger. "So he tells Greeley, so they can funnel it through the University as a huge legit donation."

"And that's also how he gets his cut. Who notices a little missing out of thirty million?" She pondered. "And if anyone gets too close it just looks like a bonus from the University, and a monster donation for corporate goodwill."

Ino gestured with a french fry covered in cheese sauce. "The Dublahm executives go for it because if Reed goes public with whatever he found out, they go to jail." The cheese started to drip off the fry. Ino stuffed it in his mouth.

Vivian frowned. "So then what? How does he end up dead?"

Ino pondered. "I mean... with that much money involved..." He trailed off. "They say two people can keep a secret if one of them is dead." The hyena grinned, popping a handful of fries into his mouth. "Maybe Greeley decided to make that happen."

Vivian frowned. "Wow. That is almost... frighteningly plausible. But what's in it for Greeley?"

Ino raised an eyebrow. "Maybe she gets a huge bonus for rallying corporate donations?" He stuck several fries into his mouth. "Not to mention her legacy. They'll probably literally name a building after her."

The pine marten thought about it, and then nodded slowly. "That is true. It's a huge deal for a University president to secure a thirty million dollar donation so that's probably enough for motive, let alone any extra money she would have gotten out of it. Maybe she gets Reed's cut now. But if nothing else she has gold-plated her resume and cemented her legacy."

Ino nodded slowly. "It's possible."

They stared at each other.

"Jesus," Vivian said.

Ino shrugged. "Of course, this is all pure conjecture. I don't know how we would *prove* any of this."

Vivian nodded. "At best, we could probably find proof of a meeting."

Ino stared at her. "We *have* proof of a meeting. Remember the date book?"

Vivian frowned. "We have *initials*. That could be anybody with those initials." She stared. "And there's one thing you haven't thought of."

Ino cracked a smile. "Just one, huh?"

She chuckled, but moved on quickly. "Susan Greeley is maybe 5'5". Reed was half a foot taller and probably outweighed her by a hundred pounds."

Ino nodded. "Hmm. More than that, I'm guessing." He frowned. "Damn. You're right. That would make it a little hard to overpower him. Or drag his body around."

They both thought for a moment. Vivian inhaled half of her cheeseburger.

"This cheese sauce tastes like shit," she commented.

Ino chuckled. "Of course it does. It comes out of a can. And since it's the summer, they've probably been on *the same* can for the entire week. It's a big can, Vivian." He thought for a moment. "Hey, what about Greeley's husband?"

Vivian blinked at him. "Suh... uh... Sebastian? Sebastian Greeley? I don't know how he feels about the cheese sauce."

Ino scowled. He swallowed. "No. He's, uh, he's... pretty big."

Vivian blinked at him. After a moment, she smiled. "Does that mean he's buff and hot?"

Ino felt himself blushing immediately. "No!" he snapped. "It just means he's big enough to... you know..."

Vivian grinned savagely. "Throw you over his shoulder and carry you away from this place?"

"NO!" Ino snarled, laughing. He was fully blushing now. "Oh my God! Here, look." He took out his phone and opened up his work email. There was a recent University newsletter with a picture of them both in it. "Lookit."

He tapped a picture with the caption *University President Susan Greeley and husband Sebastian visit the site of Back Porch Music in downtown Santiago.* The slim cheetah was wearing a business suit as usual, posed with a smile at the front door of the community music center. Her massive husband towered over her. Sebastian Greeley seemed as wide in the shoulders as he was tall. The skunk's broad torso stretched a golf polo to its absolute limits and his equally-enormous fluffy tail rose behind him like a peacock's. Susan and Sebastian were both smiling gorgeously and holding cups of punch.

Vivian nodded. "Wow, he's a big fellow." She looked up. "Also, you really have a *type*, Ino."

Ino sighed. "As if you didn't know that. Anyway, look at the size of this man. He could be big enough to... you know... *take care of* Reed."

Vivian looked at the picture and truly considered, and after a moment she nodded. "You know, you just might be onto something."

Swallowing, Ino put away his phone. He frowned, still blushing.

Vivian grinned. "Ino, you know I'm just teasing you."

Ino swallowed. "Of course I know that!" After a moment he felt his ears start to cool down. "And yes, *my God, he's hot.* He could take care of *me*, too."

Vivian laughed.

"Murder *me*, skunk daddy."

"INO!"

He grinned, and then something outside caught his eye. He turned his head past Vivian, out the window, his smile fading off his face.

Vivian paled. "Oh God, is he behind me?" She turned, and followed Ino's line of sight.

It wasn't Sebastian Greeley — it was Travis MacGregor, outside, on a bicycle. He was wearing a security polo and a pair of uniform shorts, which stopped a couple inches above his knees, and a navy-blue bicycle helmet which let his ears poke out. He was making his way slowly down campus, going from shade tree to shade tree, his head and ears constantly turning. His uniform looked stretched in every direction, over his shoulders, his stomach, his upper legs, his little paunch, and even his big arms. Ino stared for a moment and then swallowed.

"*Speaking* of your type…" Vivian started.

Ino scoffed. "Stop. That guy can't even stand me." It was true. But it didn't stop him from checking out Travis' meaty ass as the dog pedaled slowly away, his fluffy tail curled up over his strained belt.

Vivian stayed turned around too. "You know, he looks a little goofy hunched over a bicycle, but *boy* does he make up for it with those shorts!"

Ino blushed as Vivian said exactly what he had been thinking. "You are *not* wrong." He frowned. "Why is he on a bike, anyway? Isn't it like ninety degrees out?"

Vivian shrugged. "We talked about this last year. I think he's on the fraternity circuit. He's probably listening for drunk frat boys. It is Friday night, after all." She grinned. "I bet he doesn't want to have to play Drunk Taxi so he left his squad car at home."

Ino thought for a moment. He leaned back in his chair. "You know, we *did* talk about this last year." He looked up. "When was that?"

Vivian shrugged. "Just last semester. Before I left. Would have been sometime between… August of last year and, I don't know, Christmas?" She shrugged. "He stopped wearing the shorts in like, November, though. That's too cold even for a husky."

He narrowed his eyes. "I don't care about the *shorts*."

Vivian frowned. "False."

He rolled his eyes. "Okay, yes, obviously, the shorts are great. But I'm more concerned with his schedule. He *does* work the fraternity circle — we see him every Friday." He thought for a moment. "Remember, we used to have dinner before my 6:30 lab last semester? He cruises by here, checks out the freshmen dorms for any drunk stupidity, and then goes sailing off headed for the frat houses. He only takes the car if it's raining. I saw him on this route last month, too, if I was feeling lazy and came here for dinner on a Friday. He's been on the same circuit every Friday for a year."

Vivian shrugged. "So what?

Ino leaned forward. "The *eleventh* was a Friday."

She stared at him. "The night of the explosion?"

"The one and only." He hefted his bag into his lap and began digging through it for his destroyed watch. "What time is it right now?"

Vivian checked her watch. "Now? It's like 5 to 6."

He located his destroyed watch and pulled it out. "The explosion was *at six!*"

The pine marten frowned at his shattered timepiece. "It's, uh, a *little* concerning that you have that, like, on your person at all times."

He ignored her. "Okay, but think about the timeline. If it was Friday at 6 pm, shouldn't he have been making his way toward the frat houses? At the very least he would have been *around* this cafeteria. But instead he was at Baker."

Vivian blinked. "But that's all the way across campus."

Ino nodded. "Right. He should have been *here*." He pointed. "On his bike. But instead he was all the way across campus. Parked in a squad car."

Vivian frowned. "Maybe it wasn't a big night for parties?"

He stared at her. "The last Friday of finals week? The frat houses were probably full-on *Animal House* for the entire weekend."

The pine marten nodded. "I see your point."

They stared at each other.

She leaned forward. "Wow, that's like... serious circumstantial evidence."

He nodded gravely. "If nothing else, it's a hell of a coincidence. The first Friday I can remember that he wasn't across campus and instead he was *outside the building* where someone was in the process of being murdered.

Someone who had an article about *his* police station being shut down under extremely suspicious circumstances."

Vivian stared at him, wide-eyed. "*Yikes,*" she said.

He nodded gravely. "Big yikes."

They were silent for a few moments.

Ino frowned. "Jack Archer should have figured this out by now," he said, flatly.

Vivian appeared lost in thought for a moment. When she finally did speak, it was much quieter than previously.

"Maybe he *did,*" she said.

Ino thought about that.

After a long time, he let out a sigh. "That would mean Jack is covering for his officer."

Vivian shrugged. "Or at the very least, he's not asking too many questions."

Ino nodded slowly. "Right. About what his officer was doing across campus. When he had plenty of opportunity, and maybe one hell of a motive."

Vivian cracked a humorless smile. "Denial is a hell of a thing, Ino."

He frowned. "Jack isn't stupid. I'm sure these things have occurred to him." He shook his head. "And the heroin theft was a very limited pool of suspects." He thought of something else. "*And* Travis got a big severance when the station was shut down."

Vivian's eyes widened. "He did?"

Ino frowned. "I mean… I think he did. I asked and Jack told me he didn't remember. But I could tell he was lying."

Vivian pondered for a moment, and then opened her mouth. "Does that bother you?"

He blinked at her. "What?"

"Does it bother you when Jack Archer lies to you?"

He shrugged. "I mean… I guess I don't really care. It's just like you said — he has nothing to gain by telling me the truth." His ears started to heat up. "It doesn't really matter to me at all."

She nodded slowly. "Mmm-hmm," she said. After a moment, she looked like she was going to say something else, but then she closed her mouth.

He narrowed his eyes. "What," he demanded, flatly.

Vivian's eyes widened. She innocently reached for another french fry and dunked it into the cheese. "Nothing!" she said. "It just seemed like you two might be... hitting it off."

He scoffed. "We're *not* hitting it off." He picked some french fries off her tray, ignoring his cheeks heating up. "I imagine he hates me, in fact. Especially after I found the phone. And yes, it pisses me off when he lies to my face. If he respected me at all, he wouldn't do it. We hate each other, in fact, I would say."

Vivian nodded.

Ino scowled at her. "We *hate each other*, *Vivian*," he insisted.

She nodded more emphatically. "Okay! Got it!" she announced. "Message received!"

Ino sighed and stuffed another few fries into his mouth. "It sucks though. He'd be super hot if he wasn't so fucking insufferable."

Vivian looked up, smiling, but then the smile fell off of her face and she looked over Ino's shoulder, eyes wide.

Ino stared at her for a moment, his stomach doing a slow, lazy, tumble, and then slowly turned around, sighing, knowing *exactly* who he was going to see.

"Chief Archer!" he said, slowly, as he turned.

The tall shepherd grinned sardonically back at him. He was wearing a shirt and tie with his sleeves rolled up to the elbow, holding a to-go bag and a large soda. He gave him the same fake, borderline-evil grin he had shown after catching Ino ransacking the storage unit. "Dr. Reamer!" he said. "Super hot, hm?" He had an evil twinkle in his eye. "Shame about that *insufferable* part." His tail wagged slowly behind him.

Ino fake-smiled back at him. "Well, yes — like many things in chemistry, your hotness is powerful, but conditional. Nice to see you've recovered from your sudden bout of shyness — I guess *that* must be conditional too."

Jack's fake smile wavered and started to turn to anger. Ino cut him off.

"Have you met Vivian Chen? She's another professor. Psychology."

Jack blinked as his brain rebooted and then he turned. He smiled winningly at Vivian and transferred his food and drink to one hand, extending his other. "Dr. Chen! Nice to meet you. Are you Dr. Reamer's partner in crime?"

Ino narrowed his eyes. *Stupid charming jerk*, he thought.

Vivian took his hand and shook it. Jack's huge black paw dwarfed hers. "Yes," she said. "But given recent events, I need to specify — only *figuratively*."

Jack blinked at her a few times and then laughed, genuinely. "Ha! That's good to hear." He gently took his hand back and turned to stare at Ino. "I'm glad someone here knows how to follow the rules," he said, flatly.

Ino smiled sweetly back. "Don't know what you mean, Chief Archer. We're *all* rule followers here." He glanced out the window. "We have to be! I just saw Officer MacGregor rolling by on his way to maintain order on Fraternity Row."

Jack nodded. "He sure is. He's an excellent officer, Dr. Reamer."

Ino nodded. "Indeed! Very diligent. In fact, we see him most Fridays! Just out here. Every single Friday."

Jack stared at him.

Ino stared. "Well... *almost* every Friday," he said, leaning forward, conspiratorially. He kept his tone light but he stared Jack down while he said it. "Right, Chief Archer?"

Vivian's eyes widened. Ino could see it in his peripheral vision.

Jack stared at him, and *just for a moment*, his fake smile faltered. Ino caught the most subtle drop in the dog's smile. He recovered it after a second, but it had definitely been there.

After a heartbeat the dog redoubled his grin and cocked his head. "I would have to check! Well, it was nice to see you both," he said. "Nice to meet you, Dr. Chen. You two enjoy the rest of your evening." He turned directly to face Ino. "Stay out of trouble," he said, grinning.

Ino cracked a smile. He nodded, slowly. "Always, Chief Archer."

The dog stared at him for one more moment, and then turned on his heel and strode swiftly out of the cafeteria.

They waited a few moments to make sure he was gone.

Vivian let out a long breath. "Wow," she said. "I see you're no more shy about confrontation than you were when I left." She shook her head.

Ino let out a shaky sigh. "I don't know, that felt a little rough. Was my voice shaking?" He rolled his shoulders, swallowing. "Do you think he got what I meant?"

Vivian nodded enthusiastically. "He sure did. Did you see his face?! I can't believe you cracked his facade."

Ino nodded. "Right?! His poker face is like… supernatural."

She chuckled. "He must hate that you can see right through it."

The hyena frowned. "So what? So can you."

She raised an eyebrow. "Yes, but I have a PhD in psychology." She picked up a fry, appeared to reconsider, and set it back down on the greasy wax paper. "And I'm quiet and disarming. You're loud and confrontational."

Ino thought about all of that. He couldn't argue. "I guess you have a point there." He leaned back in his chair. "Ugh, that was ridiculous. So, he knows that *we* know that MacGregor's schedule was off. Maybe that will force his hand."

Vivian shook her head. "Well, if Officer Travis MacGregor suddenly confesses to murder, I guess we'll know."

He nodded, frowning. "I guess we will."

Chapter 8: Transparency

Saturday, May 19, 2018

Saturday was hot and incredibly humid the whole day. It was supposed to be in the high 90s all weekend and Monday, and Ino was feeling the heat as soon as he crawled out of bed at 10 am.

The hyena spent the day working in the yard, first mowing the lawn and then digging several plant pots out of the back shed to put on the patio. He showered and ran a few errands, ending at the Home Depot on Laporte, where he bought approximately 4 times as many flowers as he actually needed for his tiny 10'x10' deck. His patio was largely shaded by a few towering silver maples, so Ino bought shade-loving purple impatiens, red and pink begonias, and a couple tiny little hostas to replace the ones that hadn't come back up after last winter's polar vortex. The start of planting season had been the beginning of May, but with the end-of-semester crunch, this was Ino's first chance to get some color in his yard, and he wasn't going to be deterred by an unsolved murder. The growing season wasn't exactly long in the upper Midwest, and Ino had already lost nearly a month of that short time.

The air in the outdoor garden center was like a wet sponge, humid and moist and overflowing with the scent of dirt. Ino had worn a dusty-red tank top and a pair of ancient cut-off khaki shorts, and he felt the heat leaching through his fur every time he passed through a sunbeam. He was happy to be shopping for only shade plants so he didn't have to stand out in the parking lot where the full-sun varieties were, out where the asphalt was softening and a delicate little hyena would be baked like a chocolate chip cookie.

By the time he checked out it was almost 6 pm.

Ino sighed. He wouldn't be able to get these plants into the deck planters until tomorrow, unless he worked until sunset. The hyena had already been getting up and staying up later and later. Class had only been out of session for a week, and his summer class was starting next week, but Ino had already adjusted to late nights and lazy mornings. He would have to be careful, or by the time classes started he would be on Samoan Island time.

As he was loading the plastic flats and bags of dirt into the back of his Jeep, Ino's phone buzzed. *Zzt-zzt!*

He paused in unloading the cart, wiped the moist dirt off his paws onto his tank top, and fished his phone out of his shorts.

It was a text message.

Hi Dr. Reamer can I talk to you

Ino grimaced. As usual, his heart leapt into his throat when he read the words: *"Can I talk to you?"* He opened the message. As he did, another message buzzed through. *Zzt!*

It's Sean. Are you on campus Monday? It's nothing serious. Thanks!

Ino cracked a smile. Well, that was good to know. As he was looking at it, another message came through.

Sean Murphy I mean. D:

Ino half-rolled his eyes and let out a sigh. *Yes, Sean, I know,* he thought. He hit REPLY and tapped out his response.

Hi Sean! Actually I'm about to drive past campus. Want to meet in the library in 15 minutes?

He slid his phone back into his pocket and prepared to load the rest of the flowers while he waited for a response.

The hyena didn't even get his hands on the first plastic flat before Sean's response buzzed in. *Zzt!*

Oh sure doc! Yah lemme put on plams and I'll be right there

Ino stared. Two more messages came through right after.

Zzt!

I mean panks

Zzt!

PANTS! oh my gOD autocorrect those aren't even WORDS SMH

Now Ino did crack up. He finished loading his car up and headed out to the library.

Ten minutes later, Ino left his Jeep windows fully open so his new plants didn't bake to death, and walked down to the basement of the library. It smelled musty down there in a way it usually didn't, as the HVAC struggled to keep up with all the extra moisture in the air. The big industrial air conditioner chugged away to cool the building down. Ino slid into a chair and wished he had brought a fresh shirt. He smelled like sweat and dirt.

He was curious to see what was going on. Sean had sounded a lot more chipper in his text exchanges. It was probably something class-related, or about the LGBT+ group. But it would be nice to see him, if for no other reason than to check up on him.

Zzt! It was another message from Sean. He looked.

`Leaving now Dr. Eater`

The hyena laughed.

Zzt!

`DR. REAMER. OH MY GOD`

Ino chuckled. He tapped out his reply.

`Okay! Lower level. I'll be here. Sincerely, Dr. Eater`

Grinning, he waited for Sean's reply, but it didn't come.

He let out a sigh. "Oh well," he said, to himself. "*I* thought it was funny."

Ino sat there playing with his phone. He could still see the main message screen.

+1-219-505-9363	Okay! Lower level. I'll be here. Sincerel...	6:19 pm
Mom	begonias love shade. Send me pics!	3:51 pm
Rufus Reamer	ask mom, i got NO fuk-ken clue what pla...	12:21 pm

Cain Seward	let's get together when you're a little l...	May 17
21525	Automated Message: INO, please pick u...	May 16
Novi	Let me know if u want to talk. Miss u	May 14
Formalwear Outlets	TODAY ONLY: extra 30% off clearance, $29...	May 13
Alan S	OK, let us know if you need anyth...	May 12
Wolf From Gym	glad your ok !! see u soon	May 12
+1-219-555-5000	Santiago ALERT: All clear issued fo...	May 11
ETHAN REED	(No Subject)	May 11

His eyes drifted down to the last message on the main screen.

If only he'd known what Reed had been trying to tell him. He lamented giving up Reed's phone so quickly. But obviously, what choice did he have in that scenario? He had been in an active crime scene with the Chief of Security angrily stalking towards him. What could he have done, stick it into his pocket? That would definitely be evidence tampering. Ino had already been dancing on that line and taking the phone would be like swan-diving into the pool of Obstruction of Justice. And the phone had clearly been wiped — so any trace of the *intended* message was probably long gone.

In any case, Jack had said that they pulled the phone records — which presumably included text messages — and they were working on it. But did Ino know that for *sure*? At the very least, Jack was covering for Travis' bizarre scheduling abnormalities. At worst... well, the theories got a lot worse from there, and every theory also included a lot of incentive for Jack Archer to lie about the message contents.

He thought about that. Vivian was right — and so was Jack himself — that the article about the heroin implicated the entire *station*, not just

Travis MacGregor. The shepherd could easily have been the one Reed was pointing to. Hell, *Travis* might be the one covering for *Jack*, not the other way around.

An image flashed in his mind of Jack Archer, blood on his hands, frantically calling his most trusted officer to help him cover up a crime scene.

He shook his head, frowning. No, that was a bit much.

But at the very least, I shouldn't accept Jack's word at face value.

Frowning, he stared at his phone.

```
+1-219-555-5000   SANTIAGO ALERT: All   May 11
                  clear issued fo...
ETHAN REED        (No Subject           May 11
```

He looked at it. *No subject.*

That was kind of weird, right?

He scrolled through the rest of his messages until he found another one with the same title.

It didn't take him long.

```
Vivian Chen and   (No Subject)          Mar 11
9 others
```

Ino tapped on it.

A picture of Vivian with her group in Turkey popped up. All of them were making peace signs at the camera. Vivian had sent it to Ino and several other donors. They looked great. Vivian had later updated her GoFundMe profile with the same photo.

He tapped the back arrow, frowning.

Ino wasn't a technical expert, but he had confirmed one thing — *No Subject* meant a file. Or an image.

His eyes widened. Did Reed send him *a picture?*

He tapped back into Reed's message. Again, a rectangle of nothing appeared. He tapped it again, instead of the back button.

Now, two little icons slid up from the bottom.

SAVE
SHARE

Ino felt his heart speed up. It *was* an image.

He tapped the SAVE button and options appeared. **Save attachment. Save as.**

It had a filename. It was already highlighted.

Current.png.

Ino stared at it. He hit the *Confirm* button and clicked through to his Pictures, just to see if it showed up.

"Downloads" was highlighted. There was a little button next to it — NEW.

It *was* an image.

"Oh my God," he said. After a moment of building horror, he tapped on the screen.

Again, a blank white rectangle expanded to fill his phone screen.

Staring at it, he blinked, and then frowned. "What the hell?" he asked.

He tapped it several more times, shrinking and expanding it over and over. Each time the same blank white rectangle popped up to cheerfully fill his phone screen. A row of little picture filters appeared at the bottom of his screen but otherwise nothing changed.

Annoyed, he tapped the screen several more times.

"What the hell is this crap?" he demanded. Realizing how loud that had been, he lifted his head and looked around. No one appeared to have heard.

Looking back down, he sighed. So had Reed sent him a blank image just to screw with him? This *was* an image, right? What kind of file had that been? A "png?" Ino didn't know anything at all about that except that it *was* an image file, seemingly one of a dozen interchangeable file types.

Opening the phone's internet browser, he went right to Google. WHAT IS A PNG, he typed. The results came up immediately.

"PNG stands for "Portable Graphics Format." It is the most frequently used uncompressed raster image format on the internet."

He stared at it. Well, that didn't help. Those letters didn't even make sense. Shouldn't it be PGF? "Great!" he announced, loudly and sarcastically. "*Very helpful!*"

"Dr. Reamer!" said a voice behind him. "You're supposed to be QUIET in here!"

Ino turned.

Sean Murphy had appeared out of the stacks behind him. The fluffy husky was beaming back at him. His tail wagged swiftly behind him.

It took Ino a second to adjust, but after a moment he grinned. "Sean! How are you doing?" Ino had been optimistic based on the messages, and one look at Sean confirmed that the husky was doing much better. Ino smiled.

The dog wagged back at him. "Good. How are you?" Sean was wearing about as little as Ino was: a bright red tank top with the name and logo of a band Ino absolutely did not recognize — it looked like PORN WIGGLERS but that couldn't possibly be right — and basketball shorts. He had a backpack over one shoulder and a big smile on his face.

Ino cocked his head. "You're looking better." He gestured to the chair next to him.

Sean slipped into it. He smiled bashfully. "Uh, yeah." He let out a little sigh. "That's what I wanted to talk to you about. You were right. I'm going home for the summer."

Ino processed that, and then leaned back in his chair. He chuckled. "That's great!" he said.

Sean nodded. "Yeah, I talked to the therapist and she asked a bunch of questions and then said that was probably a good idea. They were pissed at work but they're kind of always pissed? So I don't really care." He fidgeted in his chair. "Anyway, I was still kind of on the fence about going home but then my parents showed up to take me home and I just felt so *relieved*, like you know? So right there, I knew it was the right decision." He blushed through his fur. "So thank you."

Ino smiled. "Sean, I'm so happy to hear! You *look* relieved. I know it feels weird to be going home when you had decided to spend your first summer away, but your support network is really important in times like this. I've talked to my mom and brother a *lot* since the explosion, and I'm a lot older than you are." He chuckled. "So what the heck are you still doing here?"

Sean blinked as if surprised, and then chuckled. "Oh. They're staying in town for a couple days. I'm closing out the week at work."

Ino nodded. "You're really dedicated to this coffee shop."

Sean shrugged. "It's money!" He leaned back, crossing his arms. "And I couldn't leave without saying goodbye." He beamed innocently.

Ino stared at him.

"And pumping you for information," the evil little husky continued. "Sooo how did your conversation with Security go?"

Ino thought about that and then cracked a smile. "I'm pretty sure they think I'm crazy." He shrugged. "They're working on it, though. Chief Archer himself is investigating it."

The husky narrowed his eyes. "Hm. Kind of a long time with no arrests. If they don't have a suspect in custody by now, they probably don't even have any leads." He frowned. "Do you think they're taking it seriously?"

Ino nodded slowly. "They are, Sean. I promise you." He tried to sound convincing. Ino wasn't exactly overflowing with confidence, but the young husky had enough on his mind at the moment. If they did find something, there was a chance Sean's own uncle would be implicated. "They definitely believed me that *something* happened. I don't think anybody thinks this was really an accident anymore." He thought of the calculations that Alanna had completed and made a mental note to tell Jack when things were a little less… contentious. "At the very least, they've figured out that *I'm* not going away."

Sean smiled at that and thought for a moment. Ino was trying to think of something else encouraging to say when the husky looked up, and his blue eyes lit up. He waved across the room, grinning. "Hey! Look who it is!" he said.

Ino turned to see who was approaching.

It was Robbie Brandt, the huge white bull terrier from Ino's Introduction to Chemistry class, the other late final finisher. He was wearing a scarred and ripped football jersey in Santiago brown and a huge shapeless pair of cargo shorts, with flip flops on his big white feet. He had a black Under Armour backpack that was a perfectly normal size, but looked like a child-sized Dora the Explorer backpack on the huge terrier's wide shoulders. Thumping over, he approached the table with the two of them. As he walked his giant flip flops went *Thwock! Thwock! Thwock! Thwock! Thwock!* The noises rang through the silent library like shots from a cap gun. Robbie looked serious, but with his big cone-shaped terrier head, he always looked serious.

Ino lifted his head, grinning. "Hey, Robbie. What are you doing back here?"

The big dog grinned. "Hi, Dr. Reamer! I got a summer course I'm taking. Did you see my score on the final?" His thin tail whipped back and forth behind him.

Ino laughed. "I'm the professor, Robbie. Of course I saw it."

Robbie processed that for a moment, and then nodded, grinning dopily. "Oh yeah. Did you see what I *got?*" He dropped into the next chair in line at the table, grinning. They were all on one side of the table — Sean was between Robbie and Ino, but the bull terrier was so tall that Sean didn't even block Ino's view. He could make eye contact with the terrier right over Sean's head.

Ino nodded. "Ninety-four, if I recall. Congratulations! It pushed you up to an A." He grinned smugly at the athlete. "I believe I said you would do fine."

Robbie beamed at him, nodding, his brow furrowing. "I studied real hard, Dr. Reamer. I was up all night." He frowned. "I was really nervous. I failed my Genetics course this semester." He screwed up his face.

Ino stared at him, astonished. He blinked. "*Really?*" He leaned back in his chair. Robbie was a diligent student and he always completed the work. He wasn't a Rhodes scholar but he was definitely trying. He shouldn't have *failed.* "Was it… the material?"

Sean frowned. "The prof had it out for him."

Ino looked back to him. "Who was the prof?" he asked flatly, but he already knew the answer.

"Reed," they both said, at once.

Ino frowned. He knew how Reed operated. If Reed didn't want you to pass, you weren't going to pass. "So what happened?" He grimaced. "Do you have an F for the semester? Aren't you on a scholarship?" Mentally, Ino started scrolling through other options Robbie might have if his scholarship was in danger. Summer school, an internship, a letter of recommendation. Ino had gone to bat for many students over the years and to date it had always worked out.

Robbie shook his head gravely. "No, they couldn't find his gradebook and he hadn't put anything in the system." He frowned. "We all just got Complete's."

Ino stared. He raised his eyebrows.

Robbie nodded unhappily. "I know." He frowned. "I feel super gross about it. I even told the Registrar I was pretty sure I was failing, but they said everybody got the same grade and I should count my blessings. They said it was a school policy going back to like 1940."

Ino leaned back in his chair. "W... wow," he said.

Sean and Robbie both nodded grimly.

After a moment, Sean cleared his throat. "So, uh, in lighter topics..."

Ino looked up.

Robbie, for some reason, now looked nervous. He swallowed and his lips pulled back just a little bit.

Ino blinked. Robbie was 6'4" and 350 pounds — Ino could not conceive of a single thing about which he might be nervous. Lightning, maybe?

"There's another reason my parents are staying in town," Sean said. "I wanted everybody to meet everybody." He beamed proudly.

Ino furrowed his brow. "*Meet everybody?* What does that mean?"

Silently, Robbie leaned forward and put his hand over Sean's hand on the desk. The big athlete looked away, blushing. Sean just grinned.

There was a quiet pause.

It still took Ino a moment.

"Oh," he said, finally, and then "OH!" He blinked a few times, trying unsuccessfully to keep the grin off his face. He laughed. "*You?* Robbie! *You're* the secret football boyfriend?!"

Robbie cracked a little smile and nodded, a blush creeping through his thin white fur. He squeezed Sean's hand. Sean was still grinning like the cat who had caught the canary. A huge, buff canary.

Ino beamed. "Well, congratulations! That's great! How are things going with your, ah, big announcement?"

Robbie smiled shyly. He was nervous but he looked excited. "Yeah, so far, so good, I think," he said. "Most people are super chill?" He shrugged his massive shoulders. "I think most people don't mess with me because I'm a gigantic monster."

Ino stared at him. The dog did not appear to be joking. Ino looked down at Sean.

Sean rolled his eyes. "He *means*, everyone is going out of their way to be loving and accepting, because he's a big sweet doofus and they all love him."

Robbie blinked for a moment, and then got a big dopey smile on his face. Ino could hear the terrier's tail wagging behind him.

Oh my God, Ino thought. *Young love.*

Ino looked down to Sean. "And were there any issues with your, ah, concerns?"

Sean smiled. "Nope. More good advice from Dr. Reamer."

Robbie looked confused.

Ino looked back up at him. "So! Do you have any interest in coming to our meetings? For the campus LGBT group, I mean." He beamed. He hated to go into recruitment mode immediately, but it was summer, and he might not get another chance.

Robbie nodded with undue seriousness. "Yeah. And doing some volunteering stuff." He looked at Sean. "We've been talking about it for a long time."

Sean beamed back at him.

Oh my God, Ino thought. *They're almost too cute.*

He chuckled. "That's great! We'll start back up again in the fall. First week of classes." He thought for a second. "And I usually have a meeting right after move-in-day for anybody who needs to talk after being home all summer." That made him think of something else. "So... did you meet the folks yet?"

Robbie nodded gravely.

Ino leaned forward, eyebrows arching. "You've been out of the closet for a week and you already met your boyfriend's parents?"

Sean and Robbie stared at him.

"Is that... bad?" Sean asked.

Ino felt his eyes widen. "No! Not at all! You kids just move fast these days. I think in the '90s I did those two things over the course of like... three years."

The boys laughed.

"It's 2018, doc," Sean said. "Get with the program."

Ino smiled. "So how did it go with the folks?"

"Went fine!" Sean said. "I don't think my parents knew what to do, but that's pretty much par for the course. They seemed fine. Dad seemed kind of excited I was dating a football player."

Ino laughed. He looked up at Robbie.

The big dog shrugged. "No problems here. My parents already knew Sean. They met him after my car accident last winter."

Ino thought for a moment. "Oh, my God. The accident." He'd read about it in the campus paper. It had been a bad one. "Oh, wow. That's right." He looked away, thinking. "I do remember two students involved. And it was *you two*. Last winter, right? During that big blizzard? The city was shut down for *days*."

Sean and Robbie stared at him. Sean swallowed, hard.

Ino thought it through. It was making his fur stand up. "I remember *you* getting that Citizen's Award," — he pointed at Sean, who rolled his eyes, visibly embarrassed. "And *you* missing those classes." He pointed at Robbie, who nodded. Ino sat back in his chair. "Oh, my God. I don't think I've ever been in a room with both of you in the last two years. And you don't share any classes. I never put it together that it was the two of you involved." He marveled at it. "What happened, again?"

Sean swallowed. "Not much. Big blizzard. Robbie had an accident. I ran my car off the road kinda nearby, so I walked over and got him, and we spent the night in my car. It wasn't a big deal." The husky wouldn't make eye contact. His ears tilted ever further backwards. Robbie looked down nervously at him.

Oh God, that hit a nerve. Ino hadn't meant to upset the young dog. He changed the subject. "Hey, so, I guess Robbie's parents don't have to warm up to you," he said, amiably.

Sean brightened.

"You have *no* idea," Robbie said. "I think they're, like, thrilled, to be honest." He cracked a little smile.

Ino smiled. "Really?" He glanced down at Sean. Sean looked surprised.

The big dog nodded. "Yeah. I mean it's like… a little weird for them that I'm not dating a girl now. But like… I don't know." He leaned forward.

"They've never *liked* any of my girlfriends." He got a funny little smile on his face. "But they *love* Sean."

They both looked at Sean. The husky got a funny, startled look on his face, and then in a few moments the white parts of his face turned crimson.

Ino couldn't keep the smile off his face. He beamed. "Well, that's fantastic to hear!" he said. "I'm here for you both if you need anything at all. After we start meetings, we're going to do a charity run. And I really want to get out and do some compassionate outreach. Like… paint a house or something."

"A gay house?" Sean asked.

Ino frowned. "It doesn't HAVE to be a gay house. Just *a* house."

Robbie nodded. "We can make it gay. We'll use gay paint."

Ino let out a long sigh. "I was kind of thinking just regular paint."

They both nodded in unison.

Ino narrowed his eyes. *Dogs,* he thought. "What are you taking over the summer, Robbie?"

The big dog blinked at him. "Oh, I'm catching up on some classes."

Sean snorted. "Catching up, he says. He's taking *extra* classes." He grinned proudly.

Robbie sighed. "Don't make it sound so exciting. I'm just trying to figure out what the hell I want to do with my life."

Ino raised his eyebrows. "Oh, really?"

Robbie's eyes got very wide. "Yeah. I don't think I want to play football professionally, so I have to figure something out. I'm taking *everything.* That's why I was in your Chem class. And Genetics. But there's a ton more I want to take. Poly Sci, Shakespearean lit, Accounting. I just finished a" — he lowered his voice and looked around for anyone eavesdropping — "*Computer Science* course." He looked away, thinking. "Meteorology, too, maybe, except there's a lot of physics. But that's like, three semesters from now." He swallowed.

Ino stared at him.

Computer Science.

I cannot do this again, he thought.

"You finished a Computer Science, course, you say?" he asked, slowly.

The boys watched him. "Yyyyyyeah," Robbie said, slowly. He seemed equal parts embarrassed and suspicious.

Oh God, I'm going to do it again, he thought.

"Would you say you're... *good* with computers?" he asked.

Sean laughed. "Oh God. Are you going to ask a tech question? Dr. Reamer, you're like two years older than us."

Ino scrunched up his muzzle. "Yes, it's about image files. I am *mostly* functional, you know." He let out a long sigh. "But I'm having a problem with a text message."

Robbie scrunched up his muzzle, until Sean turned to glare at him. The big dog stared down.

Ino immediately regretted it. "Actually, forget I asked," he said.

Sean snapped his head back around. "He's just *shy*. He thinks people will think he's a nerd."

Robbie swallowed, his ears folding back. "Just don't tell anybody, okay?"

Ino sighed. Was this really a good idea? He hated the idea of spilling the beans to two more students. But if he was going to get a technical answer about a cellphone problem, who better to ask than a techie Gen-Z? He could probably be evasive on the *reason* he was asking. "Thank you. A, uh, friend sent me an image. But it looks like it's blank. I'm wondering if I'm doing something wrong."

Robbie nodded. "What's happening?"

Ino blinked at him. "Uhhh." He pulled out his phone and unlocked it. "I think it's an image file. But it just looks like nothing." He hurriedly tapped past the message screen and into the file. Again, a big white rectangle filled the screen.

Robbie gestured for the phone.

Hesitantly, Ino slid his phone over to the big dog.

Robbie chuckled. "Don't worry. I know the no-swiping rule."

Sean's eyes widened.

Ino felt his eye start to twitch. "There aren't any pictures you need to be worried about," he said. *At least not in THAT thread,* he thought.

Robbie nodded. "Sure, bro." He looked up, his ears folding back. "I mean, Doc. Doc bro."

Ino nodded awkwardly.

Swallowing, Robbie went back to the phone. He held it in his massive hands. The phone was a large model, the largest Ino had ever owned, but it looked like a toy in Robbie's oversized paws. He tapped on it with his big thumbs, his thick claws clacking loudly, and for a moment Ino was afraid he was going to crack the screen.

Robbie peered at it. Frowning, he looked up, and reached for his backpack. He slid open a tiny pocket in the top and pulled out a pair of gold wire-rim glasses.

OH. MY GOD, Ino thought. The hyena had to try very hard to keep his jaw from dropping open. The huge hulking jock looked so adorable with glasses.

"Don't. Tell. *Anybody*," Robbie growled at him.

"I won't say a word!" Ino squeaked.

Sean looked back and forth between the two of them, wagging silently.

Blushing slightly, Robbie hunched over the phone and peered at it. He zoomed way into the picture, and then pulled down the options and turned the brightness all the way up. The phone lit up like a searchlamp. It actually cast a glow on Robbie's face.

Ino frowned, confused, and then he saw it — the picture *wasn't* perfectly white. There were little flecks of cream, and even some bits of light gray. It was the first thing he had seen in the picture that suggested it might be anything other than a big white square.

"Oh my God!" Ino said. "There's something there!"

"Mmm," Robbie said. "Kind of." He slid the image around, and as he did, Ino could see the gentle curve of a big, sweeping line. "I see distortion here. I don't think it's noise, either. Is this a PNG?"

Ino felt his eyebrows jump up. "Yes!" he said. "How did you know that?"

Robbie nodded. "That's it, then."

Ino blinked at him. "*What's* it?"

Robbie swallowed. He reached up and adjusted his glasses. "Uh. PNG's can be used to store transparent files."

Ino stared blankly at him.

The big dog frowned. "You know. A transparency. An image with no background." He shrugged. "We mostly use them for Telegram stickers."

Now Ino was thoroughly confused. "Telegram? Like dot-dot-dash, STOP?"

Robbie stared at him in disbelief. "No. It's an app. Never mind, you're too ol — uh — you probably haven't heard of it." He thought for a moment.

"Uhhh… a transparency is like an image… but like…" He thought for a moment. "Okay, like, you know how in thriller movies, there's always a scene where a character writes something out with a dry erase marker on a window? Like they write out a formula or something?"

Ino chuckled. "Yes. Are you going to do that to explain this to me?"

Robbie laughed. He was slowly relaxing. "No! But that's what a transparent file is like. It's like an image drawn on glass."

Ino nodded. "Okay. Like a projector transparency."

Sean and Robbie stared at him.

Ino blinked back. "Like for an overhead projector? Printed on clear vinyl?"

More blinks.

Ino sighed. "Never mind, you're too young. Okay, a picture drawn on a piece of glass. So why can't we see anything? If it's saved as a transparency, you should be able to see the ink but not the background, right?"

Robbie cleared his throat. "Well… you would if the ink was *black*." He smiled.

Ino stared at him. It clicked almost immediately. "Oh my GOD. The picture is drawn in white ink."

Robbie nodded. "Uh-huh. But the phone can't display a transparent background. It doesn't have a setting for 'clear,' yanno? So it just picks a default color."

Ino felt his jaw come unhinged. "It defaults to white."

Robbie nodded. "Sure does! So it's like looking at black ink on a window, except it's pitch dark outside. So you only see little hints."

Ino shook his head in disbelief. "Just like this. Oh wow. I think you cracked it." *Holy shit*, he thought. *The football player cracked the case.*

Sean beamed. Robbie blushed even harder.

Ino thought for a moment. "Uh… so… how do I fix it?"

Robbie blinked at him. "That's easy. Change the background color."

Ino blinked, and then looked down at his Samsung. "Can I —"

Robbie cleared his throat. "No, you can't do that in your messaging app."

Ino cracked a smile. "Okay. How do I do it?"

Robbie frowned, and then swallowed. "You need an art program to do it. You can email it to me, or if you give me a couple minutes, I can download one onto your phone."

Ino thought about it. *Yikes.* "I would feel kind of weird emailing a personal file to your school email." He gestured. "Go ahead on my phone, please."

Sean chuckled. "I knew he would pick that. Dr. Reamer is *extremely* responsible."

Robbie nodded. "Comin' right up!" he said, brightly. He was acting like himself again — a big dopey athlete, except his thumbs flew over Ino's screen with shocking speed, and in only a minute or two, a new app called "DashArt Free" was open on Ino's phone.

"Wow, that was fast," Ino marveled.

Robbie tapped around on it. "Did you save it already?"

Ino nodded. "It's *current.png.*"

The big dog nodded. "Okay, loading it now." The picture loaded up. He looked up. "The default background color is white but I'm going to change it to black."

Ino's eyes widened. He thought of all the insane things the bizarre rhino might have sent him while being murdered. "Uhhhhh, do you mind if I hit the button?"

Robbie cracked a smile. "I thought you might say that." He slid the phone over. There was a little black paint bucket hovering over the middle of the image. "Makes sense if you don't know what the image is. Here, tap this once. It's ready to go."

Ino smiled gratefully. "Thanks. See? I knew you were an A-student."

Robbie stared at him, surprised, and then dipped his muzzle shyly.

Sean pouted. "Really?? All that and we don't even get to see what it is?!" He narrowed his eyes.

Ino laughed nervously. "I don't know if it's safe for little husky eyes," he said.

Sean shot him a death glare.

Sliding his phone away, Ino tapped the button

An image appeared *immediately.*

But it wasn't a picture — it was letters. Huge, oversized letters that filled the screen. The text was horribly pixelated but clearly readable.

Ino frowned. "Uhhhh." He blinked at it. What the hell was he looking at?

Sean made a deadly snarky husky face, his muzzle pulling up over his teeth. "Oh, is it interesting? *I wouldn't know!*" he announced, irritated.

"Here, see for yourself," Ino said. "I have no idea what this is supposed to be." He turned his phone.

Sean and Robbie looked down at the phone, and together the three of them stared at the screen.

"What the hell is that?" Sean asked.

Ino shook his head. "I have no idea. Maybe it's a coded message? What is the exclamation point doing in the middle there?"

Sean frowned. "Why don't you ask your friend?"

Ino blinked at him, and then swallowed. "Uh… that's not an option," he said.

Sean stared at him. "What does *that* mean? Like it's a game?"

Ino rolled his eyes. "It's starting to feel that way."

Robbie cleared his throat. "It kinda looks like, uhhhhhh…"

They both looked at him.

The big dog looked away, blushing.

"Spit it out," Sean said, flatly.

Robbie swallowed. "It's just that it, uh, it looks like… encryption methodology. For like… you know… a computer password."

Ino stared at him, and then turned back to the screen.

A password.

Reed had sent him his network password.

He sat back in his chair, speechless.

Reed's computer was long gone — obviously taken and dumped by whoever wiped the phone — but now Ino had access to his network files. "Oh my God," he said, softly.

After a moment he realized Sean and Robbie were staring at him, wide-eyed.

He quickly recovered, chuckling and clearing his throat. "Haha! Sorry. My friend. What a kidder." He grinned. "Thanks, Robbie! I never would have decoded that myself."

Sean frowned. "Dr. Reamer, are you okay?" He blinked.

Ino stared. "Yes! Why wouldn't I be?"

The husky narrowed his eyes. "Because you're acting weird, and you kind of smelled like dirt when I walked in here. I didn't want to say anything."

Ino frowned. "Yes, I'm fine. Thanks again for your help." He turned to Robbie. "How do I save this?"

Robbie gestured for the phone, and in a moment had tapped the right buttons.

Ino swallowed. "Thanks, boys. Unfortunately, I have someone else I need to speak to."

The bull terrier just nodded, a little alarmed. The husky just frowned.

"Dr. Reamer, are you sure you're okay? You turned white as soon as Robbie figured out this was a password. You look like you've seen a ghost."

Ino forced a smile. "Eh. Heh."

Vivian picked up on the second ring.

"Hey," Ino said. Sean and Robbie had left and he was alone in the reference stacks now. "How soon can you get to the library?"

Vivian was there in under ten minutes. She was wearing white capris, and a thin navy-blue hooded sweatshirt. She slipped silently into the seat next to him, tucking her tail in behind her.

Ino looked up. "That was fast," he said, softly.

She nodded. "I was only in my office." She frowned at him. "Are you okay? Why do you smell like dirt?"

Ino shot her a look. "Never mind that! One of my students decoded the message that Reed sent me."

Vivian stared at him for a moment, and then her eyes widened. "The blank one? From the night he was murdered?" She leaned forward. "From *the time when he was getting murdered?*"

He nodded weakly.

Vivian slipped into the seat next to him, looking conspiratorially around. "Well, what is it?"

Frowning, Ino unlocked his phone.

They both stared at it.

`HGi!CH4`

The pine marten's eyebrows went slowly up. "Uhhh, is that what I think it is?"

He frowned. "What's your guess?"

She blinked in surprise. "Looks like a computer password!"

The hyena nodded grimly. "Got it in one guess. Yes, that is what you think it is." He locked the phone, looking around again. No one but them was in the library. The building would be closing in an hour and it was pretty much empty. Even the reference desk was unattended.

She turned to him. "Have you tried it on anything?"

He frowned. "No. I should probably just give it to Security."

Vivian nodded. "Probably."

They sat still for a moment, staring at the phone.

Ino swallowed. "I'm not going to, though," he said.

She sighed. "Do you still think we can't trust Jack?"

Ino shook his head. "Absolutely not. Not until he comes clean about Travis. Besides, he probably already has access. They could just have gotten it from IT Services."

Vivian nodded. "True." She turned to him. "And Reed did send it to *you*. He could just as easily have texted it to 911. Our campus service has accepted 911 texts ever since the shooting."

He frowned. "Right. So maybe he didn't *want* the cops to get it." He cocked his head. "Or maybe there's another weird chemistry clue that only I would understand. Like the chemical files."

They looked at each other.

"Well…" he said. "Let's get to it." He had brought his work bag out of habit, and he started to slide his laptop out of it.

Vivian put her hands on top of his. "Uhhhh, maybe that isn't such a hot idea to do this from your own personal computer." She looked around. "Is there still a computer lab down here?"

Ino blinked at her. "Oh right," he said. "God, I'm *terrible* at crime." He thought for a moment. "No, I think it's just the lab upstairs."

She nodded. "Okay then. Here we go."

The lab on the 2nd floor of the library could not possibly have been *more* conspicuous. It had 20 or so clunky desktop PC's, arranged on long tables with wires snaking all over the place — to monitors, to keyboards, to PC's, and to the enormous printer at the end of the aisle. Every surface was white melamine and lit with long rows of harsh fluorescent lighting that turned the big windows into huge mirrors. Even the interior wall separating the lab from the hallway was a twenty-foot row of six-foot tall windows.

"Great!" Ino announced. "Very private." He frowned, warily looking up at the corners of the room. He felt his ears tilt back against his head and his tail trying to creep up between his legs.

"Don't look for cameras," Vivian muttered, tugging him gently along by his forearm. "You'll look suspicious."

He frowned. "We *already* look suspicious. We're at a computer lab in a library on a Saturday night when it's 90 degrees out."

Vivian glanced casually around. "It's fine. I'm sure nobody will review this unless they have a reason to." She gestured with her muzzle at a lone PC in the corner, at the head of the two long tables, the only one facing a blank wall. "There."

They slunk along the length of the lab until they got to the computer.

Ino clicked the mouse and slapped the spacebar repeatedly to wake the computer up. "C'mooonnn," he said, impatiently.

"Try to look KIND of normal!" Vivian said, through her teeth.

Ino looked around, frowning, and then forced a smile onto his face. They hadn't seen a single person in the library on the way up here, but he still felt like a hundred people were watching him hack his dead coworker's account.

"So what do we think this password is for? Santiago sign-on?" Vivian asked.

Ino shrugged, watching the computer logo as the ancient PC buzzed into life. The fan in the computer kicked in, whirring so loudly that it sounded like a helicopter taking off. "Yup. Network access and email."

Vivian nodded. "Right. Unless it's for a personal email account or something."

He nodded. "Well, yes. In which case we're going to have to do some digging. I just figured we would try this first."

She nodded. "As good a place as any to start." She frowned. "Why a transparent image, though?" Ino had explained the file type when he asked her to join him.

The hyena let out a sign. "I don't know. He was old, I guess he just wanted the password saved in case he forgot it. Like invisible ink? He could store it anywhere or keep it on his phone, and anybody who saw it would think it was just blank. It could have been his phone background and no one would ever have known. It's more secure than writing it on a post-it under his keyboard. And then he sent it to me when he saw he, uh…" He swallowed. "… wasn't gonna make it."

Vivian grit her teeth. "Yikes!"

Ino nodded. "*Yup*. Big yikes." The log-in screen finally appeared and he had to think for a moment. "I just have to remember his network login." He thought about it. Ino had been seeing Reed's printouts on the shared printer for five years — and Reed was the type who printed *everything*. Ino had probably personally handled 2,000 cover sheets with Reed's network ID splashed across the front in three-inch-tall letters. It would start with the first three letters of his last name and then some variant of his first name.

"Ummmmm… oh yeah, got it," he muttered. He carefully typed in Reed's login and the weird password.

> Login: ReeEt1001
> Password   *******

The computer thought about it, and for a moment Ino was absolutely positive they were going to get a PASSWORD INCORRECT message.

Welcome, the computer said.

"Oh my God," Ino said. "It worked." He swallowed.

They looked at each other. Vivian was nervous too; Ino could tell by her expression.

The screen loaded.

It was a generic background. It only had a handful of programs, all of them standard for the machine's OS.

Ino frowned at it. "What the hell is this? Did you ever see Reed's computer? He had like 65 icons on his desktop."

Vivian adjusted her glasses, leaning in to look at it. "Yeah, but the Desktop would be local to his machine. Remember, this is only the *network* files. This is everything he saved to his *shared* drive."

He looked back at her. "Ahh. Of course." He frowned. "Wow, I hope he didn't have the smoking gun saved to his desktop, then." He frowned. "If the killer took his laptop when he wiped the phone, the computer is probably like… at the bottom of a lake by now."

Vivian nodded. "I would say that's accurate." The pine marten thought for a moment, reaching up to rub her small chin. "So — go into Network Explorer? You'll be able to see the remote drives in there."

Ino nodded. "OK, here we go." He clicked CTRL-E.

A drive tree opened up. They stared at it.

```
This PC
3D Objects
Desktop
Documents
Downloads
Music
Pictures
```

She frowned. "You can ignore anything local — *Desktop, Downloads, Pictures, C:*. There won't be anything useful since we're just using *this* computer to look at Reed's network drive."

He nodded. "Right, I get it." He clicked the scroll wheel and slid down.

```
Network drives: Z:ReeEth1001
ANA100 AND 200
BIO204 and lab
BIO300
BIO405
BIO505
BIO510
CONFERENCES
Desktop
Documents
Downloads
```

```
email
EXPENSE REPORTS
GEN101
GEN102
GEN203
GEN210
```

They both stared at it. It went on and on.

Ino looked for anything related to the pictured molecules in the office, but didn't see anything. Damn — that must have been for a previous version of Reed's secret-filing system. The hyena let out a sigh. There was nothing obvious here. "I guess it was a bit unrealistic to expect a folder called: *"REASONS WHY SOMEONE MIGHT HAVE MURDERED ME"*."

Vivian laughed humorlessly. She brushed her hair back. "That's a bit… macabre."

He gave her a side-eye, raising one eyebrow. "*This* is a bit macabre." He stared, and then let out a long sigh. "Well… I guess I'll just start with the first file." He moved the mouse toward ANA100.

Vivian suddenly frowned. "Oh my God," she said.

He blinked at her. "What?"

She reached up. "Look at *this*." She reached up and tapped on a folder with one claw. It was the one called *Desktop*.

He frowned. "Didn't you just say to ignore the desktop? I thought that would only be the crap stored to this stupid library computer."

Vivian grinned. "Look where it's nested, Ino."

He turned and stared at it.

`Z:ReeEth1001 > Desktop`

Cocking his head, Ino stared. "I… what?" He blinked at it. "It's a desktop… *on the network?*" He turned. "That doesn't make any sense. Only *computers* have desktops. A network drive shouldn't even have one."

She smiled back at him. "*They don't.*"

He stared for a moment. It took him a few long moments to figure it out, and then it finally hit him. "Son of a bitch. It's a dummy folder." He looked at Vivian. "That's not the desktop folder. That's another network drive — that he *named Desktop*."

She nodded, grinning. "Yup. And it worked! We skipped right over it. I bet that Security skipped it, too, assuming they even got this far. We're conditioned to ignore that since you can see the desktop files on the actual desktop. *This* folder has a misleading fake name, though, so you might skip it, thinking you'd already seen everything there."

Ino let out a long breath. "Unbelievable." He shook his head. "I know he probably just did all of this for his own amusement, but I still feel like he set up a creepy funhouse ride for us to follow."

Vivian nodded. "You are not wrong!" she declared.

Sliding the ancient dirty mouse over, Ino double-clicked on DESKTOP.

The drive opened up.

It was a solid wall of icons.

Ino stared at the folder. "*Wow,*" he said.

Vivian winced. "Yikes. There must be a hundred files in here."

Ino looked at some of the file names. "I will tell you, as a Chemistry professor for most of the last decade, *none* of these look like university documents."

Vivian frowned at the files. "Maybe it's personal files?"

Ino let out a soft grunt. "I would say yes, but I saw another folder called *Personal* in the network tree. So this is... something else."

She blinked at him. "Well then — I suggest we dive in!"

The first item was called AAN05_3313_PO.PDF

It was a PDF of a 25-page document. It looked like a purchase order for some kind of huge piece of manufacturing equipment — the sale price was for $95,000 and included a 25-year warranty, including service calls. There was a huge legal disclaimer referring to the terms and conditions of the warranty. The supplier was a company called *RAGroup* in the UK, which Ino had never heard of, and the purchaser was *Westfield Brands*, which was a massive multi-billion-dollar food conglomerate that Ino had definitely heard of. The machine was being delivered to Tempe, Arizona, in a couple months.

Vivian frowned. "What the hell do you suppose you would do with a... *BP1200 Bag Placer output to Closing Machine KVG-050?*"

Ino frowned. "Well… you probably use it to place your bags."

She rolled her eyes. "Oh really? Does it output to the Closing Machine?" she snapped.

Despite himself, he chuckled. "I mean, *obviously.*"

They both stared at it.

Vivian pondered. "So… a thought."

Ino turned to her.

The pine marten continued. "Given Reed's apparent propensity for secrets… there's probably going to be a lot of crap in here that has nothing at all to do with his murder. Just creepy shit he was stockpiling."

Ino frowned at her. "Ugh. You're probably right." He turned. "So we should probably fly through these, on the theory that, if something is related, we'll know it when we see it?"

She shrugged. "That's as good an idea as any. I don't know anybody in Tempe, Arizona, so we can probably skip this one."

Ino snorted. "So noted!" He closed the PDF. "I'll file this one for the *next* time someone gets murdered."

Vivian rolled her eyes. "Well… you can always tip off Security about this folder if we don't find any kind of a smoking gun."

Ino chuckled humorlessly. "Oh, that'll be a fun conversation. *'Hey Jack, I haven't been snooping FYI, but I just remembered that Reed had a secret folder on his network filled with incomprehensible secrets, which I somehow knew about. Assuming you and your deputy didn't murder Reed yourselves, can you look into that for me?'*"

Vivian smirked. "Is that any worse than what you've been doing up to this point?"

He blinked at her, cocked his head, and then nodded. "Fair point!" he said. "Onwards!"

The next one was an Excel spreadsheet, and it was *massive.*

The column headers were VENDOR NUMBER, VENDOR NAME, ADDRESS, COST CENTER, REMITTANCE NUMBER, REMITTANCE DATE, and AMOUNT. The last column was all dollar amounts. To Ino's untrained eyes, it looked like a list of outgoing payments to businesses providing the University with services. The amount of money going out was pretty staggering.

Ino stared at it. "Huh. Vendors again." He shook his head. "Why does this keep coming up?"

Vivian stared at him. "Keep coming up? What?"

He frowned and turned to her. "That other thing I found in Reed's office. Remember? A Vendor Setup form. It was for some random landscaping company." He looked up. "I see them on this list, too." He pointed. *Triton Landscaping* was halfway down.

They both stared for a long, long time.

Ino shook his head. "No, I got nothing. What are we even *doing*, Vivian?"

She let out a sigh. "Maybe this is a dead-end. Why don't you print it out and we'll keep going."

The hyena sighed, discouraged, but he hit PRINT and moved on to the next file.

The next ten documents didn't mean anything at all to Ino or Vivian. One of them was a bunch of photocopies of phone records from 2016 for a number based in Miami, with repeated highlights of a number that turned out to be a sex line (Ino Googled the number and immediately wished he hadn't). Another was 48 pages of legal documentation of a huge property purchase in New Mexico. The next was 22 pages of serious-looking doctor's notes that Ino was too nervous to examine very closely. The next was a $240,000 insurance claim for a house fire in Chicago in 1991 that was stamped *REFER TO FRAUD DIVISION*. It went on and on and on.

Ino was starting to feel like he was working on a late-night research project. All traces of creepiness had evaporated — it was just raw data to plow through, now. They were looking through an unbelievable pile of documentation. Reed must have used the file cabinet for about ten seconds before he decided to put everything in his network drive. The old rhino had been more technologically savvy than Ino had ever thought.

"I cannot *believe* how much personal information is in here," Vivian said, frowning. "And I'm sure every one of these alludes to a secret that *someone* wants to keep hidden. Reed should have been a private investigator."

"Reed should have been in *jail*," Ino grunted. "This is all horrifying." He was looking at a series of explicit emails between Ino's former colleague and the research assistant he was sleeping with. "Look at this! These two were totally obvious about their affair — I assumed Reed just figured it out like the rest of us. But here — he's got *documentation.*"

He clicked the next one and saw FLORIDA STATE UNIVERSITY appear at the top. He laughed.

Vivian blinked. "What's so funny?"

Ino grinned and scrolled down. "Here, check it out." He scrolled down until he got to the fun part. *INVESTIGATION OF DATA FALSIFICATION CHARGES AGAINST DR. REAMER, AND THREATS AGAINST STUDENT, NAME WITHHELD.*

"Oh my God," she said. "That's… intense."

Ino nodded, cracking a humorless smile. "Yup! Want a copy? I should print one."

She frowned. "Maybe don't draw any more attention to that than you need to?"

He chuckled and nodded. "'Yeah, I guess not."

He closed the PDF, clicked over to the network drive, and tabbed down.

The next file was simply called: **VIDEO9.MP4**

They both stared at it for a moment.

Ino swallowed. The creepy feeling had come back. He didn't know if he was ready to watch a video. "Uh, ahh — I'm scared to click on this," he said.

Vivian nodded. "It's probably nothing," she said. "It's probably just security footage of a Burger King employee spitting in the food or something."

Ino chuckled. "Yeah, haha," he said, softly. He double-clicked on the file, and the computer's native video file popped open.

A small buffering circle appeared, and then the scene popped into view. It flashed white for a moment, and then the camera adjusted to the lighting in the room.

It was Reed, directly in front of the camera. His head was *huge.* They both gasped. It was like a horror movie jump scare. His horn alone took up two-thirds of the screen.

On screen, the rhinoceros stared into the camera, in a suit jacket and tie, grinning smugly. He stared directly into the camera, trying to assess the positioning. There was loud muffled microphone noise as he wiggled it back and forth.

Ino and Vivian both leaned way back.

"Oh my God," Vivian said. Her small ears tilted back.

"*Jesus*, that's creepy," the hyena whispered.

Reed stared at the camera a few seconds longer, and then cocked his large head, apparently satisfied. He took a few steps back, revealing a large and well-appointed living room with an enormous sectional sofa framing an expensive-looking wooden coffee table and a large window with blinds drawn.

"That's his house," Ino said. "I drove him home once over the winter when his car battery died. I never went inside but I recognize that huge bay window." He pointed.

Reed wandered away from the camera, up to a wall-mounted mirror, and straightened his tie.

They both watched.

Reed checked his appearance again, grunted, satisfied, and returned to the living room. He checked the camera one more time, and then moved to sit on the large sofa.

"He's waiting for someone," Vivian said.

Ino swallowed. "Yup," he agreed.

Nothing happened for several minutes.

"Is there a fast-forward on this thing?" Vivian asked.

Ino scanned the buttons on the video player. "Uhh, probably." He clicked around until he found it and the video sped up. "He set it up *way* before the person got there," he said, glancing at Vivian, still keeping his eyes on the staticky little rhino reading a book in fast-forward.

She nodded, grimacing. "I noticed that, too. He doesn't want them to have any idea that he's filming them."

Ino grimaced. "This is… *not* going to be nothing," he said.

Vivian frowned back at him.

Suddenly, on the screen, Reed's head cocked. Ino quickly pressed the "Play" button to return it to normal speed.

Reed walked to the front door and opened it. The door was just out of frame. He stood there for a moment, speaking to an unknown party.

"Who is that?!" Ino hissed.

Reed stepped back into frame, and when he did, he had a guest.

It was Susan Greeley, the President.

Ino and Vivian both gasped.

The two people on screen stared at each other for a moment, and then leaned in for a deep kiss. Reed's face dwarfed the much smaller cheetah and he all but enveloped her.

Ino and Vivian both gasped in horror.

"No," Vivian gasped.. "They were having an affair? I don't believe it."

Ino felt his fur crawling. "Ugh. Kind of hard to deny. *That's* sure a motive." He writhed in his chair.

The president and the professor on screen were still kissing. Their hands were starting to rove, too.

Vivian swallowed. "Does this go on? The camera is obviously hidden. This is both immoral *and* illegal."

Ino grimaced. "I don't know. Hold on." He was reaching for the Fast Forward button again when both people on screen reacted to a noise.

"Wait!" Vivian said.

Ino lifted his paw off the mouse.

On screen, Reed went to the door again. The big rhino stepped out of the way, and then backed into frame. A huge, well-built skunk followed, also in a suit impeccably tailored around his massive shoulders.

They both gasped again.

Vivian leaned forward, incredulous. "Is that *Greeley's husband?* Sebastian?"

Ino swallowed. "Oh my God. Are they going to fight? Is this… is this *it*, do you think?!" His stomach did a lazy nauseated flop.

Before he could venture any further, Sebastian lunged at Reed.

"This is it!" Vivian cried.

On-screen, the skunk and the rhino dove at each other's faces, and went in for a deep kiss.

Ino and Vivian stared, open-mouthed.

Sebastian reached up to lovingly hold Reed's face, closing his eyes, and the two large men aggressively made out for several long moments. Susan watched appreciatively and clearly did not mind the show.

Ino leaned back in his chair, dumbfounded.

Vivian blinked repeatedly. "Th-they're *all* having an affair?"

Ino let out a long, shaky breath. "Ahhhhhh," he said.

They looked at each other.

"What the fuck?" Ino asked.

On-screen, the two parties who were making out and the party who was observing continued to periodically shift.

Ino swallowed. He felt warm. "I guess it's all consensual? Is this even still a motive?"

Vivian considered. "Um… maybe?" She cocked her head. "Uh. I suppose it's still a career-ender for Greeley. This is *way* too kinky for the Lutheran Church." She looked down at him, blinking. "You know? She would be out of a job in a heartbeat. So yeah, I think this still qualifies as a motive. Especially with a video I'm assuming she didn't know was being taken."

Ino scrunched up his muzzle, frowning. "Ugh. Yuck. You're right. That alone might qualify as motive. How awful."

They looked at the screen. Hands were starting to roam now and things were clearly progressing.

Ino felt sick. "Agh, I can't watch this. I'm going to turn it off."

Vivian nodded. "This is pretty gross. And you clearly already have enough to take to the Chief."

Ino was reaching for the mouse when all three people on the screen reacted again. Sebastian broke away from the skunk-slobber-covered rhino and raised his head. He said something and Reed got a big smile on his face.

"Shit, what did he say?" Vivian asked.

"Hold on," Ino said, clicking the video back 10 seconds and turning up the volume.

"*This is fun,*" came Sebastian Greeley's deep voice through the cheap monitor speakers. "*But where is our fourth guest?*"

Ino and Vivian looked at each other, wide-eyed. *Another* participant?!

On screen, Reed got a big grin on his face. "Ah, yes. He's here, but unfortunately he's been a *very* bad boy. I've had him locked in his kennel all evening. By now I'm sure he's learned his place."

Open-mouthed again, Ino and Vivian looked at each other.

"I'll be right back with him," Reed rumbled smugly, and disappeared off-screen. Susan and Sebastian moved to the couch and began affectionately undressing one another.

"I am so not ready for this," Vivian said.

Ino let out a long shaky breath. "Same," he squeaked.

On-screen, Reed returned aggressively dragging a leash. Ino heard claws on hardwood, and a large muscular dog in revealing neoprene shorts appeared fighting at the end of a leash, so close to the camera that the picture went out of focus for a moment as the camera scrambled to adjust to the changing field of view.

"*THERE'S our good boy,*" Sebastian said on-screen.

When the camera refocused, Ino immediately recognized the large black diamond on the dog at the end of the leash. He could easily tell who it was, even with the black leather puppy mask.

When the dog growled on-screen a moment later, Ino was one hundred percent clear.

"*Rrrrrr-rrrrrrrf!*" whined Chief Archer.

Ino was all the way outside before he even knew what was happening.

"Ino, wait!" Vivian cried, scrambling after him.

Ino finally came to a stop on the large concrete front patio of the library. He made a beeline for a wooden bench and sank into it. He was feeling dizzy.

Vivian sat down next to him. "Hey, *breathe*, okay?" she said. She gingerly touched his forearm. "Come on. Relax. Are you going to throw up?"

He stared at her incredulously. "I don't know! Should I?"

Vivian frowned. "I mean, a lot of people are into puppy play, Ino. It's a perfectly healthy form of sexual expr —"

"*I don't feel like that's the problem, Vivian!*" Ino hissed. He leaned in. "The *problem* is that we just found a terrific motive for *both* the University President *and* the Chief of Security to commit *murder!*"

She frowned. "I know. I get it." She sighed and leaned back. "This is... pretty bad."

He nodded. "*Yeah* it's pretty bad! We just established motive for *both of them!* If Reed put that tape out, Greeley would get fired for an affair with a coworker and — I don't know, excommunicated? So much for her legacy! And *Jack* — that would just be a bloodbath! He'd get fired same as Susan, *and* the gay community would turn on him for making the rest of us look bad. *And* misrepresenting — since I guess *apparently* he's not even gay, he's bi." He shook his head. "Both of their lives would be over." He took a deep breath and let out a shaky sigh. At the very end he let out just a trace of a high-pitched hyena laugh, something he only did when he was on the verge of a panic attack.

Vivian, of course, noticed immediately. She frowned, watching him.

Ino took another deep breath, swallowing hard.

They sat in silence for a moment, staring out into the warm dark night. Across the open expanse of campus, every street lamp was surrounded by a cloud of moths, lit up white and orbiting like stars in fast forward.

"What do we *do?*" Ino asked finally.

Vivian let out a long sigh. "I don't know. If it was the Chief of Security, you would report him to the University President. If it was just the President, we could call Security." She shrugged. "Who do you tell when it's *both?*"

They pondered.

"Okay, so…" Vivian started. She cocked her head. Ino knew that look. She was deep in thought. "The affair isn't *really* the crime here, right?"

Ino thought about that. "Uhhh…" He thought about it. "Well… no? They all appeared to be consenting adults." He swallowed. "*Enthusiastically* consenting."

She nodded. "Right. So what's the real transgression here? What's the real motive?"

He blinked at her. "The tape." He turned. "The fact that Reed secretly videotaped it. I assume, for blackmail purposes."

"Exactly."

"So… whichever of them knows about the tape *now*… probably killed him."

She nodded. "That stands to reason."

Ino pondered. "So maybe we should ask some leading questions at the Gala tomorrow. See who gets nervous. Whoever does, knows about the tape, and is probably the murderer."

She nodded. "Makes sense to me."

Ino frowned. "And then we go to the other one."

Vivian nodded. "Sounds like a plan!"

Ino rolled his eyes. "Great! All we have to do is *solve this murder.*"

Vivian chuckled. "Wow, it sounds so easy when you put it like that."

Ino smiled weakly. "The more I know about this, the more complicated it gets."

Vivian shrugged. "Yeah, well, nobody said solving a murder would be easy."

He thought about it. "I suppose you're right."

She turned. "And you should go get all of your shit, including that printout, because you left it in the library." The pine marten frowned. "And for God's sake, *log off that computer.*"

He nodded and let out a sigh.

Chapter 9: The Gala

Sunday, May 20, 2018

The next day Ino woke up at 8:00 am, on the dot, and spent an incredibly long time digging out his pour-over set, weighing beans, grinding them, and obsessing over the process of making coffee. He didn't normally do this, since it felt a lot like his chemistry work at school, but today he was grateful for the distraction.

He put all of the flowers in their pots in record time, working distractedly and mechanically, and before he realized it, he had several empty plastic flats and nothing else to plant. Then he showered and had a long workout that he barely remembered, and then spent the rest of the day obsessively cleaning the rest of his townhouse. Not a surface went un-scrubbed and un-shined. He took out his suit and ironed everything.

It was going to be a big night.

He picked Vivian up at 5:00 pm.

She stepped up to the Jeep in 4" heels. She was wearing a gorgeous pink-and-cream maxi dress, patterned with large abstract tulips, with a low sweetheart neckline and thin shoulder straps.

"You ready for this?" she asked.

"Nope!" Ino announced. "Jesus. You look *stunning*. New dress?"

Vivian beamed. "Yes. I bought it for my conference next week. It has pockets." She stuck her hands in at her sides before hefting herself up into the seat.

Ino nodded. "Amazing." He pondered. "I forgot you're out of town next week." He frowned. "That doesn't leave us much time."

She looked him over. Ino was wearing a crisp French-blue shirt, light-gray linen slacks, and a navy-blue bow tie with an oversized peach-and-rose floral print on it. She frowned. "You look great. But no jacket?"

Ino frowned. "It's in the back. Who do you take me for?!"

She considered. "Want to take the roof off? And the doors? We can roll up like we just came from the Dunes. It would be a real power move." She put on a pair of gigantic oval sunglasses.

He laughed. "You always know just what to say."

He put the Jeep in drive and they rolled off.

They walked in, Ino carrying his suit jacket over his forearm.

He surveyed the scene.

The lobby of the Santiago University Center for the Arts had been dressed to the nines with several dozen little standing tables with white tablecloths. There was a portable bar set up at each end of the lobby. Ino had expected to see University Food Services catering, as they had done for this event every previous year, but it looked like the school had hired outside caterers. Ino saw them in tuxedo shirts at the back wall. The room was filled with professors, administrators, and staff members. Ino saw the hulking angry badger, wearing what appeared to be the exact same shirt and tie Ino had previously seen him in, with a group of the administrative staff in the corner.

It looked like everyone from the University staff had been invited to celebrate the festivities. There were probably three hundred people in the huge lobby, and more in the adjacent cafeteria, which was currently decked out as a banquet hall. Ino could see it similarly decorated with white table-cloths and a huge projector screen.

"Wow," he said to Vivian. "Looks like they went all out."

She gave him a strained smile. "Hundred-year anniversary! No time to skimp."

A large older caribou in a bowtie — a ridiculous *plaid* bowtie, not a fashionable *floral* bowtie like Ino was sporting — suddenly appeared in front of them. "Vivian!" he boomed. "You're back!" Ino recognized him from the Psychology department.

She smiled warmly at him. "Carl! How are you?" She turned back to Ino. "Can I catch up with you later?"

He nodded. "You bet!" He smiled, strained, and nodded at the caribou.

The large ungulate held out his arm in a comically old-fashioned and extremely adorable manner. Vivian took his arm and they strode off. "You haven't met Diane yet! She's new in the department!" They disappeared into the crowd.

Left alone, Ino looked around and sighed.

Normally, he enjoyed these functions, or at least tolerated them. He liked dressing up, and on a college campus, there weren't many opportunities. In previous years, the nice evening and a free meal more than made up for the social demands. This year the food would undoubtedly be amazing, but as Ino looked around the room he kind of just wanted to go home.

Steeling himself, Ino took a deep breath and steered himself toward the one bastion of comfort in social situations: the bar.

He waited behind a small disorganized crowd, and finally found himself at the bar. There were two bartenders, and the closest was a lion in a tuxedo, minus the jacket, facing away from him. Ino blinked with raised eyebrows. The guy was built like an Olympic weightlifter, with tree-trunk legs and a muscular butt poured into the light fabric of his pants. He was wearing a vest that strained around his thick lats, and his shoulders looked as wide as he was tall. Ino could see his muscles roiling underneath his shirt, threatening to split the seams.

As he was staring, the lion turned around, and Ino was greeted with the shocked, and then smug, face of Doug Miller from Facilities.

Ino stared in astonishment, for several reasons — not the least of which was that Doug looked gorgeous in a tux. Ino checked out his chest and stared at him, flabbergasted.

Doug just grinned knowingly at him. He had caught Ino, and he knew it. "Dr. Reamer!" he said. "Can I get you a drink? Or... are you here for something else?"

Ino felt his face turn immediately hot. He knew he must be blushing. "Doug!" he said. "So you're a bartender now, too?!"

Doug smiled toothily at him. "I am a lion of many talents!" he said. "*Many* talents."

The other bartender glanced over, rolled her eyes, and took the next customer.

Ino let out a shaky breath. "How come you have to work when nobody else does?"

Doug shrugged, his colossal shoulders rolling in his shirt. Ino wondered how it stayed tucked in. And how it didn't just split right down the middle. "I asked if I could!" he said. "They just needed a couple people and it's double overtime." He beamed. "What can I get you?"

Ino blinked and then suddenly remembered that he had come up here for a drink. "Uh, gin and tonic, if you could. Double lime, please." It was his usual summer cocktail, though he suddenly felt pretentious ordering it.

The lion zeroed right in on it. "Comin' right up! I like a man who knows exactly what he wants."

Ino felt his blush intensify.

The lion set to making the drink — and instead of a small double-rocks glass, he reached for a large tumbler, one normally reserved for soda. Ino watched him pour two-plus shots of gin and fill the rest with tonic. Doug was really making him *two* drinks in a big glass. *I guess he is still flirting after all.*

"Thanks," Ino said, weakly.

Doug dutifully squeezed two lime halves into the drink and aggressively stirred it, then popped a lime wheel onto the glass and lifted up the drink. He leaned forward. "And hey — the tux doesn't have to go back until Friday, if you're like, you know — into that." He winked, his tail lashing behind him like an unattended fire hose.

Ino smiled blankly back at him. *YES, HE IS DEFINITELY FLIRTING*, he thought. "Thanks!" he squeaked. "I would ask how to get in touch, but it looks like I just have to show up on campus and you'll find me!" He smiled awkwardly.

Doug chuckled. "Wow!" he said. "Stalker! Haha!" He made a horny face again and Ino decided he had just made it 100 times worse.

"Well, I'm obligated to mingle!" Ino said. "Maybe I'll come back and see you." *Oh God, I'm flirting back! Stop it!* he thought.

Doug nodded. "You better," he said. God, he really was cute. Maybe Ino *was* into the tux. He hoped the lion was still interested when Ino *wasn't* trying to solve a murder.

Ino swallowed, and smiled. He reached into his pocket for a single he had put in there for a tip. Unfortunately, he took a $5 bill out instead. He stuck it in the tip jar.

Doug looked at it and then smiled knowingly. "Thanks, Doc," he said. "I owe you."

The other bartender rolled her eyes again.

"Well… bye!" Ino said, and loped quickly away.

He mingled successfully for half an hour, catching up with the rest of the science department staff and a lot of admin staff members that he knew. Ino always made a point to learn the names of everyone he encountered on a regular basis and he always gave nice Christmas presents to the house-keepers who rotated through his building, so he had plenty of people to speak to. The hall was filled with the low din of a hundred conversations. Ino was actually starting to relax and enjoy himself when he felt a tap on his shoulder.

He turned and found himself face to face with Jack Archer.

"Dr. Reamer," the dog said, staring at him with piercing amber eyes, and Ino felt himself turn pink again. Jack was wearing a nice coffee-brown suit, a white shirt and a navy-blue tie. Ino immediately thought of him in tiny neoprene shorts, nothing on his big chest and shoulders, in the black leather puppy mask.

"Chief Archer!" he squeaked.

This was awful. Ino had intended to press the dog and see if he knew anything about the video. But he could barely get the man's name out without his voice cracking.

The dog frowned at him, but carried on nevertheless. "Hello, Dr. Reamer. I just wanted to, ah, thank you for speaking to Sean Murphy."

Ino thought of the password conversation and felt all the blood drain out of his face. He stared for a moment.

Jack frowned again, more severely this time. "Dr. Reamer, are you feeling all right?"

Ino forced himself to swallow. *Act like a person, dammit!* he chided himself. "Certainly!" he said. "It's just the heat." He leaned forward, smiling. "Sorry, what did you mean about Sean?" he said, too eagerly.

The dog stared. "About going home for the summer. He's been through enough. I'm glad you convinced him to quit his stupid coffee-house job and take care of himself for once."

Ino stared at him for what seemed like thirty blank seconds, and then remembered the conversation on the park bench the Monday after the explosion. It seemed like a hundred years ago.

"Oh! Right!" he said. He tried to re-engage normally. "Of course. Sorry, I'm Sean's advisor, we talk about a lot of things. I also forgot you've known him since he was a pup." He smiled in what he hoped was a reassuring way and not like a space alien occupying an earthling host. "Right. Totally agreed. He was… quite shaken up. Really, it was his decision — he's a very smart young man." Ino was rambling and he knew it. He forced himself to shut up.

Jack was clearly not buying it but he continued nonetheless. "I, ah, agree." He thought for a moment. "Truth be told, I've been mad for weeks that Admin put him in that godforsaken building on the last Friday of the semester." He rolled his eyes. "That kid works too hard already. He doesn't need any help being stressed out. No need to schedule his final in the garbage building no one on campus wants to set foot in."

Mad for WEEKS? Ino blinked at the dog. All thoughts of awkwardness left him. "S… sorry, what was that?" he asked.

Jack frowned at him. "That last final. *Your* final. I was hoping he would get a break, maybe have some time off, and then I happened to see he was scheduled for the last Final slot available, in that hideous old lab."

Ino blinked at him. Was he hearing this right? "I'm… sorry. You *knew* Sean's final was in Baker *on the night of the explosion?*" He asked it too urgently, but he didn't care.

Jack blinked at him, his eyebrows raised. "Of course I did," he said. "I'm the head of Security, Dr. Reamer."

Ino stared at him a moment, furrowing his brow. "*How,*" he asked. "I was proctoring that final and *I* didn't even realize it was scheduled for Baker until I looked it up. How did *you* know?"

Jack scowled at him. "You realize I *run* the security force on this campus, right? I need to know what buildings are open when so we can monitor them. Student Affairs sends me a list of what buildings are open late every semester, and I have to assign an officer to lock them up as they close.

The doors don't just lock themselves, you know." He raised one eyebrow and seemed annoyed with the question. "They sent me the schedule of make-up finals and I saw Sean's name on it." He stared at Ino.

Ino stared at him. "So *you knew* we would be in that building?" he asked.

Jack frowned, and now he looked truly irritated. "You seem really caught up on that fact, Dr. Reamer."

Ino stared at him. He *was* caught up on that fact. His theory all along had been that Reed's killer had blown up the building *thinking it would be empty*. If Jack knew there was a final scheduled for the same time slot, there was no way he would have triggered an explosion for a time he knew people would be in the building. He couldn't possibly have been involved. But how many people in the Security Department had known that?

Ino swallowed. "Did… anybody else see that list?" he asked, his voice barely audible.

Jack looked at him, and now he looked somewhere between confused and annoyed. "No one else *needs* to see it. I set the schedules." He frowned. "Are you sure you're all right, Dr. Reamer? You seem… unwell." He looked down at the huge liquor glass in Ino's hand. "Have you perhaps been… overserved?" He raised an accusatory eyebrow.

Ino blinked back at him. "Nope, I'm fine!" he said, too fast.

Unconvinced, Jack leaned *way* forward into Ino's personal space, an inch away from Ino, his lips parted slightly. He put a hand on Ino's shoulder and sniffed his muzzle delicately.

Shocked, Ino froze, his heart pounding. He felt the hair on the back of his neck stand up and his heart started pounding.

Jack sniffed, pondering.

Ino held perfectly still. He could smell Jack's aftershave and a light musky cologne. For some reason, he felt weak in the knees and now he was definitely flushing. Jack's hand was heavy on his shoulder.

If he leaned forward a quarter inch they would be kissing.

After staring at him for a moment, puzzled, the large dog slowly drew back and raised his eyes. "Hm. You smell like one drink so I guess not. Is that Gucci I smell?"

Ino nodded dumbly. "Guilty," he said.

The dog nodded. "It's nice." He glanced around. "All right, I have to keep circulating. Thanks again for speaking to Sean. Let me know if you'd like a glass of water." He frowned, nodded curtly and disappeared from view. "Good night, Dr. Reamer."

Ino let out a shaky breath. He was actually sweating. "Goodnight!" he squeaked.

Ino orbited for another few minutes, making small talk and frantically thinking about what he had just learned.

That was information of great importance — Jack might have killed Reed over the video, but there was no *way* he would have done it in such a way that risked killing a student, let alone one he had known since he was a pup. And if the video was truly the motive behind Reed's death — and it was absolutely the best motive that Ino knew of so far — that left the other two people in the video.

Dinner was announced and people slowly filtered through several double-doors into the cafeteria. It was similarly done up, with white linens and huge "100 YEARS!" banners. There was a projection screen on a small stage platform. Susan Greeley was in front of the stage, flanked by a few older men in suits. As Ino watched, her husband moved to join her.

Ino stared at the hulking skunk. Sebastian navigated deftly between the tables, his huge black and white tail trailing after him like it was lighter than air. Ino could see the skunk's thick muscles roiling under his button-down shirt, and the big man was wearing tailored slacks, straining to contain his huge quads. It would have been incredibly hot if Ino hadn't been terrified. The big skunk could *absolutely* have dispatched Reed, and carried him to another location too. Probably without breaking a sweat. Even now, he didn't look like Susan's husband so much as her bodyguard, or possibly a henchman.

Vivian appeared at his side. "Shall we?" she asked.

He turned to her. "Hey! I got something to share."

She stared at him. "Oh my God, already? I couldn't even get Carl to shut up." She glanced around. "Do you want to go somewhere?"

He shook his head. "Nah. Later is fine. Let's just say I'm *very* interested in Susan's speech now."

Raising her eyebrows, Vivian nodded. "Interesting!" she said.

They wandered to one of the eight-seat tables toward the outskirts of the impromptu banquet hall. They sat for a moment before people started to join them. Ino politely smiled at a bunch of people he didn't know before Clara Calder sat down near him. She was in a nice cream skirt and a flowy floral blouse, primarily red, which matched her thick red glasses.

Ino stared at her a moment and then smiled. "Clara!" he said. "Nice to see you again." He turned to Vivian. "Vivian, this is Clara Calder from Accounting. Clara, Vivian Chen, from Psychology."

They both said their niceties as they prepared for the speech to begin.

Clara smiled. "Nice to see you not in handcuffs, Dr. Reamer. Did you get any further on the matter we discussed the other day?"

Ino stared. Oh God. He hadn't seen Clara since Jack led him out of her office. He chuckled awkwardly. "Not really!" he said. "I told Chief Archer everything I know, and the matter is with Santiago's finest now."

Clara raised an eyebrow. "And what's that?"

He blinked at the cat. "What's what?"

Clara smiled at him. "What is *everything you know?*"

He forced a smile. "Basically nothing!"

Clara blinked at him, and then laughed. "I'm sorry to hear that. I was hoping for something juicy!"

Ino shrugged. "Afraid not," he said.

More guests arrived, and Clara immediately pivoted to grilling them on names and positions. Subtly, Ino looked around.

He spotted Jack Archer at a table with Travis and what must have been a half-dozen other security officers. Travis was in a white shirt and a black tie, looking even more massive than he did in his uniform. The husky shot Ino a dirty look and turned back to the table.

Ino thought about that. *Jack* had known which buildings were occupied. Would *Travis* have had that information? The husky wasn't ruled out, after all — the video was certainly very incriminating, but Travis MacGregor still had a lot of circumstantial evidence pointing his way.

While he was pondering, Susan took the stage, next to a huge projection screen showing the University torch logo. The cheetah was wearing a knee-length emerald-green wrap dress and three-inch silver heels. As usual, she looked perfect.

She didn't *look* like a murderer. Ino frowned.

"Good evening, everyone!" the cheetah said. "Welcome and thank you for attending Santiago University's 100th Anniversary Celebration Gala!"

There was long, sustained applause. Ino looked around. The open bar was definitely having an effect on the crowd's enthusiasm.

She beamed. "I *promise* this speech is going to be a short one."

The crowd laughed.

"I'm so glad to see everyone here celebrating Santiago University's one hundredth anniversary." There was a smattering of applause. "Let's take a journey through that history." She stepped back and gestured to the projection screen. Her thin tail cast a shadow for a few seconds before she moved it out of the way in a practiced gesture. She didn't even have to look. She had known it would be in the way without ever taking her eyes off the crowd. Ino marveled.

"I don't have to tell most of you that Santiago *truly* began its history as the *Santiago Male and Female College* in 1859." The image on the projection screen changed to a grainy, incredibly old photograph of a simple four-story building surrounded by what appeared to be livestock grazing grounds.

There were some exaggerated ooh's and ahh's, which Susan turned to and laughed at. "Yes, thank you," she said. "Pause for effect." The crowd laughed back.

Ino smiled.

"Santiago Male and Female College closed in the 1860s due to the ongoing Civil War, but reopened in 1872, and of course, came into its own when it was re-chartered in 1918 as Santiago University, the beginning of our esteemed institution." The picture changed to the torch logo and a current photo of the University, to assorted applause.

"We have had a long run, full of triumph and success, and, of course, we have seen our share of tragedy." The picture changed to a photo of Ethan Reed. Susan paused for the perfect period of solemnity.

Ino stared up at the giant picture of Reed. He was smiling in the photo. It didn't look authentic. Ino felt the hair on the back of his neck stand up. The room went fully silent.

"This event, of course, has been dedicated to Ethan Reed's memory. Dr. Reed graduated Santiago University in 1982, obtained his doctorate from the University of Wisconsin, and circulated a number of careers and schools before finally coming home to Santiago." The cheetah turned, stared at Reed's picture for several extremely authentic moments, and turned back to the crowd. "He will be missed."

There was another short pause. Susan took a breath and continued.

"At the same time, we have reason to celebrate. Our friends at Dublahm Chemical..." — here she gestured at one of the front tables, populated by an extremely upper class group of identical businessmen with $200 haircuts — "... have made a *very* generous donation to allow us to move forward with several much-needed renovations. They are also helping us to honor Dr. Reed's memory."

There was assorted confusion, before Susan went on. "On that note, it is here, at our 100th Anniversary Gala, I would like to formally announce the dedication of... The Reed Center."

The image changed to an artist's rendering of the imposing metal-and-glass structure Ino had seen in model form, complete with photoshopped students and a glorious blue sky in the background.

The crowd gasped.

"The Reed Center will be a state-of-the-art, three-story, 50,000 square-foot collection of laboratories and lecture halls. The building is EPA-certified 100% green and has no carbon footprint. It has a rooftop garden and self-restoring HVAC. Most importantly, the Reed Center will be the home of free supplementary AP classes for low-income Indiana high school students, recipients of the new Dublahm Endowment. Dr. Reed's memory will live on in decades of enrichment for those who need it most."

The crowd erupted in applause and Susan took it all in, smiling perfectly down at the crowd.

Ino glanced at Vivian. The pine marten was frowning.

"*That* was fast," she whispered.

Ino nodded. "That's what I said. Apparently it's been in the works for some time."

Vivian raised her eyebrows. "Convenient we'll save all that money on demolition."

The applause died down and Susan continued. "In the next ten years, we hope to modernize four additional buildings. Together, we will set this University up for the next one hundred amazing years. This will be the legacy we leave."

Ino and Vivian glanced at one another.

Susan beamed at the audience. "With support from Dublahm, we continue to move forward. Nothing is going to stop us now. *Nothing.*"

Ino felt a chill run up his back.

The crowd applauded, long and loud and sustained. There were even assorted cheers. Susan left the stage and sat at the donor table with her hulking husband.

"Wow," Ino said. "This is going to be… some legacy."

Vivian nodded. "She's really cementing it."

"I *cannot* believe the Ethics Board approved that donation," Clara said suddenly, from next to Ino.

Ino and Vivian both blinked, and then stared at her. "Why?" Ino asked finally. "Because of the amount?"

Clara blinked at them. "No. Haven't you figured it out?"

Ino grinned. "As per usual, no."

The cat chuckled. "At least you admit it!" She leaned forward and lowered her voice. "Susan never took her husband's name when she got married." She glanced around.

Ino leaned forward. "Wait, his name *isn't* Sebastian Greeley?" He and Vivian exchanged a glance.

Grinning, Clara shook her head. "It certainly is not. I suggest a trip to Google very quickly." She leaned forward, excitedly. "Go ahead now please! I want to see the looks on your faces."

Frowning, Ino and Vivian both took out their phones and started Googling. Vivian found it first.

"Susan Greeley and Sebastian… *Dublahm?*" They looked at each other.

"As in… Dublahm Chemical?" Ino asked, sharply, his eyes wide. He and Vivian exchanged a look.

Relishing the gossip, Clara grinned. "One and the same! He's not on their board but his brother is. And one uncle I believe."

"Wow!" Ino said. "Isn't that a huge conflict of interest?"

Clara chuckled. "A 29 million dollar donation from your husband's family's company?" She grinned. "In a fiscal year where that company has a *massive* liability exposure from an accident, which will hit their books as an expense? I would think so. But hey," she said, grinning. "I'm not the Ethics Board."

Ino nodded. "Wow." He and Vivian made eye contact.

The crowd was still applauding.

After dinner, and dessert, and drinks, and even some dancing, Ino got another gin and tonic — from the *other* bar — and walked out to the deserted back patio.

It was almost 11:00 pm. Susan had left. So had Jack. There were only a few dozen people inside. Ino's drink was mostly melted ice. The hyena was lightly sweating and ready to get home and get into the shower.

Vivian circulated a little longer and then joined him. Her heels were loud and sharp on the deck as she approached him.

Ino was leaning on the patio railing, his elbows on the top edge, staring out into the distance, listening to the whine of mosquitos over the retention pond behind the Center for the Arts.

She smiled. "I see you staring in the general direction of the future *Reed Center!*"

He chuckled. "I guess I am." He shook his head. "Man, that's a little gross."

"What is?"

He frowned. "Guy was a straight-up criminal and he gets a building named after him. And an endowment program."

Vivian chuckled darkly. "I have bad news for you about literally every historical figure with a building named after him."

Ino processed that, and then laughed. "Fair point."

Vivian glanced around the patio, and leaned in. "So, what was it you wanted to tell me?"

Ino leaned against the railing overlooking the little pond behind the Center.

Ino turned. "Jack *knew* about the finals schedule. There's no way he blew up Baker."

Vivian stared at him. "Really? He did? How?"

Ino turned to her. "He had a list of all the late finals. They clear it with Security, so they know when to schedule their walkthroughs. Jack knew his deputy's nephew was going to be in Baker at 6:00 pm. There's no way he was the one to set up the explosion."

Vivian blinked. "Impressive! How did you get *that* out of him?"

Ino thought for a moment. "Uh… he volunteered it while I was trying to remember how to talk like a person."

The pine marten nodded. "Ah." She pondered. "Well. I didn't get anything remotely so useful out of Susan — she wouldn't even talk about Reed. So I guess you'll be going to Jack."

Ino nodded. "Yup. I'm going to download the video to my phone and I'll show it to him tomorrow."

Vivian let out a low whistle. "Wow. Make sure you take precautions. I can't imagine he's going to take that very well. I would confront him *at* the Security building, in fact. He's going to be pissed."

Ino glanced at her. "*I'm* pissed. That man knows damn well who two of the best suspects on campus are. Either he's covering for them or he's too chicken to really dig — and either way the psycho who almost blew me up is walking free." He finished his drink in one long pull. It was mostly water. "I'm going to tell him I know he's either covering for Susan Greeley or covering for Travis MacGregor, and I know why. I'll tell him he has to take himself off the case and reveal the tape, or I'll leak the tape and get him *taken* off. This has got to stop."

Vivian nodded. "I get it. And not that you asked — but I think if you ask him to recuse the case he *will* cave. Just… don't put yourself in a position where you're isolated with him."

Ino stared at her. "W… what does that mean?"

Vivian frowned. "You should be fine at the Security building. Behind a closed door." She stared at him pointedly. "But not a locked one."

Ino felt all of his fur bristle.

Vivian stared at him.

Ino swallowed. "Y-you think he's *dangerous?*" he stammered.

Vivian frowned. "No, absolutely not. But you're revealing that you know a very deep secret. You're going to push him pretty far. I don't think he's going to panic-murder you, but… let's just say, I wouldn't have this conversation on the overlook platform at Niagara Falls. You know?"

Ino nodded. "Right. I get it." He swallowed.

They were silent for a moment.

Ino finally cleared his throat. "Speaking of which," he said.

Vivian took a breath and let out a long sigh. "I imagine you don't mean Niagara Falls."

Ino turned. "There *is* a chance I'm wrong. Purely statistically. And if I *am* wrong, I'm going to be doing exactly what Reed did — reveal a secret that Jack would kill to *keep* secret. If I'm wrong."

She nodded. "I hear you. I don't like where you're going with this."

He smiled humorlessly. "If that happens, he'll come after me next. And if he succeeds… you're next in line after me."

Vivian nodded slowly, looking out into the night. "So I figured. It stands to reason that anything you know, I know too."

"Right," Ino said. "So… if you don't want me to confront him… I won't."

The pine marten frowned very seriously. "Ino, this situation is… extremely hypothetical."

He shook his head. "I'm not taking any chances. Take some time. Think about it. We can talk in the —"

The pine marten stared at him. "Do it."

He sighed. "*That* was taking some time?"

She shrugged. "I can take care of myself."

"Do you want me to wait until you're on your next mission trip? He'd have a lot harder time coming after you overseas." He stared at her.

Vivian processed that for a moment and then laughed loudly. "Sure! Please wait until I'm safe and secure in the comforting embrace of a war zone."

He stared at her, and then the absurdity overcame him and he laughed, too. He lifted his drink, realized he had finished it already, and lowered his hand. "God. I can't believe we're even having this conversation."

She nodded. "It has been a weird week, hasn't it."

Ino turned back to the night and rubbed his eyes with his free hand. "I'm sorry. I'm probably being totally paranoid."

Vivian cleared her throat. "No, I don't think so," she mused, quietly.

He lifted his head, and stared at her, his eyebrows rising.

The pine marten cocked her head. "I don't think you're being paranoid at all."

He leaned back, scrunching his muzzle up into a frown. "Really?"

Vivian shrugged. "Not in the least. Because one thing is true in all this, Ino… *someone* on this campus is a killer."

Ino thought about that for a moment, and stared out over the prairie, and tried to ignore the chill creeping up his spine.

They watched the night in silence.

Chapter 10: The Storm

Monday, May 21, 2018

Monday morning, there was a *lot* of activity at the Security building.

Ino had spent twenty-five minutes over breakfast thinking of what he would say to Officer Reese, or Officer Hahn (he thought the wolf was Hahn), or whoever happened to be covering the front window, but when he got through the vestibule just before noon, there was no one even at the front desk. Ino sailed right through to the main station. He was wearing golf shorts and a short-sleeve, powder-blue linen button-up.

Inside, there was a group of security officers gathered around one of the big communal tables. There were several students and a civilian in the bullpen, one that Ino recognized from a handful of faculty functions. He was a small fruit bat, even shorter than Ino, in a turquoise collared shirt with the sleeves rolled up. He was black and dark brown with some graying and Ino was pretty sure he worked in the Meteorology department. He had a handful of students, and all of them had laptops and were chattering excitedly. Ino slipped into the bullpen and several officers looked up, but no one rushed to speak to him as they had done previously.

Chief Archer was amongst them, in a white shirt and black tie, listening intently. "So how much more powerful is this than a regular thunderstorm?" he was saying.

The professor frowned. "It's difficult to say. Fifty miles an hour is easy for most structures to withstand, but it will knock you down in a parking lot. I think there might be some damage, however. There could be damaging hail and there will definitely be some branches down. We've had some storms this year but nothing with really powerful winds yet, so any vegetation that died over the winter will be coming down. You'll have some minor road blockages, minor flooding, probably some damaged cars. If nothing else, it's not going to be fun."

Jack nodded. "All right. We'll issue a warning using the text system and the PA's. And I'll get officers out in the field in case anyone needs assistance. Does that sound like it will cover it?"

The bat nodded. "Should do it. We'll stay on it, though."

Jack grinned. "All right. Nice to have our own storm chasers on-site."

The bat chuckled. "We're not chasers today, Chief Archer. *This* one is coming to *us!*" The professor and the students filed away and occupied a set of tall tables near the front door, all chattering amongst themselves.

Jack turned to Reese, the ferret officer who Ino had spoken to before. "Could you please get that text out? Don't use the Shelter in Place template, maybe use the…" He thought for a moment. "Severe Weather should cover it. Okay?"

She nodded. "Sure thing, boss." She turned away, nodded briefly at Ino, and then disappeared deeper into the station.

Jack looked up and saw Ino. "Not now," he said, turning away and heading for the dispatch.

Ino frowned. "It's *important.*" He frowned. This was hardly the first thunderstorm to hit Santiago University. Is this what security spent their time on? "More so than you humoring the Meteorology Department." He followed the German shepherd.

Jack flashed him a dirty look and walked away from him. He leaned over and spoke to the person at the dispatch desk, handing him a yellow sticky note covered in spiky handwriting. "Put this out to the field officers and see if Simmons is close enough to get on campus. If he isn't, tell him to stay home. Tell the field officers to get students inside if they see them outside."

Ino appeared at the dog's side. "I think you've been putting me off enough, Chief Archer."

Jack looked up at him. "I *do not* have time for you today, Dr. Reamer. We have a storm coming in, and it looks like a bad one. You should go somewhere safe. Somewhere other than here."

The hyena frowned.

Jack walked directly past him.

Ino let him go, bristling.

The shepherd was hovering over Reese and the computer which presumably controlled the text message service. He was talking to her.

Ino glared at him. *Okay. So this was how it was going to be.*

Pulling out his phone, Ino queued up the video he had found on Reed's computer. He slid his thumb along the video scrubber until he found the frame he wanted, and moved well out of the way of traffic. It was a corner of the bullpen near the hallway to Jack's office. He waited.

The shepherd buzzed around giving several more snappy orders, and then forcefully loped over to where Ino was standing.

"Dr. Reamer," he said, fake-cheerfully, smiling dangerously. "I am not *asking* you. Please —"

Ino casually held up the phone, so only Jack could see it.

Jack furrowed his brow. It took the dog a moment to process what he was looking at — which was not a surprise, how often would he see himself naked from behind? Minus the neoprene shorts and the puppy mask, of course. But Reed was in the image, too, yanking violently on Jack's leash, so that probably provided some context.

Jack frowned at the phone for a moment, and then his eyes snapped open in pure, unadulterated horror. The dog's mouth opened and his ears folded back and all the color drained out of his face. He pulled his head back — actually physically *recoiled* — and even his pupils dilated. He let out a little involuntary gasp.

Ino shouldn't have, but he found the reaction… gratifying. It might be the first truly genuine reaction he had gotten out of Jack Archer since he'd met him.

The shepherd stared in horror and shock for another few seconds, and then turned to look at Ino. He looked terrified, but he also looked *hurt* — but just for a second.

Then he looked *enraged*.

Uh-oh, Ino thought.

Ino struggled to stay on his feet as Jack dragged him down the hallway by his elbow.

The dog snatched the phone out of his hand and threw him into his office. He followed half a step behind, slamming the door hard behind him.

Ino turned.

Jack's eyes were wide, crazy, white visible all around his golden pupils. He was panting. "*WHAT THE FUCK IS THIS?!*" he roared, waving Ino's phone around like a bank robber waving a gun.

Ino frowned. "I figured out what my message was from Reed," he snapped, raising his voice to meet the shepherd's. "It was a password. Want to guess what I found on his computer?"

Jack didn't answer. He was looking at the phone. "It's a *v-video?!*" he whimpered, struggling to tap the screen with one thick thumb. "How long does it — " He tapped something on the screen. The phone started making noise again. It was his own voice, grunting loudly. He looked horrified.

Ino grabbed the phone out of the dog's hands and quickly backed out of the video. Based on the amount of black and white filling the screen drowning out the black and tan, Sebastian Dublahm was now... involved. Ino didn't know for sure — he hadn't watched the video that far.

He looked up at Jack. The dog was visibly panting now, his pink tongue poking out the end of his muzzle. He stared at Ino, frantic and helpless.

There was no question in Ino's mind that it was an authentic reaction.

The hyena grimaced. "You didn't know there was a video, did you," he said, flatly.

Jack was still panting. "That son of a *bitch*," he whispered, his voice quiet, but pitch high and panicked. "He *insisted* on hosting. He said he wanted to do it at his place because he already had a k-" — " Wide-eyed, he cut himself off, looking up at Ino.

Ino couldn't tell if the dog had been about to say "cage" or "kennel," but he didn't think he needed to ask.

Jack just stared back at him, his eyebrows slanted in panic. His hands were shaking, Ino noticed.

The hyena frowned. "Breathe, Jack," he said. "Nobody else has seen this," he lied.

The dog stared at him for another long, scared moment, and then swallowed.

"Why are you here?" Jack whispered.

Ino stared at him over the top of his glasses, and then let out a long sigh. "Jack," he said. "You have to recuse yourself from this case."

The dog looked genuinely startled. Some of the panic started to subside. "What?" he gasped. "Why?" he demanded.

Ino held up the phone. "Because you're *implicated* in it!" He narrowed his eyes. "And it's pretty obvious you're stalling the investigation to cover for somebody you already guessed did it."

Jack looked shocked, and then his face clouded over with rage. "*Fuck you, Reamer,*" he spat. He was shaking with anger. "How *dare* you! I am doing the job I swore to uph —"

"*It was Susan, Jack!*" Ino snarled. "They met the day of the murder. Reed let it slip that he had a video that would ruin her career." He closed the distance between them and stabbed Jack in the chest with one thick finger. "*She killed him!* Or her huge beefcake husband did. And then they called the Dublahm Chemical *fixers* to come clean up the mess."

"It's not her!" Jack snarled. He was showing his teeth now. He actually kept growling long after he finished talking, low and deep and threatening. It made Ino's fur reflexively rise.

"*Oh really?*" Ino snapped. "Then maybe it's your husky officer, with the secret of how he got his bonus finally revealed! The one who you have conveniently failed to notice was all the fuck way across campus from where he should have been, *outside a building where someone was being murdered!*"

"IT'S NOT HIM, EITHER!" Jack roared, his eyes wide and crazed.

Ino should have been scared, but now he wasn't anything but enraged. "*Well, it was one of them, Jack!* Why don't you get the fuck out of the way and let someone figure out which!"

The shepherd stared back at him, his eyes wide. Ino could see the white around his eyes.

Ino narrowed his eyes. "You have to recuse yourself from this case."

There was a loud knocking at the door.

"*Not now!*" Jack roared.

Ino didn't take his eyes off of him. He leaned forward. "You take yourself off this case, or I'll show the city cops the video and you'll be *taken* off it," he growled.

The shepherd stared at him with something Ino didn't expect — genuine, murderous anger. He curled his lips up and Ino saw a lot of teeth.

There was loud pounding again, and now the door swung violently inward.

They both snapped around to look.

It was Reese. "Sorry, Chief!" the ferret cried. "This isn't gonna wait!" She burst into the room, followed by the small bat professor Ino had seen on the way in. The bat was holding a laptop and looking concerned. Very concerned. He didn't even seem to notice the state of things in the office.

Ino frowned.

"What is it?" Jack snapped.

Reese patted the bat's back. "Go ahead," she told him.

"Th-the storm, it's intensifying," the bat said, his eyes a little wide. "It's *really* intensifying. Merrillville Doppler is showing winds a *lot* higher than fifty — they're peaking at *eighty* now," he said. "And Chesterton is reporting microbursts!"

The dog stared at him. His ears perked forward. "What kind of damage?"

The bat swallowed. "*Trees* down now, not just branches. Hail — *big* hail. Golf ball. Maybe tennis balls. Flying debris. Broken windows — big ones — cafeterias, dorms, the Union." He was talking fast now. "If we see microbursts there will be structural damage. Maybe serious. We have to hit the sirens."

Jack frowned tightly. "'How far out?"

The bat looked down at his computer and processed for a moment. "Ten minutes. Fifteen tops."

Jack nodded curtly. "Thank you, Professor." He turned to Reese. "Put out a text and email alert — Shelter in Place now, and Seek Shelter Immediately in five minutes. Interior room, away from windows. Hit the storm sirens when you send the second message."

"On it," Reese said, and strode briskly away.

Jack strode briskly out of the office and down the hall. They all trailed after him. "Rose! Radio all patrol officers we have a damaging storm inbound, nine minutes out. Get them in the wagon wheel formation on the campus perimeter — the roads could be impassable so they had better get in position right now. We're gonna lose some squad cars." He pivoted again. "Hahn! Get Facilities on the phone NOW and tell them we might have infrastructure damage in ten minutes. Ask for … uhhh…" He thought for a moment. "Ramaninov is on call right now. Tell him to drop what he's doing and be at the main shut offs in three minutes."

He turned one final time, and looked dead-on at Ino.

"Dr. Reamer," he said, without a trace of emotion in his voice. "Go home."

Ino stared unyieldingly back at him, and finally he turned away.

The bat professor cleared his throat. "Uh, I would stay put if I was you," he said. He rushed after Ino and tugged on his sleeve, hard. "It's *not* going to be nice out there." He pointed to his computer, which had an unintelligible map on it, swirled with so many thick bands of red, green and white that the lines on the county map underneath were indistinguishable.

Ino frowned. He glanced behind him at the shepherd, who was still barking orders. "I don't think I'm very safe here, either." He looked at the bat. "I live five minutes from here. Do I have enough time?"

The bat stared at him as if he was crazy. "EXACTLY five minutes?"

Ino nodded. "Four minutes and forty-five seconds. Straight shot down Sturdy. And I have a basement."

The bat grimaced, his huge ears folding back. "I wouldn't. But if you're going to do it, which you *should not*, you should leave *right this second*."

Ino nodded. "Thanks doc!"

Turning over his shoulder, he very deliberately slipped his phone into his front pants pocket.

Across the room, still talking, Jack definitely noticed. His eyes darkened.

Ino hurried for the door.

Ino fast-walked back to his car in the Security Department parking lot.

It was hot out, stiflingly hot, humid, like a sauna or a laundromat with a dozen dryers running. The air was wet and sticky and immobile. There were colossal white fluffy clouds climbing tens of thousands of feet into the sky, their edges as clearly-defined as cauliflower.

There wasn't enough wind to stir a single blade of grass at this point. Everything was perfectly still. But Ino had seen enough ripping Midwestern thunderstorms to know that it would not be still for long.

His heart pounding, he dashed the last few feet to his Jeep and slipped behind the wheel. The top was on so he wouldn't get soaked, but it was the plastic top and Ino didn't know if it would stop tennis-ball-sized hail. Hopefully he would be safely back home by then.

He tossed his backpack on the seat next to him and checked over his shoulder as he buckled his safety belt.

Ino turned the key, and the small but powerful engine rolled into life. He backed swiftly out of his space, and then hit the gas so firmly that the slip control of the four-wheel-drive engaged in the parking lot. The little car seemed to know he meant business.

Turning onto the part of Church Street that exited the campus, Ino banged a right and zipped swiftly out of the parking lot.

He made it just over a mile.

Ino's route took him from Church Street to Sturdy Road, which was a straight shot past Lakeview Cemetery, then through a series of vacant green lots and farmers' fields. On either side of it was a drainage ditch and fifteen or twenty feet of green space — unrestricted growth of pine trees and tall silver maples and assorted random conifers, growing wild on unused lots and as windbreaks on either side of the road. It was only a two-mile stretch down Sturdy Road into Ino's tiny subdivision.

As he crested the last hill on Sturdy before the home stretch, he saw red lights at the railroad crossing light up in front of him. The crossing arms were just coming down. They settled down and bounced gently in place.

Shit, he thought.

He zipped his little Jeep the half-mile to the railroad crossing, up the hill to meet the railroad grade. As he did, the first locomotive came into view from his left. Then the second one, and the first freight car. The railroad crossing was on a slight incline, raised about ten feet over the rest of the road with a long runup to the tracks, and Ino had a good view to see nothing but train down one or two miles of tracks.

He came to a begrudging stop. The Jeep's engine rumbled solemnly.

"*Shit!*" he said, out loud now. This was a freight train, which would take much longer to cross than a passenger train. A double-locomotive probably meant a lot of cars. He might be sitting here for ten minutes or more.

In front of him, massive two-story train car after train car passed slowly in front of him. The huge cars loomed overhead, as tall as a strip mall storefront.

How long had the bat said? Fifteen minutes total?

His heart was starting to pound.

It suddenly got darker out. Startled, Ino looked up and around. The sky was still mostly clear, but over the trees, to the west, the entire sky was darkening.

Silently, the automatic headlights clicked on and the dashboard lit up.

"Okay, this was a bad idea," Ino announced. Maybe he had time to get back to campus, or at least into a gas station on 30, though that might not be better than sitting here in the open. He looked back down, putting his hand on the gearshift to throw the car into reverse and go back the other way.

Reflexively, he checked the rearview mirror.

He had time to register two things: one, a set of headlights flying up behind him, attached to something big, like a truck or a van.

Two, they were *definitely* not going to stop before they hit him.

Ino had just enough time to gasp, his entire body clenching, before the truck plowed into the back of his car.

He managed to get out half a swear and then *BOOM!*

The impact was a crack-crunch, loud, *terrifyingly* loud in Ino's immediate vicinity. There was a terrific crash as the rear-mounted spare annihilated the rear door and came straight into the cargo bay. The hard foam of the seat launched forward into Ino, the headrest cracking him in the back of the skull. Tiny jagged fragments of the rear window blasted forward up into the front seats, bouncing off of every surface and showering Ino like confetti.

"*Awrk!*" Ino cried, ricocheting between the seat and his seatbelt.

The Jeep launched forward as if fired from a slingshot, the front end bucking up so hard that for a second all Ino could see was sky. It shot forward at least ten feet in a second or two, fast, *too* fast to do anything, and Ino screamed as he shot toward the train thundering before him. The crossing arm crashed against the windshield, cracking the glass and flying over the roof. Ino slammed his foot back down on the brake pedal, as hard as he could, so hard that he could feel the jolt through his entire body. It went down as far as it would go and pushed back, the metal flexing.

The Jeep came to a halt with a rubber shriek, a loud staccato howl from all four tires, bucking forward like an amusement park ride. Ino's seatbelt locked again and his backpack shot off the passenger seat, flying into the glove compartment hard enough to crack the latch. As the Jeep bucked backwards, the glove box dropped open.

Terrified, heart pounding, Ino lifted his head. He could *feel* the train. The hyena forced himself to look through the spiderwebbed windshield.

The Jeep had stopped perhaps fifteen inches from the thundering train. It might have been less.

The train was so close it completely filled Ino's view through the cracked windshield. The car was so close the only thing he could see through the split windshield was the *bottom half* of the train cars, wheels as tall as his roof, undercarriage at eye level. The train was huge. It was like an apartment building rolling past, or a cruise ship. Ino could easily feel the thundering vibrations up through the wheels and shocks. The wheels went *clack-clack-clack-clack* and from that close, each *clack* was like a gunshot.

He had just barely avoided flying under the moving train. He didn't even have enough room to turn — any forward movement would be into the train.

Gasping, reeling, he whirled around in his seat. Had someone really managed to rear-end him at a railroad crossing?!

The back window was gone and the spare tire was mostly in the trunk but still seemed to be attached to the mangled back door. The center brake light had torn out of its housing in one piece and was swinging wildly back and forth, still glowing red. Ino could see jagged daylight along the length of the back, where the detachable roof had formerly been connected to the lower half of the vehicle.

The truck was directly behind him, idling gently. Both headlights were still lit, filling the gaping maw of the destroyed rear window. All he could see was a grille and two big headlights.

It didn't even look damaged. And it wasn't moving.

That was... not an accident, Ino suddenly realized.

The truck engine roared behind him and the vehicle lurched forward with startling speed. There was another deafening crunch, and Ino was thrown back in his seat, and now in addition to the bits of plastic flying up from the rear, the metal brackets connecting the roof to the windshield all failed, one after another. They cracked like fireworks, *POP-POP-POP-POP*, and the last one shot off and whizzed past Ino's left ear.

"No no no no *no no no no!*" Ino screamed, his voice drowned out by the train, as the car went under.

Ino's Jeep slid into the wide stretch between wheels, crunching brutally into the underside of a moving freight car, which was so far off the ground that it hit the middle of the windshield. The glass splat-crackled all along its length, and both A-pillars bent into the car an inch or more, shedding their plastic housings with a loud, wet crunch. The rearview mirror shot off its post like a rock from a slingshot. It was a loud, deafening, metal-on-metal shriek, as the train was still moving, and then the boulder-sized wheel assembly hit the front of Ino's car.

The wheel itself was probably three or four feet tall, and it hit the front driver's quarter of Ino's little Jeep like a bulldozer flying along at 20 MPH. The front of the Jeep launched toward the passenger side, leaving a scattered mess of engine and body parts, the airbags exploding out of the side pillars and the dashboard. Ino's side window exploded into tiny jagged chunks as the body of the car twisted, and rained more glass all over him.

The Jeep spun almost a full hundred and eighty degrees as Ino flew off the seat and into the airbags. The Jeep slammed back down on its front end, facing the way it had come, missing about two-thirds of the engine block and the front left wheel.

Ino had no time at all to orient himself, as the vehicle crashed back down onto its three remaining wheels and teetered on the edge of the raised crossing. He felt a sickening sense of scraping and then falling, as the car slid — and then dropped — nose-first down into the drainage canal.

"*Oh no!*" Ino cried as his car dropped eight feet almost straight down and landed in three feet of water on what was left of its front end. His seatbelt was the only thing that kept Ino from dropping straight into the windshield, as bits of glass from the back window and black plastic pieces of the roof cascaded down into the car.

Water blasted away from the impact. The jagged mass at the front of the car dug down into the mud, and then the entire vehicle tipped very gently forward. The Jeep tilted back-over-front, flopping squarely over onto its roof, into the water, with a thundering splash.

Ino had about three-tenths of a second to scream.

He was flung toward the roof now, again caught by his safety belt, head snapping to a stop just inches from the headliner, his feet and knees smashing into the underside of the dashboard and steering wheel. He hadn't even stopped swinging in his seatbelt when water gushed into the exposed cabin. It poured in from all sides. In seconds, rushing white water roiled over the headliner and rose until it covered Ino's face. It was cold and it went up his nose immediately.

Sputtering and then holding his breath, Ino frantically clawed at his seatbelt, struggling to release it. The water climbed up his chest. He finally sank his thumb into the belt release, and it slipped out, but there was so much water in the car that he didn't even fall, he just floated. He opened his eyes but it was impossible to see.

His feet were still dry up in the footwell so Ino tried to struggle around in place. The seatbelt was still caught around his arm and for several panicked moments he couldn't get it out, but he finally freed himself and wriggled around in place. There were objects in the water with him, and the space was so confined and alien that Ino felt like he was inside a clothes washer. There was barely enough room to move.

He felt the seats and pulled himself between them, into the backseat. Running out of air, he lifted his head up into the rear footwell.

"GHHGLLHGHKKK!" he hissed, gasping for breath. There was barely enough room in the footwell for his muzzle. He stood, uncomfortably hunched over, on the inside roof of the car. There was one little light shining into the footwell, a tiny little incandescent bulb, and with it Ino saw the water level rising. He gasped. The footwell was an air pocket, but it wasn't air tight. It would only be a few more seconds before that filled up, too. He had maybe ten seconds and then he would have to find another way out.

Suddenly, a hand closed around his ankle.

He screamed.

The hand yanked, *hard*, and Ino went gushing back under the water, flailing his hands against the wet upholstery, scrambling for a grip on something, anything. But the person had a death grip and was a hell of a lot stronger than Ino. It had to be a man, the hand was big, *huge*, and he pulled Ino out of the car like he was reeling in a fish. Ino sailed through the tiny cargo area and out the back window without so much as landing a handhold. He hit his shoulders on what was left of the spare tire and felt his entire shirt rip.

There was another moment where Ino thought he was going to drown and then he resurfaced again. His lungs exploded and he gasped, coughing up muddy water, and he could tell by the smell of the air he was outside the car.

Wild-eyed, he shook the water off his head and looked around. The skies were dark. The freight train was still thundering past. A foot away, his fur matted to his skin, standing in the same waist-deep water in the drainage ditch, was Travis MacGregor.

Ino spotted the husky and recoiled as best he could, splashing in the water. "GET AWAY FROM ME!" he screamed.

Travis jerked in shock and lurched back, eyes wide. "I just *saved* you!" he yelled. He was in uniform, missing his baseball cap and the bandage — he must have lost it pulling Ino out of the car — and Ino saw the left side of his head was shaved, a huge nasty wound and stitches starting behind his left eye and moving back toward the back of his head.

Ino stared at him. He looked back up at the road.

The train was still rumbling by, blissfully unaware of the drama unfolding on Sturdy Road. The only vehicle in sight was a navy-blue Silverado, stopped diagonally across the shoulder with its headlights on and its driver's door hanging open, pointed right at Ino's sunken car.

The front end was undamaged.

It hadn't been Travis.

Ino looked around frantically. He tried to get to his feet, which was impossible in the muddy bottom of the ditch. He flailed, wide-eyed, pulling himself up on the smashed rear bumper of the car. He cut his hand and barely felt it. "Did you see anybody else?!" He looked to the road. He sloshed toward the edge of the ditch. His legs didn't quite want to work right.

"Only tail lights!" the husky called, over the noise of the freight train. "Looked like a pickup truck, couldn't tell the color in the dark. Are you okay?!" he yelled. He sloshed after the hyena, lunging for his arms.

Ino reached the edge of the ditch, tried to get up onto his feet, and could only get as far as his knees. He knelt there, panting, dripping, shaking.

Travis dropped to his knees next to him. "Hey, take it easy!" the husky rumbled. "Breathe! You're safe now!"

Ino had only just turned to look at him when the storm hit them.

In a moment, the air went from deadly still to churning. A huge mass of roiling air moved in, crashing out of the storm and spreading out, sweeping over the prairie. All the trees around them bowed over, the rustling of leaves and branches and that peculiar throaty hiss that strong winds make in the highest branches of tall trees. It filled the air, from all around them, audible even over the train.

Leaves skittered across the road like insects. They made high-pitched little ticks as they bounced down the pavement. The scent of the air suddenly changed, picking up a hint of moisture, and in the distance there was a deep rumble. The wind pushed again, and somewhere in the trees above them, a huge dead branch snapped with a deep wooden CRACK! It rang out like a gunshot.

In the distance, the city storm sirens began howling. *Whurrr-rrrRRRRMMMMMMMMMMMMMM!* He realized he could already hear Santiago's in the distance as all the sirens built up to a horrible discordant cacophony.

"You have got to be kidding me," Ino groaned.

Travis appeared at his side. "C'mere," he rumbled, simply, and grabbed Ino by the shoulders.

The husky hustled him back toward the upended Jeep, back down into the water-filled ditch.

The rain started, and it roared in like only a Midwestern thunderstorm could, in one long, wet sheet. It was like a fire sprinkler unleashing its flow, one huge curtain of water, and as it touched them it soaked them both to the skin with shockingly cold water.

Now the wind *really* came roaring in, carrying great horizontal curtains of water. It whipped into a frenzy of mist and vapor, stinging like hailstones, and then there *were* hailstones. Ino hunched his shoulders as he was pelted with tiny bits of ice. Above them, more branches broke with loud, deep *crack* sounds and the air was filled with the sound of smaller branches being sheared off and leaves being shredded.

"*Go, go!*" Travis howled, shoving Ino toward the up-ended sunken Jeep. The husky pushed past Ino and reached down to grope for the passenger door handle. He wrenched the door open, throwing up a great torrent of water, and pushed Ino inside. "*In there!*"

Ino could see the base of the passenger seat, and the underside of the dash, and if he crammed in there would be just enough air space between the door and the center console for his head. The passenger floor mat was gone, Ino noticed, and it irrationally annoyed him. The set had been really expensive.

Travis pushed his way in behind him. There wasn't enough room for both of them, and the huge husky pinned him in place, holding onto the gearshift and the seat anchor, pressed hard up against him.

Ino writhed, crouching neck-deep in water and squished into place. "*How is this better?!*" Ino demanded.

More hail began raining down on the underside of the Jeep, and now it sounded like river rocks falling onto sheet metal. It made Ino's ears sting. Ino cowered and Travis pushed in tighter. "*Hold on!*" the husky yelled directly into his ear. "It's about to really start u — !"

Then the wind roared so loudly that it was all Ino could hear, an all-encompassing roar that sounded like the whole atmosphere was venting into space.

It made unholy noises — a whistle, a scream, a roar, a rumble, and his ears started ringing with the sound. There was a horrible bang above them and then the train's brakes locked, the distinctive high-pitched metal-on-metal train-scream yowling above them, echoing into the Jeep like the sound of a dying animal. Lightning flashed, over and over and over, and thunder rumbled and made the ground shake but was too chopped up by the wind to travel very far. It was just a constant, low-level vibration. It occurred to Ino that they were in a water-filled ditch but he couldn't think of anywhere that might possibly be dry so he tried not to think about it.

Now the tree branches snapping went from an occasional cymbal crash to an all-out orchestra, *CRACK CRACK crack CRACK*, like fireworks, branches huge and small crashing down outside the Jeep and blowing across the road. Ino could see a tiny bit of the outside world through the gap in the back of the car. Huge hailstones pelted the pavement and grass, throwing up great splashes everywhere they hit, and with that he knew the water was falling so fast it couldn't even run off of the road. All the trees were snapping back and forth now, whipping back and forth like carwash arms, spraying water and mist back into the wet air. Water flooded into the car, in vapor, and mist. Thunder exploded near them, and this time Ino felt the vibrations. He hoped they were too far away to be electrocuted.

There was an incredibly deep crack close to them, somewhere between a branch break and a rifle shot, followed by a deep bass crash that felt like a small earthquake. A car horn nearby made a long, mangled squeal, and chopped up by the wind it sounded like a wildebeest falling victim to a crocodile, and Ino realized one of the colossal sixty-foot roadside trees had come crashing down on Travis' truck.

There was another heavy gust that felt like it was sucking the air out of the car, and a massive branch, thirty feet long and as big around as a utility pole, an object *way* too big for Ino's brain to handle just flying around in the atmosphere, crashed into the ditch behind the car. A waterfall of branches and bark came down with it, raining down on the underside of the car. The Jeep lurched violently underneath them as the smaller end of the branch landed on the SUV's back end.

"HEAD DOWN!" Travis yelled, directly into his ear, and Ino could barely hear him.

Shaking, he tucked his head down, shaking, waiting for the onslaught to pass.

It went on and on and on like that, as Ino crouched in the ditch water, held in place by the husky, Travis holding him so hard in place that Ino could feel the butt of the dog's gun digging into his back. Ino kept his head down and shivered. The water rose slowly but steadily around them.

Travis was saying something, *shouting* something, directly into his ear, and it took Ino a few moments to realize what it was.

"*Just breathe — just breathe — just breathe!*" he was yelling.

Ino tucked his head down and squeezed his eyes shut and waited for it to finish.

It was over in less than five minutes but it felt like an eternity.

The leading edge of the storm roared through and then just as quickly tapered off. Some last few stubborn branches still broke with sharp staccato cracks and snaps, but the sounds were a lot less frequent. The wind slowly died down. It was still windy, rippling the water around them, but the roar lessened and then dissipated altogether.

Things rained down on the underside of the Jeep, small branches and fat raindrops, making sharp *pang! PANG! Pang!* noises.

Eventually, light returned outside. It wasn't full daylight but it was more than the pitch-black false night that had rolled in a few minutes ago.

Travis eased back behind him, and Ino dared to raise his head.

The husky turned around, peering, and just by leaning backward was outside of the car. Ino frowned at that. If a tree had fallen in the wrong place, or even a big enough branch, Travis would have been scraped out of the Jeep like a bug off a windshield and squashed flat in the drainage ditch. A big enough hailstone could have killed him.

He frowned, his stomach flopping over. The husky had just risked his life to keep Ino safe, not to mention passed up a prime opportunity to drown him in the ditch. No, there was no question in Ino's mind — Travis was innocent.

Totally oblivious to this, the big husky slid out of the Jeep and lifted himself to his feet. It was still pouring, a cold, penetrating rain, and water coursed off of him. He shook his head every few seconds, water spraying off, and then new rain soaking in immediately. Ino watched him blink water out of his eyes.

Travis cleared his throat. "Let's go," he said. "I think the worst is over."

Ino slowly wriggled out after him. His whole body hurt, already. Both his legs were banged up and his hand was throbbing. His head hurt, too. He was sure he would have a black eye and a tender snout for weeks because of the airbag.

Cautiously, he splashed out of the upended Jeep.

Travis climbed up out of the ditch first, sticking his head out and looking cautiously around, as if the storm had dissipated as a trick and might rush back to catch them off-guard.

It was still pouring rain in sheets. Travis held one paw over his face to shield his eyes from the water, and then gestured to Ino to follow him out. He took a few steps and extended an arm.

Ino labored to climb out, reaching for the big dog's hand. The air felt at least twenty degrees cooler, and the rain pouring down was bone-chillingly cold. His teeth started chattering immediately, but that could have been from the situation just as well as from the cold. Water dripped off the end of his muzzle.

He looked around.

His Jeep barely protruded from the water in the drainage ditch, only its wheels completely visible. The rims looked familiar — he had washed them a hundred times — but his brain wouldn't connect that it was *his* Jeep, especially with the odd number of wheels. The water in the ditch was deeper and rising. The headlights and the tail lights were both completely missing, but the running lights were still illuminated, casting a weird red glow into the water.

A 40-foot pine with a trunk as wide around as a utility pole had crashed down onto Travis' blue Silverado, the trunk squashing the cab at the base of the windshield. The middle of the truck was almost touching the ground, and to Ino it looked like an overstuffed men's wallet that wouldn't quite close. The truck's lights were still on and its engine was still running but it didn't sound good. It was making an unhappy, frantic *knock-knock-knock-knock* as it tried to operate with its engine block partially smushed. Ino was glad they had sheltered in the Jeep and not in the Silverado.

The train had finally stopped sometime during the onslaught, and now it was blocking the embankment, water coursing off of it, presenting a gigantic wall blocking Sturdy Road. Scattered all over the embankment were bright-yellow pieces of plastic and shattered bits of glass, and in the middle of the road was Ino's mangled front wheel, off-road tire still attached, complete with half of its lug nuts and studs, which had ripped right out of the wheel housing.

The road was a sea of green and brown, almost completely coated with shredded leaves and bits of sticks. Ino looked down the way they had come and he couldn't believe it was the same road — every ten or fifteen feet there was a branch at least ten or twelve inches across. It was *carpeted* in leaves and pieces of branches. Ino could only see about a mile, and there were at least ten or fifteen big silver maples and pines that had crashed down across the road, completely blocking it.

He stared in disbelief. The road looked like it had been abandoned for a hundred years. There was more green than asphalt.

Travis was looking at it too, and then nodded grimly. Suddenly the husky was in front of him.

He was frowning, his blue eyes searching. "Are you okay?"

"I'm fine," Ino mumbled. He looked up at the husky's crew cut and big stitched wound. "You lost your hat."

Travis nodded. "You could be in shock. Hold still." The husky patted him down, feeling up and down his arms and legs, and while Ino was pretty confident the husky was checking him for injuries, it still felt like he was being frisked. "You're bleeding," the dog said.

Ino looked down. His left hand was, indeed, dripping blood on the wet street, from a cut running down the side of his paw, from the base of the pinky down to his wrist. It didn't hurt until he looked at it, and then it stung like crazy.

Travis took Ino's right hand and put it over his left hand. "Hold this," he said. "Hard. Hard enough to hurt."

Ino did as he said. Warm blood seeped out from between his fingers. "What the hell was that?" the hyena asked. "It wasn't a tornado. We would both be dead."

Travis was behind him, checking his mane. "Nope, not a tornado. Just straight-line winds," he said, simply. The big husky finished looking him over, and stepped in front of him, holding Ino's muzzle and face in his big hands. "That was a supercell and we just saw the wind coming out of the front of it." He forcibly lifted Ino's chin, holding his entire face.

The hyena stared at him, wide-eyed. "What are you doing?" he asked, squirming, his face stuck in the dog's huge paws.

Travis stared at him suspiciously. "Trying to see if you're going into shock."

Ino blinked at him from inches away. "I don't think so," he said, shakily. He swallowed. "Somebody tried to kill me," he said, softly.

Travis stared intently into his eyes, and after a moment, he let go. "I know," he said. "Did you see anything?"

Ino shook his head. "Just headlights," he said, softly.

Travis nodded. "Yeah, I just saw tail lights. It was already dark. Did you see what kind of vehicle it was?"

Ino shrugged. He thought of Susan Greeley's enormous Infiniti SUV. "Big," he said. "Silver, maybe. That might just have been the grille. It was hard to tell."

Travis nodded.

Ino looked down the road. "Th-they can't have gotten far," he said, gesturing with his muzzle at the tree-cratered Sturdy.

The husky frowned. "They might have, unfortunately," he said. "I saw them go into this outlet." He gestured with his muzzle at a road that was little more than asphalt dust. It had two posts on either side. A long chain was stuck to one of them, the other end discarded in the grass like a dead snake. There was a NO ENTRY sign still attached to the middle of the chain. "This runs along the railroad tracks, up into the People's Propane lot, and then right out onto 30. You'd be right in town and you could go anywhere." He frowned. "Do you have your phone? Mine's in the truck."

Ino blinked at him. He felt his pockets and slid his phone out of his wet jeans. As he held it up, water coursed out of it. It was an older model, and it hadn't been waterproof; the phone was dark and dead. It had survived the explosion only to drown in the ditch.

Ino had very nearly met the same fate.

Travis saw the dead phone and frowned. He turned to the remains of his truck. "I'm gonna call this in, don't go anywhere! I don't got the townies' radio frequency — I need the phone." The big husky turned and lunged into the crown of the fallen tree squishing the Silverado. He clambered over and under branches with surprising gracefulness. The dog disappeared for a moment and then popped up in the branches behind the squashed cab, planted one big booted foot on the side of the car, and yanked at the cab's small rear door until it popped open with a metal-on-metal squeal. He climbed up into the back and a second later the Silverado's engine went dead.

There was rummaging, and then over the rain Ino heard the husky's booming voice. "This is Officer MacGregor of Santiago University Security, I need to report a 10-57 hit and run at the train crossing on Sturdy, attempted vehicular homicide, suspect vehicle is a large SUV or pickup and fled westbound on an access road toward Route 30 —"

Ino tuned out the rest of the conversation as he looked around at the shattered bits of yellow plastic all over the road, all while coursing rain cascaded down onto him. Thunder rumbled in the distance as the storm started to ease. It was probably blowing over now. He was still shivering.

Had that just *happened?*

Had someone really tried to kill him by pushing his car into a freight train? He shivered. Or maybe the plan had been to drown him. Either way, it had come frighteningly close to working.

Was Susan Greeley really capable of such a thing? She had a monster SUV. She could easily have done it. Or maybe her enormous husband had some problems with impulse control.

Ino frowned. It probably *hadn't* been Jack. Unless the shepherd had followed him. Or tipped off Susan or Sebastian. And any of them could have noticed when he logged into Reed's network drive from his own PC the previous night to download the video. The only one who was clearly innocent at this point was Travis.

Ino shook his head, still holding his bleeding hand. This was stupid. He was being stupid. He was truly in danger. And most likely, so was anyone who knew the truth.

He gasped. *Vivian!* He reflexively reached for his phone again, but of course that wasn't going to work.

A gym bag flew out of the truck, sailed over the downed tree, and crashed down next to him, along with two travel umbrellas, followed by the husky officer crashing his way through the flattened pine. "I got an ambulance coming, but they won't be able to get closer than the cemetery. Can you walk?"

Ino stared at him. "Are you in radio range for campus?"

Travis blinked, raising his eyebrows. "Yuh. Why?"

"Can you have someone find Dr. Vivian Chen? I think she's in danger as well. She's probably in her office." He swallowed, his heart pounding.

The husky cocked his head, his eyes widening, but he reached for the school's radio key on his shoulder, turning up the volume. Ino was amazed the radio was still attached. "Dispatch! This is 47!" he said.

Ino vaguely recognized the harried voice on the other end of the radio as one of the other security employees, and there was a loud clatter in the background on the other end of the radio. "MacGregor! Where the hell are you?!" the other cop cried. "The whole campus is dark and we got three buildings flooded! Half the windows on campus are broken!"

Travis frowned. "Dispatch, someone just tried to murder Dr. Reamer with a train south of campus. I need someone to find Dr. Vivian Chen right now, that's C-H-E-N, *Charlie Hotel Echo November*. She's also a target. Start with the offices. Find her *now.*"

Ino stared at him. He shivered again.

There was a long pause.

Travis clicked the button again. "You might want to tell the Chief," he added.

There was a short crackle and then the voice came on, considerably more harried. "Copy, 47! Stay on this channel!"

Travis nodded. "Copy. I am currently without a vehicle; I will get a ride back to campus. Good luck, Dispatch. Out."

"Acknowledged!" squeaked the radio dispatch. It was the most upset Ino had ever heard someone over a radio.

Travis nodded and looked up at Ino. "All right. They'll find her." He had a big Ace bandage and he stepped toward Ino. "Give me your hand," he said.

Ino held out his bleeding hand, the rain rinsing off the wound. It didn't look *too* deep but it did look jagged. He frowned. When had that happened?

Travis roughly tied off the wound, blood spotting through the light cream of the fabric immediately, and wrapped the rest of it around Ino's hand. It was tight and it hurt, but Ino knew basic first aid and it was the right thing to do. At least they wouldn't have to shave his hand again — the fur still hadn't grown back from last time.

"Make sure they wash this out *really well* at the hospital," the husky said. "That ditch is probably full of crap." He scooped up the items on the ground and handed Ino one of the umbrellas. "Open this," he said.

Ino was shivering now, so he popped the umbrella open without protest. There was elaborate script writing on it. "*Yankee Candle*", it said. "*America's Best Loved Candle™.*"

Ino frowned at the umbrella, and then stared with confusion at the big husky officer.

Travis scowled at him. "That is *not* mine so don't even ask. Take off your shirt."

Ino blinked at him. "What?" He was already shivering. It was making his teeth chatter, literally clacking against each other, like in a cartoon.

Travis opened the other umbrella and let the gym bag dangle from a strap while he rummaged through it. "Take off your shirt!" he insisted. "You're soaking wet. I didn't save you just so you could get hypothermia." He pulled out a light-gray sweatshirt. "You're going to go into shock and then I'll have to carry your spotted ass for two miles. Do you need help with the buttons?"

Ino stared at him and finally decided he didn't have the energy to protest. "Whatever you say," he said, unbuttoning his shirt. Passing the umbrella back and forth between his hands, he wriggled out of his shirt. He wasn't wearing an undershirt, so he brushed and flattened his chest fur, wringing some of the water out and letting it run down his pants. He was truly soaked to the bone, and he smelled like rotting leaves. The light-blue shirt was ripped down the back and stained a green-brown color so he just threw it on the ground.

"Here," Travis said. "Gimmie that." He took the umbrella from Ino and lifted it up over the hyena's head, handing him a ratty-looking gym towel.

Ino leaned away to shake violently and then dried himself off as best he could while the husky held the umbrella over his head. He squeezed most of the water out of his fur, though that didn't get rid of the ditch smell. The towel smelled like husky sweat, so if anything, this had added a *new* smell, but it did feel better to dry his dripping face fur.

Travis nodded. "Good. Now put this on." He offered up the sweatshirt. It said "POPCORN FAIR SANTIAGO, INDIANA 2016, because of course it did.

Ino took it, frowning. It felt huge in his hands, like a fleece blanket. He pulled it over his head and the neck hole almost fell over his shoulders. It was massive and it stank.

Ino poked his head through and gagged. The shirt fit him like a tent and fully covered him, hanging so low he could feel it on his tail. "Oh my God, this thing *reeks*," he complained.

Travis stared at him for a moment and then laughed. "Yeah, it does. It's better than hypothermia, though."

Ino lifted up his hands, which the sleeves overhang by a good five inches, and clumsily tugged the wrist holes down over his hand, unfortunately smearing the left sleeve with blood. The shirt must have been a quadruple-X. Travis was bigger than Ino but he wasn't *that* big. Ino was trying to figure out the logistics of Travis working out in a shirt this size when he started to warm up and instantly felt a hundred times better. The oversized shirt was like being wrapped in a big blanket. A big, smelly blanket.

Travis handed him back the umbrella. "See? Isn't that better?"

Ino nodded at the husky and then frowned. Travis was still standing in the rain, his face fur matted and dripping, water coursing off his uniform pants and short-sleeve shirt. Even his vest was fully saturated and dripping. He shook aggressively, making himself the center of a husky fountain, but it barely helped with his clothes and even his face fur was still matted down to his skin.

The hyena frowned. "What about you? Aren't you cold?"

Travis cracked a smile. "I'm a husky. I don't *get* cold." He sat down in the road and started to pull off his boots, which Ino was surprised to see were huge mid-calf cowboy boots. He was about to ask what the hell Travis was doing when the husky upended the boot and poured a half gallon of ditch water onto the road.

Ino stared at him in disbelief, and thought of Sean getting blown out of his sneakers at Baker. He shivered.

"Thanks for the shirt," he said, quietly. "Thanks for... all of this."

Pouring a similar volume of water and a few leaves out of his other boot, Travis grunted in acknowledgment.

Ino watched him. "So... what's next?" he asked.

Travis let out another grunt as he wrenched himself to his feet and opened the other umbrella. This one was just black, Ino noted. The husky lifted it up over his head and shook again. Ino took a step back.

The husky took a deep breath. "Well, this is a crime scene. We're going to have to walk to the end of this road, but there will be an ambulance waiting. They'll check you out and warm you up. As soon as the road is cleared I'll have the county sheriffs check this out. I'll go to the hospital with you to make a statement but I'll have to get back to the University. They're gonna need me."

Ino nodded slowly.

The husky nodded quickly. "Okay," he said. "You ready to go?"

Clutching his umbrella, Ino nodded.

They set off into the rain.

They didn't get ten feet before Travis asked the question Ino had been dreading. "So who do you think might have been trying to kill you?"

Ino let out a long sigh. He couldn't possibly just start telling everyone his theory. He pulled the sweatshirt closer around him. "I have some ideas," he said, raising his voice to be audible over the rain. "Nothing I really want to talk about right this second."

Travis frowned. "You should. In case they succeed next time."

Ino shot him a look.

The husky blinked innocently back at him. He seemed genuinely surprised at Ino's anger. "What? You don't want to leave a cold case, do you?"

Ino shook his head. "*Jesus.* What a morbid thought. Do you know, everybody keeps telling me how *nice* you are?"

Travis ignored the jab. "Well, do you know *why* someone tried to kill you?"

Ino nodded. "Ayup. Pretty sure."

There was silence, and then the husky suddenly changed direction. He turned and stopped dead in front of Ino, staring defiantly and blocking his path.

Ino let out a long sigh. "All right, all right. I saw something I shouldn't have."

The husky frowned at him, clearly trying to determine if he was lying or not. Eventually he decided not. "Somehow, that doesn't surprise me," he grumbled.

Ino chuckled humorlessly.

Travis narrowed his eyes. "Okay. Here's the deal. You need to tell me what it was, right now, so I can call it in and we can start investigating."

Ino stared at him, feeling the blood drain from his face. *Sure, let me just show you a video of your boss having a puppy-play four-way with two suspects and a murder victim, and THEN let's broadcast that over an open radio.* "Uhhhhh," he said. "I don't think that's a good idea. For several reasons."

Travis set his jaw in a deadly frown, and Ino saw the legendary husky stubbornness he'd often glimpsed in Sean. However, Travis was a *fully-developed* stubborn husky and he might as well have been a physical brick wall in Ino's path.

Ino let out a long sigh. "It's... sensitive, okay?!" he demanded. "*Very* sensitive."

Travis frowned. "Dr. Reamer, someone tried to kill you in broad daylight. They're probably going to try again. And if they try on campus they could easily hurt other people in the process. Or they might come after Dr. Chen."

Ino grumbled. "I would have to talk to your boss again before I shared anything."

The husky blinked at him. "My boss? Chief Archer? He knows about what you saw?"

Ino thought of the shepherd's whine-growl on the video. He shivered. "Yeah. He knows *aallllll* about it." He tried to keep the frown off of his face.

The husky blinked at him. "Oh. Well never mind then." He turned and immediately started walking again. "C'mon. Shake a leg."

Ino blinked and hopped after him. He had to jog a couple feet to catch up, splashing as he went. "What? Really? That's all you needed to hear?!"

Travis turned to him and nodded. "Yeah," he said.

Ino frowned. "And you're not the least bit curious?"

The big husky shrugged. "If I need to know, he'll tell me."

Ino stared at him. "Wow. Guess you think pretty highly of him."

The husky cracked a smile. "I would trust him with my life, so... yeah."

They walked in silence for a moment. The possibility of Jack being the murderer seemed to grow more remote by the moment. That would mean that either Jack was legendarily manipulative or Travis was legendarily stupid.

They walked in silence for a few more minutes. The rain picked up a little but nothing anywhere near what had just rolled through. Ino's shoes were still completely soaked.

Ino thought about Travis and how many times he had suspected the dog of being the killer. He frowned.

"By the way..." Ino cleared his throat. "Thanks for saving my life."

Travis nodded. "Don't mention it."

There was a pause.

Travis glanced at him sideways. "I *mean* it," the husky added. "Don't mention it. Don't tell anybody."

Ino stared, and thought for a good long moment, and finally decided the husky was joking.

Travis glanced back at him, and now Ino could see the faintest glimmer of a smile in his blue eyes.

Ino chuckled. "You've got a dry sense of humor, Officer MacGregor," he said.

Facing down the road, still walking half a step ahead of him, the husky cracked a smile.

Ino decided to risk a friendly jab. "So — it's a source of great comfort to me to learn that you're not actually a gigantic asshole after all."

Travis turned to him, blue eyes wide and startled, and then smiled brightly. His curled tail even wagged a little. "Well! I do what I can. Don't get used to it."

Ino grinned silently back at him.

The husky chuckled, and then fell silent. "You should have heard Jack after he heard me snap at you. He almost wrote me up." He lowered his voice. "*I will not have one of my officers held to a lower standard than a Starbucks barista!*" The voice was deep and stodgy.

Ino couldn't keep the smile off his face. "Is that your *Jack Archer* voice?"

Travis laughed again. "Yeah. I guess so."

Suddenly Travis' radio cracked. "47!" squeaked a harried-sounding voice. They both jumped.

Travis keyed the mic at his shoulder. "47, go ahead," he said.

The radio crackled. They must have been right at the edge of the broadcast range. "47, your request has been, ah, fulfilled. Second professor is at the station. Safe and sound."

Ino and Travis made eye contact. Travis nodded and Ino let out a big sigh of relief.

The big husky keyed his mic again. "Thanks, Dispatch. I'll be back as soon as I can!"

"Roger, out!" crackled the response.

They walked on for a moment. Travis walked a little way ahead of the hyena. The husky was better-suited to challenging overland travel, a fact that was not particularly surprising.

Something occurred to Ino.

"Travis… how did you know I was here?" he asked, softly.

Shrugging, the husky glanced over his shoulder. "Jack sent me," he said. "He told me to make sure you were okay." He climbed easily over the trunk of a twenty-foot evergreen that had fallen across the road and flattened out like a broken umbrella.

Ino stared at him, eyes wide. "Really?"

Now facing him, Travis was half-smiling again. "Really." He chuckled. "I think he kinda likes you."

Now Ino stopped dead in his tracks.

Travis started to turn away but glanced back. He stopped. "Oh, come *on*," he said, raising an exasperated eyebrow. "You must have noticed."

Ino shook his head, wide-eyed.

The husky let out an annoyed sigh. "Okay, you've made your point." He turned and started walking again.

Shaking his head, Ino scrambled over the little evergreen and caught up. They set off again. "I'm afraid I don't have any evidence to support your theory," he called after Travis. "I'm pretty sure he hates me, in fact."

Travis rolled his eyes.

They walked. Summer rain coursed down on both of them and everything around them, making a gentle waterfall around the edges of their umbrellas.

He cleared his throat. "Hey," he said softly. "Do… do *you* hate me?"

Travis stiffened, and then took another few steps. He glanced back at Ino and frowned, quickly breaking eye contact. "I… uhhhhh…"

Ino chuckled humorlessly. "It's okay. I couldn't possibly hold it against you after you still saved my li —"

"No," Travis interrupted. He swallowed, his ears folding back, and he looked deeply embarrassed. "I don't hate you."

Ino stared at him. This was not the reaction he had expected.

"I just… it was just all of the…" Travis struggled for the words. "I couldn't handle the…" Finally he trailed off, growling. "I'm not good with words," he grumbled.

Ino blinked at him. "I mean, you can just *say* I'm annoying, Officer," he said, shrugging. "It's not like, a *secret*…"

"NO, it's not that." The husky rolled his eyes. "Jesus, not everything is about *you*, Reamer!"

The hyena stared at him. He elected to shut his mouth and let the husky continue.

They walked along as the husky searched for the words. The two of them came to a dip in the road with a four-inch-deep lake spanning the entire roadway with a thousand leaves and branches floating in it. Since both of them were already soaked from the waist down, they didn't bother to change course. They just splashed directly through it.

Finally, Travis let out a resigned sigh. "You can't repeat *any* of this," he grumbled. He looked at Ino with dangerous eyes.

Surprised, the hyena shook his head.

"Uhhhhhhhhhhhgh," the husky groaned, rolling his eyes again. "So… you need to know something about Sean."

Ino tried to keep his jaw from dropping open. "Sean?" he asked. "Sean *Murphy*? Your nephew?"

Travis nodded grimly. "Yeah. He's… adopted."

Ino blinked at him. "He's… whuh…" He trailed off. "He's adopted?" He frowned. "So what?" He shrugged. "So am I. It's not a big deal anymore."

Travis scrunched his muzzle up into an annoyed husky sneer.

Ino stared at him a moment and then the reason suddenly clicked. He did not succeed in keeping his jaw from dropping open.

"He doesn't *know*?!" Ino gasped. It came out louder than he intended.

Frowning, Travis shook his head. "If any of this gets back to him I swear to *God* —"

Ino held his hand up disarmingly. "I won't say a word!"

Travis nodded, and then let out a long shaky breath. "Anyway. That's the background. My sister and her husband, they… they tried for a long time, you know? They had a couple promising starts, but nothing…" He frowned. "Nothing that… worked out."

Ino frowned, and nodded slowly. There was a lot that went unsaid in that sentence.

Travis continued. "After a couple years and a lot of disappointment they finally stopped trying. I was right out of the academy at that point, and we did some work with an orphanage, and I kinda mentioned it, and like… I didn't expect it to go anywhere but, they had a couple meetings and… one day… now there's this little puppy in the picture."

Ino nodded. He cracked a smile, picturing little baby Sean.

The two of them came to a huge silver maple splayed across the entire length of the street. They wouldn't have a hope of getting through the crown, so they went wide around the roots, off the road, picking their way through the edge of the greenbelt. They splashed through a sodden corn-field on the other side, and edged back to the road. The tree's root base, ripped out of the ground, was as wide across as a garden shed, and towered higher than both of their heads.

"I don't even like kids," Travis said, on the other side. "But Sean showed up, and he was just like…" He trailed off, his eyes losing focus. "He was just so *small*. He was *so* small. I never really like, realized, how tiny babies are…" He swallowed, and glanced at Ino. "And he was little even for a puppy. You could hold his entire body in your palm and forearm." He gave Ino a goofy smile.

Ino couldn't help but smile back.

Travis continued. "And things were fine for a while. He was never really *big* for his age, but he got bigger. And then he, like… started moving around, and then it was…"

Ino smiled. "Heartwarming?"

Eyes wide, Travis shook his head. "*Terrifying.*"

Ino cocked his head. "*Terrifying?*" he repeated, startled.

Travis nodded. "Babies, man. They get into *everything*. They're like magnets for every single thing that can kill you. They're like tiny suicidal drunks. Sean got into *everything*. He could open cabinets, he could climb… you know those little plastic things they put in electrical outlets? He used to pull those out, and *eat them*."

Ino stifled a laugh.

Travis frowned at him. "It's not funny! Sean got into so many things. I didn't think he was going to make it to five." He frowned. "You answer a couple 911 calls, you see people sobbing in their living rooms, surrounded by toys. It's not funny anymore." He swallowed, hard.

Ino thought about that, his arm fur standing up. "Jesus Christ," he said. "I never thought about that."

Travis shook his head. "And like… I… I think there was something wrong with me, because…" He frowned, starting to fidget again. "It was all I could think about. Is Sean okay? Is something going to happen to Sean. Did he find something, did he get into something, did someone break in and try to hurt him." He looked down at his feet. "I would wake up in the middle of the night in a panic about it."

Ino watched him. It didn't look like the husky was lying or exaggerating. It sounded… pretty serious, actually.

Travis shook his head. "Sometimes I drove over to their house just to check on them. In the middle of the night. Or after a shift." He swallowed, his ears folding back, and let out a long sigh. "Real stupid, right? Not even my kid." He swallowed, looking away.

Ino let out a breath. "I don't think that stupid is the word I would use."

Travis tossed him a crooked humorless smile. "Yeah. Maybe not. Anyway, it faded a little as he got older, but I would still like, cruise past their house on my way home after a shift. Just to make sure that everything was okay."

Ino nodded gently. "And did you… ever talk to anyone about that?" he asked, carefully.

Travis let out a long, dejected sigh. "No. I'm sure it was anxiety or clinical depression or something but it went away and it didn't come back so I never did." He looked away, frowning tightly.

Ino nodded.

"Anyway… one day when Sean was about five, when I was doing my usual stalker check-in after a shift and driving past their house in the middle of the night, I saw a light in the garage. You remember those garage door windows everybody used to have? It was lit up."

Ino stared at him. "Like… a burglar?"

Travis stared at him, dangerously. "Like, a *flickering* light."

Ino leaned forward, eyes wide. "A *fire?*"

Travis nodded slowly. "Yup," he said flatly. "A fire. A car fire. In an attached garage."

Ino waited for him to continue.

"So I slammed on the brakes, and by the time I got out of the car, the garage window blew out, and flames just gushed out into the street. I could *feel* the heat, twenty feet away, and all the siding started to melt, and the roof overhang caught in an instant. And that's flashover, and if you're still in the house and you're still alive, you got like… seconds after that." He took a long, deep breath.

Ino watched him, eyes wide.

"So, I was running up the driveway when the kitchen lit up, an' I knew the fire was out of the garage. I ran around to the side and pounded on my sister's window." He told the story flatly, mechanically. "I got them out, but Sean's bedroom was on the second floor."

Ino swallowed. He had to tell himself to take another breath. "Did you run in?"

Travis smiled grimly. "Naw, when a fire hits flashover, it's like seven, eight hundred degrees in there. Unsurvivable." He glanced at Ino. "I ran back to my cruiser — a big Expedition — and pulled it up to the side of the house, like grinding up against it. I climbed on top of it, and I smashed the window, and I climbed in. There was smoke in his bedroom but the door wasn't open. Their *downstairs* bedroom door was open, so by the time I got the kid, the fire was coming out the window and the truck was burning." He took a long deep breath. "So I took a leap off the back of it and broke my ankle in the yard. My sister and her husband grabbed the kid and dragged me to the street."

Ino stared, open-mouthed.

Travis nodded. "Ayup."

The hyena shook his head. "Jesus. What happened?"

Travis shrugged. "The Murphy house burned to the ground. My cruiser blew up. I got a medal." He shrugged, his mouth curling up into a little smile. "The tread melted off my boots. Still got 'em."

Ino stared at him, incredulously. "And Sean?!"

Travis cracked a smile. "Not a scratch. Not one little scratch."

They came to another mid-sized pine across the road, only 30 feet or so tall. The branches were thin near the top, so they crossed to the far side of the road and wriggled through the lush green branches.

Ino didn't know what to say. He was in shock.

It was another few moments before Travis started talking again. "Anyway, after *that*, I kind of felt better, you know?"

Ino chuckled. "I can see why. You did kind of... save the day."

Travis grinned. "Right? Like it was like... what did somebody say. *Preordained*. Something really horrible happened, but I was there." He looked at Ino. "Y'know? I was *there*," he repeated. "I kept telling myself it was just chance, but it like... felt right. Like it was supposed to happen that way." He smiled. "So I kind of got over it." He shrugged. "I always kinda thought, if something else ever happened, I would be there again. I woke up feeling great, and I felt pretty good ever since then."

Ino smiled a little. It was a nice little story.

Except that wasn't the end, he thought. He already knew the end.

The end happened at 6:03 pm on Friday, May 11.

It hit him all at once. The dirty looks. The hostility. That look that Travis had given him in the Security Department parking lot, somewhere between rage and horror.

He slowed down, unconsciously, and then he couldn't walk any more so he stopped. "Oh, my God," he said. "Until Baker blew up, you mean. You felt pretty good… *until Baker blew up."* He grit his teeth.

Travis slowed to a stop, too, and then turned to glance at Ino. He smiled weakly. "Yup! Until Baker blew up," he agreed, chuckling humorlessly. "When he needed me again. And I wasn't there."

Ino swallowed.

Travis leveled his gaze on him. "*You* were there," he said, low and dangerous.

Ino grimaced. "Travis…" He felt like he had to say something but couldn't get any words together.

Travis thought for a moment and then let out a heavy sigh. "I… I couldn't even *look* at you." He glanced warily at Ino. "You were like this… *walking reminder."* He looked up. "Of me telling myself I was his fuckin' guardian or something for fifteen years." He kicked a branch and it landed with a wet thud. "That I lied to myself for his whole life. That I could just as easily have gone for a burger after my shift and they'd all be — " He trailed off.

Ino grimaced.

Travis swallowed, letting out a long, shaky sigh, and turned to glance at Ino, his ears flat. He looked devastated. "It was… a lot."

"Travis," Ino said, softly. "We don't have to talk about this if you don't want to."

"No, we do," Travis growled. "I'm sorry I was such an asshole," Travis rumbled, through clenched teeth. "I just… I was *so mad* at you." He shook his head. "I felt like I was losing my mind. All I could think about, for *days,* was that *you* were saving Sean's life while *I* was smoking a fucking joint next to a goddamn dumpster."

Ino blinked in surprise, and then slowly closed his eyes.

So that's what Jack had been covering for. Smoking weed on a boring security job. That was all.

Travis heaved another sigh. He looked up at Ino.

Ino let out a breath. "Hey, I'm sorry, too. I never should have said such a dick thing to you in the parking lot of the Security building." He clenched his teeth. "That was horrible. I'm sorry."

Travis let out a long sigh. "It's okay. I deserved it. I deserve *this*, too." He gestured at the spiderweb of wounds criss-crossing his mangled head. "You were *right*. You're the only reason he's still alive." He looked at Ino, his lower jaw set in a miserable frown, and he looked so despondent that Ino could barely take a breath.

Ino grimaced. "C'mon… you don't know that. He's a smart kid. He would have gotten out of that building. He smelled the gas before I did anyway."

The husky stared at him, and then scowled. "Yeah? How much do you know about that car accident over the winter? Sean and that other boy."

Ino thought about it, blinking. The "other boy" was Robbie Brandt. He pictured them together.

"A little," he said, hesitantly.

Travis nodded blankly at him. "Let me guess. Sean told you they both crashed and he *walked* to the other boy's car, and they spent a cozy little night together."

Ino stared at him, eyes wide. Dumbly, he nodded.

Travis narrowed his eyes. "He walked a *quarter. Mile.* In a whiteout blizzard. With two feet of snow already on the ground. To save some kid he barely knew. Do you remember that fucking storm, Reamer?"

Ino stared at him. He *did* remember the storm — of course he did. Staring through his picture window, watching his neighbor's cars get buried hour by hour. By morning he couldn't tell whose car was whose. During the whiteout, he hadn't even been able to see across the street. A quarter mile seemed inconceivable.

The husky's muzzle scrunched up. "Did he happen to mention how many people *died* during that blizzard? Or how many of them were on the highway? Two of them were on Route 49. Same as Sean and Robbie." He frowned. "I talked to him. That night." He swallowed. "Told him to stay in the car. He didn't. I *told him* to *stay in the fucking car.*"

"Yeah, but Sean saved him, right?" Ino asked, softly. "I… I remember the articles. I saw pictures of the car. Robbie's car was destroyed." He swallowed. "What would have happened if Sean had stayed in the car?"

Travis glanced at him guiltily. "He — …" It took him a few moments to answer. "He wouldn't have lasted long."

Ino thought about big sweet Robbie, panicking over question 26 on his final. He felt all the blood drain out of his face. The sound of the rain got far away for a moment.

Travis glanced at him, and shriveled under his gaze. His tail curled up between his legs. "Don't look at me like that!" he growled. "Sean did a good thing. That's not the *point.*"

Ino stared at him. "I don't understand."

"The *point* is that neither of them *should* have made it," Travis snapped. "Stepping out of that car was a fucking death sentence. We pulled that truck out of a snowdrift *seven feet deep.* It's a goddamn miracle that either of them survived." He stammered for a moment and then threw his hands up. "He didn't *think!* He saw somebody in trouble and just went charging in. So what do you think that means about the fucking lab and the gas, Dr. Reamer?"

Ino stared at him, stunned. He could barely take a full breath at this point.

Travis watched him for a few long moments. He frowned. "Yeah. You get it."

Ino looked up at him. "God."

Travis let out a long sigh. "He's just a kid. You know?"

Ino nodded. "I get it." It was still sinking in. It was pointless to argue with Travis, because of course, he was right.

Travis grunted. "He doesn't know about hard choices. Sometimes you fight. Sometimes, you gotta run. Dying in the hallway isn't gonna help anybody. He would have tried to get into that lab until the moment that… that… th —"

The husky's voice cracked, and he cut off.

Ino looked up, surprised, and found Travis looking away, clenching his jaw. The husky tried to get something out, failed, held up one finger for a moment, and then turned away, gritting his teeth, squeezing his eyes shut, and Ino could tell he was holding back a wave that was about to crash over him. Silently, his shoulders shook, casting off little droplets of water.

Ino stood in respectful silence.

After a minute or two Travis regained his composure, and they settled into a slow walk again. They walked on in silence for a few minutes.

The husky finally let out a long, shuddery sigh.

Ino didn't look at him, but he did reach over and squeeze the big man's shoulder.

Travis cleared his throat, and took a few deep breaths. "You know, ah," he said. "When we found 'em they were fuckin'."

It took Ino a few moments to figure out who Travis was talking about. "Wh… Sean and Robbie?" He gaped. "Are you *serious?*"

Travis looked up at him, shaking his head in disbelief. "Yeah. Me and Reese found them. I didn't work here yet but I hitched a ride in to help look for Sean. We found 'em in the morning and they had been up all night screwing." He scrunched his face into a grimace. "I about had a seizure."

Ino stifled a laugh. "Are you *kidding?* Even with all that peril?!"

Travis nodded. "Yeah. Well… teenagers, man. Peril makes 'em horny."

Ino grinned. "Wow. That's… quite a story."

The husky snorted. "Yeah, wish I could forget it."

Ino chuckled for a moment. "Have you, ah, followed their exploits since then?"

Travis glanced up at him, and then grinned evilly. "You mean, did they tell me that they're *secretly dating?*" Behind him, his still-dripping tail slowly started to wag.

Ino couldn't keep the grin off his face. "Ayup," he said. "Cute, aren't they?"

Travis chuckled. "Yeah. My brother-in-law hasn't said anything, but I can tell he's psyched that our boy landed a football player."

Ino burst out laughing.

They had a few easy moments.

Ino heard a radio squawk in the distance and he looked up, lifting his umbrella. Up ahead, on the other side of a toppled tree, Ino saw red and blue emergency lights.

"Looks like our ride is here!" he announced.

"Thank you," Travis said, suddenly. "For what you did. In the lab."

Ino turned. "Hey. God. Of course." He chuckled. "Considering you just saved my life, I'm quite comfortable saying we're even."

Travis narrowed his eyes. "No, we are not," he growled.

Ino looked up, eyes wide. The growl made his arm fur stand on end. It was deep and terrifying and it didn't sound like a noise that Travis should have been capable of producing. He turned to Travis, stunned.

The husky raised his upper lip, furrowing his brows and narrowing his icy blue eyes. He looked like a black and white demon. "Not until we find the fucker that started this."

Ino didn't know what to say to that, so he just nodded.

In the distance there was a soft, keening wail of a train horn.

Later, Ino was sitting on a hospital bed in the Emergency Room of Beirne Memorial Hospital in Santiago. He was wearing athletic shorts and a hospital gown and had seven fresh stitches in his left hand. It was almost 6 pm.

Vivian was in the hard plastic chair next to him. She had shown up only ten minutes after he did, carrying Ino's gym bag and spare glasses from his office, and dragging a junior SU security officer who was now her de facto escort. The junior officer was taking his role very seriously and was now waiting outside their room.

Ino had been cleaned up and stitched up by the ER doctors and swarmed by cops at the same time. The stitches only took fifteen minutes, but the questioning took a lot longer. After that he had been shuttled into a private room so the police could continue their barrage of questions. He had told the story about thirty-five times to several duty cops, and even to a detective. The Santiago city police had eventually concluded that he wasn't in immediate danger of another attempted murder again, but had been very clear that he should not travel alone. Plus, he would have a squad car outside of his house once an hour for the foreseeable future.

Now he was just waiting to be discharged. The ER had been swamped ever since the storm, mostly folks hit by flying debris and a lot of cuts from glass. Almost every other person seemed to be holding a blood-soaked dishtowel against a forearm or head. The doctors and nurses were understandably occupied. So Ino and Vivian waited.

The hospital had lost city power by the time they got there. The building was running off a series of huge generators now, which meant the equipment and most of the lights worked, but none of the non-essential items. The TV in Ino's room was dark, and even though it had been off the whole time Ino had been at the site, he still found himself staring blankly at it, as if an old episode of *Seinfeld* or *Friends* might pop on at any moment.

"Hey," Vivian said suddenly.

Ino turned to her.

"Did you ever get the check engine light fixed in your Jeep?"

Staring at her, wide-eyed, he slowly shook his head.

The marten nodded thoughtfully. "Well," she said. "Now you don't have to."

Ino stared at her for a moment before finally smiling. After another few seconds, the absurdity of her statement sank in, and he cracked up laughing.

"Wow, you're *really* good at this," he told her.

She beamed. "Aren't I, though?"

There were loud footfalls from the hall.

Ino narrowed his eyes. "I know those plodding footsteps."

Vivian looked up, and then turned frowning toward the door.

They heard Jack Archer say something to the officer outside, and then burst through the door without knocking. He was frowning. "Dr. Reamer!"

Ino looked him over. The shepherd was missing his tie. His dress shirt sleeves were rolled up to his elbows, and there were sweat stains under both of his arms. He had sweat in a large V down the center of the shirt, and his hair was messed up. There was a big smear of dirt across the front of his shirt.

Ino stared at him. "Wow. You look almost as bad as I do."

The shepherd looked him over, his eyes taking in the mess of stitches, and the fresh surgical wrappings. "Are you all right?"

Ino nodded. "I am. Thanks to Travis MacGregor."

Jack loped up to him, frowning. He actually looked shaken up. "Are you? You look terrible. I apologize that I couldn't get away sooner."

Ino glared at him. "Oh, is *that* why you're apologizing? I thought you might want to apologize because you haven't solved this case yet, and I almost fucking died because of you."

The dog stared at him a moment, perfectly still, his expression showing absolutely no emotion.

Finally, he spoke. "Dr. Chen, could you please give us a moment alone?" he said, without taking his eyes off Ino.

Ino felt his heart speed up.

Vivian stood up and looked between the two of them, frowning. "Sure," she said. "Ino, I'll be right outside." She turned to Jack. "And I have to tell you I'll be listening."

Jack glanced at her. "Do whatever you feel you need to, Doctor."

Vivian disappeared. She left the door part way open.

Ino waited.

The dog took a deep breath, and let out a long, weary sigh. "You're right," he finally said.

Ino blinked at him. "I am?" he asked, softly.

The shepherd stepped closer into the room, approaching the hard plastic chair. "Mind if I sit?"

Ino nodded. He gestured at the chair with his bandaged hand.

Jack stared at it as he slid into the chair. "How many stitches?"

Ino tried to remember. "Seven, I think? Maybe eight."

Jack leaned in and looked at Ino's forehead, where he had a nasty abrasion. His mouth tightened in displeasure.

Ino stared at him, and after a moment he could smell sweat. Jack radiated deodorant and dog musk. He wrinkled his nose. "You kind of stink, Chief Archer."

Jack scrunched up his muzzle, irritated, and then sniffed profoundly. "You, too," he said. "You smell like rotting leaves and wet husky."

Ino narrowed his eyes. "How are things on campus?"

The dog stared at him a moment, and then brightened. "Good! All things considered. Nobody has power, and we have broken windows everywhere — the Union, the library. A tree came down onto Hagerman, a real big one. Some minor flooding, but nothing Maintenance can't handle. Lots of branches down, lots of cars damaged. No serious injuries," he said, nodding.

Ino nodded. "That's good to hear."

Jack cracked a smile. "Yeah. I think we did okay."

There was a pause.

Ino stared at him. "So. You were saying."

Jack let out a long sigh. "You're right. I'm sorry. It's my fault you were in danger. I should have turned the case over a week ago." He leaned back, avoiding eye contact. "I AM turning the case over, as soon as possible. I'm meeting with Santiago city PD tomorrow afternoon and I'm going to give them everything I've got."

Ino stared at him. "Including the video?"

The dog looked up. "Including the video."

There was another pause.

Ino frowned at him. "Well, good. I'm glad all it took was my attempted murder for you to get your shit together."

Jack sighed. "Go ahead. Get it out."

Ino grit his teeth. He sat up. "I'm not kidding, Jack. I could have been *killed* because you were *stalling!*" He put his hands up in exasperation.

Jack winced, frowning. "I... I know." He opened his mouth to say something else, and then closed it. His ears drooped. "I... I can't tell you how sorry I am. This never should have happened."

Ino glared at him. "Damn right. You should have turned the case over as soon as you saw the calendar appointment and the paperweight in Reed's office. Susan and her husband should both be in custody already!"

Jack frowned. "Ino, that's not going to happen. Even if the video is a hell of a motive, it's not *evidence*. It's circumstantial at best." He let out a sigh. "Besides, I was still investigating Travis."

Ino blinked at him, and then lowered his eyes in a glare. "Oh, were you?" he snapped, sarcastically.

Jack narrowed his eyes. "Yes, I was!"

Ino snorted. "*You* were investigating Travis," he said, skeptically.

Jack glared at him. "*Yes*," he said, through his teeth. "You asked when the call came in." The dog patted down his pockets until he found his cellphone. He scrolled through files until he came to one and angrily handed the phone to Ino. "Well, here you go, Dr. Reamer."

The phone was playing a video. It was a dash camera, filming through the windshield of a car. It was night in the video. Ino could see streetlights in the distance. There was a building right next to the vehicle. Classic rock was softly playing on the car's radio.

The video was timestamped. FRI MAY 11 18:02:31. UNIT 47 0 MPH.

"*Do do do DOO DOO*," hummed a voice along with the car radio. Ino recognized it immediately as Travis MacGregor. "*Twenty-first night of Sep-TEM-BER*," he sang, softly. Ino could hear a soft inhalation as Travis took a drag on his joint.

Suddenly there was a terrific crash and the video went red and white, making the phone glow in Ino's hands, a mess of flying particles and bright white dust in front of the camera as the car rocked violently back and forth. The microphone on the camera was overwhelmed, and the phone played only *WHKK-KKH-KKT-KKSH* of electronic distortion. Ino writhed, and through some trick of his brain, he swore he could feel the heat of the fire again.

The screen went back from explosion-white to nighttime-dark but the only thing visible in front of the camera was shattered safety glass and dust. Several car warning chimes were ringing close to the camera, *Ding ding ding ding ding!*

Travis' voice came back over the speakers, and even through the tinny phone speakers Ino could hear the agony in his voice. For a solid ten seconds there was only gasping breathing and pained whimpering. Ino grimaced.

Finally Travis' voice came over the speaker. "*D... Dispatch*," he gasped. "*Dispatch, this is 47!*"

A staticky voice came over the radio in the video, and even through a shitty microphone and the phone's terrible speakers Ino could hear the concern. "*47, go ahead! Are you okay?!*"

Travis grunted, gasping in pain, and relied. "*Dispatch, Baker just exploded! It's gone, it's fucking gone! Lock it down, get everything out here.*" There was a click and then more agonized whimpering. "*Big... big fire. Get 'em down here. Get EVERYONE down here. Oh my God,*" he moaned.

Jack reached over and tapped PAUSE.

Ino grimaced. "God," he said. "He was hurt bad."

Jack nodded. "Yup. And he still crawled out the window of his cruiser and was looking for victims when the rest of us showed up." He tapped the time stamp with one thick claw. "Look, though."

Ino looked at the white text at the bottom of the screen. It took him a moment to read it through all the noise on the screen, but it said 18:03:05.

Jack held up an unfolded piece of paper. It was a computer text print-out of activity. The first line, which was highlighted, read:

```
03/18/18 18:03:15 SANTSC DISPATCH MESSAGE
SEND: ALL USERS. TEXT TEMPLATE01

SANTIAGO  ALERT:  SHELTER  IN  PLACE.  An
unspecified  event  is  threatening  campus.
Please  shelter  in  place  NOW.Lock  Doors.
Turn  Off  Lights.Stay  Quiet.Wait  for  All
Clear. THIS IS NOT A DRILL.
```

18:03:15. The timestamp was circled — ten seconds *after* Travis had called it in. The rest of the page continued with the rest of the alerts.

Ino nodded. "So my watch *was* fast after all. And I guess that clears Travis for calling in the lockdown before the explosion happened." He sighed. "Not that he's a suspect anymore." He narrowed his eyes at Jack. "So did you see that *before* or *after* you sent him alone after me in a thunderstorm?"

Jack's face went from smug to furious. "Jesus Christ, Reamer, he *saved your life.*"

Ino grit his teeth. "I know he did. But he could just as easily have drowned me in that drainage ditch with no witnesses. Did you see the video before or after?!"

Jack scrunched his muzzle angrily. "*Before!*" he snapped.

Ino narrowed his eyes. "I still don't feel like you're taking this seriously. How many days did we lose before you admitted this was even a murder?"

Jack looked like he was going to scream, his eyes wide and his mouth open, but after a moment he calmed down. "Dr. Reamer, I knew this was a murder from day one. This was *always* a murder investigation." He frowned. "I shouldn't even tell you this, but Reed didn't die from the gas. He had a crushed hyoid bone. Most likely he was strangled or choked to death."

Ino felt his jaw drop. "Are... are you kidding me? Then what was all that *Swiss cheese* bullshit?!" he demanded.

Jack narrowed his eyes. "I was trying to keep *you* out of it." He frowned. "Dr. Reamer, you're a college professor. You have no business investigating a murder."

Ino stared at him, and something occurred to him. "Oh my GOD," he said. "That's why you *let it slip* that Reed was already dead when I saw him. You did that on purpose!" He leaned forward, mad now. "You wanted to see what my reaction was so you could tell if I knew he was dead already — to tell you if *I killed him!*"

Jack frowned at him, and Ino knew he was right.

Ino glared.

The shepherd shook his head. "You should have stayed out of it. When civilians try to do police work, people get hurt." He gestured around the hospital room. "Case in point."

Ino leaned forward. "If you knew it was a murder, then why didn't you recuse yourself *from the beginning* if you had a *sexual relationship with the victim and two suspects?!*" he hissed.

Jack stared at him, eyes wide, and then after a moment the dog seemed to deflate. He leaned back in his chair, putting his arms up on the armrests, sighing. He broke eye contact. "That… was the wrong call," he said, softly.

Ino watched him, frowning, and after a moment his fury dissipated, leaving a dull frustration.

Jack looked up at him, sullenly, and then leaned forward. "Look, it was…" He searched for the words. "It was really a blow to lose my station. Back in Ohio. Back home…" He frowned. "You know? Before *this* was home. I was lost for a long time." He looked away. "If Travis hadn't pushed me for almost a year to get out of bed and go back into the world I would never even have applied for this job." He swallowed, looking up at Ino. "And that's all it was to me, at first, a job. But this place… it grew on me. I feel like I found a home here. We were doing good things." He smiled vacantly, thinking about it, and then abruptly looked away, embarrassed. "I'm sorry, that probably sounds stupid."

Ino blinked at him. He frowned.

The shepherd grimaced. "Anyway, that clouded my judgement. I just didn't want it all to come crashing down again so soon." He stared wistfully into space for a moment, his golden eyes losing focus, before blinking and coming back to reality. He glanced guiltily at Ino, his ears folding back against his head. "Sorry. That's not an excuse." He let out a sigh. "Just an explanation."

Ino frowned at him. "What do you mean *all come crashing down?*" he asked.

Jack's eyes cleared, and he looked up, frowning. "What do you *think* I mean? What do you think will happen when that video surfaces?"

Ino leaned forward, baffled. "*Surfaces?* Why would that happen?"

The shepherd leaned forward, incredulous. "Why would that *happen?*" he repeated, astonished. "Are you serious?"

Ino frowned. "Why is that a foregone conclusion? What if it never gets out?"

Jack's jaw dropped and he stared. "Reamer, are you *kidding?* If Susan is the killer, that video will be *featured in court.* It will be Exhibit A. That's *primary motive.* It's not just going to get out, it's going to be front-page news for six months! My life here is over. It's done."

Ino stared at him, and then he realized that Jack was right. He leaned back, shocked. Of *course* he was right.

Frowning, Ino thought about it. Newspapers and TV news couldn't show the footage, but everyone *in court* would see it. There would be court reporters on hand to arduously describe every gory detail. Some censored photos would even get out. *Everyone* would know what had happened. He imagined a newscaster on CNN gleefully describing the University President and Chief of Security's salacious affair with a murder victim, over a barely-blurred photo of Jack in his puppy mask and little shorts.

Oh God.

He looked at the dog. "I… I'm so sorry. I didn't even think of that. I was just thinking about proving a motive. I never thought the video would get out beyond the police. I never thought about fallout for you if you *weren't* the killer."

Jack frowned miserably back at him. He let out a heavy sigh. "I can't say I blame you. We have bigger problems to solve." He leaned back in his chair. "I'm just… collateral damage."

They sat in silence for a moment.

After half a minute passed, Jack looked up. "Anyway. That shouldn't have affected my decision to turn this case over, but it did. I'm sorry." He looked up. "I *never* thought the murderer would strike twice. This had all the hallmarks of an altercation that went too far and a clumsy, panicked cover-up." He frowned. "If I had thought for a moment that anyone else was in danger, I would have recused myself immediately."

Ino stared at the dog for a long time. Jack held his gaze, and after just a couple seconds, Ino decided that he was telling the truth.

The hyena nodded. "It's okay." He thought. "I mean… it's *not* okay, but I understand."

Jack blinked at him, and then smiled humorlessly. "That's about the best I can hope for."

There was another moment of silence.

"So now what?" Ino finally asked.

Jack shrugged. "I have my meeting tomorrow, which gives me a day to get everything together. I'll talk to Susan and see if I can get anything useful out of her before I turn the case over." He frowned. "And then I guess I'll get my affairs in order."

Ino frowned. "Do you really think you'll lose your job over this?"

Jack smiled humorlessly. "At a small religious college? *On camera,* fucking the president and her husband *and their murder victim?* In a puppy mask? Yes, I do." He chuckled. "I don't know. Maybe they'll keep me on and I can do the landscaping."

Ino winced. "I'm sorry, Jack."

The dog shrugged. "Don't worry about me, Dr. Reamer. At least I won't take anyone down with me this time."

Ino stared at him. "*This* time? What do you mean? Didn't you get closed for budget cuts last time?"

Jack blinked at him, and then another humorless smile spread across his face. "I mean, on paper. What *actually* happened is I had two officers who I thought were being too violent. Neither of them would change and I was finally bringing them up on charges. One of them was the brother-in-law of the State Comptroller. Suddenly there's no more room in the budget for Jack Archer's outpost. Twelve people lost their jobs because I wouldn't play by the code of silence."

Ino grimaced.

Jack chuckled. "Yeah. You know the worst part? They're both still cops, and I'm a glorified security guard." He raised an eyebrow, smiling. "And soon I won't even be that."

Ino let out a sigh.

Jack shrugged. "Still, thank you for pushing it. The most important thing here is prosecuting whoever is responsible here." He stared. "And keeping *you* safe in the meantime." He frowned. "Speaking of which. Now it's time for you to listen to me, Dr. Reamer."

Ino stared at him, his eyes widening. The change in Jack's demeanor was palpable. He was all business again.

Jack frowned at him. "I'm sure the city police put you under surveillance, but that's not enough. Based on that stunt at the train crossing this killer is reckless and impulsive, and that makes them incredibly dangerous." He frowned. "You need to get out of town for a while," the dog said. "Do you know anybody? Close but not too close?"

Ino thought for a moment. "I have a brother in Chicago."

Jack nodded. "Good. That's *perfect*. Call him and tell him you're coming to visit. Leave tomorrow."

Ino grimaced. "Do you really think that's necessary? The summer semester starts in a week."

The dog nodded. "I do. Do you need a car?"

Ino shook his head. "No, I'll get a rental." He let out a sigh. "I'll go."

Jack nodded. "Good. Thank you, Dr. Reamer."

Ino pondered. "One more thing. Do you know if Susan was on campus during the storm?"

Jack nodded grimly. "I do. I went to see her. She was at her office. She was there, but her big SUV was mysteriously missing."

Ino's eyes widened.

The dog nodded. "Right." He nodded. "Don't worry, Dr. Reamer. I'll take care of it."

The hyena let out a shaky breath.

Jack cocked his head. "Can I give you a ride home?"

Ino thought about it, and then frowned. "That's... probably not a great idea." He looked up. "You know, just for optics? They're going to be looking pretty closely at you. And someone did just try to kill me. I don't know if we should be seen alone together."

Jack stared at him, his expression betraying absolutely nothing. It was Cop Face again. Finally, he nodded. "Of course." He rose to his feet. "Good night then, Dr. Reamer." When he was at the door he turned and looked back at the hyena. "Be safe," he said, and turned to leave.

Ino stared at him. He watched the dog slip through the door, and just before the dog disappeared, he leaned forward. "Jack," he called out.

Stopping, surprised, the dog turned to look at him.

Ino watched him for a moment. "Are you, uhhh…" He didn't quite know how to phrase it. "Are you gonna be okay?"

The shepherd stared at him for a moment, and then smiled a sad, quiet smile. "I'll be fine, Dr. Reamer." He paused a moment. "Always am," he said. He smiled his little melancholy smile at Ino another moment, and then turned and slipped out the doorway without a sound.

And then he was gone.

CHAPTER 11: MISSING

TUESDAY, MAY 22, 2018

Ino was up early the next day, and out of bed by 7:00 am. He jerked awake as soon as sunlight started creeping around the edges of his bedroom curtains. His injured hand was throbbing, and he started thinking and couldn't stop, so half an hour later he finally just got out of bed. As he opened the curtains, he saw a Santiago PD squad car cruising slowly past his house. The sight did not make him feel better.

The hyena's whole body ached. He staggered down the stairs to make some coffee.

The doorbell rang at 8:30 am.

Surprised, Ino tied his plaid bathrobe around his boxer shorts. He peered through the side window and saw Vivian's gray CR-V in the driveway.

He threw the door open. "Vivian! What are you *doing* here? Isn't your flight in a few hours?"

She nodded. "It sure is!" The pine marten was dressed smartly, in a black pencil skirt and a silver camisole. She was wearing black heels, which Ino thought was insane for a 4-hour flight plus hiking through two airports, but Vivian was never one to appear a slouch. It made Ino feel even more like he was in his pajamas than he felt for literally being in his pajamas.

He raised his eyebrows, holding the door open for her. "Well, you didn't have to come over. You could have just texted!" he said. "I got a new phone last night."

She slipped past him into the foyer. "I know. But I have to ask you something and I need to *see* your reaction."

He stared. "Uhhhhh," he said.

She turned. "Do you want me to cancel my trip?"

The hyena stared, and then furrowed his brow. "No!" he snapped.

Vivian smiled. "Great. Now do you actually want to think about it?" She wandered into the kitchen. "Is there coffee?" she called, her dark tail disappearing around the corner.

Sighing, Ino padded after her. "There's cold brew in the fridge. I can make you a pour-over if you want it hot. And no, you're not skipping an entire conference because I had a car accident." He followed her into the kitchen.

Pulling a big pitcher out of the fridge, Vivian took a glass from an upper cabinet. "Oh yes, a car accident. That's exactly what *that* was." She filled her glass and took a pink sweetener out of a drawer.

"Wait," he said. "I made vanilla syrup." He opened the fridge again and pulled out a little squeeze bottle.

"Of course you did!" Vivian said. She held her glass out.

Ino took her glass and squirted a teaspoon of syrup into it, then stuck it under the ice dispenser. He swirled it around and handed it back to her.

Vivian took a long, savory sip. "Jesus, that's good," she said.

Ino beamed proudly.

She looked at him. "Shall I ask again?"

He sighed, and then really considered it.

After a moment, he frowned again. "N... no, it doesn't make sense. I'm leaving town anyway."

She raised an eyebrow. "Are you?"

He nodded. "Yes I am. I *really* am. Rufus is going to put me up on his couch. It'll be weird to stay in Boystown with all the Party Gays, and his couch sucks, but like..." he shrugged. "I can't think of anywhere else to go." He frowned. "And Jack's right, this person tried to kill me with a freight train in broad daylight. I'm not safe here."

They stared at each other. Vivian watched him.

He sighed. "This is weird. I don't like it."

She nodded. "I can imagine." She leaned against the counter.

Ino let out a long sigh. He picked his mug off the island and poured himself another cup of coffee. He frowned. "I just feel like..." He thought about it. "I just feel *bad*. Reed was a creepy psychopath, Susan's a murderer. Jack's life is over. Travis is traumatized." He shrugged. "Sean is traumatized. *I'm* traumatized." He stared off into space. "Like, I've seen all these thriller novels where the hero is driven and dynamic, and it ends in a sexy car chase, but like…" He let out a long sigh. "I just want *out*. This sucks, you know?"

Vivian smiled sadly back at him. She shrugged. "I get it. It's not fun when it's real life. Are you okay for your classes if you have to stay away for a while?"

He nodded. "Yeah. Two of my classes are online and I have a TA who can run the show in-person for the third one, at least for a week or two. Not my preference, but like…"

Vivian smiled. "Better than being murdered."

He cracked a humorless smile. "Yeah. Better than being murdered."

They were silent for a moment.

Vivian nodded. "Okay. I actually believe you're going out of town, and I think you're going to be okay. Just leave *today*. Like in the next couple hours."

He nodded. "Don't worry. I won't stay a minute longer than I need to."

She nodded. "My train leaves in an hour, and then it's two hours to O'Hare, and then security for God only knows how long after that. If you change your mind and want me to stay, *call me*."

He grinned. "I will. Truly. Thank you."

She nodded, and set her cup down. "I bought trip insurance, so I can reschedule until the moment the plane takes off. And don't be afraid to — " She suddenly stopped talking, staring at something on the kitchen island.

Ino stared, and then followed her eyes.

It was a copy of the journal entry from Reed's office. He'd left it on the kitchen island along with all of his mail and his car keys.

Ino frowned. "Ignore that. I made a copy before I went to see Clara. Jack took the original."

She nodded. "I figured." She picked it up and adjusted her glasses.

There were a couple moments of silence.

Ino frowned. "What are you doing?" he asked, low and accusatory.

Vivian glanced casually at him over the top of the journal entry. "Nothing. We determined the only clue in this was the phone number… right?"

He stared at her.

She looked innocently back at him.

He rolled his eyes. "Oh God. I know that look. Here we go." He frowned. "Yes, the only thing that stands out is the secret phone number. *My* phone number."

Vivian nodded. "Interesting. Very interesting."

Silence.

Ino shook his head. "*What is it, woman?*"

Vivian set the document down. "It's just…" She pondered, choosing her words. "There's a lot… going on here. You know? Lots of opportunities to convey a lot of information."

The hyena blinked at her. Dumbly, he shook his head. "I don't get it."

Vivian thought for a moment. "Okay, so think about it. If his *entire intention* was to point to you in case something happened to him, because you knew about his little games, there are a lot more *direct* ways to do that, right?"

Ino frowned. "I still don't get it."

Vivian nodded. "Think of it this way — if *you* had to steer investigators to *me*, think of all the ways you could do that. How would you do it? Give me a method."

Ino blinked at her, and then thought about it. "Uh. A photograph. With the two of us circled. Maybe… a note — *if I am indisposed, speak to Vivian Chen.* An email out of office. My voicemail greeting."

She nodded, smiling. "Right. So how far down the list would you have to go before you got to encoding my phone number in a fake accounting document?"

He thought about it. "I see," he said, finally.

Vivian nodded. "Like that's kind of weird, right? And very *specific*."

Ino stared at her. He didn't like the way this was going.

"So, my question is, *why? Why this?* What was his motive for choosing *this* method?" The pine marten leaned forward. "I'm trying to get into his head for how he settled on this, and I can't."

Ino processed that for a moment.

"*Shit,*" he groaned. "I think you're on to something here." He stepped up to the island and stared down at the document.

JOURNAL ENTRY		1/8/18
ACCOUNT	**DEBIT**	**CREDIT**
Investment dividends 4042300	$2,565,400.70	
Vacation accrual 303030	$27,750.08	
Raw materials purchased 206000	$6,560.10	
Interest Payable 3710000	$21,320.02	
Cash JP Morgan ***51015 3010101		$24,576,577.30
TOTAL	$2,621,030.90	$24,576,577.30
Variance check		$0.00

They studied it.

Vivian stared at it. "The date? Any significance there?"

He considered. "Well… I saw an accounting textbook and all the examples were random generic dates like that. So I doubt it." He pointed. "Look, it just says "One Eight One Eight.""

They both pored over it.

"Okay, I see something," Vivian said.

Ino frowned. "I'm scared to ask," he said.

She pointed to the last line. CASH, it said. JPMORGAN 51015. "This is a bank account, right? That's cash money coming out of the University bank account. So all this other stuff on here, *this* should be the stuff you bought with the money, right?" She pointed at all the other lines.

"Yesss," Ino said, cautiously.

"Well, I don't think these other accounts are real. I'm not an accountant, but I know we don't pay dividends. We certainly don't buy raw materials or have a factory, and I'm pretty sure we don't have any huge loans out that we would be paying interest on. So that's all junk and anyone who works at a school would know that immediately. But *this*" — she pointed to the bank account — "is real. I think that's Santiago's *actual* bank account, Ino. I got a direct expense repayment once and the information on the check sure looked like this."

He stared at it. She was right. The number looked familiar.

She tapped it with one claw. "Okay. So what is the *point?*"

He frowned. "So… following the logic, part of this transaction is real. That's actual money, leaving our actual bank account."

She nodded. "Stands to reason. But it's not *going* toward any real purchases."

Both their eyes widened.

Ino swallowed. "Wow, that sounds a lot like embezzlement, doesn't it?" He felt excited. And lightheaded. He swallowed, hard.

Vivian looked down at it. "Hm. Real money out. Fake purchases to account for it." She looked up. "Yep. That's fraud, all right."

He nodded. "Shit. Yes. Jesus. I never even thought about that. It's fraud. It's accounting fraud. That's why he used this document." He swallowed. "But who does that *point* to? The angry badger? He's doing something and Reed found out?"

Vivian pondered. "Mm. The prime suspect. Didn't he basically point to himself? Saying he wished he'd been the one to kill Reed over making somebody quit?" She narrowed her eyes, deep in thought.

Ino nodded. He frowned. "You're getting an idea. I can tell by your face."

She thought for another moment and then nodded slowly. "Well — I was just thinking, if you killed someone, that would be a great way to obfuscate your motive."

He furrowed his brow. "What? How?"

"Go out of your way to point to yourself. But for the *wrong reason*."

Ino thought about it. "Oh my God. So you get them all over you for something obvious, but then you get cleared."

She nodded. "And draw attention away from your *real* motive — the fraud."

Ino grit his teeth. "And the cops move right on to the next person."

They stared at each other.

Vivian suddenly shook her head. "Wait, no. It only works if you have an airtight alibi. Otherwise regardless of motive, the police would investigate you for the crime and still figure out you did it. The badger had an alibi. Right?"

Ino thought. His heart was starting to pound. "Security got alibis for the wrong times."

Vivian leaned forward. "*Pardon?*" she asked, her eyebrows threatening to leap off her face.

He looked up. "My smartest student ran the numbers for how long it would take a room that size to fill up with enough gas to explode. Even if you opened all of the gas jets it would take two to four hours, *at least*, to reach combustion density. Reed was lying in that lab for a lot longer than they think."

Vivian leaned forward. "Are you serious?!" she demanded. "Did you tell Security?"

He shook his head. "No, we only figured it out right before you and I found that video. And then we thought it was Jack or maybe Travis and after the train thing I completely forgot about it."

Vivian frowned. "So it could be the badger."

Ino nodded. "Right, they probably only have his alibi for the hour or so before the explosion." He frowned. "During which he was inexplicably smoking *in front of* the admin building, where everyone would see him. *Instead of* where I saw him smoking the other day — in back of the building. Where the ashtrays are," he added, slowly.

Vivian grimaced. "Yikes! That's exactly what you would want to do if you were establishing an alibi for yourself. Be out front and center."

He nodded. "Yeah. Jesus."

Vivian leaned forward. "I think it's time to let someone know."

Ino nodded. "I'll make the call," he said, picking his new cellphone up off the counter, padding up the stairs to put on some clothes.

Jack was there in ten minutes.

It was just before 9 am, and the dog was impeccably dressed in dark-brown slacks and a crisp beige shirt. He smelled good, and he had a navy-blue tie and even his crew cut looked freshly touched-up. Ino wondered if he was putting in the extra effort because his days at the University were numbered, but of course he didn't ask.

"Dr. Reamer," the dog said, stepping into the front room. He followed him into the kitchen and nodded at Vivian too. "Dr. Chen." He turned back to face Ino. "I thought you were leaving for Chicago," he said curtly.

Ino stared at him. This was clearly All Business Jack. He gave no hint that the previous evening's conversation had ever happened.

Ino let out a long sigh. "In a few hours. I couldn't get a rental car before 11."

The shepherd nodded. "I understand there was something you wanted to show me?"

Ino and Vivian filled him in. Jack was interested but not surprised as they told him about the various accounts on the documents, but his eyes widened when Ino showed him the math for the gas level flow rates.

Jack frowned at the evidence, his brow furrowed, and then finally looked up. "I think… you may be on to something here."

They looked at each other.

Jack grimaced, and then let out a long sigh. "Well… I guess this changes my day." He frowned. 'I believe I'll go pay our accounting friend a visit. With any luck I can get something useful before I turn this all over." He pointed at Ino. "And *you* had better be on the highway as soon as you get that car."

Ino frowned. "I will. You're not going alone, are you?" He swallowed.

Jack gave him a tight-lipped frown. "I haven't decided. Probably not. I know what I'm doing, Dr. Reamer," he said.

Ino sighed. "Of course." He thought. "Would you mind, uh, giving me a call this afternoon anyway? I'm… worried."

Vivian was watching him very closely. Ino felt himself start to blush.

Jack stared at him, and then slowly nodded. "I can do that."

Ino let out a relieved sigh. "Thank you."

Jack raised an eyebrow. "I'm still going to talk to Susan." He narrowed his eyes. "And I'm still going to turn the case over." He frowned. "I did have an undisclosed personal relationship with the victim. I shouldn't be the one issuing charges for his murder."

They both nodded.

"Are you looking forward to being off the case?" Vivian asked, quietly.

Ino felt his eyes widen. What kind of question was that?!

Jack thought for a moment, his eyes narrowing suspiciously, and then he softened. "If I'm honest, yeah. I thought this was a test, this conversation just now." He shook his head, letting out a sigh. "I'm not looking forward to the fallout, but this case has been a nightmare. It's messing with my head."

Ino almost let his jaw drop. Vivian had gotten a shockingly straight answer out of the shepherd.

She nodded. "Good luck, Chief."

Jack smiled weakly. "Thank you," he said, softly. The dog turned to Ino. "All right, Dr. Reamer. I'll let you be on your way. Please give me a call when you get to Chicago. Hopefully you won't have to be there long."

Ino nodded. "That's really the least of my concerns at this point. But thank you."

Jack cracked a smile. He nodded at both of them. "Thank you, both of you. Take care now." He turned, and slipped silently out the door.

Ino watched him lope to his cruiser through the front picture window.

When he turned, Vivian was staring at him.

He blinked at her. "What?"

She raised an eyebrow. "Do you have a thing for him?"

Ino blinked, and then frowned. "No!" he snapped.

The pine marten stared. "Mmmm-hmm," she said.

Ino let out a long sigh. "We didn't exactly get off on the right foot." He wrinkled his nose. "Or any of the right subsequent feet." He shrugged. "Why do you ask?"

She shrugged. "I don't know. Giving up the case really struck me. He's terrified of the consequences, but he knows he can't solve this. He's turning it over, because it's the right thing to do." She shrugged. "I think it's admirable."

He nodded, and thought about it. "Me too, I guess. I just wish the consequences weren't so... extreme."

She nodded. "Yeah."

They both looked up at the clock.

Vivian sighed. "I guess it's that time."

Ino put his arms out. They slid into a tight hug.

"I'll miss youuuuuuu!" Ino squealed into her ear.

Vivian laughed. "I'll be back before you know it. It's just a couple days. If there was hotel space, I would just take you with me. But I'm already rooming with someone else."

Ino chuckled. "Wow, a Psych conference! I should be so lucky." He squeezed her. "Have a safe flight."

She nodded. "I will. Send me a text when you get to Chicago." She grinned. "Say hi to Rufus for me."

"I will!"

She smiled devilishly. "I want to hear all about the new guy he's dating."

"Ah yes, the mystery man." He chuckled. "Me, too. I'll see if I can get some pics."

She nodded. "Perfect!" She stared at him a moment longer. "I'm so sorry to leave without this all resolved. I'm sure they'll solve the case in no time." She nodded.

Ino cracked a humorless smile. "I sure hope so."

She nodded, and they hugged again. He walked her to her car, they hugged one last time, and then she pulled out of the driveway and Ino was left standing on the sidewalk, waving, alone.

After Jack and Vivian left, Ino got into the shower. He spent a long time in there. His entire body still hurt and the hot water felt good on him, even with a plastic grocery bag wrapped around the stitches on his hand. He had showered the previous night, but that had just been to get the smell of drainage ditch out of his fur. Today he enjoyed the slow, relaxed pace and the smell of flowery soap in his fur.

Since he was headed to Boystown, he decided to dress a little more fashionably. He put on just-tight-enough navy-blue shorts that hit him just above the knee, and a bright-blue tank top with an abstract wave pattern on it. It was tight enough to hold onto his chest and his arms looked great in it. He checked his reflection. He looked like a respectably hot 35-year-old, and *not* like he was trying to pass for 22. Perfect.

The storms yesterday had ushered in a mass of cold, dry air, and it was only 72 degrees today. It was sunny, dry, and beautiful. There was still evidence of yesterday's storms everywhere, mostly shredded leaves and branches scattered every few feet, but the weather itself was shockingly beautiful.

The rental car place was only a half mile away. Ino's fur was still a little damp but he would air-dry in the sun on the way. He slipped on a pair of gray sneakers, locked his front door, and set off.

Half an hour later, he was back at his apartment with a brand-new white Chevrolet Sonic with only 12,000 miles on it. It was a tiny, awkward little car, but it would get him to Chicago.

It was 11:45. Still no call from Jack.

He frowned at his new cellphone. He had only added a handful of phone numbers to it — Vivian, Rufus, his mom, and Jack.

He called Jack Archer's phone.

No answer. It rang 4 or 5 times, and then went to voicemail.

Hm.

By 1:30 pm, Ino was starting to get worried.

He called Jack again. Again, after 5 rings, it went to voicemail.

He checked his watch.

He called the campus security office.

"Santiago Security, this is Officer Reese, how may I help you?"

Ino brightened. That was the helpful ferret he had met a couple times. "Hi, Officer Reese. This is Ino Reamer. Do you know if Jack Archer is in the office right now?"

"Hi again, Dr. Reamer! Hold on." There was a pause. Ino heard movement on the other line. "Hmm. Looks like his door is closed. He was around earlier but I think he's busy now. Want me to have him call you when he's available?"

Ino nodded. "Yes, please. That would be very helpful. Thank you very much."

"Will do, Dr. Reamer! Have a good afternoon."

"Thanks, Officer Reese. You too."

Only slightly satisfied, Ino hung up.

By 3:15 pm, Ino eyed his rental car in the driveway. He kept walking past the front window and seeing it where his familiar yellow Jeep should be. But it was just the white Sonic, staring dopily back at him with its stupid bubble headlights, like vacant, wide eyes. *Are we going?* it seemed to say.

Ino eyed his suitcase, sitting packed on his coffee table. It was everything he would need for a few days at Rufus'.

He should probably leave now, if he wanted to get to Chicago before rush hour. In fact, he probably should have left a few hours ago. Now was really his last chance.

He looked from the suitcase to the car.

The hyena slipped his phone out again.

No new messages.

Frowning, he sat back down on the couch.

At a quarter to 5, Ino called the campus Security non-emergency number again.

"Santiago Security, this is Officer Hahn, can I help you?"

Ino thought feverishly. Hahn? Which one was Hahn? He blinked. "Officer Hahn? I thought Reese was on the phones today." Had his message been misplaced? He hoped that was the answer.

There was a grunt. "She's on patrol. We rotate, so you get me now. Can I help you with something?"

Ino cleared his throat. "Is Jack Archer in? I've been trying to get in touch with him all day."

Hahn grunted. "So I've heard. No, he's not in yet. Generally, the Chief doesn't tell us what he's doing with his day."

Ino paused, and then frowned. "Can you have him call me please?

"You bet, Dr. Reamer," the officer said, way too fake-cheerful. "Anything else?"

Ino rolled his eyes. "No, thanks. Just that."

"Thanks for calling Santiago Security!" the officer said.

Annoyed, Ino hung up.

At 6:31 pm, Ino's phone rang. It was a number he didn't recognize, but it looked like a campus number.

"Hello?" he answered, tentatively.

"*Reamer!*" snapped Travis MacGregor. "What the hell is going on?"

"Wh-what?" Ino stammered.

"I just heard that you've been trying to find Jack Archer all day. Nobody has seen him since this morning, and now *I* can't find him. He's not answering his phone and it's been hours. So what's going on?"

The hyena gasped. "This morning? You saw him?"

Travis grunted. "*Yes*, he wanted me to go with him to see a suspect. A guy in the admin building. We went to see him together. Total dead-end. We just got yelled at. What's going on?"

Ino blinked. "The badger, right? He, uh, he's not in custody?"

There was a long pause. "*Custody?* Why would he be?" Travis asked slowly. He sounded suspicious.

Ino frowned. "We found some more clues this morning. The badger seemed to be a more likely suspect."

Travis groaned. "Is that why Jack was asking about the guy's alibi?" He swore. "I wondered about that. No, the badger was in the office for twelve hours the day of the explosion. The guy has a conference call about once every twenty minutes. He's cleared for the entire week."

Cleared for the entire week?? Ino thought. Had they been wrong about the accounting fraud? *That makes Susan the most likely suspect again.* Maybe the accounting document was meant to suggest her skimming off the top of the massive donation? *Uh-oh.*

"Shit," Ino said. "Where did Jack go after that?"

Another pause. "He didn't say. He said he had one more thing to check."

Ino felt his blood run cold. "Did he say *where?* Or with *whom?*"

"No!" Travis snapped. "And I didn't ask. Reamer, what is this about? You better spill, or when I find Jack, I'll —"

"I think Jack is in trouble."

There was a long pause.

"Go on," Travis said, deadly serious.

Ino took a deep breath. "Listen, Jack is turning the case over to the city PD."

"He's *what?!*"

"*Listen to me!*" Ino snapped. "He's turning the case over. He has a connection to the victim. That's all I can say. He has a connection to Reed and it implicates him. It's bad."

"Jesus Christ," Travis groaned.

"He's turning over the case *tonight* and when he does the fallout is going to be awful. So I don't know what other leads he's working, but I think he might be in trouble."

"Ughh, Reamer, you son of a bitch," Travis growled. "Okay. I'm gonna go look for him myself."

"Okay, there's something else you need to know," Ino said. "Don't tell anybody, okay? But before the badger, President Greeley was our prime suspect."

"*What?!*" Travis demanded. "Are you serious, Reamer?"

Ino swallowed. "And her husband. Check them out first, okay? And *be careful.*"

There was an annoyed husky growl on the other end of the line. "You cannot be serious with this shit." Travis came back on the line. "Okay, I'm going to go find Jack. Keep your ringer on, okay?"

Ino nodded. "Yes. Absolutely. Thank you."

"And listen to me, Reamer," Travis growled. "Under *no circumstances whatsoever* are you to set foot on this campus. Do you understand me? Stay away. In fact, get in your car and get on the road right now. Go to Chicago. Go *anywhere*. It's not safe for you here."

Ino let out a sigh. "Fine," he mumbled. "Just… find Jack, okay?"

There was a grunt. "Try and stop me," he rumbled.

The line went dead.

At 7:15 pm Ino texted the number Travis had called from.

```
7:16:01          Any luck?
```

The response came in a few moments.

```
7:16:25          No. r u in Chicago?
```

Ino rolled his eyes and sighed.

At 7:45 pm Ino called the station again. He felt silly harassing them, but he also had a well-formed ball of dread in the pit of his stomach. It was almost

8:00 pm, and the sun was starting to descend over the horizon. It was getting dark out. He frowned.

Someone picked up immediately. "Santiago Security, Hahn speaking," someone said, immediately.

Ino swallowed. His mouth felt dry. "Hi, Officer Hahn. It's Ino Reamer. Sorry, to bother you, but I'm —"

"Dr. Reamer!" the cop said. "Are you calling about Chief Archer?"

Ino felt his heart pound.

"Do you know where he is?" Hahn demanded.

Ino was silent for a moment. "Uhh, no. That's why I'm calling."

"Damn," Hahn said. "Tell me everything you know about where he was going."

Ino frowned. "You still haven't found him yet?" He swallowed. *Shit.* "I, uh, I told Travis MacGregor everything I know a couple hours ago."

"Okay, good, he's the one leading the search."

"The *search?!*" Ino gasped. "Do you need help?"

"*No!*" the officer snapped. "We'll find him, Dr. Reamer." There was a pause. "That's the other line. I have to go. Please call us back immediately if you hear *anything*, okay?"

Ino swallowed. "Yeah. I will," he said.

The line went dead.

At 8:00 pm, Ino had had enough. The sun was almost all the way down and it was nearly fully dark. It would be a lot harder to spot clues, cars, and a German shepherd.

What had happened to Jack? Obviously foul play was most likely. He'd clearly talked to the wrong person after he'd left Travis. If the mystery killer had tried to add Ino to the list of victims, they probably would have no qualms about murdering Jack, too, especially if the chief came alone and was asking too many questions. But who had he talked to?

Susan was the obvious choice. But Ino had sent Travis right to her, so if she had Jack tied up in the closet or a new blood stain on her office floor, he likely would have seen it. But Jack was still missing.

Ino took one last look at his suitcase. Everyone had told him to stay away — Jack, Travis, even Vivian. But Jack was obviously in danger. If he wasn't dead already, minutes could make the difference.

Sighing, Ino scooped the keys to his rental off the counter and strode quickly out to the parking lot.

He left the suitcase on the coffee table behind him.

Santiago University was only a few minutes away. Ino was surprised to see how badly-damaged the campus was. There were branches and even trees down everywhere, some of them cordoned off with yellow caution tape. Some of the buildings on Old Campus had big pieces of plywood in place of smashed-out windows, and there were tiles missing off of the roofs of the smaller buildings close to campus. One of the freshman dorms had a 30' maple tree down in the lawn and a University landscaping truck parked out front.

Ino shook his head. It had been a hell of a storm.

He passed the site where Baker Brown Science Center had stood. The big white tent that had been over the wreckage of Baker had been flattened — which was not a surprise given that it was a banquet tent. It had been crushed into a huge, crumpled, messy heap of white canvas, thirty feet tall, shoved up against the fence of the athletic center. The Baker wreckage was mostly cleared, leaving a footprint that ranged from flat concrete to a deep hole. There was orange construction fencing in place around it, but it was only a couple feet tall.

Ino came to a slow stop on the side of the road, and could see the entire expanse of campus. For the first time in fifty years there was an uninter-rupted view from the athletic field all the way to the Chapel. Ino stopped and let his jaw hang open. It just looked *wrong*. He stared.

He drove five more minutes to his office and parked next to the build-ing. He killed the engine, looking in the direction of the administration building with Susan's office in it.

Suddenly, a Santiago Security cruiser sailed into view, a big Ford Crown Victoria, roaring fast down Church Street. Travis was driving and it looked like Reese in the passenger seat. The searchlight was on.

Ino yelped and sank down into his front seat. He slid down and hid himself from view. If Travis saw him, that would be the end of his search.

The light swept the area around him, and for a brief moment, settled on Ino's rental car. Ino's heart started pounding, but the light only lingered for a moment, and then swept away.

After a few seconds, Ino risked a peek up over the windowsill.

Travis and Reese's cruiser flew into the Admin building parking lot, the tires emitting sharp little squeaks, and came to a hard stop in the turn-around. The husky and the ferret burst out of the car, striding with purpose toward the front doors.

Ino stared. Hmmm. On the one hand, Travis and the other officers were clearly covering a lot of ground and they most likely had Susan under control. But on the other hand, if they were going back to old leads, that meant they had nothing. He frowned.

Maybe he should go with, and mention the video. That would certainly get a reaction out of the President. But Travis would never hear him out before he threw him off campus. And he might not even believe the story about the video — it was certainly a lot to take in. And Ino wasn't even really sure it was Susan, instead of the badger accountant.

But what if he could *prove* which of them it was?

That gave him an idea. He glanced at Rose Hall, the nearest building to his office in Malerich. Rose was mainly devoted to Meteorology and Communications, but also housed a couple of smaller offices, including Accounting. If Ino could get definitive proof of who was committing fraud, he could tell Travis, and the entire Security Department could go in with guns blazing. If not, he would wait until the officers had left Susan's office, and go in and blackmail her with the video until she either gave up Jack or… something.

He frowned. It was a plan. It wasn't a great one, but it could work.

He looked at the car dash clock. 8:17 pm. Almost twelve hours since he had last seen Jack Archer.

Sighing, Ino slipped out of the car and walked quickly toward Rose Hall.

Dr. Calder was just locking up her office on the second floor.

Ino stepped up behind her. "Hi, Clara, so sorry to bother you."

The calico turned and stared at him. "Dr. Reamer!" she said. She frowned. "Are you quite all right? You look upset."

He shook his head. "Not exactly. Could you take a look at something for me?" He swallowed. "It's… important."

She blinked at him, considered for a moment, and then nodded. She twisted her key and the door lock snapped back open. "Of course, Dr. Reamer. Come right in."

Ino pulled his bag off his shoulder before he was two steps into the office. "I need you to help me with something," he said. "There's…" He frowned, debating what to say. "There's a problem." He slipped out the journal entry in the plastic bag.

Clara frowned at it, with that mixture of suspicion and annoyance that only cats could truly muster. "Now I'm *quite* sure you were lying when you said that isn't evidence, Dr. Reamer," she said.

He frowned, nodding. "I'm sorry. I wasn't sure. We figured out something about this document. I can identify the cash account. I need your help with the other ones." He set the document on the desk.

She blinked at him. "What do you mean, *the cash account?*"

Ino pointed at it. "That's our real bank account. For the University. We missed the big tell on this — this document is a clue about accounting fraud."

The cat stared at him. "WHAT?" she asked.

Ino shook his head. "I know. It's hard to believe. But that's our real cash account, and it shows money going out but not coming in. I need you to look at the other accounts and tell me if there are any more clues for what *kind* of accounting fraud." He frowned. "Like if there's names on them. Or certain departments. Jack talked to someone this morning, and I need a clue for who it was."

She blinked and stared at them. "That's quite a tall order, Ino. Accounting strings vary by company or entity. There's no guarantee these are real."

He clenched his teeth. "Please? Can you take a look?"

Clara nodded. "Of course." She thought for a moment, and then turned. "I have a list of the real University strings around here somewhere. Everything is electronic now, but they let me keep the paper copy as a visual aid." She turned to her bookshelves. "I can't imagine they've changed the account numbers. Give me a moment, won't you?"

He nodded. "Of course." He slid into one of the guest chairs facing Clara's desk. "Here, I'll write them down for you."

"Mmm, yes," Clara muttered behind him, digging through the book shelf.

Ino reached for a Post-It and a pen. There was one of the huge glass 100th Anniversary paperweights on Clara's desk. Ino saw it, thought of Susan, and frowned.

Ino grabbed the journal entry and started writing down accounts. He wrote the amounts down too, just in case.

4042300	$2,565,400.70
3030300	$27,750.08
2060000	$6560.10
3710000	$21,320.02
3010101	$24,576,577.30

And then under that, he wrote down his phone number, for reference.

219-555-4637

As soon as he wrote the last number, it felt wrong.

He frowned.

4-6-3-7 was his extension. It ended in a 7.

And yet, in the cents column, was a little parade of round numbers. 0. 0. 0. 8, add that to the 2, you got 10. 0 in the cents column again. Not even any odd numbers.

So where the hell did the 7 come from?

Frowning, Ino glanced behind him, to where the older cat was still picking through the books on her shelves. Had Clara calculated the clue *incorrectly*? Were they missing another vital piece of information?

Reaching for the big calculator on her desk, he tapped the numbers back out.

2,565,400.70 + 27,750.08 + 6560.10 + 21,320.02 - 24,576,577.30 =

The number popped up before him — 219-555-4640. Ino didn't know many campus phone numbers, but he knew this one — he'd dialed it a few days ago, to announce he was coming. The first time he had come to visit Clara Calder.

It was *her* number.

Whoops, he thought, his blood turning to ice.

"Actually, I just thought of something!" he announced, rising to his feet and turning quickly around. "Got to go, thank you for your —"

He froze. The calico was standing behind him, holding a little black-covered reference book in one hand, and a large black pistol in the other. It was a semiautomatic and it looked too big for her hands, which meant it was at least a .45 caliber and maybe something bigger. Ino didn't know enough about guns to be sure on sight alone, but he knew that it was enough to put an end to his sleuthing. For good.

He swallowed.

"Don't you want to see the account strings, Dr. Reamer?" Clara purred, pushing the door closed behind her.

It took Ino a few moments to catch his breath, and then he slid back down into the chair.

Clara slipped back around her desk, keeping the gun trained on him. She wasn't between him and the door anymore, but she was still pointing the gun at him.

"*YOU???*" was all he could think to say.

She laughed. "Is that so shocking, Dr. Reamer?"

He stammered for a moment. "But you seem so... so *nice!*"

She shrugged. "I am nice. For instance, I haven't shot you yet."

Ino swallowed. He had to stall while he thought of a plan. "But *why?* Dr. Reed?! You didn't even work in the same department!"

"Do you know what the beauty is in accounting, Dr. Reamer?"

He stared. *Maybe I don't need to stall — this sounds like it could go on for a while.*

"The *beauty* of accounting, Dr. Reamer, is that you can't hide *anything*. There are two sides to every transaction, each one adjudicated by a different person. You can't steal from *your* account because I'll see it in *mine*. Everything has to be offset — every dollar. Every *cent*. It's all out in the open. Nowhere to hide. No sin goes unseen."

Ino swallowed. He was pretty sure that wasn't how accounting worked, but he wasn't about to tell Clara so.

"But that beauty is also accounting's greatest weakness," she said. She leaned forward. "Because if you can find *someone else* to handle the *other side* of that fraudulent transaction..." She leaned back. "You can do anything you want."

I Ie stared at her. "You mean..."

She nodded. "I do. *Collusion*. The act of two people working together, nefariously, to circumvent revenue controls. Two people doing a crime together. They each bury the other's fraud. And nobody ever finds them." She leaned forward, grinning evilly. "It's poetic. Romantic, even."

Ino swallowed. He felt his blood run cold.

"Would you like to meet my collusion partner, Dr. Reamer?" Clara purred.

Behind him, the doorknob clacked loudly. The door creaked open with a long, piercing squeal. Slowly, Ino turned.

In the doorway stood Chief Jack Archer.

The German shepherd stared at Ino.

Ino felt his stomach drop.

For a moment, he just couldn't breathe, and then that moment went on and on and on, and then he felt like he was going to pass out.

Jack opened his mouth. "Ino — " the dog started to say, and then he *launched* into the room, shoved from behind, and crashed into a heap on the floor. The dog landed hard on his chest with a pained grunt, and as he flattened out Ino saw he was covered in blood, *a lot* of blood, all over the back of the dog's head and back. It was soaked into his neck fur, matting it up in points, and had dripped down the back of his shirt like candle wax.

"*Jack!*" Ino gasped, dropping out of his chair. He put his hands on the dog's shoulders. Jack just groaned. He was alive, but he had a serious wound on the back of his head. He had a big lump and a gash that looked like blunt-force trauma. The injury was at least a couple hours old.

Ino looked up, astonished and horrified, at the person who had shoved the dog into the room.

Grinning savagely, Doug Miller, the maintenance lion, stepped into the room and pushed the door shut behind him. It closed with a bang.

"YOU!" Ino gasped, astonished.

"Hey doc," the lion growled down at him, still grinning sadistically. "Help you with something?"

It wasn't Jack. It was Doug. Ino didn't understand but at the moment he didn't particularly care. Stunned, he leaned down, peering into Jack's face.

The shepherd stared back at him, dazed, his eyes unfocused. He lay with his chin on the office floor, his mouth partially open, breathing shallowly. Most of the blood on the back of his head had dried, but one of these two had clearly hit him with something hard. It must have happened early in the afternoon, and they'd been keeping him since then.

Ino felt a wave of panic wash over him. Jack was badly hurt. He needed medical attention, now. He looked like he could lose consciousness at any moment. He looked like he could *die* at any moment, right here on the floor.

Okay, Ino. Think. Think! Thoughts raced through his head.

Jack needed help. They needed to escape. Obviously the two cats couldn't possibly shoot him right in Clara's office, where someone might hear and they would leave evidence everywhere, but they clearly weren't planning on letting them escape.

Doug was between Ino and the door. Clara was behind him with a gun. Ino was in a 6-foot by 8-foot space between Clara's guest chairs and the door to the office, which was closed. The side walls were lined with bookcases, covered in a lot of soft textbooks which would be of absolutely no help to Ino.

The objects within Ino's reach were: two chairs, a pair of monitors, a cup of pens and a letter opener on the desk, and a glass paperweight.

Glancing up, Ino made a quick check of the ceiling, and with that he determined his plan.

Now he just needed to stall.

Swiftly, the hyena stood up.

Doug pulled a gun out of his waistband, too. "Not so fast, doc," he growled.

Great! Ino thought. *They both have guns.* "You're not really going to shoot me with Security right outside, are you? There's about twenty of them within earshot." He looked down at the lion's gun. "That's a revolver. It's even louder than hers." His eyes drifted from the gun to Doug's shirt.

There was a logo on the lion's green polo.

Triton Landscaping, it said.

And suddenly, Ino figured it all out.

His jaw dropping, he turned. "*Triton Landscaping*," he said, to Clara.

She grinned proudly back at him. She knew he'd solved the mystery.

He shook his head. "Oh my God. I found the wrong fucking *clue!*" he wailed. "This doesn't have *anything* to do with the video, or the big corporate donation." He looked back and forth between them. "Does it?!" he demanded.

Doug frowned. "What video?"

He narrowed his eyes. "Triton Landscaping is an official service provider of Santiago University But..." He thought of the Santiago University truck full of sod outside the remains of Baker Brown Science Center. "But we don't *have* any landscaping vendors. Maintenance does all of it. *That's* the fraud!" He whipped around to face Clara. "You're paying an outside vendor for services we *already do ourselves!*"

Clara grinned proudly back at him.

Ino shook his head. He pointed. "*You* set up a fake vendor!"

As he pointed, he took a step toward the desk.

Clara laughed. "I most certainly did not," she said. "I set up a *perfectly legitimate* vendor. You saw my Vendor Form, I'm sure. All my approvals were in order. I can submit under ten thousand dollars, same as you, Dr. Reamer. Same as any professor."

Ino snorted. "And nobody noticed an accounting professor hiring a landscaping vendor?"

Clara raised an eyebrow. "Dr. Reed noticed. And look where it got him."

Ino felt his eyebrows raise. *Uh-oh. Change topic.* "So how did you pay him?" He pointed back at Doug. As he did, he took another half-step back toward the desk.

This time Doug answered. He chuckled deeply. "Same as any business pays their landscaper. I send 'em an invoice, and they pay me."

Ino looked back and forth between them, skeptically. "I don't believe it," he said, flatly. "It's too easy."

Clara chuckled. "That's the beauty of it, Dr. Reamer. It's *designed* to be easy. It's part of doing business! As long as you follow all the rules, and submit all the right forms, the money keeps rolling out. I submitted a Vendor Request form with the proper signatures and sign-offs, and our stupid corporate accounting department didn't even question it." She leaned forward. "And for *four years*, Triton Landscaping has been dutifully submitting invoices for $9,800, which is coincidentally just under the corporate approval level. And for four years, Santiago has been paying!"

Ino stared, his jaw hanging open. Assuming a monthly invoice, that was like... half a million dollars. He leaned forward. "Are you *serious?*"

Clara shrugged, smiling proudly, a sadistic gleam in her eyes. "What can I say! I've been teaching this for thirty years, Dr. Reamer. I know where the holes are."

He shook his head. "Incredible." He glanced down at the desk. He was just about in reach. "So how did you get caught?" He glanced back at Doug. The lion glared at him. "Did somebody notice you never actually mowed the lawn?"

The big lion snorted. "How closely do you look at the guy mowing the lawn, Doc?"

Ino thought about that. That was true. He looked back at Clara.

Clara's face turned down in anger. "Through no fault of my own, I assure you. We were going to stop at the end of this fiscal year — one more short month. We had enough to abscond to some nice equatorial nation and sit tight while our interest compounded. I was going to quietly retire. No one would even know a crime had occurred. And then *Ethan Reed* does an *audit* of all University vendors."

Ino stared at her, his mouth slightly open. He leaned forward. "Seriously?" Subtly, he planted one foot a half-step closer to the desk. He was directly next to it now. "He audited... the University... vendors."

She shrugged.

"Okay, but *why*, though?" he asked.

Clara chuckled. "You know perfectly well, don't you, Dr. Reamer? Dr. Reed liked *secrets*. And he was *looking for them*. All day, every day. It was a game to him. A game he was very good at."

Ino frowned. "Is that how he got all his little bits of information?"

The calico smiled, raising an eyebrow. "Ahh, I see he must have had something on you, too. Yes sir, that's where he got all his information — he was a dutiful researcher. I would say..." She raised her gun. "*Too* dutiful."

Ino grit his teeth. "So he had to go," he said, grimly.

Clara shrugged. "I mean, he didn't *have* to go. I was going to try to bribe him. I think that's what he was *really* after." She leaned back against the counter behind her desk. "But Doug here didn't take too kindly to the way Reed was talking to me, and, as the police are wont to say... one thing led to another."

His fur standing on end, Ino turned to glance at the huge lion blocking the door. Dipping his head, Doug grinned evilly back at him.

Jesus. Ino felt all his fur stand up.

Ino turned. Clara frowned at him sympathetically. "We're working on impulse control," she told him. She looked past him at the lion. "So we don't do things like try to *kill someone with a freight train*. Which would never, ever work," she snapped.

Ino glanced back, his eyes wide. Doug frowned angrily. "Hey, babe, you miss a hundred percent of the shots you don't take." He shrugged his big shoulders. "Once this nerd saw the building plans, I knew he would eventually get to the maintenance man."

Ino turned and furrowed his brow. "The maintenance man? Why would I get to..." He thought for a moment. "Oh my God, the flow rate." He looked up.

Doug scowled at him. "Ayup. I'm sure you two thought I was too stupid to know what you were talking about, when you asked for the friggin' blueprints of the building we blew up."

Ino felt realization crash down on him. "So you didn't even *open* the gas valves. You probably just like... disconnected the main supply line or something. Didn't you?" Ino worked it out as he said it. "That's why the room filled with gas so fast, *way* faster than it could have filled through just the nozzles." He thought about it, his jaw hanging open. "You just cracked the pipes wide open." He stared. "And then disabled the door lock. You knew exactly how to do it."

Doug frowned a big angry lion frown. "I sure did!" He glared at Clara across Ino's face. "See? Sooner or later they would have got back to the guy with all the wrenches and the wire cutters. That's why *he* had to go. I took my chance."

Clara rolled her eyes. "Honestly. We'll talk about this later. Right now, we have business to attend to." She gestured at Ino with the gun.

Ino's eyes widened. *Uh-oh.* He swallowed. "I think you should reconsider. You won't get away with two more murders." Ino glanced down at Jack, who had stirred a little and was looking up at him, panting. The hyena looked up. "You didn't even get away with the first one!" His heart was pounding.

Clara snorted. "I don't *need* to get away with anything, Dr. Reamer. I *need* you two out of my way, and then a day or so to get to a tiny South Pacific island with poor extradition treaties and a favorable exchange rate! Then it won't matter if they know who did it, I can spend the rest of my life in a tropical paradise. We were going to leave tonight and then your bumbling dog came snooping. And you *followed!* Now we have to take care of both of you!"

He grimaced. "How are you going to do it?" He grit his teeth.

Clara blinked, and then grinned down at him conspiratorially. "Do you really want to know?"

Ino considered. "I mean... I think it's only fair."

She nodded, and then leaned forward, excited. "We're going to blow up... another building."

Ino stared at her. "*Really?*" he asked. He was genuinely astonished.

The cat nodded, excited. "It's brilliant! The media will go *insane*. One University with two deadly gas explosions. There will be 24-7 coverage about the ticking time bomb that is Santiago University. They'll have experts talking about methane pockets and international terrorism. It'll be *weeks* before anyone even thinks of anything as boring as stealing half a million dollars. We never planned for the first explosion to be that big but now it's the perfect excuse."

Staring at her, Ino frowned. He had a weird dissociative feeling. Furtively, he glanced down at the shepherd at his feet. Ino's plan required him to leave Jack behind.

But he had to. It was their only chance.

He heard Travis' voice in his head. *Sometimes, you gotta run.*

Jack and Ino made eye contact. The dog stared up at him, his expression betraying nothing. As per usual.

Ino swallowed.

"I just have one more question," he said.

Clara rolled her eyes. "Oh, what now?" she demanded.

Ino narrowed his eyes. "Why did you *give me the answer* to the journal entry clue?" He frowned.

Clara laughed. She showed a lot of teeth.

Ino clenched his jaw. "We never would have figured out that was a phone number. And once you told us it was, *eventually* someone was going to check your math, and find out that the real clue was *your* number. And that you lied about it."

Clara smiled evilly back at him. "Why, Dr. Reamer… because it was fun."

He stared at her.

"It was a thrill to do it wrong right under your stupid noses." She leaned forward. "I enjoy being smarter than the men around me, Dr. Reamer."

He frowned. "Is that so," he said, flatly.

"It is. For instance, don't think I don't see you inching toward the desk," Clara snapped, snatching the pencil cup with the letter opener off the desk.

Ino narrowed his eyes. "Not quite," he grunted, lunging forward for the glass paperweight.

He couldn't throw it at either of them — whoever he didn't hit, would shoot him.

So he swung his powerful arm around like he was winding up for a pitch, and let the paperweight go rocketing away in a thunderous, underhand lob.

Straight up.

Into the fire sprinkler.

Clara's office, like all the offices in the building, like all of the labs, like every room on the entire campus, had a 3" metal fire sprinkler protruding from the ceiling, directly over Ino's head. The heavy glass globe hit the nozzle with a sharp *crack!* and water *exploded* from it. *FSSSSSSSSSSSSSSSSSSSSSSHHHHHHHHHHH!*

Ino had been expecting a lot of water, but he would never have expected what blasted out of the ceiling nozzle. It was like a fire hose poked through the roof. It made the storm from yesterday feel like a lawn sprinkler.

Ino stumbled, blinded by the water and mist and instantly soaked to the skin, staggering under the weight of the blast from the ceiling. He could barely breathe and he struggled to stay on his feet. Seeing anything was out of the question.

"AWWKRKRHK!" the lion roared; the rest of them were too shocked to do anything at all.

Ino launched himself away from the desk and shot toward the door, navigating from memory since he could barely see from the water and mist filling the air and coursing over his face. He aimed wrong and slammed into the bookshelf next to the door, jarring his chest hard; he grabbed the side of the shelf and yanked it over. He could feel the moment when the bookcase tipped and gravity took over. It toppled into the mist with a huge crash and he heard a thud and a scream as it hit Doug behind him. Clara screamed something too, but Ino couldn't even make it out over the roar of the blasted sprinkler head.

Feeling for the door handle, Ino found the knob and twisted violently. He yanked the door open, staggered into the hallway, and slammed the door in a panic behind him. Water immediately began gushing through the crack under the door.

Ino took off at a dead sprint down the hallway, the water splashing out of his shoes as he went. He shook his head reflexively as he ran, water spraying off of him in all directions.

Ino had no idea where he was going, he was just going *away.* The hyena bolted down the 2nd floor hallway, racing past offices and classrooms.

From down the hall came a *roar* as Doug burst from the office. The waterfall in the room was suddenly louder. Ino flinched as he sprinted away.

"GET HIM!" Clara screamed somewhere down the hall.

Shit shit shit SHIT SHIT, Ino thought, trying to take a hard left down a side hallway. His wet shoes shot out from under him and he went down like a sandbag, skidding across the floor and crashing feet-first into the far wall and crushing his tail.

As he dropped, a gunshot rang out down the hall.

He heard the bullet whip over his head, and a glass display case exploded in the wall above him. Big jagged panes of glass coursed down over him.

"*Ahhk!*" he squealed, scrambling around the corner on all fours, staggering to his feet as he skittered away.

"*Damn, lost him!*" Doug yelled. Ino could hear heavy footsteps pounding after him.

Ino took off like an Olympic sprinter.

The side hallway was only fifty feet or so. The hyena hit the stairwell door crash bar at a full run.

There was a fire alarm and an Emergency Help Button in the stairwell. Ino jabbed the "HELP" button and yanked the fire alarm next to it before dashing down the concrete steps two at a time, landing precariously on wet feet with every step, held upright only by his death grip on the metal railing. The concrete stairwell filled and reverberated with the deafening ringing fire siren.

As he rounded the bottom, swinging himself around the railing, the lion exploded into the top of the stairwell.

"*YARP!*" Ino yelped, ducking and covering his head and lunging for the ground floor door. Doug shot at him three times, firing wildly down into the stairwell, *BANG BANG BANG!* In the stairwell the gunshots were ear-shattering. Little chips of concrete bounced off of Ino but he wasn't hit. His heart felt like it was going to explode.

He flung himself into the exit door onto the first floor, careening through it so hard it swung wide and slammed against the wall it was mounted to. He raced forward, down a short hallway, then a sharp turn into another hallway. This time he purposefully ricocheted off the far wall, so he wouldn't lose any speed or slip again. The lights were off on the ground floor except for the emergency strobes from the fire alarm, snapping like camera flashes every few feet. It was like a haunted house.

"*GET BACK HERE!*" Doug roared, deep in the building. HIs voice carried like thunder, even over the blaring alarm bells. He wasn't far behind.

Ino didn't bother replying. Abruptly, he ran out of hallways, and zeroed in on the nearest exit.

It was about sixty feet away. He would dash out the door and hopefully into enough witnesses that Doug wouldn't murder him right on the steps.

Ino hit high gear and sprinted toward the door.

"THERE YOU ARE!" Doug roared down the hall behind him.

Ino's entire body jerked in shock, even as he shot down the hallway, and he braced himself to hit the exit door at a full run. Ten feet. He could make it ten more feet!

Suddenly, the door in front of him swung violently open.

Jerking in shock again, the hyena frantically tried to skid to a halt, and again his feet flew out from under him. He crashed painfully onto his ass and tail, and screeched to a halt on the vinyl floor, crashing into the legs of the person who had just pulled open the door.

Standing in the doorway, his gun out, his face a mask of astonishment, was Travis MacGregor.

He looked astonished. "WHAT — " he started.

"*LOOK OUT HE'S GOT A GUN!*" Ino screamed.

Standing over him, Travis raised his gun in both hands and pointed it down the hall. "DROP THE WEAPON!" he roared.

Doug didn't, and before Travis' voice even finished echoing off the walls, a gunshot exploded like thunder.

"*Aaah!*" Ino screamed. Still lying flattened on the floor, he jerked in shock, and then forced himself to open his eyes.

Travis was standing. Eyes wide, gun still raised. Still standing.

Scrambling onto his side, heart pounding, Ino looked down the hallway.

Doug Miller was lying on his back down the hallway, writhing in pain. "*Aaaahh!*" the lion moaned. His gun had slid a few more feet down the hallway and was halfway between Ino and himself. A dark crimson stain had formed in the shoulder of his Triton Landscaping polo and was slowly spreading out. "You *SHOT ME,* you *ASSHOLE,*" he moaned.

Officer Reese appeared from the other end of the hallway. "Clear this side!" she called. She was holding her gun high. It was a search pattern. They must have heard the shots from outside.

Ino scrambled to his feet. "There's another one," he gasped. "Second floor. Clara Calder. She's got Jack!"

Travis' eyes widened. He looked at Reese.

The ferret gestured with her head. "Go! I got this!" She moved toward the prone lion with a pair of handcuffs. "GO!"

Travis turned to him.

"This way!" Ino gasped. He took off toward the stairwell, the big husky a step behind him.

They burst into the stairwell with the bullet holes in it. "Up there! End of the hall!" Ino announced.

Travis nodded, and took point, charging up the stairs. Ino was right behind him.

Travis' radio started squawking — it was Reese downstairs, calling for an ambulance — and the dog reached up to turn it off without looking. The husky pulled open the stairwell door and swung into the hallway, gun first. He disappeared down the hall, and Ino raced after him.

When the husky rounded the last corner, his ears perked and he put his finger over the trigger guard. "SECURITY, FREEZE!" he boomed.

Ino stuck his head out.

Clara Calder was standing in the middle of the hallway, dripping wet and scowling, her glasses fogged up and her calico fur matted to her face. She had her hands over her head and a deathly glare on her face. Her gun was twenty feet ahead of her, well out of reach.

She was surrendering.

Ino looked at the office door. Water was pouring out of the office. It had flooded the entire hallway, soaking the vinyl all the way down to the corner of the hall. A half-inch deep river had already reached the place where they were standing. It started waterfalling down the stairs behind him.

"GET ON THE GROUND!" Travis ordered. "HANDS OVER YOUR HEAD!"

"Is that *really* necessary, Officer?" Clara pouted.

"*GET ON THE FUCKING GROUND!*" the husky screamed, his voice echoing over the blaring alarm.

Rolling her eyes, the cat slowly lowered herself to her knees in the water. "Honestly," she said.

"Do not move!" Still holding his gun up, Travis moved toward the kneeling cat.

Ino looked between the two of them, and took off. He raced down the hallway, his feet splashing underneath him.

"Reamer, *wait!*" Travis ordered.

His heart pounding, Ino launched himself into the office.

The sprinkler was still blasting away, making it nearly impossible to see, blasting out so hard it stung his skin. He covered his eyes. The first thing he found — by accident — was the bookshelf he had pulled over onto Doug. He tripped over it and crashed face-first onto the shelf and the floor.

"*Ungh!*" he grunted as he landed hard on both of his shins and his hands. He shook his head and lifted himself onto all fours. The water was *freezing.* "JACK!" he called.

He crawled forward, feeling his way into the office. The water on the floor was at least four inches deep and roiled beneath him. He felt his way over the bookcase, toward where he had last seen the dog.

He found the wet mess of shepherd. "*JACK!*" he cried. He couldn't see him, only feel him.

The dog felt cold.

Ino felt his stomach drop again. He was shaking now, big involuntary shivers that wracked his entire body. "Jack!" he moaned, grabbing the dog's shoulders and shaking him.

Suddenly, the other man moved. "Nnnnggghhh," the dog groaned, writhing weakly under Ino's grasp.

Ino gasped. "C'mon! I got you!" He put his hands under the dog's arms and pulled.

"Aaaaggghhh," Jack grunted. He was barely moving.

Ino pulled. He backed over the bookcase, taking Jack with him. He felt Jack's shirt start to tear and he definitely pulled out some fur, but he knew he had to get Jack out of the blasting water if he had any chance at all. He pulled, functioning on sheer adrenaline and nothing else.

As soon as he made it to the doorway, the fire bell abruptly cut out. The sudden lack of bells made Ino's ears ring. He could hear the rushing of blood in his ears.

Travis had Clara handcuffed face-down on the hallway floor, feeling her for other weapons.

Ino pulled the shepherd backward a few more feet, and with that they were out in the hallway.

He shook his head so he could see and dropped to his knees. "Jack," he said.

The dog didn't respond. He was laying on his chest, his eyes half closed and unfocused. His lips were blue and his skin looked white underneath his wet, matted-down fur. The dried blood had mostly washed off the back of his head, but the gash and the lump it showed were somehow worse, the edges of the cut white and ragged under the fur. He was still breathing, but he looked like a corpse.

Behind him, Travis gasped, sharp and alarmed. Ino did not take that as a particularly good sign. The husky clawed at his radio. "Dispatch, we need an ambulance to Rose Hall right now. Second floor! Officer down!" Travis said, into his radio. "Repeat, officer down!"

Jack was still laying in the water, but the entire hallway was flooded, so Ino didn't know what to do about it. He lay next to the shepherd. "Jack, c'mon, stay with us," he pleaded. He squeezed the dog's shoulder. "Hang on, help is on the way."

Jack just groaned. He didn't give any indication that he had heard or understood what Ino had said.

Travis dropped on his other side. "C'mon, Sarge, keep it together," he whispered. His voice was shaking.

Footsteps thundered down the hall.

It was two EMTs — Ino recognized them from the night of the explosion. He slid back from the injured shepherd, and with that, his brain started to disengage again, and he just watched.

The evening rushed by in a haze after that. Jack was carted away immediately. Travis went with him and promised to keep Ino updated. The Rose building was swarmed with police, EMTs, maintenance personnel — everyone. Two paramedics checked him out and gave him a blanket to wrap around his wet tank top. Ino gave his statement a dozen times, at least, to campus security, to city cops, to a detective, to another detective. It was surreal, but he knew the drill at this point.

The various law enforcement finished up by midnight, and Officer Reese offered to drive him home, but Ino declined. The wireless key fob of his rental had died in the water but the key still worked. It was a warm night and he drove home with the radio off and the windows down. It was quiet and peaceful.

As he rounded the corner from Route 30 to Sturdy Road he saw that the railroad crossing lights were red and a freight train was lumbering past. He slowed down as he approached the crossing, but just as he arrived the last train car thundered through, and the crossing lights came up, clearing the path. Ino rolled on the rest of the way home.

Travis wasn't incredibly descriptive, but he did keep his promise to keep Ino informed. His first message at 12:30 am said "BRAIN SWELLING" which gave Ino a full-on panic attack, but his next message at 1:15 am said "DOING BETTER," and then at 2:45 am, "THEY'RE KEEPING HIM A COUPLE DAYS," which Ino took as a good sign.

He fell asleep on his couch around 3:00 am.

Chapter 12: Visiting Hours

Wednesday, May 23, 2018

Riiiiiiiiiiinnnngggggggggggggggg!

Grunting, Ino jerked groggily awake. It was his desk phone, an old, sharp bell ringer.

He sat up, bleary-eyed, and looked around.

He was in his living room. His cellphone was on the coffee table, shrilly ringing and vibrating itself angrily in circles. He was on the couch.

Rolling his eyes, Ino realized he had never changed the default ringtone, which had been set to "old timey phone." He'd only had the phone for a day. Or was it two days? At least the new phone was waterproof. He snatched it up off the table. It was 8:04 am. and his phone was at 9% battery. It said: MISSED CALL: TRAVIS SECURITY.

Eyes widening, Ino hit redial. Travis answered immediately.

"How is he?" Ino gasped.

On the other end of the phone, Travis grunted. "He's… okay. Those bastards really did a number on him. The docs say his brain was swelling. He didn't have a lot of time left."

Ino swallowed, hard. His heart was pounding. "Jesus," he said, softly.

"Yeah. Anyway, he's awake now. You can come visit. He's a little out of it but he'll be glad to see you."

Ino blinked. "Glad to see *me?*" he asked. He frowned. "Travis, we talked about this. He doesn't even like me." He let out a sigh.

Travis laughed into the phone. "Yeah, okay, Reamer. Come see him. It'll do him good."

Ino swallowed. "Okay," he said. He felt his face start to heat up.

"And take a shower," Travis added. "You stank last night."

Ino rolled his eyes. "HOW did you convince everyone that you're a nice person?"

"Ha!" the husky barked. "If I don't see you here, have a good rest of your week, Dr. Reamer." And with that he hung up.

Ino cracked a smile, laying back on his couch.

Abruptly, the phone rang in his hands again. *Rinnnnnnnnnnnnnng!* Ino stared at it.

VIVIAN CELL.

Uh-oh, he thought. He slid the phone to TALK.

"Hhhhhhhhiiiiiiiii," he said, cautiously. "This is Ino."

"Can I *REALLY NOT LEAVE YOU FOR ONE SINGLE DAY?*" Vivian demanded through the phone.

Despite himself, Ino laughed. "Hey, Viv. Did you have a nice flight?"

"PLUG IN YOUR PHONE AND TELL ME EVERYTHING," Vivian ordered him.

Ino chuckled. "Okay. But it's gonna have to be the condensed version. I have to go see somebody."

Ino's heart started pounding as soon as he parked the rental car at Beirne Memorial Hospital.

He started at the reception desk and got a name tag sticker and directions. It wasn't a huge hospital, so it didn't take him long to negotiate from the reception desk to the observation rooms on the fourth floor. His heart kept thumping harder as he got closer. Jack had been in pretty bad shape last night. Surely Travis would have told him if Jack had sustained something like permanent brain damage. But that did nothing to calm the hyena's nerves. He swallowed hard, willing himself not to shake.

His elevator reached the fourth floor and Ino followed the wall directions to Room 444. The hospital was absolutely bustling with doctors and nurses, and Ino tried his best to look like he knew exactly where he was going, lest someone identify his cluelessness.

He rounded the last corner and almost ran smack into two huskies, one in gym shorts and one in a security uniform.

"DOCTOR REAMER!" Sean shouted, zipping forward and throwing his arms around Ino's chest. He hit him hard and squeezed him tightly.

"*Oof!*" Ino grunted. He staggered back a few steps. "Hi, Sean!" he said. "How are you doing?" He awkwardly patted the small husky's shoulder, making eye contact with Travis and nodding. Travis smiled, amused at Ino's discomfort.

"Oh my God I'm so glad you're okay," Sean said, in one breath. "What is the *matter* with you? Stop getting into trouble! I heard about the car and the train too!" He looked up with horrified blue eyes, ears back, still clinging to Ino's chest.

Ino chuckled. "I'm fine. It's all over now. I don't have any reason to get into trouble anymore." He patted the top of the husky's head.

Sean grunted and released him. He took a step back and gave Ino the same annoyed husky sneer that Travis had occasionally sported. "You BETTER be!" He pouted.

Ino grinned at him. "Really. I'm *so* done. You have no idea how done I am. I literally cannot even with this." He looked up at the other dog. "Hello, Officer MacGregor. Thanks for saving my life *again* last night."

Travis cracked a smile. "Happy to, Dr. Reamer. Thanks for saving my nephew *and* my boss."

Ino chuckled. "Well then, I suppose *now* we're even, then?" He grinned.

Travis nodded gravely. "We are." Without warning, he leaned forward and enveloped Ino in a massive bearhug.

"*Oooomphh!*" Ino gasped, as Travis lifted him off of his feet. Something popped in his back. "*Don't mention it!*" he gasped, writhing in Travis' grasp. The big dog was ridiculously strong.

Travis squeezed him for another moment, and just when Ino thought he was going to pass out, relaxed his grip. Ino felt his feet touch the floor again and sucked in a deep breath.

The husky nodded at him. "Nice work yesterday," he said simply, cracking the faintest of smiles. With one final head tilt, he put his hand on Sean's shoulder, and set off gently toward the elevators.

"Bye, Dr. Reamer!" Sean called, as he was steered away. "I'm finally going home! I'll see you in the fall!"

Smiling, Ino waved at both of them. Then the smile dropped off his face. "Wait, where's the room?!" he called after them.

Travis pointed. "End of the hall!" said both huskies, in unison.

Ino nodded. "Thanks!" He turned and walked to the end of the hall.

Ino found the room and paused in the doorway. The room had a big industrial door propped open against the wall, and a bevy of medical equipment visible from outside. Ino leaned in, knocking gently. He remembered how Jack had looked last night, with blue lips and pale skin, and his stomach did a slow nauseated turn.

Jack was in a large hospital bed, angled upward behind his back, with a freestanding tray that covered his lap. He was clean and dry and all of his color was back. He was wearing a hospital gown and nestled into a pile of blankets. As Ino knocked and leaned in, the shepherd looked up, curiously. He still looked a little dazed, his eyes half-closed, but at least his eyes were focusing. And when he saw Ino, he brightened up immediately. His ears perked up and he straightened up in bed.

"Dr. Reamer!" he said. His voice was soft and raspy, but he looked happy to see him.

Ino stepped into the room, grinning. "You really need to start calling me Ino." He walked up to Jack's bedside. "I think we've been through enough."

The dog smiled sleepily back at him, his eyes half-closed. Both of his eyes were bloodshot and he didn't look steady, but otherwise the shepherd looked a thousand times better than last night. He didn't even really look injured — if Ino didn't know better he would just think the shepherd was just tired, or maybe a little drunk. It made Ino's heart leap seeing Jack in such better condition.

Ino laughed. "Can I hug you? Oh my God."

Smiling dopily, Jack nodded and held out his arms.

Ino leaned in and put one hand across Jack's chest, squeezing him. Jack reached up and gently hugged Ino's arm. The shepherd felt solid and strong in his grip, the opposite of the cold dead weight from the previous evening. Jack was warm and soft and smelled good.

"Oh my *God*," Ino said. "I was so worried. Holy shit. You looked *so bad*." He squeezed the dog as hard as he dared, and after a few moments they both released their grip.

Ino grabbed the hard plastic chair next to the bed and slipped into it. He pulled it up to the bed. "How *are* you? Are you okay? How's your *brain swelling?*"

Jack chuckled softly. "Gonna be in here a couple days while things calm down. But they don't think I have any permanent damage." He cracked a smile.

Ino nodded intently. "Good, good. You feel all right?"

The dog shrugged, cracking a smile. "Still got a headache. But the drugs are good."

Ino nodded. He looked the dog over again. "God, Jack. You look *amazing*. Last night I thought... I thought..." He swallowed, wondering how he could possibly end that sentence, and then finally just trailed off. "Well, you didn't look so good."

Jack cracked a little smile. "Yeah. I know. Travis told me." He adjusted himself in the bed, leaning back. "Think I freaked him out a little."

Ino let out a shaky breath. "Yeah. I know just how he feels." He frowned.

Jack stared at him for a moment, leaned back, eyes half closed, and reached for him with one big black paw.

Ino blinked at him, for a moment, raising his eyebrows.

Jack frowned. "C'mon," he grunted, holding his fingers open.

Blushing, Ino reached up and took the shepherd's hand. Jack's grip was strong and his paw pads were hot to the touch. Ino felt himself start to blush immediately.

The shepherd squeezed his hand, looking him in the eye. "Thank you," he said. "For finding me. For *looking* for me."

Ino felt his face heating up and his heart racing. He looked away, embarrassed. "Don't thank *me*," he mumbled. "I left you with those psychopaths."

Jack watched him. "We both know you had to."

Ino shook his head, still holding Jack's hand. "I don't know about that." He finally looked up, and to his surprise he suddenly found himself blinking back tears. "I should have stayed."

The shepherd frowned at him. "Ino. I wasn't going anywhere. You weren't going to get me out of that room. If you'd stayed, that story would only have one ending — we would both be dead right now."

Ino looked up at him, frowning. Jack was right, so Ino didn't say anything at all.

The shepherd squeezed his hand again. "Anyway. Thank you for looking for me. You didn't have to do that." He let go of Ino's hand.

Ino reached up with his other hand to wipe the tears out of his eyes. "Yeah, I did," he muttered.

The dog stared at him, eyes wide. "Did you?" he asked, softly.

Ino finished wiping his eyes. "Yes, of *course* I did, you *idiot*," he snapped.

Jack watched him, amused, and then smiled a broad, genuine smile.

Ino swallowed, willing both his blush and his tears away, and shook his head gently. "Ugh," he said, softly. He cleared his throat. "Anyway," he said. "Do you remember anything?" he asked. "From last night?"

Jack blinked at him, and then gave a little shrug. "Bits. Pieces." He frowned, looking away as he thought about it. "I heard a little of their scheme. I don't remember much after the morning."

Ino nodded, considering. "Where did you go after interviewing the badger in the accounting department?"

Jack looked at him and frowned. "Somewhere stupid," he rumbled. "I was checking Susan's SUV in the parking lot for yellow paint an' I saw some of the maintenance guys cleaning up branches. And then I figured out what had been bothering me about that vendor form."

Ino nodded slowly. "Let me guess. You wondered why we were paying money to a vendor for an outside landscaping service, when *our own employees* already do the landscaping."

Jack nodded, cracking a smile. "Yup. Wish I'd made that connection a little sooner."

Ino rolled his eyes. "You're telling me. There were clues about that *everywhere*. How many times in the last week have I driven past a University landscaping truck?"

The shepherd nodded. "Ayup. So I went to check out the address we had on file for Triton Landscaping. Just wanted to take a quick look."

Ino grimaced. "Is that where they got you?"

Jack glared at him darkly with bloodshot eyes. "Didn't get ten steps out of my cruiser." He shook his head, frowning sourly. "I remember thinking it looked like a residence, not a business, some shitty little trailer out in the sticks, and they only had one truck, and wondering if I even had the right address. I heard a rustle behind me and that's all I remember." He shook his head angrily.

Ino winced. "Do you know what they hit you with?"

Jack let out an annoyed sigh. "Docs say it was probably a thick tree branch or something." He frowned. "Nothing like a pipe or it woulda killed me immediately." He sighed. "As it was, I was in and out for a while, and I'm pretty sure I was handcuffed, and they must have dragged me back to campus. Risky as hell, but I guess they needed it for their plan to blow both of us up."

Ino processed that, and then shivered. "God," he said, softly.

Jack nodded. "Mm-hmm."

The hyena shook his head in wonder. "They seemed so *nice*."

The dog chuckled. "They always do." He thought for a moment, frowning, considering. "Well, that's not really true. *Sometimes* they do."

"So did Travis fill you in on how their whole scheme worked?"

Jack raised his eyebrows. "Yeah. That was... a wild one."

Ino cracked a smile. "It didn't even occur to me until I had all the pieces in front of me. And even then they had to explain it."

Jack chuckled. "It's one for the books, all right."

Ino shook his head slowly. "So this had nothing to do with Susan."

Jack shook his head. "No. If she's been a little weird lately, she's probably just really taking it rough that Reed died." He frowned. "They've known each other thirty years. They both graduated Santiago together, three decades ago." He shrugged. "I think she's just throwing herself into her University work. They were close."

Ino nodded. "And the paperweight?"

"A goodbye. She left it in his office the morning after the explosion."

"Mm. That explains that, then. And this whole thing had nothing to do with the missing heroin from your police station."

Jack shrugged. "I guess not. I did look into it — a couple people got a decent severance but not decent enough to risk a felony. If you can solve *that* mystery, you'll be the first." He gave a little tight-lipped frown. "And if Reed figured out who did it... he's not telling."

Ino nodded thoughtfully. "Yikes. Jesus." He thought about it. "I just kind of expected a neat little bow on that one."

Jack cracked a little smile. "Mmm. Doesn't always work out like that."

Ino frowned. "Speaking of which, what about the missed cellphone? How did that happen? I heard both you and Susan say the other one hired the crime scene investigators."

Jack blinked at him, and then looked away. "They were pretty bad. I think we both screwed that one up. We picked them together, and neither of us loved the team we ended up with." He frowned. "I guess next time I'll call in some experts to help pick our experts." He rolled his eyes.

Ino blinked. "Huh. It's always so organized on TV."

Jack grinned. "Yeah well. It's a lot messier in real life." He gave Ino a private little grin. "Y'know?" He smiled a dopey little smile at him.

Ino felt his heart flutter a little. He looked away, his blush creeping back.

Jack stared at him. "How are *you* doing?"

The hyena frowned back at him. "What? Me?" He swallowed, flustered. "I'm fine. I'm not sitting in a hospital bed right now, for starters."

Jack cracked a smile. "Doesn't mean everything is fine."

Ino scowled at him. "Ugh. You sound like Vivian." He thought for a moment. "I guess... I don't know. It was pretty scary, but we got the bad guys." He looked up. "Not the *method* I would have chosen, but I can't argue with the results. And you don't have to give up the case anymore."

Jack processed that, and then stared at him pointedly, his eyes widening a little. "Uhhhh," he said.

Ino blinked at him. "What?"

Jack swallowed, and then looked away. "Uh, I didn't know what to do about that. Whether to go through with it or not."

Ino frowned. "You have enough to charge them, right?"

Jack slowly nodded. "More than enough. Doug Miller is on camera trying to shoot a civilian and a security officer. And you're a witness for everything else." He paused for a moment. "Personally, I bet they flip on each other during questioning. They don't strike me as the particularly loyal type." He shrugged. "The University will probably share jurisdiction with the city cops and use one of their detectives for the interrogation, and then it goes to a local prosecutor. I don't think they'll have any problems nailing it."

Ino shrugged. "Then keep the case. You don't have a conflict anymore. I can see the headlines now." He held up his hands. "*Campus Cops Catch Killer.*"

Jack watched him. He cracked a little smile. "I mean... if you're sure. You can think about it if you want."

Ino watched him. "Jack. Seriously. I know your relationship with Reed had nothing to do with this case. I saw that first-hand. If you want to disclose to the prosecutor that you had a" — he lowered his voice — "*sexual relationship* with the victim, just to be perfectly open, that's fine. But this is a small town. Everyone here has *some* kind of relation to the victim. I knew him for half a decade."

Jack watched him for a moment, and then chuckled. "Well, yes, I will, especially because *somebody's* forensics team will be going through that drive for evidence of any other crimes, and they're going to see it anyway. It won't be evidence, but I will disclose it. I… I just want to make sure I'm not burning any bridges with you by keeping the case."

Ino blinked at him. "Why not? Why would you care what *I* think?"

Jack blinked at him, and then looked away.

It looked like he was blushing.

Ino watched him. He liked what he saw, so he decided to push it.

"You know…" the hyena said, leaning forward, smiling. "Vivian thinks you have a *thing* for me."

The shepherd swallowed hard, still refusing to make eye contact, and now he was *definitely* blushing. His muzzle turned crimson under the black fur, and red even started to creep into the cream and white parts of his neck and face.

Ino leaned forward, grinning slyly. "She also thinks I have a thing for *you.*"

Jack was in the process of turning fluorescent pink when an alarm erupted out of a machine next to the bed. *Beep beep beep beep beep beep beep!*

Startled, they both looked at each other and then back at the machine. It looked like a heart rate monitor. It had a little bouncing line on it. It went on and on.

"Is that — " Ino started.

A nurse appeared in the doorway. "Mr. Archer!" she said, striding to the machine. "What are you up to in here?"

Alarmed, the dog looked at her. "Nothing!" he said, eyes wide. "Just sitting here in bed." His ears folded back against his head.

The nurse chuckled, hitting a button on the keening machine and silencing it. "Are you sure? I think you must be doing gymnastics. Your heart rate suddenly skyrocketed."

Ino processed that for a moment, and then grinned.

Squirming, Jack looked like he wanted to sink into the bedsheets.

The nurse turned to him. "Try to relax, won't you? You're supposed to be resting."

The shepherd swallowed. "I *am* resting!" he protested.

The hyena grinned smugly. "Sorry, that's my fault," he said. He looked at Jack. "I guess I'll wait until you're better before I ask you out on a date."

Jack turned to look at him, stammering, his ears flattening again.

Beep beep beep beep beep beep beep! went the machine again.

Jack broke eye contact and sank into his bedsheets, coloring deep crimson.

The nurse laughed. "Well," she said. "I guess I'm interrupting." She silenced the machine again and pointed at Ino. "Cute, but cut it out. He needs to rest. His encephalitis takes precedence over your flirting."

Jack made a little whimpering noise, and tried to hide behind his tray table.

Ino nodded, still grinning smugly. "Understood. Doctor's orders."

She nodded. "That's right. There will be plenty of time for cuteness later."

Ino nodded back. "Of course!"

She nodded one final time. "Thank you." She turned to Jack. "Do you need anything while I'm here? Water? How's your pain?"

Jack swallowed. "I'm fine," he squeaked.

She chuckled. "Okay. They'll be around for lunch orders in a little while."

The shepherd nodded without making eye contact. Smiling, the nurse disappeared out the door.

Ino just beamed at the shepherd. Jack wouldn't look at him.

The hyena chuckled. "Well. I guess we're back to boring topics. I don't want to get you too excited again."

Jack let out a shuddering breath. "You know…" he mumbled. "I *usually* have a pretty good poker face," he said, softly.

Ino grinned smugly. "I notice your poker face is getting worse and worse around me."

Jack rolled his eyes, blushing.

Ino smiled. "That's okay. I like it."

Jack glanced briefly at him, and gave him a shy little smile.

They sat in silence for a comfortable moment.

"You mind if I stay a bit?" Ino asked.

Jack looked up at him, and cracked a little smile. "Would you? That would be great. I hate hospitals." He frowned. "I might fall asleep, though. It comes up on me pretty quick." He sat back, his eyes drooping shut. "In fact… I think it's coming up on me right now."

Ino nodded, smiling. "That's fine. I don't mind. I'll probably sleep in this chair. I had kind of a rough night."

Jack laughed, low and deep. "Oh yeah? What'd you get up to?"

Ino chuckled. "Oh, you know. Nothing much. Caught up with somebody from the Accounting department."

Jack closed his eyes and laughed.

Ino reached over and squeezed his hand. "Get some sleep. I'll be hanging out right here."

Jack gave him a grateful, sleepy smile, and leaned back, nestling into the covers. "Thank you, Ino," he said, softly. "For everything."

Ino nodded. "Any time, Jack." He leaned forward and kissed the shepherd on the cheek.

Nodding, and yawning, smiling, Jack's eyes drifted closed.

Letting out a happy sigh, Ino settled back in the plastic chair.

Chapter 13: Epilogue

Friday, May 25, 2018

The following Friday, standing in front of Chaney Cafeteria, Ino checked his watch once again. It was brand new — a cool new smart watch that he had bought himself after the incident in Rose Hall. This watch set its own time based on its connection to his phone, so Ino didn't have to worry about its accuracy — it would always be exactly on time.

Ino paced back and forth, hefting his backpack on his shoulders. He was wearing khaki shorts and a bright-yellow t-shirt with flip flops. The outfit was probably overly casual for campus, but it was a beautiful summer Friday, so it felt fine.

"Hey, nerd," said a voice behind him.

He turned. "Dr. Chen!" he announced.

She nodded. "Dr. Reamer!" They hugged. Vivian squeezed him extra tight, which hurt since his entire body was still injured, but he didn't mind. She'd gotten back from the conference late the night before and she was looking cute in skinny jeans and a flowy pink blouse. "I can't believe I'm seeing you after *yet another* terrifying personal attack." She leaned back and frowned. "And why are we meeting at school?" she demanded. "We do have *houses*, you know."

Ino shrugged. "One of us would have to cook."

Vivian nodded. "Excellent point! I'll lead the way!"

They selected and paid for their food. Leading the way, Vivian bypassed their usual bar table and instead settled into a cushy booth.

Ino eyed Vivian's strawberry and spinach salad. "I see you're back on a real food diet," he said, grinning. "I knew you couldn't last on burgers and fries."

Vivian rolled her eyes. "Ugh, yes. I ate like crap at the conference. I was actually craving a salad. Isn't that just *depraved?*"

Ino chuckled. He started in on his chicken tenders. "I don't know, my baseline for depraved has made a … considerable migration, as of late."

She nodded, sipping her iced tea, frowning thoughtfully. "Mmm. Go on. How are you feeling after a few days to digest?"

He shrugged. "Fine, I guess? The second attempt on my life wasn't too different from the first attempt on my life."

She nodded thoughtfully.

He gestured with a french fry. "Also, similarly: extremely wet. I would not have guessed. I expected it to be terrifying. I did not expect it to be quite so… moist."

The pine marten wrinkled her nose. "Ugh, I hate that word." She leaned forward watching him. "But you're feeling okay?"

Ino considered, furrowing his brow. "I think I am… like, genuinely. The lingering sense of doubt is gone. Everything is pretty much solved. Miller and Calder are both in jail. Mystery solved!"

She chuckled. "Literally."

He nodded, gesturing with a french fry. "*Literally.*"

She considered for a moment. "Well, that's good to hear. You're pretty resilient. I thought you'd be okay but I wanted to check in. And listen, if you're *not* okay, that's okay too, you know?" She reached over and squeezed his hand.

Ino beamed. "Awww," he said. "You're so good to me."

She nodded. "I am. I am good to you." She tucked in on her salad. "How's the prosecution going? Hear anything yet?"

Ino chuckled. "Oh yeah, besides Doug chasing me with a gun through the Rose building, which was all on camera by the way, there was another big piece. The landscaping truck they found registered to Triton Landscaping — Doug's fake company — has a front bumper full of yellow paint."

Vivian nodded. "From your car."

Ino shook his head. "No, he rear-ended a school bus." He frowned. "Unrelated. But it looks very bad." He pursed his lips.

She narrowed her eyes at him.

Ino grinned. "Yes, from my car. Obviously!"

Vivian rolled her eyes. "*This* is why people keep trying to murder you."

Ino choked on his fries laughing. "Wow. First of all, that is so rude. Second, *one* person tried to murder me, *on several occasions*. That is *not* the same as 'people.'"

Vivian nodded, stealing a french fry off his tray. "That is true, I suppose, yes." She popped it into her mouth. "Speaking of which, are they both on trial for murder? Or is the accounting professor just an accessory and the hot lion did the dirty work?"

Ino frowned. "I don't know yet. We don't *actually* know which of them did it. Jack says they'll both probably implicate the other one, but one of them will have evidence to back it up. And either way they'll both be tried for conspiracy to commit murder for me and Jack."

Vivian smiled. "And how *is* Jack?"

Ino chuckled. "He's good! He's out of the hospital. They expect him to make a full recovery. It was a nasty blow but they got to him before any damage became permanent." He let out a relieved sigh. "He's way too stubborn to be affected by trivial matters like a serious brain injury."

Vivian chuckled. "And how are you *and* Jack?"

Ino blinked innocently. "Me and Jack? There is no 'me and Jack.'"

Vivian raised an eyebrow, smiling.

The hyena chuckled. "I haven't officially asked him out yet. But I'm working up to it."

She grinned. "You have a goofy look on your face. That's cute."

Ino frowned. "What? No I don't. There's not a trace of goof on my face."

She nodded, beaming. "There's *maximum* goof. I am an expert, Ino. Goof falls *directly* under my purview." The pine marten smiled. "Seriously, though, I'm happy for you. I always had a feeling. I can't wait to see your little mutant hyena-shepherd babies."

Ino was drinking and spit his Diet Coke out onto the table. "VIVIAN!" he gasped, laughing.

Vivian recoiled. "Eugh! More moist-ness!"

He reached for a fistful of napkins. "I'm not an English professor, but I'm pretty sure the word you're looking for is *moisture*."

"We could always go ask an English professor."

Ino snorted again. "Great suggestion! That worked out terrific for me *last* time." He finished mopping the cola out of his facial fur. "Anyway,

Jack needs a break from the dating scene. He was working the Reed-as-a-swinger angle."

Vivian raised her eyebrows. "*Really,*" she said. Now she was interested.

Ino nodded. "Yup. Reed liked married couples, as you know… so Jack was investigating the crime as a probable lover's quarrel. So he spent two weeks on all of Reed's social media hookup profiles."

Vivian leaned forward. "You're kidding!" She thought about it. "And yet, I am not surprised."

Ino nodded. "*Right?* Given what we know now, it sounds extremely plausible. If this had been a normal murder he would have solved it in three days. But because of this stupid *accounting conspiracy*, he pretended to be a rhino on hookups-dot-com for two weeks, and all it got him was a branch to the brain." He shook his head sadly.

Vivian let out a slow breath. "Wow. That is… just so stupid."

He nodded. "It sure is. And it explains why he avoided the main University suspects for so long." He took another big sip of his soda. "So everything's pretty much wrapped up." He paused. "Except… there's just one thing that still does not make any sense to me."

Vivian's smile dropped off her face. "*One* thing?" she repeated in disbelief.

Ino rolled his eyes. "Well — one *major* thing. Why all the stupid clues?"

Vivian frowned. "How do you mean?"

Ino narrowed his eyes. "Why the journal entry? Why message me nothing but a password? Ethan could've left a note that said IF I DISAPPEAR CLARA CALDER AND HER SEXY BOYFRIEND KILLED ME."

Vivian leaned back, nodding. "Ohhhh, I got it. Why not just come out and say it?"

Ino nodded, furrowing his brow. "Right. It would have saved me an awful lot of work."

Vivian nodded. "Well… the password is probably because he was… incapacitated."

Ino grimaced. "Ugh, you mean, dying on the floor."

The pine marten considered her words. "In… no shape to write a long, detailed message. And as for the fake accounting document… how do you know that's the only thing he left? He probably *did* leave a note. I bet you anything Doug scrubbed the office."

Ino blinked at her. "Scrubbed?"

She stared. "Not *literally*. But he probably checked Reed's office. Think about it — they knew that Reed had figured out their fraud. He probably ransacked the office looking for any obvious evidence that would point the blame to them." She shrugged. "It's not like the man doesn't have keys to the entire school."

Ino stared at her, his eyes widening. "That's probably where Reed's laptop went."

Vivian nodded. "And he was probably the one in the storage unit before you. Did Jack figure out if the phone really belonged to Reed?"

Ino shook his head. "No, it was a dummy. It was another University-issued phone, one Miller probably stole earlier, since he was such an upstanding citizen. Jack says he probably swapped Reed's phone in case there was evidence on it, and planted the new one before blowing up the place. They assumed we would only find pieces of the phone — they never thought it would still be in working condition."

Vivian nodded. "Right. So he took care of all the obvious evidence. But not the journal entry. It had all the information we needed to solve the case, but it could have been sitting right out on top of Reed's desk and a guy like Doug wouldn't even know it was evidence. It was genius, really."

Ino nodded slowly. "I never thought of that. Based on where I found it, it *was* on top of Reed's desk."

Vivian nodded. "Right. Reed left it out in plain sight. But he made it purposely confusing. And it's a good thing he did, or it would be sitting at the bottom of Silver Lake with the security tapes, and Reed's computer, and his real cellphone. Whatever Miller did with the evidence he did find in Reed's office."

The hyena nodded. "Wow, I bet you're right." After a moment he frowned. "Oh God. When do you think Miller ransacked the office?" He felt a lump in the pit of his stomach.

Vivian blinked. She thought about it for a moment. "Well... if the murder was unplanned... I would think he would clean up as soon as he could afterwards. Probably the night of the explosion?" She shrugged.

Ino grimaced. The fur on the back of his neck stood up. "I slept in my office the night of the explosion."

Vivian blinked at him, and then frowned. "Oh, gross. Right across the hall." She grit her teeth and writhed. "Oh, that's *horrible*. You were asleep on your couch, twenty feet from where a murderer was ransacking a dead man's office." She shuddered. "That makes my skin crawl. What if you'd left in the middle of the night and bumped into him?"

Ino winced. "Uggghh," he grunted. He thought about it. "I guess we both know what would have happened."

Vivian shivered. "God. I'm glad you're a heavy sleeper."

They both pondered that for an uneasy moment.

Vivian finally shook it off. "Ugh! No point in dwelling on that, I guess." She looked up at him. "So now what?"

Ino thought about it. "Now... nothing, I guess. I'm going to try to have a normal summer. Teach my courses. My brother is going to visit in the fall. Maybe we'll go to the Popcorn Fair." He chuckled and looked at her conspiratorially. "Maybe I'll take Jack."

Vivian laughed. "Good. Sounds like fun."

Ino nodded. "It *does* sound like fun." After a moment, he smiled.

It was shaping up to be a pretty great summer after all.

Contributor Page

Bill Siracusa, Author. Bill can be found on social media as UnstableBill, a completely reasonable name. Bill has been writing since the late '90s, making his internet debut with some deeply cursed fanfiction of Keenspot webcomics that you should absolutely not search for. Bill lives in the Chicago suburbs with his hyena husband and 3 rescue cats, because of course. He is ecstatic to be presenting his first full-length novel and is already hard at work on the 2nd through 18th entries. Dr. Reamer will return in *A Spot Of Murder 2: Spot Harder.*

Jay Fitzmaurice, Illustrator. Jay lives in New Jersey, on purpose, and is a fearless internet veteran who uses his Actual For Real name on social media (so feel free to say hello). When he isn't busy being The Gym Tiger, he's working on character design to compensate for his buddy Bill, who doesn't "know" what things "look like." His cat daughter Madeline sends her regards.

Theresa Hahn, Editor. Theresa has been assiduously avoiding social media since 2007 — she still prefers a good old-fashioned phone call to catch up with friends. She has known Bill since the late 90's, and sat next to him in one infamous college English class. Theresa lives in Chicagoland, where she is still waiting to be adopted by her next cat -- she just needs to find one that's calm enough not to worry about being crushed by the 3,000 books lining the walls of her apartment.

KC Alpinus, Contributing Editor. KC is a prolific author and editor and has a long list of credits of books better than this one (Edit: Bill wrote that). She cherishes each and every book she has had the privilege and opportunity to work on, and every author who has had the patience to work with a chaos gremlin like her. She lives in Alberta, with the snow, hot tea, and her purple-striped spouse, Ocean, who happily enables her love of sushi, boardgames, and general chaos. You can find her @SwirlyTales on Twitter. Come chat with her about books, board games, or just dholes in general.

Ajax B. Coriander, Contributing Editor. Ajax is an editor, writer, publisher, woodworker, layout designer, dog, and Dad-enthusiast. He currently lives in Dallas with his domestic wolves, and in a house that is 20% FurPlanet books by volume. He can be found at @saintajax33 on twitter and he has a website at http://www.ajaxwriter.com/